State of Vengeance

Jake J. Harrison

State of Vengeance

WorldMaker Media
www.worldmakermedia.com

Copyright 2017 WorldMaker Media
All rights reserved.
First published by WorldMaker Media, a division of TheNextBigWriter, LLC in June 2017.
ISBN: 978-0-9838934-9-3

Learn more at www.stateofvengeance.com

Dedication

To Alison, who never stopped believing that I could make it happen.

Sometime in the not-to-distant future...

Part I
The Forge

Chapter 1

Undergrad from Harvard, MBA from the Wharton School, a job after graduation at a prestigious investment bank. People expected big things from Zeke. He watched as his former classmates and friends received promotions, large bonuses, accolades and prestigious positions while he toiled away on his idea, bereft of income, reliant on his wife to support them. He spent many sleepless nights tossing and turning, wondering if he made the right decision, wondering if his path was persistence or folly. When his wife's ex-boyfriend struck it rich with some type of chirping animal app, Zeke almost gave up, but Rachel urged him forward, told him he would make it, that their sacrifice would be worth it.

Today, he would find out.

He finished peering at his reflection through the circular hole he brushed in the steamed mirror and walked out of the bathroom into their cramped bedroom. His phone dinged from the top of the dresser. He reached over and picked it up.

"Issues with the deviation. Do you want me to increase the buying range?" Adele wrote. Stay calm, stick with the plan. As Zeke typed an answer on his phone, he felt a tug at his pants.

"Hi Sam," he said, taking a quick glance down at his eighteen-month old son. Sam replied with some baby talk and pulled his pants again.

"One second, Sam. I need one more second."

"Zeke! Do you see what Sam is doing. He's playing with a battery. Don't let him put it in his mouth!" Rachel shouted from the bedroom doorway.

"Sorry, I was trying to..." He fixed a typo in his text.

"You're not listening to me, are you, Zeke?"

"Sorry, did you say something?" he asked, finishing the message and hitting the send button.

"Zeke! Get the battery!" Rachel said rushing in." Alarmed, he put down the phone and plucked it out of Sam's hand a second before he tried to take a bite." Sam's cries started up, like a lawnmower sputtering to life, and Zeke scooped him up and gave him a tickle.

Rachel walked in from the bathroom, nodding her head.

"Sorry. I needed to get back to Adele. She had to calibrate the position again."

Sam flailed his arms for a second before settling in and enjoying Zeke's light touches on his arm. Rachel's icy demeanor thawed a bit and she flashed a small smile.

"Don't be mad, Rachel. I'm sorry but we're almost there."

"It's okay," she said. She put out her hands to calm herself. "You can neglect us, but just today. Even though you won't see us for a week, I understand."

Could he have found a more wonderful woman? She had sacrificed more than anyone living in this roach infested, slumlord apartment so they could pursue his plan, or folly, as his father-in-law called it.

"Do you have to leave?" he asked. "Wait a day."

"Zeke, you know we have to fly out today or we'll miss the boat. My parents will be waiting. If things work out, why don't you try to meet us in Sicily."

"You know how I feel about your parents." Although Zeke's paternal granfather was Jewish, he had been raised Episcopalian, a compromise between his Catholic mother and Methodist father. Rachel's parents had commanded their daughter to end the relationship. Although their attitude towards him had softened a bit with Sam's birth, he still found them hostile and cold.

"That's in the past. This trip is their peace offering."

"Really?" More like some ploy. They knew how bad the timing was for him. That they had paid for the trip only made it worse. He agreed to go only because he knew how much it meant to Rachel.

"What time does your flight leave again?"

"We've got about four-and-a-half hours. It leaves at twelve thirty."

"I'll give you a ride to the airport."

Sam gave him a hug and and then squirmed to be put down.

"No more batteries, okay." Zeke said.

Sam crawled off into the other room.

Rachel disappeared into the bathroom, giving him a minute to quickly scroll through the headlines. The President was traveling to the UN for an address to the General Assembly, heavy rain threatened flooding in Louisiana, the Patriots won their first regular season game. For the moment, the universe remained in harmony. He didn't see any event that could disrupt the complex financial positions they had built over the last three months. According to his calculations, only a black swan, the financial term for a totally unpredictable event, could disrupt the plan. As long as Adele properly calibrated the buying algorithim, they would be ready to go.

The forecast called for clear skies and unseasonably warm temperatures for mid-March, perfect flying weather.

He grabbed an iron, plugged it in, and waited for the bottom to heat up. In the meantime, he walked to the closet to get the ironing board and found a pile of plastic bags, baby toys, and furniture, all stacked haphazardly. Hurricane Rachel had blown through recently. After moving a few of his wife's knick-nacks, he grabbed the board, turned, and found Rachel leaning against the door, eyebrows raised, face pale.

"Rach, is everything okay?"

"I just received the strangest text."

"Okay," he said, putting down the ironing board.

"What did it say?" She didn't speak. "Rachel?"

"It said not to leave today on the trip."

Chapter 2

"What? It said not to take the trip today?"

She nodded.

His phone pinged. What was it now?

"Who sent it?" he asked.

"I don't know. I don't recognize the number."

"Can I see your phone?" he asked, reaching forward and taking it from her hand.

"Do not leave today on your trip," the message said. He looked at the recipient number: 1091212914. Below it he saw two texts Rachel sent in reply:

"Who is this?"

"Who are you?"

No reponse.

His phone dinged again. Adele needed more advice on the calibration, Patric had a technical question about the model initiation. He needed to get to the office ASAP.

He pressed the phone symbol next to the mystery number and waited. It rang once and then gave him the standard "this message is not in service" recording. Strange.

"The number isn't active. Maybe you should delay a day. Skip the flight and go tomorrow," he said, looking up. That would make things easier for everyone and allow him to focus on the model execution.

Sam crawled into the room and began to tug at Rachel's leg. She reached down to scoop him up and Zeke noticed the tears streaming down her cheeks.

"We'll miss the boat. I've been looking forward to this vacation for so long." She had worked long shifts the last year to make extra money and the hours took their toll, leaving dark circles under her eyes. She wiped the tears away and sniffled. "It must have been a prank," she said as Sam wriggled in her arms. "We're nobodies in the grand scheme of things. Why would anyone text something like that to us?"

He bristled at the thought of being a nobody, but had to admit she was right. When he Googled his name, the only results that appeared besides social networking links were a article about his string of one hundred straight chess tournament wins in high school and Sam's birth announcement.

"But how did the sender know you're going on a trip?" Zeke asked.

She thought for a moment. "It could have been someone at work. Yes," she said, more confidently, "I bet Lorna put someone up to it. She was mad at having to cover my shift."

"Would she stoop that low?" Rachel told him stories about the woman cutting her boyfriends' shirts in anger and spiking co-workers drinks with laxative.

"I've told you about her. Yes, it has to be Lorna."

"Still, maybe you should..."

"There is no way I'm giving that witch the satisfaction of ruining my vacation," she said.

Another message made his phone vibrate.

"They're texting you, aren't they?"

He nodded. "Patric and Adele are having some trouble with the model."

"Is it serious?"

"No, I don't think so. They're not entirely sure how to resolve the issue though."

"Go to the office. We'll take a car. I'm sorry we have to leave today. You know if it wasn't for my parents I would stay with you. Plus, I know you need to concentrate. It's better that we'll be away."

"No, I'll take you," he said. His phone pinged again and Rachel smiled and shook her head.

"We'll user Uber. You need to go and make this thing work, Zeke. I'm counting on you."

* * *

Zeke carried their luggage down four flights of stairs and they waited outside, basking in the sunlight. A homeless man passed by, stuck out his empty pan, and squawked at them:

"Spare some change? Spare some change?" Rachel pulled a five dollar bill out of her purse and dropped it in.

"You know they buy booze with it," he said.

She shrugged.

They lived in Dorchester, a hardscrabble part of the city, far from most of their friends who years earlier moved to the affluent suburbs.

"There's our ride," Rachel said as an all-electric Toyota Camry glided to a stop next to the curb. The driver, a young, Arab-looking man, stepped out and walked over.

"Rachel Katz?" he asked.

She nodded.

He clicked a button on his key chain and popped the trunk. Zeke and the driver grabbed the two luggage bags and loaded them while Rachel worked to secure the car seat.

When they finished, Zeke met Rachel and Sam back on the sidewalk.

"Okay, I guess this is goodbye," she said. Rachel looked beautiful, dark brown hair falling in pretty waves down to her shoulders and glistening in the sun. She smiled, but he could see tears.

Sam grabbed his father's pant leg with his little hand. Zeke hoisted Sam into the air and blew a big raspberry onto his soft cheek. His son squealed and wriggled in his arms. Zeke went over to Rachel and clasped both of them in a group bear hug.

"Stay safe."

"Of course. You stay safe without us," she said, trying to lighten the moment.

"I'll be over as soon as I can."

"Meet us in Sicily," Rachel said, giving him the eye and reminding him of his promise. They broke their embrace and he buckled Sam into the car seat.

"If all goes well, we'll buy Sicily," he said. "Save me some wine and pasta."

"Remember, call me right away."

"Put your phone on," he shot back.

She giggled. "Good luck, Zeke. Love you." She cupped his cheek and gave him a soft kiss.

"Rachel," he said, pausing, and in that moment he almost told her not to go. She should wait one more day and they would all go together. They had never traveled apart before, and he didn't like splitting up, especially after the weird text. But his phone dinged and interrupted the thought.

"It's going to work," he whispered instead, sounding confident and hoping she didn't sense just how nervous and scared he felt.

"I know," she said, "I believe in you."

"I love you," he responded, fighting the tears in his eyes and giving her a lingering kiss.

"I love you too." One more long kiss before Rachel broke the moment. "We'll see you in Sicily." She hopped into the car and he closed the door. Rachel and Sam blew a few kisses as the Toyota pulled away. For one last moment he watched his son looking back, his little face crinkling up into a smile, his little hand waving, before another car drove by and blocked his view.

Chapter 3

*Do not look nervous. They watch for any sign you are hiding
something.*

The email provided precise instructions on how to get
through airport security. The encrypted message, the latest of
thirty messages received over a three year period were signed
with the letter E, and Walid would have considered them trash
except for the value they contained: precise instructions on the
schedules for TSO officers, the easiest airports to penetrate,
unpublished flight schedules, and classified itineraries of
government officials. Despite the accuracy of the previous
emails, Walid felt anxious as he approached the x-ray
machines at Boston Logan International Airport.

Walid took the bag from around his shoulder, placed it on
the moving conveyor belt, and watched as it disappeared under
the curtain. Heart pounding, he heard a high-pitched whine
which always happened whenever he was nervous. He forced
himself to calmly peer up and smile at the old woman manning
the x-ray scanner. She had straight dark hair, thick, blue
makeup around her eyes, and Cassandra printed on her name
tag. Cassandra, the Greek goddess of prophecy. In early
school, before he truly committed himself to the true God,
Allah, he studied the false gods of the ancient Greeks. How
odd he should come upon the name of a false god today. Could
it be an omen? A message from almighty Allah that his
mission would be successful? Yes, it must have been a sign
and the woman's name calmed his thoughts.

For the past week, he noticed the signs everywhere.
Praised be Allah, the clues had been small but unmistakable.
On the flight from Saudi Arabia to the United States he sat
next to an obese American woman whose enormous girth
spilled over the arm rest onto his seat. He shifted away as
much as possible but could not prevent contact. Halfway

through the flight, her nose opened like a Qasba'a after rain, dripping red splotches onto her tray, where it coated the piece of chicken she hungrily attacked. Disgusting. Although she attempted to staunch the flow, it kept recurring, surely a sign that America, the land of gluttony would soon be awash in its own blood, and like the woman, be unable to stop or prevent it from happening.

Walking down Boston's Boylston Street the other night, the sight of the blessed marathon attack, a bird started following him, chirping a distinct song. He took a taxi several miles back to his hotel, but the next morning as he left the building, he heard the same distinctive call and spotted the bird peering down from the telephone wires. Surely, this was a sign he walked the right path, the path of the Prophet, and like the bird, others would follow him in completing Allah's mission.

Of course, Allah would be most proud of the meticulous way he planned this project. Using the emails, he'd spent years finding the right people, choosing the correct dates, and selecting the proper targets. The airports thought themselves secure. Who would be crazy enough to hijack a plane? After 9/11, the government and airlines implemented new security procedures which they thought foolproof. False believers. Any human system could be beaten, especially by someone who knew its weaknesses. Even without the emails, Walid didn't think it would be hard to fool these people. Would Cassandra know how to spot plastic explosive if he hid it in his bag? Doubtful. Would she understand how a simple tourist trinket like a mirror or a lamp could be turned into a sharp weapon? No. If they plugged one hole, Walid would find another.

For the last ten years, Allah tested Fist of Allah, banishing them from the Caliphate in the Levent, sending them into hiding in Oman and Paksitan. Today marked the beginning of the group's rebirth.

Cassandra finished scanning his bag, pushed it forward, and it rolled out the other side of the machine. A large man with a bushy mustache waved at him and indicated he should walk through the detector. Walid moved into the tube, placed his feet in the correct place, raised his arms above his head as they instructed, and watched the machine spin. The man indicated he should walk forward and Walid headed towards his bags when a man wearing a gold badge came towards him.

You will most likely be searched. Be polite and respectful. Again, do not show you are nervous.

"Get your stuff and come over here," the man pointed. Taking a deep breath to relax, Walid gathered his carry-on bag, shoes, and jacket before following him to the corner where several other travelers stood, their jackets open and their shoes off. "Raise your arms, please," the soldier asked. The man frisked him. "Your shoes, please," the agent said pointing to the pair in his hands.

He handed them over. The man pulled up the foam arch before running a brush over them, dabbing the results on a piece of paper and then inserting it into a machine. Nothing. He would find nothing.

"Please open your suitcase," he said pointing to his leather satchel. Walid placed it on the table and let the man open it.

Put Western books and magazines in your carry-on.

He pulled out a book by Sigmund Freud, a *Sports Illustrated* swimsuit edition, an iPhone, a *People Magazine,* and a New York Yankees cap.

Satisfied with his search, the TSO agent put the items back into his satchel.

"Thank you," he said as Walid walked to the gate. On the LCD screen above the ticket agent, a sign said: Gate 35: Flight 2718. Below that: Sevilla. Other travelers sat in front of the gate, checking their email on their phones, chatting, eating. He found an open seat, opened his satchel, and pulled out the book, pretending to read.

Walid looked up and noticed a pimple faced, balding man sitting several rows across from him also reading a book. They traded an almost imperceptible nod. Khalid. Across the gateway, he spied a muscular, blond-haired passenger wearing a Cubs cap and drinking a cup of something– something vile knowing Hassan. Their eyes met for an instant. He made one more scan of the other travelers and saw Bin Gaudi talking on his phone, his bushy beard gone. Praise be Allah, they were all there. He said a small prayer and then settled back into his seat.

Walid watched the crowd walking down the terminal for several minutes, mostly obese Americans laughing and talking about trivial subjects, oblivious to the world around them, cocooned in their blissful sloth. A young woman, with a baseball cap pulled down over her face, walked beside a man in a polo shirt and khakis.

Walid pulled out the *People Magazine* from his satchel and flipped to the right page. Yes, it was her, Victoria Vison, the Vice President's daughter. The email had been right about her departure date and plane number. Walid offered a silent prayer for Allah's beneficence. He had been fearful they would change her plane at the last minute as a security precaution, throwing his entire plan into disarray, but the email had been adamant this was the flight. The girl and her protector walked over to the gate, disappearing through the door and down the walkway to the plane. If someone hadn't been paying attention, they wouldn't have spotted what just happened.

He closed his eyes and started to pray but a piercing wail pulled him from his concentration. A mother tried to console a small boy, bouncing him in her arms and whispering into his ear. The woman saw him staring and flashed an apologetic smile. Walid glared back, annoyed and irritated at the interruption. He had no sympathy for women who didn't know how to handle their children. The boy eventually calmed down and he resumed his prayers.

A few minutes later, flight 2718 started boarding.

Chapter 4

Zeke glanced at his watch: 11:00 am. He calculated the plane to be halfway across the Atlantic. He stepped out of the elevator into a tastefully decorated beige lobby, turned left and walked through a set of heavy glass doors with the name Spinnaker Investments imprinted in silver. He named the firm after one of his passions, sailing. As a boy, he had often snuck out of the foster homes and run to the river, where he managed to convince the dock hands to let him take a boat out after-hours. The tug of the wind, keel of the boat, and heat of the sun helped him forget what happened to his parents, and for a few minutes escape the foster homes. The spinnaker, a second sail, provided the boat with more speed and maneuverability. It seemed an apt name for the firm.

"Good morning, Margaret," he called to a well-dressed older woman sitting behind a curved desk.

She looked up from her computer and smiled. "Good morning to you, Zeke. Did Rachel and Sam get off okay?"

"Right on time. I took them to the airport myself."

She nodded approvingly. Margaret acted like the grandmother he never knew. Thin, graying, impeccably dressed, she exuded a steadying influence and managed the office efficiently.

"I'm sure Rachel appreciated it." She picked up a pink note and handed it to Zeke. "Ms. Broadhurst has called several times today already. She asked you to call her when you got in."

Zeke sighed. He didn't relish the conversation; he never did. "She's checking on her money," Zeke mumbled.

"Probably more than that," Margaret added.

He ignored the comment. "Could you see if there are any flights to Sicily, departing sometime early tomorrow morning?"

"I'll look into it, but if my memory is correct, it's difficult to get to Sicily by air. You may want to fly into Reggio Calabria and take a car to the ferry."

"Whatever you think is best, Margaret," he said, walking down the hallway. She nodded as if to say, that's right, let me take care of it.

The office, with its plush beige carpeting, covered three thousand square feet. Pictures of famous America's Cup sailboats lined the wall, their sails billowing, sea spray blowing into the faces of many of the stout crews. The site of them energized him each morning. Recessed LED lights led a trail down the main hallway, which served as the spine of the office. Individual offices branched from it like ribs, and a conference room sat at the end, like a brain.

The office was much too ostentatious for his taste and budget but Lilly insisted on the decor. "You can't work in a dump, like your apartment," she quipped. He almost cancelled the deal that day.

He stopped at the slightly ajar door to the first office and noticed a pair of sneakers perched on a desk, squeezed between two flat screen computer monitors, surrounded by a haze of smoke.

"Patric, this is a no smoking office."

"Since when?" a voice asked with a slight Swiss accent.

"Since forever."

"Come on boss, you know what's happening today. I need the cigi, it helps me deal with the stress." A well-tanned face with a shock full of unruly hair poked out from behind the screens. Until Patric, Zeke had never met a vain computer programmer. Patric constantly adjusted his hair and shopped on Newbury Street, picking up the latest styles, spending most of his free time either clubbing or using his computer savvy to digitally remix club tracks. But even while clubbing, Zeke knew Patric's mind spun through intricate problems, an intellect that marked him as one of the rising computer science stars at MIT before the school expelled him.

"Okay, just for today. How is the system working? Are we ready?"

Patric tapped one of the screens. "Oh, we're ready. I've been following the price discrepancy between the May Canadian Dollar and the July American. It's starting to move into the range the model predicted. Several orders will execute soon and once those have cleared we should be ready to party." He eyed Zeke. "Want a drag? You look a tad bit uptight."

"No, but thanks for the thought."

"Anytime, jefe," Patric said before turning back to his screens.

Zeke continued walking down the hallway and passed Amir, one of his technical analysts. Amir's face glittered with sweat.

"Oh, you decided to show up?" Amir deadpanned. "I thought you were sleeping off another hangover."

"Funny."

"It's going to happen very soon, perhaps in the next hour. The positions are starting to move as the model predicted." Originally from Kuwait, his family had been left near destitute after Saddam invaded the oil-rich country in the nineteen nineties. Although shy and unassuming, Amir developed a knack for spotting hidden correlations in the data, using the information to enhance the model buying opportunities.

"Let me know when, Amir, and I'll buy."

"Yes, of course, of course, as long as *HE*," he said nodding towards Patric's office, "keeps the data flowing correctly."

Zeke knew each of them felt the other encroached on their turf and to some degree that was expected in the laissez-faire climate he had established. He believed in finding and hiring the best in their respective fields, providing the overall direction, and getting out of the way to let them do their job. He made the ultimate decisions and developed the model that drew them together, but Zeke trusted and respected the advice he received from his other team members.

"Just let me know," he repeated before continuing down the hallway. His corner office, the one perk he allowed himself, provided a view of the city from two different angles. From the left window he could see the Prudential Building in the forefront and the other skyscrapers from Boston's financial district while the other window gave him a view of the Charles River and MIT's Great Dome sitting atop Building 10.

He sat down, picked up the phone, and dialed her private cellphone number. Lilly's moods varied and his calls with her could either be unpleasant, or extremely unpleasant, especially when she began to talk about their college days.

"Hello, Zeke," she cooed with a Texas drawl, her voice husky and sensual as if she rolled out of bed after a morning of making love. "It's your sugar momma." Most of it was a tease, although the affection was very real. He tried to square her religious upbringing with the wild girl who did body shots in college, who he kissed by the Trevi Fountain, and who had been best friends with Rachel before he drove a wedge the size of the Grand Canyon through their friendship. He wanted to forget the whole incident.

"Good morning, Lilly. Margaret told me you called."

"Of course I called. I wanted to wish you good luck." When Lilly's father passed away three years ago, she inherited control of the largest oil company in Texas. After not hearing from her in five years, she suddenly approached him about investing in his company. "I want to invest in your business," she stated. "I know how smart you are and all of these chauvanistic pricks need to see a woman can make money." Against Rachel's advice, he accepted her offer. She become his "sugar momma" as she called it, a fact Lilly didn't tire of reminding him.

"Thanks, Lilly."

"Well, I sure am ready for you to make me even richer," she said laughing. "After you've been spectacularly successful, you'll come to Texas and we'll celebrate. I'll throw a huge party like the one we went to. Remember that, Zeke?"

He did remember feeling totally uncomfortable amidst the socialite set of Dallas.

Lilly rolled on. "Mom would love to see you. It will be so much fun."

"Maybe," he told her although he knew the real answer was no.

"And you can bring your son. What's his name?"

"Sam."

"That's right. Bring him, but leave Cinderella at home. She doesn't get to go to the ball."

"Lilly–"

"Lighten up, Zeke, I was only joking. But you can still leave her at home."

"Thanks," he said again, wanting to end the conversation.

"Ta-ta now," she said. "Got business to take care of here. I'll be waiting for the good news!"

"Bye," he said and the line went dead. Overall, not a horrible call.

He turned on his computer, checked a few relatively unimportant emails, and walked over to the largest room in the office up near the head of the spine. On the wall sat a giant one hundred inch screen projecting a continuous flow of data: stock quotes, currency prices, future contracts, option contracts, bond yields, commodity prices, and other lifeblood of the global economy. Today, Patric programmed the screen to focus on the US and Canadian dollars. A downward sloping graph showed the trend of the USD versus the CD for the last year while a second graph displayed a minute-by-minute analysis of the same trend for the last twenty-four hours. For the day, the Canadian dollar was up 2.25 basis points against its US counterpart with one basis point equaling one cent.

If he were to trade straight Canadian and US dollars it would have been impossible for him to make a significant return. But Zeke traded derivatives, or the option values of these dollars, speculating on the future values of each of these currencies.

Derivatives tied to mortgages had almost brought down the financial world, precipitating the Great Recession at the dawn of the century. Many amateur traders didn't understand how options worked; they could be opaque and hard to model – a bet upon a bet, upon a bet. Today, he would test his own knowledge.

Adele stood alone in the room, looking up at the screen. A tall, blonde Stanford MBA who crunched numbers with the same ease that most people breathed, Adele modeled the trading scenarios to determine their best opportunity to profit. She was also Lilly's cousin, and the heiress made Adele's hire the one condition attached to the funding.

Only a black swan could derail his calculations and cause the model to fail. The term, coined by the economist and philosopher Nassim Nicholas Taleb, referred to a shock surprise that could only be explained with the benefit of hindsight. The attacks of 9/11 were black swan events as was the collapse of Lehman Brothers. He tried to extend the algorithim to detect and account for black swan events but hadn't been successful and therein lay the primary risk to the model. Still, as he often told himself: no risk, no reward.

"Adele, are we ready?" She turned from the screen.

"Ready. As soon as Amir gives the word. I'm tracking several buying opportunities. There are three other market makers looking to take a position but we've been able to identify them and I don't think they will be a problem. They don't have the algorithm so they shouldn't be able to interfere with our trade execution."

Zeke reached into his pocket and turned off his mobile phone. During the heat of trading he liked all of his attention focused on the numbers and he didn't accept calls.

Amir walked over. "When the Canadian dollar drops another penny to $.969, we should start buying. The pricing inefficiency should last about two hours so that is the time we have to open and close the position. The Canadian dollar should start to rise after that and will probably level off at .997

17

before dropping again. If the Canadian dollar falls below $.9570 cents something has gone wrong."

Zeke nodded. Patric and Margaret entered the room and sat down.

They all watched the Canadian dollar drop - .979, .9787, .978, .9775, .9773. The numbers began rising but Amir raised his hand as if to say it's okay, and no sooner had he done it the descent continued—.9773, ..9772, .9771…

Zeke's mouth felt dry.

Adele's hands rested on the keyboard, waiting to input the orders. .9770, .9697, .9695, .9692, and finally .9690. Adele pressed a key, confirming the order and Patric's computer program executed, buying enormous quantities of option contracts for the Canadian dollar at the price of .9690.

Zeke exhaled. Now they waited. The higher the Canadian dollar moved above the .9690 exchange rate, the better the position and the more profit they would make.

Approximately fifteen minutes after entering the initial order, the Canadian dollar began a slow and inexorable rise from their purchase point, rising on tenth of a cent and then two tenths. Zeke did a quick calculation. They made $50 MM and the position was still running.

He felt giddy, light, and realized how much the stress weighed on him. His professors, the bankers, the finance experts— they all told him it couldn't be done, and until this moment, when he saw the actual position beginning to make money, he felt their nagging doubt. Now, he realized, their words didn't mean anything. The "experts" weren't so smart after all.

This is what it must have felt like to shoot a kilo of cocaine into your body. Pure adrenalin. Rachel deserved to experience this and he missed the smile he could imagine on her face as their dream became a reality.

"Something's happening," Adele said, "the position is moving more than the model predicted." Zeke snapped back from his daydream. The Canadian dollar suddenly gained a whole nickel against the American dollar and Patric's fingers moved furiously over the keyboard. On the screen, red lines appeared and when it came to money, red was never a good color.

"The model is breaking down," Amir said. "There is a black swan."

Chapter 5

Sam squirmed in her arms and accidentally clipped the woman beside them with his foot. They sat in first class–an indulgence they splurged on in anticipation of money to come– and while the seats were spacious, they still couldn't contain a rambunctious two-year old.

"I'm so sorry about that," Rachel said.

"That is quite all right," the older woman said with a thick, French accent. Her pale skin, perfectly coiffed dark hair, designer clothes, and enormous ruby perched on her bony middle finger made her appear like a European aristocrat.

"How old is your son?"

"He's almost two, eighteen-months."

"Il est précieux mignon. He is very cute."

"Merci," she said, using one of the few words she remembered from French class. "I'm going to take him for a little walk before he turns into a devil." The woman smiled and waved her hand. As she stood, Rachel's eyes wandered to the seat bed beside them and she noticed a familiar looking woman curled up, trying to sleep. Straight blonde hair, freckles, and a Harvard t-shirt gave her an all-American girl look. A clean-cut man in a white collared shirt and a blue blazer kept his seat upright beside her, watching a movie. Who was she? Rachel tried to place the face.

The girl's identity wouldn't click so she gave up and guided Sam down the aisle.

The plane settled into a drowsy calm, the roar of the engines providing a soothing background noise as twilight enveloped the plane. Most of the travelers spread their blankets and turned off the overhead lights, although a few typed on computers or listened to music while even fewer watched a movie.

A small girl played patty-cake with Sam for a few minutes. While they played, Rachel's thoughts turned to Zeke's gamble. They had scrimped and saved while her girlfriends bought five bedroom houses and nice cars, traveled to Europe for shopping trips, and furnished their living rooms from magazines. The lack of material goods didn't bother her so much. She grew up in a middle-class class family with everything at her disposal and didn't need a lot – a small house, a car that worked, and lots of love would suffice. A nurse could always get a job, and they would have food and a place sleep. But how would Zeke react to failure? She didn't know if he could recover so easily. Everyone, except for Lilly, thought his idea wouldn't work. While she never admitted it to Zeke, Rachel knew Lilly had ulterior motives for giving the money.

They started walking back to their seats when the plane shook. She hated turbulence. On the one trip she took as a girl to her grandfather's funeral, her mother assured her the bumps were nothing more than potholes in the sky, which relieved her because cars never crashed from potholes. The plane shook again and the seat belt sign pinged on. Just as she reached the first-class cabin, the plane dropped slightly and then lurched to the left, forcing her off balance and nearly pitching them into a sleeping couple. Sam fell into the aisle but she managed to maintain her balance and pull her son off the floor. A man with a Yankees cap pulled over blond hair stood in the aisle, watching them with a scowl on his face that made her shiver. With cold eyes, he watched them struggle on the floor, making no attempt to offer assistance. After a moment, she noticed a gun in left hand, pointed right at her face.

"Sit down," the man ordered in perfect English.

Chapter 6

Walid wanted to check the moment he boarded the plane but fought against the desire and told himself to wait for the right moment. Getting caught at this point would be a fool's move. No, patience, Walid counseled himself. Be patient and you will be rewarded.

The man sitting next to him opened a thick book almost immediately after sitting down and kept his nose in it. Walid watched him and waited, praying that the reading would make him tired so he would turn off the light and go to sleep, but an hour passed and still the man read his book. Walid peeked at the title: Steven King – *The Stand*. Mindless American rubbish. Someday, this man would spend his time reading the Koran, the only literature worthy of study. Sheikh Imaad said: *The brain is like a sponge and can absorb a finite amount. Would you fill it with offal, or fill it with gold?* One could spend a lifetime delving into the Koran and only scratch the surface.

Finally, the man yawned, shoved the book into the seat pocket in front of him, rubbed his eyes, and turned out the light.

Walid waited and the minutes passed like hours. Eventually the man's breathing deepened. Walid, judging the man asleep, bent down and reached under his seat as if grabbing for his satchel. His hand closed around a hard object wrapped in cloth.

Praise be Allah, it was there. They successfully placed it on the plane. Hopefully, the other items made it as well.

"Would you like something to drink, sir?" He almost followed his instinct and jerked his hand up, but he fought the impulse and calmly withdrew it. Hopefully, it didn't look out of place. Women possessed a keen sense for danger and he knew the airlines trained these attendants to spot anything that did not look normal. They were like the Amazon whores he read about as a boy - big, strong, overly opinionated, and not to be trusted.

He smiled.

"Yes. Please. I think I'd like some tea, ice tea if you have it." She nodded and poured him a plastic cup full of the American drink. "Thank you."

She smiled back. "Let me know if you need anything else." She moved on with the beverage cart. He pulled down his neighbor's tray and put his cup on it before standing and looking up and down the cabin.

Five rows behind him Khalid stared out the window. What could he see? Out his window he saw only the blinking of a light on the wing of the plane and endless black. Hassan turned and saw him looking. He nodded and gave him his usual blood curdling smile. Walid didn't want the American convert on the mission, but Sheikh Imaad insisted, explaining that Hassan knew the ways of the enemy, having grown up in Iowa. Walid doubted it. Hassan's eyes appeared empty, devoid of emotion and Walid didn't trust him. Somehow, the American wound up with a gun and Walid prayed to Allah that the man followed the plan.

Bin Gaudi waited for them in first class, hopefully with the target.

The plane shook from turbulence and Walid steadied himself. The cabin light blinked on followed by the captain's voice over the plane's speakers.

"Hello ladies and gentleman, we've picked up a bit of turbulence at thirty-thousand feet. We're going to move up to thirty-three thousand to try and go over it. In the meantime, we've turned the seatbelt light on so please return to your seats. Thank you."

Now. He reached down, pulled the cloth-covered object out from under the seat, and walked up towards the first class cabin. Looking back, he could see Hassan moving up the aisle towards a woman and her small child. He reached Amir and

23

gave him a nod, indicating that he should stay in his seat and scout the plane for any sky marshals.

"Praise be to Allah, praise be to Allah," he recited to try and calm his pounding heart and cool the sweat beading up on his forehead. He opened himself to the fear as the sheik trained him to do: let the belly sink, exhale, recognize that death is invetiable, accept Allah's glory overcomes everything.

"You must fear death if its probability approaches. For life is sacred and your sacrifice would mean nothing if you did not value what you were giving. But know that Allah understands your sacrifice in his name and he will protect you either in life or in death."

He swung the first-class curtain open, turned to the teen-age girl's seat, and fired three shots into the man sitting next to her. The gun shots roared through the plane, much louder than he had imagined, breaking through even the background noise of the engines. The first bullet hit the man in the face, forcing him back into the seat. The second bullet tore a gaping hole in his neck. The third caused a stain of blood to spread across his chest as if an invisible painter had decided to drip thick splotches of red dye down his shirt. Perfect. All the shots hit the agent and none breached the hull of the plane. The Secret Service agent collapsed back into the seat like a deflating tube.

Screams erupted and he noticed someone try to stand behind him. Amir clubbed the man in the face and knocked him back into the seat. No heroes today.

Blood covered the girl's pretty face. She feebly tried to wipe it off, clearly in shock. Good, let them know fear, he thought. Someone started shouting in a language other than English, maybe French. Amir nodded, and made the OK sign with his fingers–no more Secret Service or Sky Marshals. Email twenty-seven had detailed how many they should expect.

A stewardess started to move out of first class and he motioned for her to come over. "There is no need to be afraid. Just submit to my orders and you will not be harmed. I promise on Allah's word," he said.

"What do you want?" the woman asked in a quivering voice.

"Show me the phone to the cockpit." Email twenty-eight made it clear the pilot would immediately secure the cockpit door and radio back to the tower.

She pointed to a phone at the front of first class.

"Thank you, now sit down," he ordered. He spoke loudly so that everyone around could hear. "Khalid, show them your carry-on package." A thin man stood up and lifted his shirt, revealing white packets strapped to his chest. "That's plastic explosive," Walid said. "Enough to blow an immense hole in this plane. Everyone stay seated and you will be fine. But remember, we're watching." Hassan pushed a woman and a sobbing little boy back to their seats in first class. Why did Hassan make everything difficult? Why couldn't he have just sat them back in coach instead of bringing them to the front of the plane, especially if the boy couldn't stop crying? He recognized the child from the airport lounge. "Make him stop crying," he ordered. The mother grabbed her son and tried to rock him to silence but the child continued to sob.

Walid went over to the phone.

"Hello, I know that you can hear me. One of us has a belt of C4 explosive strapped around his waist." Silence from the cockpit. "This is what I want. You will open the door to the cockpit within ten seconds after I hang up this phone. If you do not, I will begin to kill a person for every sixty seconds that the door remains closed. If after five minutes the door is not open, I will detonate the C4. The clock starts now," he said hanging up the phone.

It didn't take more than five seconds for the cockpit door to click open and a man with a blue jacket to peek out.

"Are you the captain?" Walid asked.

"Yes."

"Fly to this location," Walid said removing a piece of paper from his pocket and handing it to the man. "I assure you, this is not a suicide mission. If you follow my instructions, you may escape with your lives."

The man studied the coordinates.

"This is the first point you will fly to. Once we are there, I will provide you with the final coordinates." He pulled a small black device out of the same pocket and pressed a button, causing a red light to flash.

"This is a GPS positioning device. If the flight path deviates from these coordinates, we will detonate the C4. Do you understand?"

The man nodded.

"Now, return to the cockpit and get the Vice President on the line. I have some business to discuss with him."

"I can't just get the Vice President–"

"Just do it!" Walid yelled. "I have his daughter on the plane. He will talk to us." The man scurried back towards the cockpit. "Oh captain, Bin Gaudi will be joining you." Bin Gaudi stepped forward, the explosive belt hanging from his hip and absently cuffed the captain in the head before following him into the cabin. Walid frowned.

He picked up the intercom and addressed the cabin. "Ladies and gentleman, good evening. Praise be Allah. This flight is going to be taking a detour. It is now under my control. I want to assure you that this is not a suicide mission and if Allah allows it, you will arrive safe and secure. In the meantime, please stay in your seats. If you need to relieve yourself, please beep and we will escort you to the restrooms. We have a bomb on the plane and any resistance will trigger its detonation. In the meantime, I suggest that each of you pray to Allah, the one and only God, for mercy and deliverance."

A murmur went through the passengers and he could hear brief snippets of conservation.

"A bomb, did he say a bomb?"

"Oh my God, we're going to die."

"How could this happen to us? What about the sky marshalls?"

In first class, Victoria Vison managed to remove most of the blood from her face and she curled up against the window, sniffling, her lips moving in prayer. He respected her faith but it would not help, unless she called to Allah, which he doubted. The little boy started to cry. Her nerves frayed, he couldn't tolerate the sound.

"Make him stop crying!" Walid yelled. The wails pulsed through his head. It needed to stop.

"I'm trying, please, I'm trying," the woman replied.

"Try harder!"

She nodded and rocked the boy.

"Walid," Bin Gaudi yelled from the cockpit in his heavy Algerian accent, "they are on the line!" Walid entered the cockpit and placed the earphones over his ears.

"Allahu Akbar," he shouted into the microphone. "God is great."

"Who is this?" came a voice.

"No, it is I who will do the asking," Walid replied. "We are now in control of American Air Flight 2718. Victoria Vison is one of our passengers. If you want to see her or any of the rest of the plane alive, you will answer my questions. Is that understood?"

No answer.

"Is that understood!" he yelled into the phone.

Finally after a short pause, "Yes."

"Good. This is not a suicide mission. If my conditions are met, I will release them unharmed."

"Has anyone been injured or hurt already?"

"One of your agents, David Lloyd, is dead," Walid said looking at the dead Secret Service agent's ID.

"What do you want?"

Walid spent enough hours listening to the Vice President's speeches to know the voice on the phone was not his. Instead, they insulted him with some low-level negotiator, wasting time so their experts could develop profiles and understand Walid's motivations and psychology. Western drivel. He would make it easy for them.

"First, who am I talking to?"

"This is Harold Stimson, the Secretary of Defense. Who are you?"

Stimson. He hated the man. Stimson ordered the massacre of Din Bah where Salim and Fares died. Now, three years later he, a simple man from Saudi Arabia, held the advantage over this man. Walid recited a small prayer and his confidence surged.

"My name is Walid bin Ibrahim and these are my demands," he said, ready to move the conversation along. "By noon tomorrow, Eastern Standard Time, October eighth, you will release Sheikh Abdul Imaad from his unjust and criminal incarceration. You will place him on a plane and fly him to Hamburg, Germany. You will deposit one hundred million dollars into bank account number 5633456 of Banco de Argentina. There will be no negotiation. If this is not done by the timeframe outlined, we will begin killing the passengers on the plane, including the Vice President's daughter. If you make any attempt to stop this plane, or interfere with our flight plan, we will kill the Vice President's daughter." He motioned for Bin Gaudi to grab the girl and drag her into the cockpit, which he did with relish. He grunted and smiled as he pulled the stricken girl forward.

"Give your father a message," Bin Gaudi said, pinching her breast.

Walid frowned.

"H-h-h-help us," she managed to say between sobs. "P-p-p-please Daddy, help us," she stuttered, teeth chattering, mouth quivering, snot flowing down her face.

Bin Gaudi smiled.

Walid did not take pleasure in the suffering of others but the girl's discomfort could not be avoided. He saw Mouna's face and his doubts vanished. *Remember what happened to Mouna and do not grow weak.* He pulled off the headphones and said curtly.

"I trust you will provide us with what we want." Walid motioned for the captain to close the channel.

"Get back to your seat," he ordered the sobbing girl, giving her a rough shove. "Don't bother her anymore," he said to Bin Gaudi and Hassan who both watched her stumble back with hungry eyes.

Other than a few other sobs and sniffles, the rest of the cockpit became quiet. Until the little boy began to cry again.

Chapter 7

"Aminah, can you please take the cookies out of the oven?" an older woman's voice called from the other room.

"Cookies," returned the voice of a girl. "I want cookies!" she exclaimed.

Aminah could smell the heavenly scent coming from the kitchen, just like when she was a little girl, and it relieved her to see that her mother had not lost any cooking skills. She walked across the small one-bedroom apartment. A worn sofa rested against the wall, flanked by a pair of outdated armchairs. A picture of her parents taken forty years before in Lebanon hung above the sofa. They stood on the beach in Beirut with the ocean to their backs, staring solemnly into the lens. Several other pictures hung beside it—her graduation from high school, her sister graduating from college, and a recent picture of Daayana, her niece, looking up at the camera with a huge smile on her face.

Aminah entered the kitchen, turned off the oven, and reached down to remove the tray of cookies. Her arm grazed the hot stove, sending a jolt of pain through her hand, and making her release the pan. It tipped over, spilling the cookies across the floor.

"Aminah, are you allright?" her mother called.

"Fine, fine," she said, on her knees, frantically scooping their desert onto the tray.

"Did you drop the cookies?" her mother called.

Her mother was well aware of her lack of coordination and she didn't want to reinforce the perception.

"Just a small accident. I think they're okay."

Aminah returned to the living room and Daayana sat on the coach watching some big stuffed toy dance in circles. Her brother and sister-in-law had left Daayana in their care while they vacationed in Mexico.

"Eh, much better," her mother said, coming down the hallway. "I needed an extra sweater and shirt. It feels like Siberia here."

"It's almost fifty degrees today, Mom."

"In Beirut this would be considered freezing."

Aminah shrugged.

"Let's take a look at these cookies," her mother muttered, ambling into the kitchen and to inspect her handiwork. "It looks like you dropped them. Well, some things don't change," she said.

Aminah gritted her teeth and used every ounce of willpower to hold back a reply.

"So," her mother said, switching to Arabic, "how are you feeling?"

"I'm fine. I'm finally starting to feel better."

Her mother munched on a cookie and Aminah could see the wheels spinning in her head.

"Good. Good. I was speaking to Mrs. Habibah and she mentioned that her son also lived in Washington."

"You promised me you wouldn't talk about this if I came for a visit."

"Well, I changed my mind. It is my duty as a mother. John has been dead for a year. It's time for you to move on and find someone else to help you. You need some children. Dayaana needs some cousins." Her niece glanced up for a moment at the mention of her name and then went back to the television.

"I don't need anyone else!"

"You cannot marry a kufar!"

"Don't use that word; you know I don't like it."

"You did that once and look what happened. Please Aminah, reconsider, understand. You will be making life hard on yourself. What if your children do not become Muslims?"

Aminah suspected her mother had been relieved at John's death, for it provided her daugher with a chance to start over. Although her mother never spoke the thought, she expressed it through body language, sighs, and her unceasing attempt to find Aminah another husband as soon as possible.

"Ami," her mother said, using her pet name, irritating her further. "The world has changed in many ways, but in other ways, it's still the same. Women appear stronger, but in reality they are also weaker."

She was about to tell her mother to keep her antiquated opinions to herself when her cellphone rang. Aminah looked at the number and frowned: 213-435-3343. A call from the Executive Mansion, the office building for the Vice President's staff.

"Hello," she answered. Her heart skipped a beat.

"Ms. O' Connor?"

"Yes?"

"Please provide your passcode."

She took out a thin card with six numbers flashing on one side in red. The numbers changed every fifteen minutes and needed to be read in a certain order.

"471171," she said, reading the third number first, the fourth number second, and so on.

"You're confirmed," he said, and his tone softened. "Ms. O' Connor, I'm calling from the office of the Vice President. Stephen Ambrose gave us your name. About thirty minutes ago, terrorists took control of American Air Flight 2718 en route from Boston to Sevilla. The terrorists are demanding the release of Sheikh Walid bin Imaad from his confinement in Virginia as well as one hundred million dollars in cash."

She expected some type of rescue attempt to happen eventually, for Sheikh Imaad commanded a fiery loyalty throughout what remained of the militant Islamic fundamentalist world.

"How many hostages?" she asked.

"Two hundred and seventy-five, including the Vice President's daughter."

Vison's daughter? How did they get to her? Commercial flights for top officials and their families were chosen at the last minute and the itinerary kept secret. The probability of terrorists randomly stumbling on the correct flight was exceedingly small.

"The Vice President requests your presence in Washington, immediately. He apologizes for the inconvenience but believes you understand the gravity of the situation."

"Yes, of course," she said.

"We've chartered a flight for you departing out of JFK."

"That's fine," she replied, thinking about her last encounter with Sheikh Imaad. She'd been on the CIA team that helped find him in the deserts of Morocco. The operation cost John his life.

"I'll be in Washington within the next two hours."

"Thank you. I'd like to ask you a couple more questions. Can you stay on the line?"

"Give me your phone number and I'll call you back in five minutes. I need to say goodbye to my family."

He gave her the number and hung up.

Worry forrowed her mother's brow. She never approved of Aminah's profession. When Aminah thought about it, her mother didn't approve of much but maybe that was the role of a mother.

"I have to go to Washington. There's been an emergency."

"What happened? Is everything all right?"

"Someone hijacked a plane about thirty minutes ago with the Vice President's daughter onboard."

"Hijacked a plane? Were they Arab?"

"It appears so."

"Uh," she said throwing her hands into the air. "Why is it always the Arabs? Don't they understand how it impacts us? I'm going to get more nasty stares at Bingo this week. I wish they'd just get those fanatics."

"We're trying," Aminah replied. Aminah wanted to laugh at her mother's melodramatics but a kernel of truth lay in her words. Every time Arab extremists perpetuated another act of violence, it reflected poorly on the whole community and made life more unpleasant and difficult. She had been harassed several times in the past, especially before she married John and changed her last name. Most Arabs hated the extremists as much as the general population. She looked up at the picture of her father on the mantle, and she remembered his dark, bushy mustache tickling her face. The extremists had killed him for believing in a modern Lebanon.

"Hopefully it won't be for more than a few days."

"Dayaana grabbed her hand.

"Auntie, do you have to go?" She stared up with big, brown eyes.

The plea broke Aminah's heart. She had been so looking forward to spending a few days with her niece. She bent down and brushed the hair off the girl's small face.

"Honey, I do need to leave for a little while. But you'll be here with Nani and your parents will be back soon."

Daayana nodded. "Be safe Auntie." She smiled.

"I always am."

Chapter 8

"The code is fine. The feed is fine. I just checked prices on several back-up data streams," said Amir. The line on the screen dropped like a rock thrown off a cliff.

Zeke forced himself to swallow and balled his hands into fists. Amir punched away at the keyboard.

"There's nothing wrong with the algorithm. Something happened to jolt the market," Zeke said. The algorithm predicted a maximum increase of one penny and suddenly it was down ten times that amount.

What would he tell Rachel? How could he face her parents and Lilly? He learned that events often were not as bad as they seemed, or as good.

They all held their breaths and then the line began to climb.

"This is really whipsawing," Amir said. "It's very unusual."

"Patric, check the news." Now the line had come all the way back and began to climb.

"We're getting another big divergence," Amir said. "But it's going in the other direction. The Canadian dollar is climbing."

Zeke did a quick calculation and realized the position was now worth over thirty-million dollars.

"What's causing the jump? Should we get out now?" Adele asked. The Canadian dollar rose another tenth of a penny and they had just made another ten-million dollars.

Logic said they should close the position since the results deviated from the model but he didn't feel satisfied with forty-million dollars. No, he needed more to truly show that his ideas had merit. "It's still going up," Zeke said, "let's ride it until it begins to come down again. Go with the trend." No risk, no reward, stay resolute and steadfast, don't panic.

Every tick up felt like another shot of adrenaline, like the force of gravity that tied him to the planet became a bit less able to hold him and his ideas tethered to the ground. Zeke allowed himself a brief smile and feeling of achievement. This was going to work. He envisioned himself getting off the plane in Italy, hugging Rachel and Sam, swinging them both as he explained that money was no longer a problem. The look on her parents' faces would also be priceless.

Patric typed furiously, stopped, and stared at the screen. "There's been a plane hijacking," he said.

Zeke processed the information. For some reason the news had first strengthened the US dollar but now it moved against the currency, exaggerating their position in the Canadian dollar and producing the profit. He studied hijackings as well as hundreds of other market shocks while building the model and none of them created this kind of divergence.

He turned to tell Adele to close the position just as Patric started reading from the article.

"…according to government sources, American Flight #2718 was hijacked approximately two hours after takeoff. It is unclear how the hijackers eluded airport security or what kind of weapons they might have onboard. What is known is that Victoria Vison, daughter of Vice President Edward Vison, is a passenger.

Sources at the State Department also confirm that a conversation occurred between the plane and a high-level official in the administration shortly after the terrorists took control of the airplane. In the transmission, one of the hijackers reportedly demanded the release of jailed terrorist leader Sheikh Abdul Imaad and one hundred million dollars. Radar is tracking the plane and it remains on course to reach its intended destination, Sevilla."

"Where?" Zeke asked, dropping his phone and finding it difficult to draw a breathe. "What was the plane number and where did you say it is going?" he managed to whisper as a stab of fear made his gut ache.

"American Air flight 2718 en route to Sevilla, Spain." Only Margaret understood his panic. He rushed out of the room, oblivious to the numbers dancing on the screen, and grabbed his iPhone. His fingers felt like kielbasa sausages as he fumbled to pull up Rachel's flight itinerary. Beside the blinking cursor, he saw the information he had entered on his phone: AmAir, Flt #2718.

Margaret walked into the office with a dour look on her face. "Was that their flight?" she asked.

His hands shook. "I think I took it down wrong. I was distracted and rushed when Rachel gave it to me."

"I'm going to call the airline to see if they are on the flight," she said softly. "Maybe they missed the plane or took a different one."

"Yes, that's a good idea," he mumbled. He sat at his desk, starting numbly at the numbers on the screen. His wife, his son, his life, were at this moment all up in the air– literally.

He wouldn't let himself lose a family again.

* * *

Margaret returned a few minutes later and her expression confirmed what he dreaded. Rachel and Sam were on flight 2718.

"They were on the plane, weren't they?" he asked.

"Yes, I'm sorry. The State Department set up a hotline for family members," she said, slipping him a piece of paper.

He stared out the window, focusing on a woman shuffling papers in another tower across the street.

"Women and children are usually let go from these situations, Zeke."

In the other hijackings he studied, the women and children managed to get out alive. Didn't they? He tried to remember a specific example, and for once his excellent memory failed him.

Zeke could see the other three walking tentatively towards his office.

"Are Rachel and Sam on the plane?" Adele asked.

"It appears they are."

Patric held up a middle finger towards the ceiling. "Fuckers!"

"I'm sorry this is happening," Amir said. "I hope they will be okay."

The phone rang and a number he didn't recognize flashed across the LCD display. He picked it up, hoping to speak to an official from the airline or the government.

"Hello."

"Zeke, It's Lilly."

"Lilly, now is really not a good—"

"Weren't your wife and daughter going to Sevilla today?"

Zeke closed his eyes. "Rachel is with Sam, my son. Yes, they are on the plane."

She sighed. "My God. I'm sorry. Have you heard anything?" She sounded sympathetic and very un-Lilly-like.

"No, I don't even know where to start."

"I might be able to help. The Secretarty of State is a close friend of mine. I've done a few favors for him in the past. He might be able to help."

Rachel would be aghast but he had no choice.

"Lilly, thank you, I appreciate it."

"Of course. I'm going to send you his personal number. He'll probably send you to one of his assistants, but Vance will know where to start."

"Thanks."

"Stop thanking me. We're not just business partners, we're friends. Remember? I care about you. Let me know if you run into any problems. I would be remiss though if I didn't ask about the position. How is it doing?"

"I don't know. The hijacking disturbed the model. It's a black swan event."

"A what?"

"Nothing. It's just a financial term. The position is up at this point and the team is monitoring it closely."

"Of course, well let's hope everything turns out well."

"Thank you, Lilly," he said, meaning it. He ended the conversation and began dialing Lilly's contact when Patric entered the room.

"The terrorists snuck a bomb on the plane," the computer whiz said somberly.

Zeke stopped dialing, paralyzed momentarily by the news.

"And the position is going haywire."

Chapter 9

Rachel needed to go to the bathroom and her bladder ached. Sam's weight on top of her lap only added to the discomfort but she didn't dare move, fearful of waking Sam and drawing White Guy's attention. Even as she thought about her full bladder, Sam stirred, stretched an arm, kicked a leg out, and fell into a deep slumber in his new position. She gently wiped a sheen of sweat from his upper lip.

Sam had finally fallen asleep, which allowed her to relax a bit. White Guy, as she now thought of him, made it clear he wanted the baby to stop crying. The third time he mentioned it, Rachel caught a look in his eye that told her he would make her son shut up if she didn't find a way to do it. She had bounced Sam on her knee and rubbed his back while singing one of his favorite songs, *Little Boy Sam*. Zeke made it up when Sam was just an infant.

"Who's the little boy lying in his bed?
It's a little baby, covered on the head.
He's going to grow up and do wonderful things-
Like travel to Saskatchewan;
And play Carnegie Hall;
And hit a home run for the Red Sox;
And write a great novel;
And run a marathon;
And meet a wonderful girl;
And have some kids.
He'll be higher in the sky
Then the greatest of kites.

So who's the little ball lying in his bed?
It's my little boy Sam
And I love him in red."

The last line needed work. Listening to the familiar words had calmed her son and his eyes had closed.

Only after his eyes closed did she begin to ponder their predicament. At first, she panicked. She didn't want her baby to die! She didn't want to die! She took a couple of deep breaths and managed to stop the building crescendo of fear. Breathe in, breathe out, relax. Rachel still couldn't believe terrorists hijacked the plane. This only happened in the movies.

Feeling a bit more calm, Rachel's eyes wandered to the poor secret service man slumped in the next aisle. How was his family going to feel? Blood crusted the front of his shirt. The Vice President's daughter– was her name Virginia?–sat curled up with her face against the window, a sob wracking her body every so often. She wanted to comfort the young girl, but the bastards wouldn't let any of them move and she needed to look after Sam.

She took a moment to assess the hijackers. Not an impressive looking group at first sight. The man giving orders, the one who shot the secret service agent was a dark-skinned man. Definitely Arab. He appeared clean-cut, with almond-shaped eyes that darted across the plane, and a Yankees hat on his head. She named him Leader Guy.

The white supremacist look-alike from the cornfields of Nebraska she named White Guy. How he wound up on a plane with Arab terrorists instead of painting swastikas on tombstones must have been quite a story. He seemed dangerous, striding angrily about the cabin, smacking the passengers in the head or the face, leering like a high school bully at the terror he inflicted.

The third hijacker, a homely, pimpled, dark-complexioned reed of a man with two missing front teeth glared at the passengers and mumbled to himself. He took orders from the others, so she named him Mule. The fourth hijacker, the one with the bomb, remained in the cabin so she named him No Show.

Rachel considered their chances of being released. The US government *claimed* that it didn't negotiate with terrorists, but everyone knew that to be untrue. The Vice President's daughter's presence on the plane mattered.

She imagined a flash and the cabin breaking apart, the pieces falling, her body plummeting through the sky as she clutched Sam to her chest. She would protect her baby for as long as she could.

Her bladder ached and she shifted her body to relieve the pressure. Except for the occasional cough or sneeze, the plane remained quiet. Behind her, in the galley between first class and coach, all but No Show huddled in discussion. White Guy and Leader Guy seemed to be arguing. Dissension amongst the ranks was probably a good thing.

Rachel desperately wanted to let Zeke know they were unharmed but earlier White Guy had collected all the phones and dumped them into a bag.

She should have listened to the warning and cancelled the trip. Damn Lorna. It didn't look her evil co-worker sent the message after all. Who then? Goosebumps rippled up her arms as she watched the hijcakers continue to talk amongst themselves. Someone knew the plane would be hijacked. Who? None of it made any sense.

After several minutes, the party broke up. White Guy went to the front of the first class cabin and asked a man in a business suit for his passport. The man hastily pulled a briefcase up from below his seat, clicked it open, and withdrew an EU passport. White Guy examined it, looked at the name and then asked him a question.

"Are you Spanish?"

"Si."

"Catholic?"

"Si."

"Get up." The man rose, trembling. "Go with him."

"Donde? Donde voy?"

White Guy raised his hand and violently swept his gun into the man's face. The Spaniard staggered back but kept himself upright by grabbing the tops of the seats. Blood spurted from his nose and his left eye filled with red.

"Go with him," White Guy said again. Mule approached, grabbed the man by the arm and took him out of first class. They repeated the process with two other passengers and then came to an olive-skinned man sitting in front of Rachel.

"Passport." White Guy stuck out his hand. The well dressed, middle-aged man pointed up towards the luggage bins.

"It's up there," he said.

"Get it."

He rose, opened the bin, and brought down a carry-on bag. He rifled through it and withdrew his passport before White Guy pushed him back into his seat. Rachel could see that he enjoyed the dominance and power he held over the passengers. She hated him.

White Guy examined the passport and then spoke much more respectfully. "Inshallah," he said. "I am sorry that you must be a part of this and I apologize for the inconvenience."

"Let the plane go," the man said. "This is not what Allah wants." She expected White Guy to get angry but instead, he smiled.

"My friend, I know you think we are walking the wrong path, but soon you will see that it is you who have been deceived. In the meantime, I tell you that you will not be harmed. Please once again accept my apologies. This will all hopefully be over soon. Allah Akbar," he said again. White Guy collected a few other passports, sending two more passengers to the back of the plane.

White Guy finally came to their row. Her heart pounded madly, her breath caught in her lungs. A mother's protective instinct, honed through thousands of years of persecution, came alive. When White Guy had started his rounds, Rachel had tucked her necklace with a Jewish Star into her shirt and she hoped now he wouldn't notice it.

Her grandfather gave her the star as a Bat-Mitzvah gift when she turned thirteen.

"This was your grandmother's," he said. "On the train to Auschwitz, she gave it to me and told me that it was her last piece of jewelry. Some day, she prayed that I could wear it and be proud and not have to worry about being singled out or killed. She knew that she was going to die and she wanted to pass it along to me, hoping that I would survive the gas chambers and the death that awaited us all to see a better day. When we got to the camp, I dug a hole and hid the necklace near the barracks where they housed us to die. My mother divined her own fate; she died in the ovens. For the next three months, I managed to survive in the camp, scraping by, feeling barely human, but remembering some shred of dignity. Finally, when the Americans liberated the camp, I dug up the necklace and placed it around my neck. I became so stooped and thin that it dangled to my belly. But in front of the NAZI pigs, I put the necklace on and never again took it off."

"But I can't take this, Papa."

He gave her a big hug. "Yes, of course you can. Don't worry, I'm not going to die. I just want the pleasure of seeing it on someone I love. Wear it proudly, Rachel, for those who couldn't."

Her grandfather hadn't survived Auschwitz by being stupid though.

"Passport," he said staring down at her. His cold blue eyes appraised her and then passed over sleeping Sam. She handed it to him. He studied it for a moment before his lips twisted into a smile.

"Katz, what kind of name is that?"

"It's German," she said to White Guy. That was a lie. Zeke was Episcopelian but had a Jewish paternal grandfather who passed the name to his grandson.

"You don't look German to me."

"My father was German and my mother was Spanish, which is why I am traveling to Sevilla."

The woman sitting beside them suddenly spoke in a thick French accent. "Oh no, no, she's not German or Spanish. I saw, I saw what she did with the necklace that she tucked under her shirt. She's a Jew. The woman and her baby are Jews. They're Jews, I saw the star on her necklace."

The betrayal stunned Rachel.

White Guy smirked. "I knew that she was a Jew. You can smell a Jew, just like you can smell a monkey."

"Khalid, take these two Jews back." Mule lurched forward and grabbed her arm. She tried to get up, forgetting that her seatbelt remained fastened, and bounced back down. Sam shifted in her arms and his eyes fluttered open. He stretched, saw his mother, and smiled.

"Come," Khalid said. He pulled her arm and she managed to unbuckle the lap belt and stagger to her feet. As she stood, the need to urinate became nearly unbearable and she struggled to hold Sam and step forward.

"Move!" Nasser yelled. Sam smiled at the French bitch. Rachel turned to glare at her betrayer but the woman stared out the window.

"Momma," Sam said.

The Muslim passenger stood up. "What are you doing to them?" the man asked. "She is a woman with a child. This is not right."

"My friend, this is not your business. Sit down."

"No Muslim would do this. This is not Allah's will. It is thuloum. The Koran forbids doing harm to women and children."

White Guy pointed his gun at the man's head. "I will ask you nicely one more time– sit down. Jews are monkeys and dogs. They do not receive the same consideration as the rest of the people in the Koran. That is all I will say."

The man pursed his lips, slowly turned, and sat in his seat.

"Now go!" White Guy said and Khalid pulled her and Sam out of first class and down the coach aisle.

"May I use the restroom?" she asked as they neared the back of the plane. He shook his head no and indicated that she should sit in the empty last row, right next to the latrine door.

Rachel sat and clutched Sam, who began to squirm. He wanted to walk and squealed as she held him down.

"Please Sam," she whispered, trying to manage her son. She felt an enormous release mixed with shame as a warm feeling spread down her buttocks and legs.

Rachel often wondered what her grandfather, grandmother, and other family members experienced during the NAZI terror. What did it feel like to be singled out, humiliated, degraded, and killed? Now she knew. This bond with her ancestors calmed her nerves and strengthened her resolve. She would not go passively to her death, like sheep led to the slaughterhouse—she would fight. Rachel banished her desire to cry, focused her mind, and reviewed her options. She needed to save herself and her child. And if it was their destiny to die, it would at least be a noble death.

Chapter 10

"What can you tell me about Sheikh Abdul Imaad?" Harold Stimson, the Secretary of Defense asked.

Stimson was a thin, short man, with blue flinty blue eyes and a patch of whitish, grey hair on his large head. Stubble shadowed his face and small tufts of hair poked out from his ears. In the middle of the desk sat a three foot long, 1:500 scale die-cast model of the USS Enterprise. He fiddled with a black stapler, opening and closing it with surprisngly delicate and nimble hands.

Her boss, Stephen Ambrose, sat next to Aminah. He ran the Office of Counter Intelligence, a small, secretive group outside of the main military establishment. The OCT didn't report to either the Secretary of Defense or to the intelligence community, but to the Vice President. President Rodriguez and Vice President Vison considered the DOD and the CIA too leak-prone and set up the OCT to handle the most classified information related to terrorism. The capture and apprehension of Sheikh Imaad ranked as the group's biggest success.

Ambrose celebrated his sixty-third birthday a month earlier and he remained spry and stronger than most men half his age. A former Green Beret, he kept himself in shape, working out every day and taking five mile runs around the mall.

He flashed her a reassuring smile that eased the anxiety – a bit. On the other side of the table, next to Stimson sat General Hague, the head of the Joint Chiefs of Staff.

In the back seat of the Lincoln Town Car on the way to the meeting, Stephen had given her a few quick words of wisdom.

"Don't be intimidated. You're the foremost expert on Fist of Allah. They'll go gentle. They know what happened to John."

Stimson continued. "I know we locked him away about seven years ago along with a bunch of other fundamentalist, but what does he want, what is he thinking?" Stimson asked as a follow up.

You've got this, she told herself. "He is an extremely radical man, Mr. Secretary. He was born in Egypt in 1957 and grew up during the era of Pan-Arab nationalism that thrived during Nasser's rule. He spent several years in Nasser's movement before he became disenchanted and joined the Muslim Brotherhood."

"In Egypt?"

"Yes. Although he became much more radical than the Brotherhood there. He believes the Brotherhood has been tainted and corrupted, Westernized, which is the worst possible insult.

"Mubarak forced him to leave Egypt with his family in 1991 and he appeared in Sudan, Afghanistan, Oman, Eden, and Indonesia at various times.

"During his travel through these countries, he made contacts with other fundamentalist cells and became further radicalized. The basic ideologies of these groups revolve around the creation of an Islamic state throughout the world. They believe that they are following a holy edict and that God himself will help them in their quest. Imaad believes any means is justified in pursuing this holy goal." She paused to see if there were any questions. None.

"After his exile from Egypt, Imaad became more active in the actual planning of terrorist attacks. He also emerged as a leader, attracting a group of adherents to his radical views. His group was implicated in the bombing of several oil tankers in the Persian Gulf and the ignition of the natural gas pipeline in Austin, Texas. The United States tracked him to Mali where Special Ops forces apprehended him after a bloody battle. During the operation, one of his wives and two children were killed. It is believed he is survived by a son and a granddaughter. As I'm sure you know, he is in Virginia serving a life sentence."

"You were part of the team that found him, isn't that right?" Secretary Stimson asked.

"I provided intelligence that OCT used to track him down."

"And your husband died in the operation? He was part of the Mali kill team?"

"Yes," she replied. "John died on the mission." Or so the official report stated. The OCT never recovered his body and while the government told her he died in the hunt for the Sheikh, something about the story seemed...incomplete. Who killed him? When? Where? The report omitted these facts. She forced John from her mind. She needed to focus on this crisis.

The Secretary nodded and clicked the stapler closed before proceeding. "Do you know a Walid bin Ibrahim?"

"No. I haven't heard the name before."

"He seems to be one of the central hijackers," Ambrose said. "He spoke to us. We checked the passenger list and didn't find his name on the flight. Walid's English is excellent."

"I'm not surprised you didn't find him on the list. Fist of Allah is adept at frequently changing identities to evade the law and cover their tracks. It also doesn't surprise me that he spoke English so fluently. Many of the group's members have lived or studied in the United States. Lately, they've managed to recruit American-born citizens to their cause.

"We always thought native terrorists comprised the soft underbelly of our security system," Ambrose added. "Over the past ten years, Fist of Allah has made inroads recruiting in U.S. jails. We've received reports of the group intentionally placing its members in prison to help with their recruitment efforts. Imaad has also been successful personally recruiting inmates."

Ambrose turned back to Aminah. "The plane is over Germany. Do you have any idea about where it might go?" he asked.

Softball question. *Thank you, Stephen.*

"Undoubtedly to some country in the Middle East. A location the United States would have trouble reaching quickly and where the local law is relatively weak or unable to interfere. "

The Secretary clicked the stapler closed again and then put it down on his desk. He fiddled with a pen and looked up.

"So what do you think is going to happen if we don't let him go and pay the money?" he asked.

Aminah had spent so many years studying Sheik Imaad and researching the ethos of Fist of Allah that she didn't need to even think about the answer. "They will kill everyone on the plane. These people are committed and willing to lose their lives. In their minds the passengers on that plane are part of a system they want to destroy. Because citizens from Western democracies support the system, every man, woman, and child are as much the enemy as the soldier holding a gun or manning a tank. There are no innocent civilians in their ideology."

"Mrs. O' Connor, in your opinion, what do you think we should do?" Stimson asked.

It was the first time he called her by name. "If you want to save the passenger's lives, I would recommend letting Imaad go and sending the money."

"Could we just storm the plane and surprise them?" General Hague asked, breaking his silence.

"You could try, but first you'd have to get men out there and set them up. Before you could do that, I expect the plane would be blown to dust," she answered.

The Secretary folded his hands in front of him and took a deep sigh. "We do not. as a course of policy, negotiate with terrorist. Of course, we've broken that directive on several occasions. The Vice President, as you can imagine, is deeply concerned about the situation as well as the fate of his daughter. He directed me to find a way to resolve this problem with minimal loss of life. He is comfortable releasing the Sheikh but doesn't like the idea of paying their blood money. It's too blatant, something the Democrats would surely discover and use in the next election." He clicked the stapler and scanned the room. I'd like some ideas on my desk within one hour. That's it for now," he said, abruptly ending the meeting. "Ambrose, stick around."

Ambrose walked her to the door, taking her arm and bending over to whisper in her ear. His breathe smelled sour.

"Stay close by. We may need you shortly." He gave her a wink and closed the door.

* * *

She took a sip of coffee from a white Styrofoam cup and although it tasted terrible, the warmth felt good. She found a cafeteria in the bowels of the Pentagon and listened to two women at the next table talking and laughing.

Her phone vibrated against the table. "Hello," she said, expecting it to be Ambrose or someone from the CIA.

"Aminah O' Connor?" asked an unfamiliar voice.

"Yes."

"My name is Zeke Katz. Felix Arroyo at the State Department gave me your number." Felix manned the Middle Eastern affairs desk at State and had been a good friend of John's. Since John's death, he visited her a couple of times to see if she needed anything. She could guess what he thought she needed and had politely declined his offers to grab a bite to eat. So much for friendship. When you died, the vultures moved in.

The man paused for a moment before continuing. "Aminah, my wife and son are on American Air 2718, the hijacked flight."

Her heart dropped at hearing his news but she stayed silent. She didn't want to breach protocol. Felix shouldn't have passed him on to her.

He continued. "Felix told me that you might have some information, something more than what they are saying on the news."

"I'm sorry, Mr…"

"Katz."

"Mr. Katz. I'd like to, but I can't. The highest levels of the government are involved and are determined to resolve this issue in the best possible way. I'm sorry." He sighed and Aminah realized she sounded exactly like a soulless government bureaucrat.

He didn't let the conversation end. "I understand there's a demand for $100 million. Is that true?"

She hesitated. "Yes, it's true," she finally said.

"I don't know if the government is willing to pay the ransom but I've recently come into some money, and I'm willing to pay it out of my own pocket if necessary."

She was about to give him another bout of government speak and decline his offer when she realized Mr. Katz might hold the solution. While the US government might be hesitant to pay the ransom, a private citizen could do whatever he or she wanted. Of course, ransom money from a private citizen still sent a message that America paid to free hostages and that might encourage more hijackings down the line, but if it resolved the problem today, who knew about the future?

"That's an interesting proposal. Let me run it by some of my colleagues and let you know." She took down his number and promised to provide an update shortly.

Before she hung up, Aminah couldn't stop herself from asking: "How old is your son?" She had been trained not to get personally involved in a hostage situation, but she could never resist the urge to connect personally with those impacted by an event. When John died, she wanted to be treated like a human-being. The blank faces and stonewalling only made the grief worse and she refused to treat another person the same way.

"He's a little over two."

She remembered Dayaana at two. "I'll be praying for him and your wife."

"Thank you, I appreciate that."

She hung up the phone and wondered if she had made the right move. Getting a civilian involved might be a brilliant stroke, or it could end her career.

Chapter 11

Rachel's watch read 11:00 pm. It had been a little over twelve hours since they had taken off from Logan and her legs felt like wood while her back ached from the sitting. While rowing crew in college, she herniated a disc and prolonged sitting and stress tended to reawaken the old injury. Rachel couldn't stop shivering even though others on the plane looked rather hot. She fiddled with the air nozzle but only varying degrees of cold air blew out.

She sat in hell the last three hours. Sam wanted to get up and move around but Mule, his real name Khalid made it very obvious he was not to do that. The acne pocked terrorist skulked around with a permanent sneer, his unibrow and jutting eye ridge making him look like a troll.

When he wasn't able to get up, Sam began to struggle, and then to squeal in anger. At first, his cries sounded more like grunts as he fought against her arms. Showing no real prrogress, his objections became louder and the wailing started. Her head throbbed, her hands shook as she rocked him in a frantic effort to quiet her son.

"Sam, please, stop. Just sit on Momma's lap." She knew he understood but he struggled even harder and shrieked at the top of his lungs.

"Sam, stop crying!" she hissed. His lower lip jutted out and then he put his head against her chest and lay back, big tears coursing down his cheeks. He sobbed for a few minutes before lifting his head.

"Out. Out," he said pointing towards the window. She started to cry herself.

"I know you want to go out. Hopefully we will soon." She rubbed his hair. "I'm sorry for yelling at you. I really am. You're a good boy." He lay back down and shortly after fell asleep. She prayed that he slept for another couple of hours.

The lightening sky told her that they must have traveled quite a distance west. Europe was six hours ahead of the East Coast and she thought the Middle East was eight. If it was 7:00 am, then they would be seeing the dawn of the new day.

The cabin remained quiet. She and Sam sat in the very back, alone, while the rest of the Americans sat ten rows in front of them, and the Europeans one row further up. Passengers from mostly developing countries filled the front of the plane and Muslims sat in first class. It had all been arranged in a hierarchy.

Two of the hijackers – Mule and White Guy patrolled the coach aisle, keeping an eye on them and occasionally investigating something that looked amiss. At one point White Guy came with Bin Gaudi to discuss their captives.

"Imagine, a whole plane of people and we only caught ourselves two Jews. I thought you people traveled in hordes. I expected at least three or four of you."

She shivered and clutched Sam tighter.

He gave her an icy smirk and then walked back to the front.

Occasionally, another passenger came back to use the bathroom. Some tried to smile but the vast majority took furtive peeks, looking quickly away to avoid any eye contact. Was it guilt or shame, or something else that made people turn away? She and Sam occupied the lowest rung on the totem pole, like a villager branded with a scarlet letter. In college, she studied psychology and understood the terrorists' methods. Separate and divide the plane, create classes of victims to break the morale and cohesiveness of the group.

The sun's rays glinted off the side of the fusalage and the vast white dessert sparkled below them: rippling dunes and an occasional black dot that might have been a structure or a rock formation. Her ears popped as the features on the ground became clearer and closer. The plane was descending. They would be on the ground shortly.

As the sky brightened further, other passengers peered out of their windows. Sand rippled like fish scales in the glittering sun and the terrain stretched off beyond the horizon. Rachel knew that a large jumbo jet could not land in the sand– the plane would be torn apart without a hard runway– and needed a sizable landing strip. Still, the plane continued to drop.

Sam stirred and grimaced. His ears must have been popping. The ground grew closer, perhaps 1,000 feet below them and now she could see spots of color mixed into the shimmering ground– a splash of black signifying some rocky outcrop or a dash of color showing a cluster of cactus. The plane dropped:

500 feet.

400 feet.

300 feet.

Could the hijackers be crazy? What would they accomplish by crashing the plane into the desert? The absurdity of flying thousands of miles just to crash the jet kept her from panicking. There had to be another plan. Further up, a woman began to scream.

"We're going to crash into the desert! Please God, no!" She stood and the man beside her, probably her husband, frantically yanked on her arm to pull her back to her seat. "I don't want to die!" she sobbed.

Two hundred feet.

One hundred feet.

Small shrubs and cacti whipped by and the peaks and troughs of the dunes became clearer, the air shimmying around them, incandescent, resplendescent, like thousands of diamonds strewn over the land. She squinted at the glare.

Fifty-feet.

Thirty feet.

Still no visible runway. She grasped Sam tightly and planted a kiss on his forehead.

Chapter 12

Ten miles from the airport he spotted the bright glint, like a supernova in a sky full of stars. Walid sighed in relief. Twelve other beacons flashed through the sun and sand. They found the spot. Now the captain needed to land the plane.

"There." Walid pointed to the shimmering reflections. "That is where we'll land."

"If we land in the dessert, we're going to die. You might as well have detonated your bomb over the ocean," the pilot replied.

Fool.

"Have you no faith in Allah? Just point the plane in that direction and bring it down." He placed the muzzle of the gun against the captain's thin neck to dispel any lingering doubts.

The captain sighed.

"Bring it down, captain, right on those beacons. I hope you can fly." A sheen of perspiration covered the bald pate of the pilot's head. Weak unbeliever.

Allah rewarded His believers graciously. He held the Vice President's daughter as well as two hundred and forty-five passengers as hostages. Walid fully expected Sheikh Imaad would soon be free and their account flush with the money they needed for phase two. Once that happened, their dream of destroying the enemy and wakening the Muslim masses, of spreading the power of Islam across the globe would become a reality. If Allah wished it so.

One step at a time, he told himself.

The plane descended rapidly and Walid saw the beautiful dunes. After being away for three years, he basked in the majesty of the desert, his home. The Prophet's feet touched these grains, trod through this landscape, and he felt Allah's presence in the stark beauty.

A flat strip of ground cut through the sea of dunes, like the parting of the Red Sea – a landing strip. On either side of the strip silver lights flashed, his beacons.

"You want me to land on that?" Sweat glistened off the captain's bald head.

"Yes, is there a problem?"

"The runway is too short. We won't be able to stop in time."

"You must find a way to do it. Put your trust in Allah." Why couldn't these dhimmi understand that true peace and clarity came through fidelity to Allah? He decided when it was time for you to die; He chose your path. Walid did not worry about things he could not control for Allah controlled his destiny and He alone would decide when Walid's mission would end. If Allah willed him to die today, then let that be his fate.

As the plane descended, his mind remained clear and calm, even as his heart rate increased and sweat slicked the back of his neck. The ground sped by underneath and he wondered if the runway could support the plane. Yes, with Allah's guidance, it would be all right.

They blasted by several parked trucks and then the tires met the ground, letting out a shriek of protest. A jolt shook the plane before it lifted, and the wheels touched down again. The captain pushed the throttle back and Walid flew forward, hitting the front console and smashing his face into a bank of dials and switches. As he staggered back, blood oozing down his face, he groggily observed the end of the runway rushing towards them.

"Stop the plane!" he tried to scream but it came out as a muffled groan.

"The runway isn't long enough. There's not enough space!"

"Stop it!" he managed to stammer, tasting the blood coursing down his face. The warm blood reinvigorated him and Walid placed the muzzle of the gun back against the Captain's head.

"I said stop the plane!"

"I'm trying! It's as far back as it will go." Before either of them could say or do anything else, the runway ended, and the plane plowed into the soft dunes. Walid gaped as an enormous wave of sand washed over the window. He plowed forward again, hit something hard, and staggered back into the first class aisle before collapsing to the floor.

Groaning, he blinked blood from his eyes, and saw Hassan staring down at him. They had landed.

Chapter 13

Aminah's attempt to stay clear of politics had only been successful some of the time. The United States' intelligence agencies clawed at each others' throats, angling for influence, for funds, for exposure. On any given day, one of the directors could be on top, just to be toppled in an internecine power shuffle.

Sitting in the Secretary of Defense's office for the third time in the last seven hours, Aminah realized politics, not sound policy, dictated the decision-making process. Just as she opened her mouth to voice her concern, the door to the conference room flung open and the Vice President strode into the room, his long legs propelling him to the conference room table in three strides. Andrew Mills Vison played football in college and she could see he still kept in shape. He moved easily, confidently, like someone who knew where he was going and what he wanted. In many ways, he reminded her of an older version of John, with the square jaw and the same fluid motion of an athlete.

Focus. Don't let everything bring you back to John, especially not now. How ridiculous would she look if she started crying in front of the most powerful men the world?

President Rodriquez won the election as a moderate Republican from California and the first Hispanic President, while Vison was a religious conservative from Texas. They made an odd but effective ticket. Most pundits thought Rodriguez a bit intellectual and bookish while they described Vison as a cocktail of Southern bravado mixed with an ex-preacher's charm.

John once told her that most of Washington believed the Raqaa civilian massacre had destroyed Vison's chances of ever becoming President. While the panel of inquiry never directly implicated him, Vison commanded two of the units, and the official report blamed his take-no-prisoners, hate thy enemy approach for contributing to a climate of "military excesses."

Despite his reputation, Aminah liked him. John worked with him more closely and seemed charmed by the ex-General and his gruff bravado. Vison surprised her by coming to John's funeral, where he had appoached Aminah and told her how much he enjoyed getting to know her husband.

"Hello Dick and Stephen," he said, shaking hands before taking his seat.

Aminah felt the level of tension rise in the room as it was well known in Washington that the Secretary and Vice President did not like each other. Vison considered Secretary Stimson unqualified to serve because he had used a medical deferment to get out of Vietnam. At least that was what Ambrose told her.

"Andrew, we're awfully sorry to hear about your daughter," Secretary Stimson said.

"Don't make apologies, Dick. Just tell me what we're doing to resolve the situation."

Stimson glared at him before nodding to a bald CIA analyst named Harold Finnman.

Aminah turned to Ambrose and although he appeared calm she knew his blood boiled watching the CIA take lead on the presentation.

Harold stood in front of an image of the Arabian Peninsula. A plane icon appeared on the lower right portion of a white land mass surrounded by water.

"The plane landed in a remote part of the Arabian Peninsula, approximately three hundred miles from Medina, and four hundred and fifty miles from Abu Dhabi."

Harold clicked a button and a grainy image displayed a dark strip cutting across a blanket of white. Several square objects lined the runway and at the end sat a black bug-like mark. "Pan-Sat took this image about one hour ago." He pointed to the strip and the square shapes. "This is a landing strip that must have been constructed over the last several months. An image from six months ago doesn't show the structure. Beside the landing strip, are several temporary buildings. At the end of the strip, actually off the end, is the plane. The hijacking was well planned. "

"Do we have any men on the ground? Can we surround the plane?" Vison asked.

"The Saudis gave us permission to send in a team," he replied. "It'll take a day to gather the group and get them to the plane."

"That's too much time," Vison said. "Don't we have a team on standby, Stephen?"

"We did but they were deployed to Pakistan. It will take at least twelve hours to get them back and into position. We'll need to buy some time. We can string the bastards along, tell them it will take a few hours to get the money together while we get our men into position."

"What about the Saudis? Do they have anyone we can send in?" asked Vison.

"No," Stimson said.

"Goddamit!" Vison hissed, nostrils flaring, eyes glaring from across the table. "My daugher is on that plane! They said they were going to start killing hostages if their demands were not met within the next hour!"

"Andrew—" Secretary Stimson started before Vison cut him off.

"Mr. Vice President."

Stimson glared at him. "Mr. Vice President, they won't kill Victoria first, you know that. She's too valuable for them. It may not be possible to prevent a total loss of life but we can probably save most of the plane."

Save most of the plane? Aminah couldn't believe what she just heard. Since when did they concede casualties during an operation? The plan also underestimated the terrorists. This Walid somehow managed to hijack a plane and land it on a pre-built runway strip. He undoubtedly already thought through the US response and prepared for it.

Aminah tried to open her mouth but nothing came out. What if she was wrong? Where was Harold? She saw he had sunk into a chair and she watched him dab the the perspiration from his face with a paper bathroom towel. Ah hell, Harold managed to present and since when did she hold her tongue? "Releasing Sheikh—"

Before she could finish her sentence, the Vice President cut her off. "I spoke with the President before the meeting," Vison said. "He wants this situation resolved with a minimal loss of life. He gave his authorization to start the process for granting clemency to Sheik Imaad. The Sheik's an old, ill man whose best years are behind him. We can claim that we were going to do this anyway because of his poor health."

"That's a mistake," she blurted out.

All eyes turned to her. She had their attention.

"Sheikh Imaad is the leader. Fist of Allah revolves around him. He's vicious and far from done. He inspires his followers to fanatical acts on behalf of his radical interpretation of Islam. According to Imaad's worldview, a perpetual state of Jihad exists until Allah gains worldwide dominance. His men follow him with a cult-like devotion and they would kill as many people as necessary to further the group's goals. He's far from retired. Some of our contacts tell us he's busy recruiting inmates while in prison."

Did she go too far? Ambrose's face looked blank. Not a good sign.

"It's been decided," Vison replied.

Plucking up courage she didn't know existed, Aminah straightened her back and turned to the Vice President. "So, you're just going to release my husband's killer?"

"Aminah," Ambrose interjected, "give us another option." Unable to think of one on the spot, Aminah felt the bravado deflate. She knew from experience that Vison tolerated objections as long as an alternative was also presented. Stupid. How could she have stumbled forward without a plan?

Vison eyed her like she had three eyes and continued. "We're willing to release Imaad, but not pay the ransom. Paying a ransom is against U.S. policy."

Yeah, and so is letting a convicted felon out of prison, she thought.

Vison continued: "There needs to be another way—a donor who is willing to lend the money outside of government circles."

She wet her lips and looked over at Stephen, who flashed a tired smile. Should she mention her solution? Would they even listen or just brush her aside again? Aminah felt like an ant advising an elephant how to walk. Maybe she could redeem her previous flub.

"I believe I know someone who can provide the money," she said. Heads turned in her direction and to her relief they didn't laugh.

"It has to be totally untraceable," Vison said.

She couldn't turn back now. "Not in this case," she replied. "The person I am thinking of has a wife and son on the plane. I spoke to him about an hour ago and he volunteered to pay the ransom."

Ambrose understood immediately. "It can be a private deal between the terrorists and your contact. Our hands will be clean."

"Yes, that might work," Stimson agreed.

"Who's the source?" Vison asked her.

"His name is Zeke Katz."

"A Jew?" asked Vison.

"I'm not sure but I would guess so because of his name. Being Jewish would only increase the risk to his wife and daughter. Imaad and his followers are known to be virulently anti-Semitic."

Stimson nodded. "So how do we reach Mr. Katz?" Stimson asked.

She held up her phone. "We can call him," she said, feeling a small bit of satisfaction for getting their attention.

Chapter 14

Walid calmly sipped his steaming cup of chai from a small glass, half listening to Hassan.

"You know what the source said, the Americans will bluff and bluff. In the meantime, they are sending their helicopters over here as we speak. While we sip tea, they are getting ready to encircle us. What good will the money do if we are all dead?"

Walid and Hassan sat with two others around a short table in a small, wooden hut beside the runway. Two sheets of paper with inscriptions from the Koran adorned otherwise bare walls.

Walid couldn't remember the names of the others, but they kept themselves, like many followers of Sheikh Imaad, with long, shaggy beards and dirty, unclipped nails.

Twice in the last hour Hassan had criticized his judgment in front of them, and Walid tried to still his growing irritation by ignoring the American's incessant chatter. He found it impossible to tune it out.

Because of the relationship Hassan had forged with the Sheikh in prison, the American had gained some degree of authority. According to the tales told by Hassan, a group of white supremacists decided to kill Sheikh Imaad by stabbing him with a fork on the exercise fields. Hassan belonged to the group but Allah spoke to him while he peeled potatoes in the kitchen, telling him to save the blind man. He alerted the Sheikh to the plot and the guards found the supremacists the next day, hanging dead from the shower nozzles. Hassan performed a great deed saving the Sheik's life but Walid didn't fully trust him. The American possessed a side that existed to inflict pain, his judgment often clouded by blood lust and the enjoyment of hurting others. Fist of Allah needed to be ruthless but the violence served a purpose. In Walid's opinion such a man did not work for God, he worked for himself. But Imaad trusted the American and so chose him to also take part in the mission.

It had taken four years and twenty people to plan the operation and he wouldn't let Hassan cause problems or jeopardize it with his temper or lack of thinking. Four years he spent poring over maps, trudging through the burning desert, holding clandestine meetings, and rehashing and rehearsing every detail, expecting the CIA to burst through the door at any moment and drag him off. Now, in the comfort of the desert, they were so close to success. Of course, they still did not have the money or word of Imaad's release. Walid banished the thought. Through Allah's will they would shortly.

Hassan continued his speech in garbled Arabic. "Do you know the helicopters fly low to evade radar? They come swooping in and before you know what is happening – bang, bang, bang," he said in a mix of Allah's language and filthy English.

Walid doubted Hassan ever saw a helicopter come flying over a sea of dunes. While the American sat locked in jail, Walid had fled through the Sahara, into Mali and then back to Saudi to escape the Americans. Hassan knew nothing about the vastness of the desert, its power, and also its perils.

Walid checked his watch. They captured the plane five hours ago and according to the timetable, the money should have been deposited into the bank by now. They were falling behind schedule. What was taking so long? He considered giving the Americans a call but he didn't want to telegraph his own apprehension. No, he needed to maintain the perception of strength.

"Hassan, please be quiet. I've heard enough."

The large head snapped towards him. "I can talk if I want. No one said you can control what I say."

The others exchanged nervous glances.

"I just asked you to be quiet."

"Well, I'm trying to tell you that things are moving too slowly. We need action."

He knew Hassan wanted to kill one of the hostages.

"Everything is fine. Allah will provide."

Looking irritated, Hassan hastily rose from the table, tipping a corner and causing a cup of hot tea to spill over Walid's lap.

"You clumsy oaf!" he screamed, jumping to his feet, pulling out his gun, and pointing it at Hassan's face. The other two men shrank back and Hassan glared at him with that empty experession in his eyes. For a moment no one moved, the gun shaking ever so slightly in his hand, the air hot, the faint scent of tea coming from his lap. Walid might have pulled the trigger, regardless of Hassan's relationship with Sheikh Imaad, if Nasser hadn't burst through the door.

"Walid, a call has come through," he said.

Walid lowered the gun, glared at Hassan, and then followed the rest of them out the door. He needed to watch the American closely.

Walid accidentally left the satellite phone in the plane and now they climbed up the rope ladder into the fuselage. If possible, the plane felt even hotter than when he left, the blazing sun making the light shimmer off the silver metal.

Sweat poured off the passengers' faces and darkened their shirts, and several lay passed out in their seats as the plane became an oven in the hot Arabian sun.

He walked to the front and passed three men and one woman sitting in the Muslim section.

"Saalam Alakem," he whispered. "I am sorry for the heat and inconvenience. God willing, this will soon be finished." Over time his speech acquired the singsong calling of a true believer, rising and falling like the prayers he performed, and he enjoyed listening to its cadence. His parents gave him very little religious training and Walid envied the way the learned prayed with such ease, how Allah seemed to pour through their words and movements. Allah felt so close when He could be invoked in every sentence, every gesture.

One man nodded but the rest pulled away trying to disappear into their seats. The West cowed the Muslim people into submission. He wanted to let them off the plane but he couldn't be sure of their loyalty to the cause. In time all would support their goals. Walid scrutinized the man who defended the Jew and her baby. Some might not be redeamable. Once the masses of Islam awakened, the world would yield to their conquest; just as the world opened when Mohammad marched out of Saudi Arabia and through the Middle East, and then the world.

He walked into the empty cockpit and sat down in the captain's chair. After landing, they moved the crew to the American section of the plane. Nasser handed him the satellite phone. Hassan hung over his shoulder.

"Are you ready to meet my demands?" he asked.

A deep melodious voice responded. "I would like to speak to you first. I would like to speak to you because I fear you are injuring yourself in the eyes of Allah. Allah would never support this kind of action."

Walid bristled in anger but held his tongue. He wanted to hear the words of this kafir.

"The Koran says that civilians shall not be injured. I am Sheik Abbadi, the head of the Muslim community in the United States. You have been taught the wrong path but there is still time to change. Let the hostages go. Turn yourself over to Allah."

He chuckled softly. How could he be angry at such an ignorant and brainwashed brother? Could one be angry at a child for not knowing how to spell or how to read the Koran? This man was a child in Allah's eyes.

"No my friend, it is you who are brainwashed and made into a pawn by the West. They do not care about Islam, or about truth, or about justice. The word of God has been supplanted by a greedy society that wants more cars, more computers, more Big Macs. And they will do anything they can to keep their voracious appetites fed, including sacrificing the Muslim world at their alter of consumption. Islam is but an obstacle to them. Wake up my brother. See that you have been deceived. See that there is an alternate way."

Silence for several seconds.

"Praise Allah you gain wisdom in His ways," the man said.

Walid heard a thump as the receiver was passed and another voice came on. It boomed through the phone, older, authoritative, tinged with an accent. Southern maybe. He imagined the man wearing a cowboy hat and jeans, spinning his lasso as he spoke. The voice, though, sounded deadly serious.

"Hello, Walid. You must be pretty hot in that desert. That's right, we know where you are. I can see the plane just slightly off the runway. I'm guessing the landing went pretty rough. Let the hostages go and you can escape. There are helicopters on the way and you are in the Arabian desert, hundreds of miles from the nearest city. How can you hope to escape?"

Walid thought about Hassan's ramblings on helicopters and almost panicked. No, this blustering, old government official held no power over him. Nothing the man said surprised him, and he just needed to play the game correctly. He needed to push him a bit.

"Who are you?" Walid asked.

"That's not really important, is it?"

"I want to know who I am talking to," Walid said calmly into the phone. "Tell me your name and position or I will begin the executions with you listening on the phone and saying goodbye to each of the victims.

"And if I hang up?"

"Allah help me, I will kill the Vice President's daughter. I will cut her open like a pig and send the tape to Mr. Vice President so he can see how you contributed to his daughter's disembowelment."

A pause and Walid realized with wonder that the man bowed to his word. Praise Allah!

"My name is Stephen Ambrose and I am the special assistant to the Vice President."

"Mr. Ambrose, you do not understand the ways of Islam or Allah. We are all ready to lay down our lives and sacrifice ourselves to His cause. If I die a martyr, I will be blessed in the afterlife," he said, speaking earnestly. "So your threats do not scare me. But the others on this flight, the unbelievers fear death. They have not embraced Islam and to them death would be truly terrifying."

"Let the hostages go, Walid, the United States does not negotiate with terrorists."

"Oh, you know that is not true." It was time to put the next part of his plan into action. He expected they would try to stonewall and delay, using psychological babble, intimidation, and tired slogans about how they didn't negotiate with terrorists. Every freedom fighter knew that the right pressure could bring anyone to its knees, even the United States government.

"Stephen," he said switching to the familiar. "Please excuse me one moment. I will be right back. Do not hang up or I swear on Allah I will kill your Vice President's daughter."

"Where are you going..." Stephen asked as Walid put the phone down and started to head out of the cockpit.

"It's time to make them understand," he said to Hassan and the blond-haired devil's wide grin almost made him shiver. *Hassan was insane.*

"Good, leave this to me." Hassan headed towards the back of the plane and for just an instant Walid wondered if this was how things should be, if this was what Allah really wanted. But the words of Sheikh Imaad strengthened his resolve:

"Do not feel pity or show mercy. The Jews and the West feel neither when they exterminate our cities, kill our children and steal our resources."

Let Allah guide the way, he thought.

Chapter 15

In the back, far from the door, the plane turned into an oven, the heat sucking the moisture from Rachel's lips, sending sweat streaming down her face and back, making her thoughts turn to glasses of water. Water, she needed water. The air became heavy, thick, and drawing a breathe required effort. The heat stewed the latrines, drawing out the putrid odor and at first she struggled not to gag. Now, she was almost used to the smell and it seemed a minor inconvenience compared to her parched tongue.

Sam lay on her sweat-soaked shirt, his small chest rising with every inhalation. His cheeks were flushed and his hair soaked with sweat. In the beginning he'd squirmed and cried, although she tried to quiet him, but as the time passed, his breathing became heavy and irregular, his eyes glazed over into a trance-like half-sleep, and his head lolled back like when he had been an infant. She could feel him slipping away and steeled herself to do something to save his life, although what that would be she didn't know. Before she came to a decision, a man walked down the aisle toward the bathroom. At first, Rachel didn't think anything of it. Other passengers passed without saying a word or making eye contact.

He stopped in front of her and waited for the bathroom to become vacant. As he waited, he turned, stared out the window, and pressed a small Dixie cup of water into her hand.

"Hurry, hurry, give him the water. Hurry."

She raised the cup and dripped water onto Sam's parched lips.

"Thank you," she mouthed, holding back tears as she recognized the Muslim man who had tried to intervene with White Guy.

He walked into the bathroom without acknowledging her thanks. Every hour, the man made another trip to the bathroom and slipped a Dixie cup of water into her hands. After four or five trips, Sam revived slightly, becoming a bit less listless, moving in her arms and opening his eyes.

She was singing softly to Sam when she noticed White Guy coming down the aisle towards them, a particularly smug look on his face, like he just thought of something witty, which she doubted. People like White Guy weren't witty and their pleasure came from the pain of others. Rachel's stomach tightened and her heart raced. She reached under her leg and grabbed a pen she had put aside as a makeshift weapon.

"I love you, Sam," she said, touching his forehead and giving him a kiss. He looked up and gave her a small smile. She would have cried but she needed to be strong.

Clear your head Rachel, be strong for Sam.

White Guy's eyes fastened on them. All heads turned slightly as he walked by and she could see he enjoyed the terror he spread throughout the cabin; he wanted people to fear him. He stopped in front of her.

"Hello, Jewess. Give me the boy."

"Never," she said in a firm voice. "I'll never hand my baby over to you." She met his stare with icy resolve and determination.

"Fine, if that's how you want to be," he said, raising his gun.

Goodby Zeke, goodbye Sam. I'll see you in a better place.

In a movement she'd practiced in her mind for the last hour, she rolled Sam onto the seat beside her and sprang at White Guy.

"Leave my baby alone!" she screamed.

White Guy fumbled with his gun but he wasn't able to bring it up in time to block the pen arcing towards his face. She hit him on the lower forehead, then ripped it down across his left eye, leaving a gashing wound. He staggered back and fell into the aisle, pulling the trigger as he fell. The bullet shot towards first class.

"You fucking bitch, I'm going to kill you! I'm going to kill you and your baby!" he said while writhing on the floor.

Rachel stared in hatred at the thrashing man and realized she had only seconds before the others came to his rescue.

"Get up," she said to the rest of the passengers. "Grab his gun, help me." She motioned to a women who could have easily stuck a foot in White Guy's balls and taken the gun from him. She didn't know if it was fear or that these people just didn't care, but no one made a move to help. Behind her, Samuel started to cry. *No time to listen, sorry my baby.* White Guy managed to crawl a few aisles up the plane. If no one else was going to help then she would have to do it herself.

She closed the distance, raised her leg and kicked him hard five or six times. He turned over and stared up at her through the blood coursing down his face.

"Fuck you," she said and kicked him in the groin. He gave a satisfying howl of pain. Rachel might have been able to grab the gun if she didn't feel a seering pain in her side. She staggered back. A dark red plume spread across her lower abdomen. Boss Man stood behind White Guy, his gun pointed at her. He looked furious. Incredible pain shot up her midsection, followed by the urge to vomit. His face began to spin and she fell into her seat beside Sam.

"Oh dear God, help me," she whispered, laboring to breathe, the pain spreading through her stomach and legs.

"Momma!" Samuel cried out before it all faded into blackness.

* * *

"Open your eyes bitch!" a voice barked.

She managed to open them a crack and stared at an injured face. A bloody gash started in the left corner of White Guy's forehead and ran down to a bandaged left eye. She only wished it had been deeper. Hopefully he would lose his eye.

"You're not going to be laughing for long," he said. "Lift her up." Hands grabbed the back of her shirt and hoisted her off the ground. Pain ripped through her abdomen and she vomited blood onto the floor.

"Fucking disgusting cunt."

She heard a hollow sound, like a vacuum cleaner running in another room. She fought to keep her eyes open.

Boss Man placed something in front of her face. A phone.

"Say your name," he ordered.

She said nothing and White Guy kicked her in the belly. Pain like she had never felt before– not even in labor– screamed through her mid-section.

"I said say your name," Boss Man repeated.

"Never," she whispered.

"Say it!" White Man screamed and rammed his fist into her abdomen. The world spun. She would give them no further satisfaction. She would not do as they asked, no matter what. She dimly heard Boss Man telling White Guy to move back.

"The Jew and her son are the first," Boss Man said. They let go of her arms and she slumped onto the floor. The hollow sound grew closer and she searched frantically for her baby.

"Sam," she whispered. "Sam." She would not let them see her sob. Someone grabbed her arms and hauled her up onto her knees. She could hear Sam's crying and the hollow sound retreated as her instincts sharpened.

"Sam."

One of the men held him like a football under his arms. Tears streamed down his face and he reached his arms out to her. White Guy took her child and with a turn of the body pitched him out of the open airplane door.

"No!" she screamed, drawing upon her last strength and lunging at White Guy. She clawed at his face, backing him towards the door and almost over the edge before hands restrained her attack.

"Look down, Jewess," White Guy panted, blood oozing from the fresh scratches on his face.

She looked and saw Samuel struggling in the sand, trying to stand.

"Throw the cunt over," he said.

She tumbled forward and landed with a thud on the sand.

My baby, I am almost there. Hold on.

A strong metallic taste filled her mouth. The sand shifted beside her, a hand caressed her face.

"Momma?"

With one last burst of energy she pulled her baby towards her and an instant later heard the gunshots from above. The hollow sound swelled around her into a symphony of beautiful noise while the brilliant desert sun flared into infinity.

Chapter 16

As night crept up on the city, Zeke sat at his desk, hands folded in front of his face, and watched the lights slowly blink on across the city skyline. In the next building, Zeke spotted a woman hunched over her desk, fingers pecking away at a keyboard. Probably some junior partner who needed to stay late to finish a brief. On another night, he might have felt sorry for her, but now he envied the normality of her work situation. How quickly a perspective on life could change.

A few minutes earlier, he had finished a call with Rachel's parents and they had been both worried and bitter, as usual.

"Zeke, you get them back. Do whatever you have to do. Get them back!" her mother shouted in a thick Long Island accent.

"You should have been on that plane with them," her father said. He expected this response and for once they were right. He should have been on the plane. Maybe he could have done something to foil the hijacking. At least he would have been with them.

Several hours after his conversation with Aminah, he received a call back from her.

"Hi, Zeke, how are you?" she had asked, concern in her voice. In his limited experience, most stressed-out government personnel displayed as much pesonality as a robot. Aminah acted differently.

"I want my wife and son back."

"We all do. We're all working on getting them back safely and that's why I'm calling you," she said and then paused for a moment. "Zeke, there are some developments that could impact you. The hijackers landed the plane. They've threanted to kill the passengers unless their demands are met. Time is short. Is your offer to help still good?"

He felt a fresh wave of anxiety as his heart-rate kicked up a notch. "Did they tell you this?"

"Yes, we've spoken to them."

"Are Rachel and Sam in danger? Are they hurt?" he asked, trying to bring his feelings under control. He couldn't afford to be overwhelmed. *You can't go through this again, a voice said. If something happens to them, it will break you.* He bunched his hand into a fist and bit deeply into his lip.

"We don't think anyone has been hurt. But I don't think there's much time. Is your offer to pay the ransom still on the table?"

"I'll do whatever it takes," he said, feeling a bit better. He could help; he could rescue Rachel and Sam and make it okay.

"The United States refuses to negotiate with terrorists. It's a dangerous precedent to set. However, as a private citizen, you are free to make a deal."

Zeke didn't care about their ethical contortions or about what the government could or couldn't do. He wanted his wife and child safe and secure, and he would do whatever needed to be done– no questions asked.

"What about the sheik they want released from prison?" he asked.

"The President is willing to parole him. He's an old man, and politically they feel it's okay. Is the money ready to go?"

"No, I need to make the arrangements, close some position." Zeke performed some rough calculations. "I'll have it in about two hours."

"Get it as fast as possible and be prepared to make a transfer. We'll negotiate with the hijackers a bit longer and then put you in direct contact with them. There is nothing you need to say other than you have the money and work out the details on how to transfer it. That's between the two of you. I'll contact you shortly when we're ready for you to take the call," she said.

He clenched his jaw at the thought of talking to the bastards who had his family. He wanted to reach through the phone and strangle them but speaking to the terrorists gave him the opportunity to better assess the situation.

"Do you think we'll get them back?" he asked her without expecting much of a reply.

"These people do not value life the same way we do. Even if we meet their demands, they may still kill the passengers. Until the passengers are released, their safety is in jeopardy. I want you to know that." She paused for a moment and he could tell she was considering whether or not to continue.

"You can speak your mind, Aminah. I appreciate your honesty."

"Your wife and child are Jewish, Mr. Katz. This group is rabidly anti-Semitic. I only hope that they are decent enough not to harm a woman and child."

He had the same fears and hoped Rachel and Sam had successfully hidden their religion.

They said goodbye and he called the staff together. Zeke barely paid attention to the trading but now it mattered again; he needed the money. The five of them – Margaret, Patric, Adele, Amir, and he sat in the screening room and he gave them a brief update.

"We need to liquidate one hundred million of the position."

"How long do we have?" Adele asked.

"Two hours."

Amir whistled. "It's a challenge. The main exchanges in the United States are closed so we will need to go into dark markets and non-U.S. markets. It will be riskier. But we will do everything we can. We might take some significant losses."

"I'll put up everything I have," Zeke said.

"I'll see if I can optimize the algorithims," Patric added.

"Thank you," he said, struggling to hold back tears.

They nodded. No doubt they would do it. The team broke up and started to liquidate the massive profit position.

* * *

He sat at his desk for the next two hours, unable to unstick his mind from circling around the same questions. Were Rachel and Sam all right? What were they doing? Were they scared and petrified? Were they being well taken care of?

Someone tapped lightly at the door.

"Come in."

Margaret entered with a steaming mug. "I thought you could use some tea," she said.

"Thanks, Margaret." He took the mug and put it down. She loitered by the door but he didn't feel like engaging in conversation.

"I hope they're safe," she said. Margaret turned and walked away. He rubbed his temples and Amir appeared.

Amir reminded him of himself ten years earlier – smart, ambitious, brimming with ideas. Did Amir feel the same way towards him? Perhaps his warmth and cooperation hid his true thoughts and intentions. Perhaps all Muslims had their own secret agenda? He loathed the thought and buried it.

"Hello, Zeke, good news. We did better than I expected and will have the one hundred million dollars within the next fifteen minutes. In the process though, we have lost about fifty million. It's after-hours and the expediency of the situation forced us to engage in less than optimal trades. We tried our best."

"You did exactly what I needed, Amir. Thank you very much."

"Zeke, you should know this is only a small part of the overall portfolio. There is no way we could liquidate it all today. It has become a whale." Zeke barely listened as Amir continued: "The plane hijacking magnified the model. The position is now worth north of three billion dollars and it is still running."

Zeke snapped to attention.

"Did you say three billion?"

"Yes. We achieved one of the largest trading profits ever recorded in a single day. You have become a very rich man."

He should have been celebrating the news with Rachel, getting ready to jump on a plane to meet them. He could at least be happy for the team. They had worked hard for this moment and deserved the success.

"Congratulations, Amir. I couldn't have done it without you and the rest of the team," he said, trying to muster some enthusiasm. Neither of them spoke for an awkward minute and then his mobile phone rang with Aminah's number. Amir gave a small wave and disappeared down the hallway.

"Hey, Aminah," he said trying to sound friendly but feeling drained. "Any news?" he asked. "What's happening down there?"

"An assault team will be on the ground near the plane in about six hours."

How long could it take to get a special ops force on the ground?

"Six hours? That's too long," he said.

"It's the best we can do. We have been in contact with the hijackers and they are willing to do a deal.

"They said that?"

"Yes."

He let out a sigh of relief. He could make everything all right.

"We'll be releasing Sheik Imaad in fifteen minutes. Do you have the money?"

"Yes," he said.

"We're going to put you in touch with someone by the name of Walid. From what we can tell, he's the leader. I'll be listening in on a line only you can hear so I can help you with instructions and advice. He's familiar with the United States. He received an engineering degree from the University of Illinois and his English is pretty good. Are you ready to speak to him?"

"Now?" he asked. He didn't realize that she wanted the conversation to happen so quickly.

"Yes. They're getting jumpy on the plane and I think the sooner this is resolved, the better."

His heart picked up a notch and adrenaline woke him from his lethargy. "Whatever you think is best. Put him on."

"Remember, don't get angry or allow yourself to be drawn into any kind of political discussion or debate. You are not on the line to argue about the merits of US policy. Focus on getting the transaction done." Her voice softened and the tone became less formal. "I'll be on the phone with you, Zeke. You'll hear a few clicks as we make the connection and then he should be on the line. Good luck."

He felt lightheaded and nauseous and he shivered even as sweat poured from his pits. He took several deep breaths and forced his mind to clear. A minute passed and Zeke began to think something had gone wrong when he heard a burst of static, several clicks, and then more static. Out of the static came a voice:

"Anyone there?" a man asked in heavily accented English.

So, this was what a terrorist sounded like.

"I asked is anyone there?"

"I'm here," Zeke said.

"Before we begin, tell your friends at the CIA and the Defense Department to hang up. This is a conversation between us, and us alone."

"We're alone," Zeke said. "What can I do to get those passengers off the plane?"

"Who are you and why are you interested in paying the money?"

"My wife and son are on the plane and I'm interested in seeing their secure release, along with the other passengers."

Silence for a moment and then the voice spoke again. "You have not spoken to Stephen Ambrose?" he asked.

"No, I don't know that name," Zeke said.

"Zeke Katz. Interesting, they send a Jew to do their work," he said, spitting out the word Jew like he had bitten into a rotten apple.

"Who am I speaking to?" Zeke asked, ignoring the comment. Zeke learned to negotiate in the foster homes, bartering items with the other kids and sometimes the parents.

"Didn't they already tell you that my name is Walid? Praise be Allah they were not lying when they told me you were a civilian. A civilian and a stupid Jew."

He ignored the comment. "I'd like to talk to my wife before we continue."

The man's tone grew angry. "I don't think you understand that you do not dictate the terms! If I want to let you speak to her after we are done, then I will."

"No, I don't think you understand *me*. If you want to see your sheikh again then you will let me speak with my wife. If not, I will personally drive to the prison where he is located and strangle him..."

"Zeke," Aminah's voice cut in. "Cool it." She didn't understand the way these people operated. He had dealt with bullies before and backing off and letting them feel powerful only emboldened them. He thought he had left this type of vicious street-fight behind but certain parts of life had a way of not letting go. With effort he forced himself to calm down.

"Are you there, Jew?" Some of the taunting had disappeared from Walid's voice. "Listen to what I say and follow my directions exactly. If you do, and if Allah believes that the path is right, the passengers will be released. Do you understand me?"

Zeke gritted his teeth. "Yes," he said.

"Perhaps all Jews aren't stupid. Interrupt me one more time and I will kill your wife and child. Within the next thirty minutes I want you to wire one hundred million dollars to a bank account in Dubai. The account number is 45537475. After the money has been deposited in the account and Sheikh Imaad has been freed, the hostages will be released and you will be reunited with your wife and son. If the money is not delivered in thirty minutes, we will start to kill every non-Muslim on this plane, starting with your Jew family. I relayed this same message to your government. The clock starts now," he said before the phone line went dead.

Chapter 17

At seven o'clock he sent everyone home. Exhausted from maintaining a brave, stoic front, he wanted to be alone.

"Zeke, I can't leave you by yourself," Margaret had complained when he told her to go.

"Go home, Margaret. Tomorrow everything will be better," he replied. She pursed her lips, looked like she wanted to say something, and nodded her head.

"Yes, well, I'll see you tomorrow. Let's get out of here and give Zeke some space," she called out like a mother hen. They each bid him goodbye. Margaret gave a small wave and closed the door.

He paced the halls, up and down, up and down, turning the news over in his mind, waiting for Aminah to contact him. He called her four times but only reached her voicemail.

Zeke sat down at his desk and pulled open the top left drawer, fumbling through business cards, a stapler, and a bunch of rubber bands before he found what he was looking for—a pack of pictures in a tattered sleeve. He pulled out the photos. A younger Rachel stood behind him with her arms wrapped around his shoulders and her hands clasped at his chest. He looked up at her and she flashed a dazzling white smile. In the background he could see the lake and to their left the red flames of a bonfire. He remembered kissing for the first time in front of the fire. He had been a different person then: shy, less open, less confident in his abilities, and so angry. He often wondered what a beautiful, happy girl like Rachel saw in him.

He flipped to another picture: the two of them on the pier in Santa Monica. On the way to Hawaii for their honeymoon they stopped in Los Angeles to break up the flight and do some sightseeing. Rachel's hair was windblown and he thought he could see the red bumps on her arms. Rachel developed an allergic reaction to the sun before they even reached Hawaii. He chuckled remembering how she had spent most of the trip in long-sleeve shirts and pants to keep the spots from getting worse. But Rachel didn't complain. If anything her condition made her more determined to enjoy the vacation, and although they stayed away from the beach they hiked up volcanoes, parasailed around one of the islands, took long walks, and spent a lot of time indoors.

He was about to flip the picture over and look at the next one when he heard something coming from the television in the other room. He quickly rose from his seat and ran down the hallway. A pretty female correspondent named Maria Arrono spoke gravely.

"...hostages were found two hundred miles from Riyadh. Many were in severe states of dehydration. The temperature inside the plane reached as high as one hundred and twenty degrees. We've been told they are being transported to hospitals in Saudi Arabia while the Americans onboard are being taken to the Rammstein air base in Germany."

Richard Corliss, the lead anchor appeared.

"That was Maria Arrono reporting from Riyadh. For those who just joined, we have received word via fax that as of six-thirty am EST the hostages were rescued. American special forces found the plane and its passengers left unguarded in the Arabian desert approximately two hundred miles from the capital of Riyadh. The rescue capped a harrowing trip that started with the plane's departure from Boston's Logan Airport before it was hijacked, diverted, and crash-landed in the Saudi Arabian desert. At this time, we do not know if there are any casualties or if Victoria Vison, the daughter of Vice President Vison is still alive. As Maria stated, there are reports of large numbers of survivors being airlifted to medical facilities in Saudi Arabia. Many are reported to be severely dehydrated. There is also no word on the hijackers. Whether they have been captured, escaped, or are being pursued by Saudi and American authorities is unclear. We do know that Sheikh

Imaad boarded a plane several hours ago although his ultimate destination remains unclear."

Zeke felt twenty pounds lighter. He scrambled to his office for the phone but before he got there, it started to ring. He picked up the receiver.

"Hello."

"Hello, Zeke." A somber voice. Aminah.

The hand holding the phone trembled; his stomach dropped. "What's happening, Aminah? I just heard on television the hostages have been released. When can I speak to Rachel and Sam?" She didn't respond for a moment and in that pause the motion of the world came to a slow, grinding halt. He stared out the window but saw nothing; his feet bounced up and down in nervous anticipation; he swallowed into a desert dry throat and found it difficult to breathe. Time stopped.

"I'm sorry, Zeke, they're gone."

He couldn't say anything.

"Zeke?"

He stared at the picture of Rachel and Sam on his desk. The picture of Rachel with her windblown hair and red bumps. "Gone?" he heard himself whisper.

"They were the only casualties. They were found dead in the sand."

"No," he responded, "No."

"We tried." Aminah sobbed.

"No!" He grabbed the phone, yanked it out of the wall, and hurled it at the window. It hit the glass, bounced back, and fell to the floor. He looked at it lying dead, inert, immobile and collapsed into his chair.

* * *

He wasn't sure how long he sat at his desk: hours, seconds, days, centuries. It didn't matter. The television broke the spell.

"We just received a statement from the purported hijackers of the plane. It has not been verified but I'm going to read it."

He wandering down the hallway.

"'With Allah's help we have been successful in our jihad against the infidels. This is just the beginning. Allah has nourished us and prepared us for war. Today, we killed two Jews, tomorrow there will be more. The days of Allah's victory over the Dini will soon be upon you all.'"

Zeke grabbed the flat-screen and hurtled it to the floor. The panel landed face down, sputtered, and went dark.

He felt like this once before in his life and he promised himself never to let it come back. Then, he managed to control the rage, to turn it inward. Not this time. *Don't go down this path,* he heard Rachel say. No, even she would understand.

He started to kick the screen. Whap– the panel rose and then settled back. Whack– his shoe flew off and sailed across the room. Whap– the side of the casing cracked, along with a small bone in his left foot. Whap– the casing split open, blood seeping through the sock Rachel picked out that morning.

The flat-screen lay a mangled, shattered mess. He limped over to the corner of the room, leaving a trail of blood in his wake. Zeke leaned against the wall and as he slowly sank to the floor, he saw a vision of Rachel and Sam dead, inert in their body bags. He started to cry.

He sat for what seemed like forever. The sun rose, bringing the city back to life: fathers and mothers pulled themselves out of bed, preparing for the day ahead; little boys and girls rubbed the sleep from their eyes; parents made breakfast; children received hugs and kisses– time ticked on and life moved forward. Across the space between the skyscrapers, he spied the woman returning to her desk. He hadn't even noticed when she left last night. For almost everyone in the world it was another normal day. Not for him. His heart beat and his lungs exhaled air but his life had ended.

Before, years ago, in what seemed like a different life, he had been a scared little boy with nothing to lose. Now, he was a man with three billion dollars and nothing to lose.

His hand reached out and touched the window as the sun's rays bathed the room. A moment later he walked out of his office, and never returned.

Part II
Divinity

Chapter 18

The students leaned forward in their chairs, eyes following Aminah as she paced across the space in front of the white board. Using a black marker, she turned and wrote: Nightmare Scenario #1.

"Terrorists sneaking a nuclear bomb into the United States is the stuff of fiction. It has become a cliché, explored endlessly in shows like *24* and thriller and terrorism-themed fiction. But terrorists don't see it as cliché or overdone, or boring. To them, the detonation of a nuclear bomb on American soil would be the ultimate achievement. Why? Because nothing causes the loss of life, sows terror, and leaves a path of long-lasting destruction like the explosion of a nuclear weapon. It *is* nightmare scenario number one," she said, holding up her pointer-finger.

"In October 2001, a month after the 9-11 attacks, a CIA agent named Dragonfire reported that Fist of Allah terrorists possessed a ten-kiloton nuclear bomb stolen from Russia. According to the agent, the nuclear weapon made it to U.S. soil and arrived in New York City. The Vice President was sent to an undisclosed location and the President dispatched Nuclear Emergency Support Teams specialists to look for the weapon. The report turned out to be false. That time." The audience remained silent, rapt, and she continued.

"Let's assume for a moment that the report had been true, and the terrorists had detonated the weapon in the middle of Manhattan, say in Times Square. Here's what would happen. The resulting blast would generate temperatures reaching into the tens of millions of degrees Fahrenheit. Times Square would vanish in a flash; the theatre district, the New York Times building, Grand Central Terminal and every other structure within one third of a mile of the detonation would be utterly destroyed. Rockefeller Center, Carnegie Hall, and the

Empire State Building would be reduced to rubble. From the United Nations complex to the eighties, structures would appear bombed out and devastated. Here, at Columbia, most of the buildings would be destroyed either by the blast or by subsequent fires, and the radiation would kill almost everyone the blast didn't."

"On a normal workday, half a million people are packed into the half-mile radius around Times Square. A detonation would kill them all. Hundreds of thousands of others would die from radiation, building collapses, fires, panic, and more.

"The threat of a nuclear terrorist attack is very real. Since the collapse of Fist of Allah in Syria and Iraq, the group, as well as other Jihadi groups, have tried to reconstitute themselves and mount a significant attack on the West. That's why limiting nuclear proliferation and securing existing stocks of nuclear weapons is so important. Any questions?"

"Is the Russian arsenal still vulnerable to theft?" a male student asked.

"The Russians have made great progress in securing their nuclear weapons, and we now believe that their arsenal is safe. But in addition to Russia, Pakistan, Iran, India, North Korea and potentially other states possess known nuclear capability. Fist of Allah began work on a crude nuclear weapon while they controlled territory in Iraq and Syria. Documents recovered after the fall of the Caliphate indicate the group intended to build and detonate a weapon.

"But don't stay up at night thinking about this. The United States runs a very active counter-intelligence program, and smuggling a weapon into this country is no easy task. A terrorist would need precise information detailing exactly how to do it. There is no indication that Fist of Allah has acquired the capability to detonate a weapon here or anywhere else in the country."

She looked at the clock on the wall. "So, on that happy note, it looks like we're out of time. Read section three in the

Life of a Terrorist. Have a nice weekend. Remember, we don't meet until next Tuesday."

Aminah watched the class leave and hoped she hadn't spooked them too badly. She considered not including the section on nuclear terrorism, but decided no class would be complete without some discussion on the topic. She walked back to the desk at the front of the room and began placing her notes in a binder.

"Pretty heavy stuff, Aminah. Do you think they can take it?" a familiar voice asked.

"Stephen, were you listening?" she asked, looking up and moving over to give him a hug. " I didn't see you."

"I'm a spook, remember? I know how to hide in the shadows. How are you doing?"

"Fine. Great. I think I've found my calling."

"It looks like it. You're a natural."

"I try. It's easier than presenting to Stimson or Vison."

He nodded. "Can we go someplace to talk?"

"You mean this wasn't just a social call?" she teased. Over the twelve years of their working relationship she had learned that Ambrose didn't do social calls. "Sure, let's go to my office." They chatted about the weather, about his wife, about teaching at Columbia until they arrived at her office. She closed the door and motioned for him to sit in a chair commonly used by visiting students.

"So, what's up? What brings you to New York?"

"I didn't come to sightsee. I came to talk to you. Aminah, the Vice President asked me to visit you."

"Stephen, I'm done."

"I know, I know. You had a tough time. I understand you needed to get away. But just listen for a second, please." He stared at her until she nodded her head.

"Okay."

"Thank you. Over the last several months we've picked up some unusual activity regarding several wanted members of Fist of Allah."

"What kind of activity?"

He reached into a satchel and pulled out several photographs. The first showed a mug shot of an unattractive bearded man with squinty eyes, acne, and a large nose.

"You remember our friend, Khalid. Airplane hijacker, small time leader of Fist of Allah. We believe he was running a small cell in Karachi. He was in the process of kidnapping an American aid worker when he and two companions were ambushed. The Pakistani police found his body along with two of his two friends in the basement of a building. As you can see, it was a rather gruesome finale for these men."

She noticed the deep cuts across both of their necks. "They've been virtually decapitated," Aminah said.

"Yup, someone really didn't like these guys. The kidnapping target, a man by the name of Francis Bacon, was found unconscious in the trunk of their car. He couldn't provide any information on what happened to his abductors. Several witnesses said they saw the car following a woman on a motorcycle."

"Woman on a motorcycle...In Karachi? That's odd," she said. "Perhaps one of them raped a woman, or stole money, or..."

Ambrose threw two more pictures down on her desk. "The top picture is Nasser al Hassdani. The maid found him floating in a bathtub in Amman, Jordan. Two of his bodyguards lay dead in the foyer. The killer left no clue."

She examined the picture: a heavyset man lay in a pool of reddish water, his head back as if he was taking a nap, his hands floating in the water above his body. A bullet hole adorned the center of his forehead.

"The third photograph is of Ali al Hakna Hussaini, a Saudi found dead in a Medina alleyway. He left a meeting at a café and ten hours later a schoolboy found his body." Ali lay face down on a cobblestone street, the angle shielding his face. She guessed he also had a bullet hole going through his forehead. "Both Ali and Nasser were active, high level members of Fist of Allah. We picked up some unhappy chatter between members of the group discussing the killings. Based on this, we don't think they turned on them. So, who did it?"

Aminah studied the pictures. "Whoever killed them knew what they were doing," she finally said. "They were looking specifically for these men. They had to find them, which is not easy. Israelis?"

"It's not the Israelis. We checked with them and while they were quite happy with the pictures, they regretted not being able to take credit."

She put the photos down. "I can't help you," she said, shuddering a bit. Just looking at Khalid brought back memories of the plane hijacking, of Zeke.

"Are you okay?" he asked.

She rubbed her temples and nodded. "I'm done, Stephen. I'm just starting to put my life back together. I can't do this. Get Ray or Carolina involved."

"Aminah, I undersand what you went through and I didn't want to disturb you. The Vice President ordered me here."

"Vison? Why?"

"He knows you're the best. You helped save his daughter." Ambrose paused. "We're also pretty sure there's an intelligence leak in the OCT. Targets seem to know we're coming. Vison won't trust anyone until we find out who it is."

Aminah had told Ambrose a week after the hijacking that Fist of Allah received inside help to successfully place knives and explosives on the plane and to escape from the Saudi desert. He had been doubtful at first, but now he seemed to be reconsidering his position.

"Who?"

"Not a clue. Vison is suspicious of everyone. He trusts you because he's worked with you before and you've been out of the business for the last two years. You couldn't be the source."

She chewed her lip, digesting the revelations. There was a certain appeal to the puzzle. Who was murdering these terrorists? Yet, her life had changed direction and these pictures threatened to pull her back to a past she wanted to forget. What would her mother say if she heard Aminah was getting back into the business? That alone was enough of a deterrent. She just wanted to teach her class, spend time with Daayana and her mother, and maybe find a nice guy.

"Stephen, I'm sorry, I'm done, I'm retired."

He said nothing for a minute. "I understand, Aminah. But before you say no for good, let me tempt you with one other enticement."

"Stephen, please."

"Hear me out. I'm aware you've been poking around about John's death."

"Poking around? I wouldn't call it that. I've called a few people. The official report is pretty dodgy and they never did find John's body."

"True, true. Word gets around though and some people aren't happy."

"Who?"

"Let's leave it at some people. I did a little digging and while I don't totally agree with your assessment, I did find some strange irregularities in the official report."

"Seriously, Stephen! After all the grief you gave me."

"I meant to tell you but I wanted to learn a bit more. Now we may be able to kill two birds with one stone."

"How?"

"I'm here to ask you to travel to Karachi and meet with Sharesh Panjababi. He's our operative in the region. Talk to him. He's collected information on the killings *and* he may know something about John's death."

"Stephen, you know I'm not a field agent."

"True, true," he said, repeating an affectation Aminah found annoying. "But this will be safe. You'll fly in, meet with him, fly out. It will all happen in a day. A private jet is fueled up and ready to depart from JFK."

This was certainly presumptive? "Bring him here."

Ambrose shook his head. "We can't. He won't come. He says it will compromise his position."

"Talk to him on the phone."

"Aminah, you know sometimes the personal connection is needed. Sharesh isn't telling us everything. He's spooked."

"I still don't see why you need me to go. I'm a chicken." When he recruited Aminah to the OCT, she had made it very clear that she didn't have the bravado to work in the field. Roller coasters made her nauseous for hours and a scary movie could keep her up for days.

"The Vice President is confident once you look over the reports and speak with Sharesh, you'll figure out what is going on." Ambrose was all business today.

"I'm a chicken," she repeated.

"This is an in and out job."

She owed her career to Ambrose and he had backed her up and supported her over the years. He never asked for repayment, until today.

Sighing, she mentally reviewed her calendar. She had five days before her next class and her mother wasn't expecting Aminah to visit until Friday, three days away. She could fly into Pakistan and be back by then. The violent deaths of these Jihadis had piqued her interest. She cursed Ambrose's ability to push her buttons and get his way. Washington insiders considered him one of the best inside political operatives in a city filled with sharks and connivers and she had to agree.

"In and out," she said.

"That's the plan."

"I need to be back by Friday so my mother never discovers I left."

"No problem."

"You're sure."

"Positive."

"It's safe?"

"Almost no one knows you're going."

"Okay, I'll do it. But if I'm not back in time you'll have to call my mother. And God help you if it comes to that."

Chapter 19

To change the world, he needed to leave the blinding brilliance of the desert and enter the darkness of the forest, and Walid hated it. The plants, the animals, the smell of dirt, living material, and decomposition assaulted him like a hostile, alien world. But he would deal with it and more in the name of Allah and Jihad.

As the trucks rumbled forward, the underbrush stirred and Walid grabbed his pistol. A creature with large eyes, black fur, and dark claws took a quick glance at them, curled its lips, and darted into the woods. Walid cursed and sat back, trying to relax. His back ached from the hours of sitting, fouling his mood even more.

In the two years since the successful hijacking, he remained focused, planning a bigger operation, something so magnificent that it would change the world and truly spread the word of Allah across the globe. No one had believed he would succeed with the airplane hijacking. Fools. In a two-day period, they had freed Sheikh Imaad and earned one-hundred and fifty million dollars, and not a single member of the group had been captured or killed. Praise Allah!

Despite his attempt to master his mind, it refused to obey, wandered where it would like a stubborn camel, turning over the news of Khalid, Nasser, and Ali. But Khalid's death bothered him the most. The killers videotaped the execution, uploading it to the Internet, and somehow placing a link in one of Fist of Allah's private message boards. The image of Khalid begging for his life played over and over in his mind. Walid clenched his fists. It had to be some Shiite group, but the cowards in the video spoke perfect English. Who?

After killing Bin Gaudi, the killers dumped his body into a sludgy pit in some dark cave and crudely covered it with sewage slop. The CIA and Israelis didn't operate this way. Who?

"We are close to the meeting location," Faisel said, peering out from behind the wheel. "Walid, are you all right?"

He turned his attention back to the forest, realizing that if he didn't focus, he would join Khalid in the gardens of paradise.

"Yes, yes, sorry, I was just thinking."

Faisel nodded. Ever since the plane, the men called him "the thinker" and Walid rather liked the name.

The trucks stopped and awaited his command. He raised his hand into a fist and stuck it out the window. Taking their cue, ten men lifted their hands in response before slipping out of the covered backs and into the woods.

"Okay, let's go," Walid said, and the trucks started off again. A few minutes later they emerged into a small clearing. Tree stumps dotted the ground and the charred remains of a fire lay in the middle. A rabbit darted across the road and disappeared into the forest. About ten feet behind the line of the rabbit waited two drab green Soviet-era military conveys identical to the ones they rode in.

"Bring the truck up behind there," Walid said pointing to the vehicle at the back of the line. "Pay attention everyone. Keep your weapons ready. Allah Akbar," he shouted and the men yelled back,"Allah Akbar."

The truck groaned forward, the tires cutting through the soft ground and leaving six-inch-deep tire marks. Faisel turned off the engine. Silence.

Heart pounding, Walid stepped out of the cab, his boot landing in soft mud. In the back sat twenty crates stuffed with one hundred dollar bills for a total of fifty million dollars, part of the money provided to Fist of Allah two years ago, courtesy of the Jew. Ali rigged plastic explosive throughout the vehicle so that if they were betrayed, the money would be incinerated.

Opposite them, the doors to the other trucks opened and four soldiers in green military fatigues jumped quickly down and held up their rifles. A massive head emerged a moment later, and a bull of a man with broad shoulders and a sizable stomach landed heavily on the ground with a grunt. Thin, gold rimmed glasses gave him a scholarly appearance despite his brutish body. Victor Kranchenko. The last email Walid had received warned of Victor.

"Be wary of Victor. He is a half-Russian, half-Tajik former general in the Russian military who has become a mid-level player in the Russian mafia. The man aspires to higher things and this is his weakness. Kranchenko likes fast cars, villas, beautiful women, and fine food. He is homicidal and killed his own stepsister after suspecting her of spying for a rival group. He will not hesitate to double cross anyone on the other side of a deal."

A cold breeze cut through Walid's jacket and he exhaled a plume of breath. Focus, he told himself. Praise Allah, let me succeed.

Faisel walked beside him and he knew the others lay silently in the woods, watching, waiting for the signal. They had simulated this moment hundreds of times and he had run the men through practice run after practice run to cover every contingency. When the men tired and complained, he drove them harder.

The two groups met in front of Walid's truck.

"You Walid?" Victor asked with a thick Russian accent.

"Yes."

Victor chuckled and said something to his men, who snickered. He was counting on their arrogance to blind them to the presence of the men stationed in the woods. The Russians possessed more men and firepower and if Victor discovered his hidden reserves, Walid might find himself buried in the dark soil he so detested.

"Do you have the bells?" he asked the Russian. Victor smiled again, revealing two gold teeth.

"Right down to business, my little Islamic friend. You must really want these bells to travel to such a godforsaken place."

"Travel is no trouble," Walid said. "We will go wherever it is needed."

Victor grunted disapprovingly.

Walid continued, taking the initiative just as he had on the airplane with the American official. Ever since he had embraced Islam, a killer like Victor no longer impressed or intimidated him. "Just to make it clear. Our truck is full of C4. If you try to kill us and take the money, we will detonate it."

Victor grunted again. "Show me the money."

"Do you have the 'Bells?'" Walid asked again.

The men on both sides shifted nervously and then the General burst into another fit of laughter that Walid found revealing, for his father had always told him that people who laughed too much were hiding something. Victor shouted in Russian and then turned back to Walid.

"You don't need to call them bells anymore. It is a bomb. A nuclear bomb. Come, I will go first. I will show you what you have come for. I will show you the bells."

"There were supposed to be two bombs," Walid said coldly. He didn't like unexpected changes to the plan, especially one that robbed him of a nuclear weapon.

The general shrugged. "Now there is only one. Do you think it was easy getting this? The Russians have destroyed much of their extra arsenal over the past ten years and they have stricter controls. To get this one bomb, I had to smuggle it out of a military base and then retrieve the access codes. I had my men go back and falsify the records so that no one will ever know it existed." He looked Walid in the eyes and smiled. "If you don't want it we can all go home."

Victor would never depart without trying to get the money. His plan would still work with one bomb, so long as it was a real nuclear weapon.

"We will continue," Walid said calming his anger.

"Good. Come." They walked through the mud to the rear of one of the trucks. Two men peeled back the canvas, revealing a wooden crate. Victor spoke in Russian and the soldiers jumped up and pried off the top. Inside the create lay a silver, conical object that looked like an oversized bullet. One side of the casing was pulled away, revealing a mass of wires, metal bars, and small circuits. A small red light blinked.

"Here is it. Ten kilotons. Enough to incinerate most of Washington DC, or half of New York if that is your objective," Victor said, growing serious.

Walid slowly reached out a hand to touch the casing and felt the cool, smooth metal under his fingers. His heart pounded, his fingers and toes tingled. Looking at the weapon, he remembered watching Sheikh Imaad dictate the Fatwa that justified the operation.

"If the Muslims can't overwhelm the infidels in any other way, they are allowed to use weapons of mass destruction to kill everyone and erase them and their descendants from the earth."

He took a breath of air, focused his thoughts, and motioned for Ali to come forward. The Professor held a black, square metal object the size of a thick book. He flipped a button and the device squawked in high pitched bursts. Ali knelt down, inspected the casing and the gangle of wires which threaded through the metal frame, and then rose, his eyes wide, his mouth curved into a slight smile.

"It is real. If you really don't believe me you can press the red button to start the detonation process," Victor said casually.

"That's not necessary," Walid replied.

"Enough!" Victor nodded at his men to put the cover back on. "You have seen that I have fulfilled my end of the bargain. Now, do you have the money?"

They walked over to Walid's truck and he pulled back the canvas cover. As they did so, Walid caught Victor making a motion to three men standing behind them. His heart raced as he ran his fingers through his hair, praying Nassar and Hakeem recognized the signal to be on alert.

Victor purred in delight at the rows of American dollars stacked neatly in the crate.

"You got this money from the plane hijacking?" Victor asked.

Walid nodded.

"You are clever. Driving here I had many, many hours to think and I wondered how you were able to hijack that plane with the Vice President's daughter. In Russia we have a saying: 'God's favor only falls on those who cheat.'"

"Then you must not believe in Allah," Walid said, unwilling to divulge anything to the Russian.

Victor grunted.

They all watched each other closely now. Walid eyed Victor's hand, waiting to see if he pulled the gun at his hip while Victor's squinty eyes followed him closely, the Russian's pupils large behind the glasses.

"It's fifty million," Walid said. "But because you only delivered one weapon, we will cut the pile in half. Half the money for half the weapons."

Kranchenko said nothing for a moment, just sticking the point of his boot into the muddy ground and adjusting his glasses.

"How about this? You give me the money and I give you nothing." Just as he finished the sentence, two men at the back of the truck lifted their Kalashnikovs and fired.

Walid turned, pulled out his Beretta and pumped two bullets in Victor's direction as the general rushed out the back. The first bullet missed but the second struck his stomach, the momentum throwing the general to the end of the truck from where he tumbled out of view. A stinging pain raced through Walid's leg. He tried to walk forward and collapsed, falling off the end of the truck and landing in the mud beside Victor. Hands grabbed his jacket and pulled him up.

About ten feet from the vehicle he could see four of his men – Pasha, Kamal, Hakeem, and Abdul Raq – kneeling, surrounded by five Russian soldiers. They dragged him over and threw him down next to the other four.

Don't detonate the truck yet!

One of the soldiers helped Victor to his feet and the general staggered over, blood seeping from the creases in his puffy down jacket. He coughed and then managed to smile.

"Did you think I was going to let a bunch of Islamic radicals just take a nuclear weapon? Do you think I'm a fool? I was a general in the Russian military," he said, coughing blood onto the front of the coat. "Now, go ahead and detonate your little bombs in the truck," he said. When no explosion occurred, he laughed. "We jammed the signal. Your belief in your God is misplaced. He will not be able to save you." As he spoke, a red dot appeared on Victor's chest.

"What is this?" Victor grumbled, noticing the dot.

"Allah feeds off your arrogance," Walid spat. The dot moved to Victor's leg and a moment later he crumpled over, writhing in agony. Walid gave specific instructions not to kill the general. Three of the Russian soldiers fell and the other two fled back towards their truck, pulling Victor with them. Ignoring the searing pain in his leg, Walid jumped to his feet, grabbed the rifle from the Russian on the ground and ran towards the trucks. He gave the men orders not to fire into the back and bullets pulverized the front of the cab– glass shot into the air, chunks of metal whizzed by, rubber tires were torn to pieces, and the trucks sank down onto the muddy ground like exhausted camels–but the back remained untouched. He trained them well and, praise Allah, they listened.

The startled Russians tried to return fire but as Walid anticipated, they couldn't recover from the flanking attack.

Walid and Abdul Raq reached the truck with the weapon and pulled the canvas aside. Victor sat beside the bomb, his blood pooling underneath him.

"General, you underestimate the power of Islam," Walid said quietly.

Victor grunted. "Fuck you."

"Get the bomb," Walid commanded two men. They returned a few minutes later with the crate and gently put it down. "Now general, give me the access code."

"Fuck you," the general said again.

Walid snapped his fingers and Abdul-Raq and Kamal stepped on the General's arms and legs with their muddy boots, squishing them into the mud.

"Get off me," he grunted. "I am a general in the Russian military. You will be hanged for this." The General grunted and tried to resist but he remained unable to move as they tied a rope to each arm and leg. Next, they attached each rope to the bumper of a truck.

Viktor's eyes swelled, his breathing ragged, his face flushed. "I am a general," he kept muttering.

Walid motioned for each truck to back up until the ropes drew taut

"No," the general squealed, acknowledging his fear for the first time. "No, this is not the way."

"Now general, I am going to ask you one more time, what are the access codes?"

"5-a-8-9-q-x-4-5," the General replied.

"Very well, we will try it. Ali, enter the code." He moved aside the lid, found the keypad, and punched in the numbers.

"He's a liar," Ali said. "His code is garbage."

Walid nodded again to the men and they descended on the General, cutting his clothes away and leaving him suspended naked, half a meter off the ground.

"Please," Kranchenko said, "please, I beg of you let me go. I will give you the code." Tears rolled down his cheeks.

Was it right to be a part of such degradation and cruelty? The general was not a man of the Koran, a man who worshipped Allah and who sought peace. Unlike Hassan though, he didn't relish inflicting unnecessary pain or suffering. He thanked Allah the blond barbarian was not with them on this mission. Surely, he would have jeopardized everything with his cruel impulses and unthinking actions. He shook away the thoughts. He planned this perfectly and he needed to follow the plan.

"The next time the code is wrong, I am going to cut off one of your testicles. The time after, I will cut off the second.

The third time we will cut a small hole in your stomach and slowly pull out your intestines. Then, we will cook them and shove them down your mouth. The fourth time we will slowly back up the trucks until you are pulled to pieces. If you are still alive, we will leave you to be eaten by the wolves. If you give me the codes, I promise you a quick, painless death. Do you understand?"

Kranchenko nodded. "Look in my jacket. Sewn into a pocket in the inner lining," he panted, saliva drooling from his mouth. The general's flabby arms, and legs quaked from the strain of keeping his bloated body suspended. Ali, injured, but not seriously, rifled through the jacket. "There," Kranchenko groaned, "there." Ali ripped open the lining and held up a piece of paper.

"Enter it," Walid commanded.

Ali went over to the bomb and entered the numbers.

Let the codes be accurate, Walid thought. He did not relish having to resort to extreme torture.

Ali smiled and gave a thumbs up.

Walid exhaled. "Good," he said, grabbing his gun, holding it to Victor's head, and pulling the trigger.

At Walid's direction, they executed the three remaining soldiers. His men wanted to tie them into one of the trucks and set it on fire, but he couldn't stomach hearing their screams and wanted it over quickly.

Shadows shifted through the trees and the temperature began to drop by the time Walid settled into his seat, shivering from the cold, adrenaline slowly draining from his body. The bullet in his leg began to throb. Abdul-Raq tried to clean the wound using a bottle of vodka found in one of the Russian trucks, claiming he had seen it done on television, but the pain seared like hellfire and Walid quickly stopped him, deciding to have a more experienced doctor remove it at the closest civilized town.

The engine coughed to life and the truck plodded through the mud. The first part of the plan had gone just as he expected, praise Allah.

Chapter 20

Aminah moved quickly through the throngs on the crowded street.

"Some barbecue?" a thin man with a black mustache asked, shoving a kebob in her face. She ignored him and pulled her robe tighter. She felt eyes on her and reflexively pulled at her veil tighter. Where did she fit in? In the States she was too Muslim; in Pakistan, she was too American.

Aminah felt like a target. She should have taken comfort walking amongst other Muslims, but didn't. The sights, smells, sounds, food, language were all alien to her. Her few memories of Lebanon included sandy beaches and the well-manicured boulevards of Beirut, not a cacophonous stew of humanity bartering, bickering, and traveling on the streets.

A couple of blocks back, near a crumbling water fountain, she spied a dark-haired man with an Adidas t-shirt looking at her and she tried to calm her imagination. Get in, grab the information, and leave. Quick, 1-2-3. Keep moving. Piece of cake. *No one knows I'm here.*

As an added measure of protection, Ambrose arranged a two-person Pakisani security detail. Mohit and Danish lurked behind, browsing the food carts and trying to look inconspicous. Their presence reassured her, slightly.

No time for reflection, she told herself, pushing her way through a mass of people to arrive at a narrow alleyway. She studied the directions before scanning her surroundings. Yes, this was it. A currency trading booth lay to her left and directly in front of her an old man sold an assortment of leather knickknacks. Her quick scan of the crowd revealed nothing amiss. She swiftly walked down the alley.

Aminah came to a door with a warped, weather-beaten, red awning. Number twenty-one. The sign on the outside said, Ali Khan – Fine Rugs. Aminah glanced across the street and

Mohit and Danish gave a nod. She pushed the door open and a set of bells jingled, making her jump. A black arrow on a laminated piece of white paper pointed up a rickety flight of stairs. Taking a deep breath, she rapidly climbed, the wood creaking with each step. So much for stealth. The hallway smelled damp, mildewy, and the worn banister by the staircase shook when she put her hand on it.

Aminah climbed to the top and came to a dark hallway with one doorway leading from it. The faint scent of tobacco reminded Aminah of her father smoking on the porch of their house. The memory and familiar scent calmed her nerves.

She touched the pistol under her chest for comfort and then pushed the door open, walking into a room stacked high with rugs and a dusty crystal chandelier hanging from the ceiling. At the back, behind a wood desk, sat a heavyset man with a shiny forehead. He took a puff from a cigar and pecked away on a tablet.

He glanced up when she walked in.

"Salaam," he said jovially, looking at her curiously.

"Salaam," she replied softly. Be firm and strong, she reminded herself.

"How can I be of assistance?" he asked in Urdu.

"I'm looking for Sharesh Panjababi."

"American," he said switching to English and eyeing her with more curiosity and interest. She nodded and he gave her a wide smile.

"Are you looking for a rug?" He let the words run like a horse out of the gate. "We sell many fine rugs here. Pakistanis make the finest rugs and our store contains the finest rugs in Pakistan. Karachi gets the best rugs. I have many fine deals."

"I'm not looking for a rug," she replied, trying to speak more firmly.

"Hmm, not a rug, then what are you looking for if I may ask?"

"I'm looking for Sharesh Panjababi."

"What is your business with Sharesh?"

"I'm looking for information."

"Information." He spoke the word slowly and his face creased into a scowl.

"He's not here anymore. Sharesh moved away several months ago. He didn't sell enough rugs, so I had to fire him. Terrible salesman. Always insulting the customers."

Heart beating wildly, she fingered her gun before reaching into her pocketbook, pulling out her identification, and showing it to the man.

"I know it's you, Sharesh," she said calmly, preparing for his reaction. Although he appeared friendly and benevolent, Sharesh had been taught to kill and she braced herself for a violent reaction. Instead he leaned back as if physically shocked.

"OCT?" he groaned. "What do you want from me? Please, I just want to sell rugs, leave me alone. I am a simple man, with simple tastes." He examined her identification more closely. "O' Connor," he said softly. "John O' Connor."

"He was my husband."

"Why did they send you? It is not safe for you here."

"What is happening to Fist of Allah? Who is killing their members?"

"How would I know?"

"I came over two thousand miles because Ambrose thinks you have information. Please don't make my trip a waste." Stay bold. Be forceful. Aminah had no idea how to actually interview or interrogate someone. She had spent a few days in training on the topic and tried to remember the lessons. Be firm and resolute came to mind.

"I'm not here to reenlist you or reactivate you, Sharesh. I just want to know what is happening."

Sharesh gaped at her for a moment, stood, and came around from his desk. She tensed up but let him firmly grab her arm.

"Leave, please leave! You are putting me, my family, and my shop in terrible danger!" he said, pointing towards the door. "I don't know anything; I don't want to know anything. It is a very dangerous time now. With the collapse of the Caliphate, Karachi is crawling with jihadis. Please, leave."

Just then the bells below jingled. He ran over to the window and peered down at the entrance to the building. Aminah peaked out and noticed an unfamiliar man with short, dark hair standing to the side of the awning. Glancing across the street, she didn't see Mohit or Danish in their agreed to spots.

"Allah curse me, what have you done!" he hissed. "You brought them. Quickly, come this way, quickly!" He brought her around a pile of rugs and into another room. "You are going to get me killed." He pushed aside a pile to reveal a door. As he fumbled with the latch, Aminah could hear footsteps coming up the hallway.

"Who is it?" she asked but Sharesh ignored her. His stubby fingers awkwardly worked the latch and finally popped it open, revealing a back staircase that he nearly pushed her down.

"Go!" he hissed again, closing the door behind him.

They scrambled down the staircase and emerged onto an alley at the side of the building which, to her relief, was empty. Who was he afraid of?

"Who are they?" Aminah asked, as Sharesh surveyed the street, his CIA training starting to assert itself. She knew from his file that he had been trained during the U.S. occupation of Afghanistan and been a valuable source of intelligence. The file described him as "crafty," "devious," but "loyal" to Western interests.

He didn't answer but instead pulled her forward.

"This way, quickly. They will find the door soon." He ran fast despite the paunch, and in a few minutes they turned a block and entered another small market. Sharesh slowed.

"How can you be OCT?" he asked. "You were being followed and didn't know it. They were Fist of Allah."

"How?" she asked. "I had a security detail with me."

"Bah, security detail. Worthless. Someone told them you were here," he said, as they rushed through the market, his head scanning everyone they passed. "Your security detail has been killed and you're next. Someone wants you dead."

The only person who knew her location was Ambrose and she couldn't believe he set her up.

"I'm not a field agent. This isn't what I was trained to do."

"Really? It isn't obvious. You're not like your husband, eh?" he asked.

"So you did know him?"

Sharesh stopped and looked directly at her. "I am going to tell you this and then I want you to go back home. It is much too dangerous here for an untrained American woman. And please do not bother me again. I am only telling you this because I was a friend of your husband. Perhaps I should have said something sooner, but...." He shrugged. "Sometimes secrets are better left dead."

"Please, tell me." Aminah's heart pounded.

"Fist of Allah did not kill your husband. The day after they said he was killed, I saw him alive in Pakistan, boarding a plane to Washington DC."

Aminah tried to reconcile what he said with what she had been told. "Are you sure? "

"Of course I am sure. I am a professional. Your husband lived when he left Pakistan."

"They told me he died in Iraq. That's what the official report indicated." Sharesh smiled but the warmth and joviality was gone from his face.

"They lied.

"Why?" she asked. "Why lie? Where is he now? "

"I can only tell you what I saw that day." He paused and moved her down another small street. "The jihadis speak of a huntress, a woman who stalks Fist of Allah like a bitch wolf. No one knows her identify."

"Is the Huntress from another jihadi group?"

"No."

"What makes you so sure?" she asked.

" No jihadi group would use a woman as a hunter."

They reached the edge of the market, but before he could say anything else, a black Mercedes sedan squealed to a stop in front of them. The back doors flew open and two men with ski masks over their faces flew out.

"Run!" Sharesh screamed. Aminah took one large leap, tripped on a stick, and tumbled onto the ground. Before she could rise, strong arms wrapped her waist and dragged her towards the Mercedes. In the brief instant before being pushed into the car, she watched one of the men pull a gun and shoot Sharesh in the head, splattering a ribbon of red across a woman at a market stall. A moment later, the car door closed and a man smelling strongly of garlic pulled a bag over her head, leaving her blind and gasping for air. It happened so fast she didn't even have time to scream.

Chapter 21

The path to Europe brought Walid across Kazakhstan into Russia, the Ukraine, and then Poland. For a week, they passed through kilometer upon kilometer of forest, farmland, and grassland, stopping only to purchase food or relieve themselves. While they traveled by highway at night, by day Walid directed them onto smaller side roads running through villages where the locals eyed their car warily, the children chasing it through the narrow streets as if running behind a horse or camel. The E letters explained how to cross national borders using old smuggling routes, the roads little more than cowpaths or old hiking trails. In Ukraine, the van sank into a meter of mud halfway up a mountain and the three of them spent four hours pushing and pulling until free. Once they arrived in Poland, via a path that looked more suited to cows than cars, they entered the EU, and Walid relaxed, a little.

Walid drove, while Ali and Abdul-Haseeb sat in the middle row of the minivan. Ali possessed technical knowledge of the weapon which might prove essential to completing the mission. He chose Abdul-Haseeb for his loyalty as the boy followed him around like a puppy dog, eager to do a favor, run an errand, and help in any way. At first, Walid had found his attention irritating but he had grown to appreciate such an assistant and rewarded the boy by asssigning him to the mission. The boy had started writing poetry, which Walid thought silly and counter-productive, but harmless.

Their destination was a small city three hours from the border called Rseszow where they would pick up the fourth member of the group. The city lay along the East-West European E40 Highway, a route that would transport them efficiently from Poland to Germany, France, and then Belgium and ultimately Holland.

They pulled off the highway and traveled down Lwowska Boulevard, reaching a bridge across the Wislok River. Walid watched a boy lug a suitcase, as an attractive couple holding hands walked behind him. He always considered the Poles a half-Jew, dirty people but the city looked neat and well-kept, the population fit and well fed. Rows of five-and-six-story apartment buildings lined the street and shrubs and hedges provided a touch of life. He read Rseszow was the largest city in southeastern Poland, with a population of about one hundred and fifty thousand. Easily accessible by car and served by an international airport, Restow had become a key destination for Fist of Allah to enter and leave Europe.

They van traveled three more blocks, reached an intersection, and continued straight through the lights. On their right, they passed a red apothecary.

"We are almost there," he told Abdul Haseeb. "Slow down." Several colored buildings lay clustered on the left followed by a modern apartment complex, all glass and steel. Across the street loomed a medieval church, a gold cross atop the tallest spire.

"If not for the loss of the Muslim army at the Battle of Vienna, minerats would dot this land instead of crosses," he said aloud to no one in particular. "Pull in there," he pointed to the right. Abdul-Haseeb steered the car off the main road to the entrance of the building's garage. Walid shifted his weight to pull a fob out of his pocket and pain rocketed up his left leg. Grimacing, he waited for the searing bolt to subside before handing the device to Abdul-Haseeb. The fool had used the Russian's dirty vodka to sterilize the bullet wound and he prayed infection hadn't set in.

The garage door opened and they drove the truck into the basement.

"Look for spot 138," Walid said. Finding it a minute later, Walid motioned for Abdul-Haseeb to park next to a Nissan van. A quick check of the license plate confirmed the vehicle. So far, so good.

"Be alert," Walid said. He patted his waist and felt the pistol's outline before opening the door and stepping down.

Pain! He took a deep breath and tried to stay upright, but sank onto one knee.

"Walid. Walid, are you okay?" asked Ali, rushing over.

He brushed him away. "I'm fine," he said through gritted teeth. He needed to find a doctor soon but first they would get the new van and pick up Ashraf. All would be done in good time.

He pulled himself erect and shuffled over to the Nissan. He touched the hood. Cold. He moved to the driver's side and opened the door. Walid bent down, groped under the seat, and his fingers brushed against a small slip of paper and a cellphone. He pulled them out. A number was printed on the paper. He pulled his shirt over the pre-paid, disposable phone and dialed the number.

"Allo," grumbled a voice. He didn't recall Ashraf speaking in such a low tone but he knew to mask his voice to avoid detection.

"Allo," he said back. "We have arrived." He hung up.

"Abdul and Ali, move the weapon. Faisel, you and I will move everything else." As he took out their travel bags and backpacks, he watched Abdul and Ali carefully withdraw the boxed warhead and move it into the back of the van. The floor at the back of the Nissan lifted to reveal a compartment big enough to house the weapon box. Ali and Abdul-Haseeb carefully laid the warhead into its new home.

"I thought you said the bomb couldn't explode from being dropped or jostled," he called out to Ali.

"Of course, of course. That's what I said. It can't, but who wants to find out," Ali replied. The Doctor had a dour, rather cautious outlook on life that Walid couldn't decide if he liked, or found irritating.

"Well, let's move quickly. We don't need to be seen." Picking up the tempo, they secured the bomb and folded the floor back into place.

Where was Ashraf? Walid checked his phone and thought of the appropriate words to berate the man for his tardiness.

An elevator dinged, the door opened at the other end of the garage. A figure exited and Walid motioned for the others to get into the van. If it was Ashraf, good; if not, they would look like a bunch of men getting ready to go.

In the dim light, Walid squinted to clearly view the approaching figure. This man wore jeans with military boots and a camouflage style jacket. A green wool cap covered his ears. No, this couldn't be Ashraf. Walid turned to get back into the van but a voice called out.

"Hey, Walid!" called a voice in an American accent. He stood still for an instant, his body chilled by the sound of the voice, his stomach tightening in distaste.

No. please he prayed to Allah, no. Anyone but him.

Walid realized he now confronted the first serious obstacle in his perfectly planned mission.

Chapter 22

The sack over Aminah's head clung to her mouth and she gasped for air. The radio played a recitation of the Koran and every few minutes two or three male voices chanted "Allahu Akbar, Allahu Akbar." The engine revved, gears changed, the car rattled as it passed over a pothole. The men spoke in a mixture of Urdu and Arabic, switching frequently back and forth.

"Is this one connected to Khalid?"

"He thinks she is."

"Should I ask her?"

"Say nothing. He instructed us not to speak to her."

The car slowed and turned right. Heart pounding, she tried to think of some way to break free and flee. Once they arrived at their destination, it would be much harder to get away. But wedged in between two bodies, with a hood over her face, escape seemed impossible.

"Open the door," the driver said and the body to her right rose. She should go now, but her legs wouldn't move. The car door thumped closed. They started slowly forward again and then the engine sputtered off. The doors opened and strong hands pulled her out.

"This way, this way," a voice said gruffly in Urdu. They half pushed, half pulled her for several hundred feet. Aminah smelled the chalky scent of aged, musty concrete and heard the scuffle of their feet. She shuddered.

Hands shoved her into a seat, forced her wrists into steel manacles, anchoring her to the chair. She needed to stay alert and look for another way to escape.

Don't panic.

They pulled the hood off her face and she blinked in the glare of a bright light.

It took a minute for the room to come into focus: bare grey concrete walls, a cheap-looking lamp in the corner. A naked lightbulb dangled from a wire above her head.

A tall, dark-haired man with a bushy beard gazed at her. Behind him, a stocky man with an empty left sleeve leered. A young man, actually more like a boy, stood next to the armless guy.

Tall man faced her in silence for several minutes before speaking. She recognized his face.

"The hand of the devil comes in the form of a woman."

Now was no time to act meek. Case outcomes showed that groveling or acting passive did little to improve a hostage's odds for survival. She played her only card, a weak one.

"The Koran says nothing about harming civilians, about holding and kidnapping women. Let me go."

"The Koran says we must wage war on the infidels and in this we should be ruthless. You are Muslim but you choose the side of the infidels. For that, you are a traitor to your people and your faith. You forsake and betray Islam."

"I am still a Muslim…"

"You are an apostate, a harlot, a defiler of Islam and Mohammad and Allah!" he screamed, banging his fist onto the table. "First you marry an infidel, then you work for the enemy, and now you do their evil bidding. These are all affronts, insults," he seethed.

So this man knew her identify. But how was that possible?

"You killed my husband."

He laughed. "If you wish to believe that. It makes no difference to me."

Once again, more riddles. Did he possess information about John?

"Now, let's begin," he said calmly. "Tell me who is responsible for killing our men," he demanded, getting right to the point. "Where they are hiding. Where is it they are staging their operations from?"

She put a name to his face. "Bin Gaudi. You were one of the hijackers," she said.

He nodded and smiled. They all had ego. Bin Gaudi had been a second-tier player on Flight 2816. But everyone associated with that mission had come out a hero in the Arab world and he clearly relished the attention.

She wanted to call him what he was: a child killer, a murderer, a perverter of her religion.

"I had the honor of helping free Sheikh Imaad," he responded. "Now," he asked her more calmly, apparently pleased with the recognition, "tell me who is hunting Fist of Allah?"

"I don't know."

Smack. Her face stung. The coppery taste of blood flooded her mouth. So much for a calmer demeanor.

"Liar!" he hissed. "Tell me and we will show you mercy."

"I told you, I don't know," she replied struggling not to cry and retain her cool. Hadn't Ambrose said the mission was safe? What the fuck was this?

"It is the Mossad, isn't it?" Bin Ghadi screamed at her, his spit covering her face. "Or is it the CIA? Some cell within the CIA? Tell me, or by Allah I will give you a thousand burning cuts with my knife!" Unstable, easily angered, she recognized the Jihadi personality.

"We heard about it but were not involved," she wheezed, finding it hard to breath. Trembling, compsure crumbling, she found it increasingly difficult to think. *Stay calm. Remember what Ambrose told you about the executed terrorists.* The wrong word could be her death. "You know more than I do. I came here looking for answers."

"In the video of Khalid's death a man spoke in English. He is American. Who is he? Who does he work for?"

Video? Ambrose never mentioned the video. "I don't know."

"You keep saying that. I'm tired of the same words!" Smack! She shrank away from him, afraid of the pain from another slap. "Please, I'm telling the truth."

Bin Ghadi retreated a few steps and glanced at his watch. "It is time to pray. Do you wish to pray?" he asked politely. With shaking hands Aminah wiped the tears from her face.

"Y-y-y-yes," she stammered, ignoring the nausea in her stomach. She knew any other answer could ignite a murderous rage.

He took out a key, unlocked her manacles, and motioned to the floor. She dropped to her knees. Her hands free, she thought again about fleeing, but the risks were too great.

"Mecca is that way," he said motioning towards a grey concrete wall. Trembling in fear, under the watchful eyes of her executioners, Aminah went through the Salat. Bin Ghadi and the men knelt next to her.

When they were done, Bin Ghadi rose. "Perhaps we can make a deal."

A deal?

"You see, we are reasonable. We are both looking for information, no? You are looking for news of your husband. We are looking for information on who is killing our warriors."

Bin Gaudi's belief that she possessed valuable information kept her alive. But she had nothing.

"Do not protect the aggressors," he said tenderly. "You are a Muslim. Your infidel husband did not die from my hand. He did not die from the sword of Allah."

"What happened to him?" she asked letting out a sniffle.

Bin Gaudi smiled. "Perhaps you should ask the devil government you work for. They can tell you more lies. Why would they be honest to a Muslim? You have prostituted yourself to them and they treat you like a whore," he said. He softened his tone. "You are a Muslim. Did you think they would treat you well? Can't you see what they have done to all of us? The children dying in the camps, the poverty, the stench of their devil ways? Even today they export their sick culture where it grows like a weed, threatening to choke everything that is great about the Arab and Muslim world."

Had Ambrose walked her into a trap? Did he want her killed because she had asked too many questions? He seemed upset that she had been poking around about the airplane hijackers and John's death.

"And yet you work for them and protect their secrets?" Bin Ghadi sat down, his eyes like drills. "Now, tell me who is killing our men and I will share information about your husband."

She needed to tell him something but she couldn't give in too quickly. "I can't tell you," she said.

Bin Gaudi smiled gently. "Of course you can. Tell me, Aminah. Tell me and return to your people."

Tears streamed down her face and she forced herself to sob. Her chest heaved.

"It's the CIA." Silence. Her control gone, she frantically embellished the lie. "They are hunting you for kidnapping the Vice President's daughter."

He shook his head. "That is the best you can do?"

"It's true!" she insisted, knowing he didn't buy the story.

"You lie!" he screamed and she shrank back. "Put her in the box," he commanded the two men behind them. "I want to know who is killing my brothers. I give you twenty-four hours to tell me before I send you to be judged by Allah."

Numb and drained, she watched the boy and the one-armed man undo her shackles, put a chain around her neck, and lead her down a set of stairs to the basement. The room ended at a three foot high steel door set into the wall. The boy took out a key, unlocked the door, and pulled it open. Human excrement mixed with blood decorated the floor, a swarm of insects scattered in the light.

"Get in," he said, giving her a shove.

She tripped on the chain and sprawled across the concrete, feeling something slither under her cheek.

"Welcome to Karachi," One Arm said with a laugh. The door clanged shut and the bolts screeched as he slid them into place.

Aminah swatted at a feathery touch on her ankle. Legs slithered across her forehead. She gave a scream and squished a mushy object with the palm of her hand. Flies buzzed, their flight paths brushing her body and face. Screaming, she flailed her arms to scare them away but she could sense the insects circling her head. She tried to hold her stomach down but a wave of bugs ascended her arm, sending her over. She bent over to vomit, smashed her head into the wall and as she bounced back the vomit spewed onto her lap, covering her robe and hands.

"You need to relax or the box can kill you," a soft voice said.

Chapter 23

The voice cut through her panic and panting. She refocused on the speaker and away from the vomit and bugs and stink and the claustrophobia of being locked in a tiny room.

"Focus on my voice and forget about the box."

"Yes, that's what I'm trying to do," she sobbed.

"Good."

After a few moments, the worst of the panic subsided.

"Breathe," he commanded. "Relax."

"You sound like my yoga instructor," she said.

"Humor helps. The class must have been pretty crappy." His body shifted. "Here, take this. You can clean yourself off a bit."

"You can see?"

"I can smell."

Her fingers probed the darkness, finding a stiff cloth. She grabbed it, wondering if the rag was any cleaner than her shirt, and worked to remove the vomit.

"Thanks. Well, the class was above a pawn shop on a street with drug dealers at the corner," she said.

"Most yoga classes my wife goes to are in seedy locations. At least in New York."

"It's a yoga class requirement. Are you from New York?" Aminah asked.

"I lived there for three years before involuntarily moving to the Middle East. You?"

"Upper East Side." Silence. How much should she reveal? "How did you wind up here?" she asked.

"In this box? Christ, that's a long story. But the short of it is, I arranged an interview with a Pakistani parliament member who allegedly supported Fist of Allah. I never conducted the interview. They grabbed me en route."

"You're David Tinely," she said, remembering the briefing about his disappearance.

"Yes," he said, a bit sadly, as if someone recognizing him made his plight that much more realistic. "Do they still talk about me?"

In truth, the media didn't anymore, but she didn't want to tell him that.

"I see your name on the news from time to time. You aren't forgotten. But that's not what really matters. The government is still working to free you. Your wife is trying hard to bring you home."

"Valerie hasn't forgotten me?"

"I met with her." His wife, a petite brunette with a large, pregnant belly, came to Columbia seeking Aminah's assistance. The woman broke down in the middle of the conversation and Aminah promised to speak with some of her contacts at the OCT. Ambrose told her what she already suspected: Fist of Allah kidnpped Tinely and OCT had no idea of his location.

"You met Valerie?" he asked, and he shuffled closer. "Why? Who are you? How is she? How is the baby?"

"She was very pregnant when we met. She visited my office last March so I'm sure you have a new child by now."

"A boy," Tinely said softly. "We planned to name him Jackson."

"I think your wife mentioned that name."

He sat quietly for a moment, seeming to savor the thought and then spoke again.

"Why did you meet her?"

"Are they listening?"

"Probably. I searched the box from top to bottom and didn't find any electronic bugs or listening devices but I'd be surprised if there wasn't one." She wasn't sure it even mattered, since Bin Gaudi already knew her identity.

"I work, worked, still work for the OCT," she whispered.

"You're an agent?"

"Not exactly. I'm an analyst." He let out a low whistle. "Your wife came to me looking for help."

"That's wonderful," he said, his voice trembling with emotion.

"You aren't forgotten."

"Thank you," he said quietly. "Thank you. What did she say? What did she look like? Please, tell me everything."

She did, the chatter helping her maintain some semblance of sanity. When she had finished describing the meeting, Tinely remained quiet for a moment.

"Do you have kids?"

"No." Tears welled in her eyes and she couldn't suppress a sniffle.

"I'm sorry," David said. "That was a poor question."

"No, it's okay," She wiped the tears, rattling the chains around her arms and legs. "I was pregnant once and had a miscarriage. We never told anyone so you are the first person to know. My husband, John, died before we could try again."

"How did he die?"

"Fist of Allah killed him," she replied. "I think."

Tinely's chains rattled. "Was he in the military?"

"No, he worked with me at the OCT. We met on the job."

David whistled. "Nice, a terrorism fighting couple."

"Yup. Both killed by Fist of Allah." She sobbed, thinking about the lost opportunities to be a mother. She wanted children when she was younger, in her teens and early twenties, when life seemed to be forever and getting married and having babies were just the normal flow of life. Oh Allah, she would never have her own baby now. She wept.

"Aminah," David asked, "is your last name O'Connor?"

"How did you know that?"

"They speak about you. Not exactly you, but I think your husband. Sometimes, they forget I'm here and can understand Arabic."

"They said something about John?" she asked.

"Once or twice, I think," David said.

125

"What did they say?"

"They called him a Khie'yen."

"A traitor," Aminah translated. "Why would they say that?"

"I may not have heard them correctly."

"I'm not sure what happened to John," she said. "The OCT never recovered his body and an operative told me they saw him alive, after he was supposedly killed."

"Strange." He shifted and his chains rattled. "I came to Pakistan because I was given a tip."

"What?" she asked.

"Someone told me to meet with a Pakistani politician who had information about the U.S. government's involvement in the airline hijacking two years ago. Rumors circulated on a couple of online boards that someone in the U.S. government helped the terrorists."

Aminah stiffened. She suspected all along that someone inside helped Fist of Allah with the operation. She spent hours pouring over TSA security tapes and tracking airline employees to find who planted the weapons and bomb on the plane. But she couldn't find anything

"Who gave you this tip?"

"Lilly Broadhurst."

"Who?" she asked again, even more surprised.

"Lilly Broadhurst, the rich oil woman."

Aminah met the tall, glamorous blonde briefly at the funeral for Zeke's wife and son. She remembered the heiress standing by Zeke's side, giving him a hug, wiping a tear from her cheek. What part did she play? From what Aminah remembered, Lilly helped fund Zeke's business venture. "How did you wind up speaking with her?"

"Several years ago I received a short text from an unknown sender. It said: 'Flight 2817. Lilly Broadhurst.' I receive a lot of texts so I didn't read it at the time. Sixteen months later as I was going through my phone during an upgrade and came across the text again."

She reached out, found a hard knee, and squeezed.

"Whoa," he said.

"What was the date of that text?"

"November 13."

"One day before the airplane hijacking,"she whispered, finding it hard to breathe. "Someone texted you a day in advance with the number of the plane that would be hijacked and Lilly Broadhurts's name?

"Yes," he replied.

"Who sent the text?"

"I did say it was anonymous, right?"

Zeke insisted his wife had received an anonymous text the morning of her flight, although Aminah had never been able to find any evidence of the message. "So, what did you do?"

"I traveled down to Texas to meet with Lilly. At first she ignored me, but I sent her a note alluding to her connection with Flight 2718. One day later, I received an invitation to lunch. She insisted her only connection to Flight 2718 was the investment in Zeke's financial company. She explained the text I received was an alert about the financial transaction she made with Zeke. The big story was in Pakistan. According to her sources, an elite American counter-terrorist group collaborated with Fist of Allah to free and protect Sheikh Imaad. She gave me Mohammed Gandapur's name."

"So you left?"

"I didn't completely buy what she was selling but a tip from one of the richest women in the world was worth investigating. The ultra-wealthy have high level connections and journalists need a good scoop."

"Never to be seen again," Aminah said softly. "Do you think she set you up?"

"She wanted me to disappear. She lied about the text."

"Just like someone from the OCT wanted me gone."

"I always thought Lilly made up the story about an inside mole," he added. "But it appears she told the truth."

Aminah's head spun, the newfound knowledge like a jumble of clothes in her dryer, spinning around, tossed and tangled without any sense or order. "I don't know what any of this means," she said. Despair returned. "I can't see how I'm going to get out of here alive, so it may not matter."

"Why are you in Pakistan,?" he asked, sounding like a reporter.

"Someone has been picking off members of Fist of Allah. OCT sent me to meet with a contact who held information about the executions. He's dead and I'm here."

"They talk about the killings," David said. "I've never seen them so agitated. They say there is a woman, a demon woman who kills them with a bullet to the forehead. These Jihadis can get very poetic," he said, chuckling.

"Bin Gaudi thinks I know. He wants me to tell him or he's threatened to kill me."

"Aminah, they plan to kill both of us. It's just a question of how and when." He leaned close to her and lowered his voice to a whisper. "The longer you can delay, the better your chances of escaping or being rescued. To stay alive, you need to convince them you have valuable information."

"But I don't." she whispered back."

"Make something up. I do it all the time. Be creative. Tell a story."

"It works?"

"Of course. They accuse me of being a CIA agent. If I don't have value to them I'm dead, so I need to give them value, keep them guessing."

"And they buy it?"

"I'm not sure they know any better. You actually work for the OCT. Spin a really crazy story."

"Maybe," she said. Creative writing had never been one of her strong suits. Silence for a moment and then:

"Aminah, if you get out of here, tell my family I love them."

"You'll make it out, we'll both make it out," she said, trying to believe her own words and dispel the lurking despair. Her mouth quivered and she let out a partial sob.

"Please, remember to tell them. Thanks." In a few moments he began to breathe deeply and she wondered how he could fall asleep so easily.

Something crawled across her leg. She swatted the bug and let out another sob, her control beginning to fray. Speaking with David provided a momentary distraction from the terror permeating every cell of her body. *Don't lose it Aminah. If you do, you're dead. Focus on the positive.* How could she stay alive? What plausible story could she tell?

Her mind turned, the darkness swirled, revealing images – buildings and faces, places, and times. Voices echoed through the chamber. Poor John. He should have lived to become a father. Zeke. A poor billionaire. Her eyes shut and jerked open. She hadn't slept or eaten in days. Thoughts about John and Zeke circled in her mind. As she drifted off, an idea came to her.

A loud clang reverberated through the box. Bright light streamed in from the open door.

"Out!" a rough voice commanded. "Get out. Both of you. Move, move, you lazy dogs!"

She rolled over, groggy, unsure of her surroundings. Where?

"Move! If I have to come in, I'll pull out your teeth."

A man in stained brown clothes and a ragged beard crawled out, receiving a kick in the side from the guard. David.

"Let's go whore!"

Whore? The box. It all rushed back except for the dream.

As she clambered towards the door, heedless of the bugs squished under her palm, Aminah tried desperately to remember the idea that came to her on the edge of sleep.

Chapter 24

The ride through Poland should have been uneventful and pleasant. The highway, straight, smooth and without traffic stretched across grassy meadows, farms, and small towns. Walid admitted a grudging admiration for the serenity of the landscape, the order of the farms, the neat rows of corn stocks and plants, the symmetry of power lines stretching across vast distances. Soon, Muslims would occupy the land.

But Hassan's blathering sucked all pleasant feelings, like a colony of leeches attached to his genitals. Since leaving Rseszow, the American questioned his every decision. How could Skeikh Imaad have replaced Ashraf with the Barbarian? Walid knew better than to question the Sheik's wisdom, but still, the choice troubled him.

"Why are we taking such a small road? This is the wrong direction! We are not making fast enough time." Five minutes ago, the American insisted they stop. His nagging so irritated Walid that he agreed to pull the van into a small convenience store near the Polish and German border.

"I'm tired of wiping my ass with grass," the Blonde Barbarian complained. Didn't the savage understand the more contact they had with others the better the chance something could derail their mission? The prominent scar the Jewess had carved into Hassan's face made him look even more like a filthy Bedouin.

They parked the van in front of a small, wooden convenience store with firewood stacked in a pile beside the entrance. Luckily, no other cars sat in the lot. They shouldn't be stopped here at all, he reminded himself. Curse Hassan!

His foot throbbed. Last night, before leaving Rseszow, Hassan directed them to the house of a Chechen named Balak who called himself a doctor. Doctor Balak removed the bullet with a knife and a bottle of rubbing alcohol.

"This is how we do it in Chechnya," the man said, his grin showing a lone gold tooth at the front of his mouth. Walid should have walked out the moment he saw the half-drunk fool, but the ache prevented him from thinking clearly. After the procedure, the pain lessened, but with each passing hour his mind turned to the wound with greater frequency.

Walid was about to open the door to check on Hassan when a woman's scream broke the silence.

"Please, someone help me! Please, they'll kill me! Please!" she screamed in heavily accented English. A short skirt barely covered her womanly parts and she ran awkwardly in bare feet. From across the parking lot he appreciated her beautiful blonde hair and perfect features. He tried to avert his gaze, but he couldn't, held spellbound by her distress. This was exactly the kind of situation he wanted to avoid.

What now?

"Stay in the van," Walid ordered Ali and Abdul-Haseeb.

She approached and banged on the windows, sccreaming, eyes wide, tears streaming down her face.

Go away.

Did he know her? Up close, she looked familiar, but he couldn't be sure. As much as he tried, he couldn't stop himself from peering at her—large eyes, wavy hair, and a body that was curvy but not too thin, not skeletal like most Western women.

Do not get involved. Turn away.

But he couldn't. He tightened his grip on the handle, recognized his own impulse, and forced his fingers to relax.

Stay focused.

"Do not help her," Walid ordered.

"Please, help me! Please!" she cried frantically banging on the glass. For one moment their eyes locked.

Her eyes are like Mouna's.

Yes, that was it. Her eyes held the same beauty and intelligence as Mouna. He prepared to open the door when headlights flashed and washed the woman's face in their bright glare.

Her screaming became even more frantic. "No! No!" She started to back towards the store entrance.

Three men jumped out of a silver Mercedes M Class sedan. One wore a leather jacket, the other two business suits.

Walid's hand tensed on the door handle and he gave new directions.

"Be ready."

The men carried themselves like the Albanian gangsters he met once in a safe house in Turkey. One choked a prostitute to death for being ten euros short on her payment.

As the woman ran towards the entrance to the shop, the door opened and Hassan came out carrying a carton of milk. She slammed into him, dropping the carton. It split open on the concrete and splashed his black athletic shoes with white drops of liquid.

"Shit!" he screamed in English. "What is going on?"

"Give me the girl, you stupid fuck," leather jacket ordered.

No Hassan, do not react.

The American picked up the dripping, half-full carton. Hassan' eyes narrowed, his mouth bent into a frown, his fingers curled into fists. Walid flung open the door. Unable to move fast enough to stop him, Walid watched Hassan take the milk carton and throw it into the man's face.

No Hassan! What are you doing? How many times had he told him remain cool, to take the insults and the taunts if that was what needed to be done? They couldn't afford to attract attention to themselves.

Walid made a quick decision. "Allah Akbar!" Walid shouted, jumping out of the van, Ali and Abdul-Haseeb close beyond. He fired his Beretta, hitting Leather Jacket in the chest. Even without the silencer, the gun barely made a sound, more like the hiss of a camel than the retort of a weapon.

"What the fuck!" the man screamed. He staggered back.

Walid fired again into his face.

Ali and Abdul-Haseeb moved just as quickly, killing the heathen's two companions.

Walid surveyed the scene. Curse Hassan!

The door to the store opened and a little man emerged with a blue apron around his waist. He glared at them, and shouted something in Polish. Hassan raised his gun and shot him in the head. *Hassan!* Perhaps it was the right move, but the Barbarian should have waited for his orders.

"Take their guns," he panted, trying to keep his voice calm and hide the seething anger. Hassan, the camel stupid, ugly American savage had already jeopardized the trip.

Think. Change the future, not the past.

He pointed to the dead men in front of them. "Kill anyone else inside, quickly! Then, wipe our prints from these guns and place them on their bodies. Take one of the men and place him over there to make it look like he shot the other two and the store owner." Maybe the setup would buy them enough time to get out of Poland.

Ali and Abdul Hasseeb stared at the dead bodies for a moment too long and Walid saw the unease on their faces. This was not an ideal situation but such was life.

"Do it!' he screamed.

"What about her?" Hassan asked. The woman cowered by the side of the store.

Walid hesitated.

"She's seen the whole thing! She could identify us!" Hassan yelled, pulling his gun.

"Please," the woman said softly in heavily accented English. "Please, don't kill me." Walid hesitated, for once unsure. Her dead body might make the scene look like some kind of lovers' quarrel. But her soft, quiet begging made him hesitate.

Her eyes are so much like Mouna's.

"We don't want to leave more of a mess. She'll come with us until we figure out what to do with her."

"That's a bad idea," Hassan said. "She'll slow us down. Better to kill her now." Hassan was right. But he so hated the American that if the savage said left, Walid would have picked right. He would not give the dhimmi the satisfaction of agreeing with him, and they could always dump her at the side of the road later on.

"She'll come with us," he repeated firmly. "Grab some of that rope and bind her wrists in the van. Let's go!"

"It's a bad idea," Hassan repeated. He motioned to her arm. "She's been cut." Walid frowned. The thin scar near her bicep certainly looked like the mark of a tracker.

"What's that on your arm?" he asked in English. The woman pointed to her arm. "Yes," he confirmed, "on your arm."

"They put it there. They no let me go, tell me I am theirs. But you kill them," she responded.

Hassan was right, she represented a threat to the mission. Pausing for a moment, he tried to clear his thoughts. He gazed at her, prepared to order her death, and couldn't. She stood silent, beautiful and submissive, ready to accept his sentence. Allah whispered in his ear: *today is not her day to die*.

"She comes with us."

Hassan spat and mumbled something in English.

Ali and Abdul-Haseeb came out of the store and reported that no one else had been inside. Good, he didn't want to complicate the situation by killing anyone else.

The girl followed compliantly but a problem arose when she climbed into the van, as neither Ali nor Abdul Haseeb wanted to sit next to her.

"No, I will not," said Abdul Haseeb. Ali eyed the woman and seemed ready to change his mind, but Abdul Haseeb folded his arms and stared at the ground.

"I'll sit next to her," Hassan volunteered, his smile like those of the men who enjoyed killing chickens on Uncle Baba's farm.

"I'll sit there!" Walid yelled. "I need to stretch my leg anyway." He climbed in and Ali followed.

Abdul-Haseeb put the vehicle into reverse and the tires squealed as they returned to the road.

"Do you know what you are doing?" Abdul-Haseeb asked him in Arabic as the vehicle accelerated.

"No, but pray Allah does."

They pulled onto a two-lane road leading back to the highway. In three hours they would be out of Poland and into Germany.

Chapter 25

Bright light streamed in from the open door, blinding her after the hours spent in the total darkness of the box.

"Move," a voice said as a blur lashed out and collided with her jaw, whipsawing her head back and numbing her face for an instant before pain bloomed across her nose. "Get out!" When she tried to rise, her legs quivered and she collapsed back against the wall.

David whispered behind her. "It'll take a minute for you to regain sensation in your legs."

"No talking!" the jihadi yelled and cuffed her again on the side of the head. Ears ringing, eyes blinded by the light, she crawled towards the entrance, trying to suppress her sobs. The chain tightened and a strong jerk sent her sprawling forward, before dragging her across the fetid bottom of the box.

The one-armed man walked into the room. He grabbed her hair and yanked her out of the cell. Her scalp burned. She reflexively tried to push his arm away.

"Get up!" he yelled, giving her a quick kick to the stomach.

She managed to kneel, blood from her nose dripping onto her knees and spotting the floor.

"Can't you do anything right?" another man snapped. "Bin Ghadi said to bring them in quickly, and you take the entire morning. Now, she's dirtying the floor! I have to do everything myself. Up!" he screamed, "Or Allah have mercy on you! I shall whip you like a beaten dog! I have to do everything," he muttered again.

She shrank down at his voice and noticed David standing beside her, head bowed, eyes resigned.

The shackles around her ankles made it difficult to walk and the older man swatted her every few feet.

"If you weren't such a whore, I'd take you as one of my wives and make you bear my babies," he said, flashing a lewd smile. Her mind focused on putting one foot in front of the other and not falling. As bad as her scalp burned, things would only get worse if she slipped.

They herded them into the room where she first met Bin Ghadi. When had it been? Yesterday? How long had she slept? They forced her into the chair and ordered David to kneel in front of her.

"Today you both will die," the older one said casually after securing her arms and legs. He smirked. "It is a shame. You would have made a handsome wife."

Her heart pounded. She didn't want to die here, out of the sun, like a caged animal. She examined David, a gaunt, balding man with a straggly beard tinged gray. A frayed, black one-piece outfit matted with blood, hair and God knew what else hung on his bony frame. Dark welts spotted his alabaster white skin. Their eyes met for a moment and he smiled slightly.

Without really thinking, she pulled on her chains, testing them, and the older one broke into laughter.

"Go ahead, try and escape. Try and break the chains. Try harder," he said and slapped her across the face.

She grimaced, refusing to cry, refusing to show her pain and terror. *Keep your head down, do not talk to this man, he is insane.*

"Go ahead, try again!" the man taunted her.

"Enough!" Bin Ghadi walked into the room and threw a scarf in her direction. "Cover your hair, harlot."

Hands shaking, she managed to wrap the scarf around her head. Aminah hadn't worn a hijab or a scarf in years and lacked practice at securing it into place.

"That's better. Now you look a bit more proper. I hope you had enough time to think about what we discussed yesterday. It is your duty as a Muslim to help us. So, I will ask you again, and I pray for your soul that you will reveal the truth, who is responsible for the death of the martyrs?"

She racked her brain for the thought that had come to her before sleep. But the more she tried, the more the thought receded.

"Tell me!" he screamed.

"Okay," she said. *Stay calm.* She grasped the arm of the chair and bit her lip. Calm down, she told herself, think. And then she remembered.

"We do not know for sure," she started, speaking slowly to give her time to create the story, "but we believe a private group is responsible for the killings."

"Go on," he said.

So far, so good.

"Who hates you? Who would stop at nothing to see you dead?"

"There are many people who resist the power of Allah and would try to strike back at us."

"But who has the resources to find and kill you?"

He looked perplexed. "Enough of these riddles, tell me!" he yelled.

"The man whose wife you killed."

"Who?"

"The American who paid you the ransom after you killed his family. The man who you cheated and lied to in the name of Allah."

"What was his name?" Bin Gaudi demanded, glaring at her.

"Zeke Katz."

"Yes," I remember him, Bin Gaudi said. He smirked, sucked in his cheeks, and started to chuckle. The one-armed man joined him. The chuckle turned to a laugh, his belly heaving, spittle flying onto his mustache and beard.

"You are funny," he said, wiping his tears and laughing again. "That lazy American Jew couldn't squash a cockroach. We killed his wife and child and he gave us money. Do you think a stupid Jew could hunt down and kill my men? We are

Allah's warriors. "Enough with the jokes," Bin Gaudi said, the laughter over. "Tell me what I want to know."

"You're going to kill me anyway," she said softly.

"Maybe, maybe not. But let me give you a little demonstration of what awaits if you do not change your attitude."

He pulled out a knife from his belt and turned towards David.

"Hold him," Bin Gaudi ordered, and the two other restrained David's arms. Bin Gaudi walked over and grabbed the reporter's face, forcing him look at Aminah.

"No," Aminah said. "No, please, don't do this."

"Tell us who is killing our warriors."

"I told you."

"She cost you your life, journalist."

David didn't speak but she could see the fear in his eyes, terror mixed with resignation.

"Remember to tell them," he whispered. His confidence in her ability to escape her own beheading seemed misplaced.

"No, please!" Aminah said franticially, "I'll tell you, "I'll tell you what you want to know!" She'd make up something else.

Bin Gaudi pushed David's head forward and ran the knife across the skin on the back of his neck. "Yes, you will tell me. After the journalist is dead." One Arm came forward with an iPhone and begin to film. "This is the American journalist David Tiley." He got the name wrong. "Today we kill him in the name of jihad as a warning to all who try to come to our lands to report lies."

David managed to shift his head up slightly towards the camera and yelled. "Valerie, I love you. I love-"

Enraged at the interruption, Bin Gaudi slashed the knife across Tinely's throat, reducing his last words to a gurgle as a fountain of blood erupted onto the floor. Bin Gaudi sawed away, hacking back and forth across the front of the journalist's neck, sawing through the spine, until only a sinewy layer of skin kept the head attached to the body. In shock, Aminah turned away, the image of the finger of sinew seared into her mind.

With a grunt, Bin Gaudi gripped David's hair and ripped the journalist's head from his body, blood coursing from the severed neck, guts smattering the floor. Holding the head in one hand, Bin Gaudi used his left hand to force Aminah to turn and stare into David's open eyes. Could he still see her? Oh Allah, why? Such cruelty.

"Now, do you see what awaits infidels? Tell us what we want to know and we might not kill you. You can still become the wife of a mujahedin. Tell us and start to return to your people." He tossed David's head across the room.

"No," she said firmly. Her shaking ceased and she looked him squarely in the eyes. "I will never tell you anything else." Faced with death, the fear had receded.

"No?" he screamed, coming towards her with the bloody knife, pieces of skin hanging from the blade. "No?" He placed the blade against her neck.

"Go ahead, kill me. But I guarantee whatever group is hunting you will find you, and it will pull you apart piece by piece."

His hands quivered in anger. "So you do know who is hunting us?"

"Oh yes," she said lying, "and they are demons. They will not stop until every single one of you is dead." The knife quivered against her skin.

"I am going to cut the answer out of you!" he screamed, slashing her across the ear. "You will tell me or I will cut and cut you until you are in pieces!"

"And then I will be dead and it will be your turn to die," she shot back, unsure where her courage came from. Perhaps someone truly didn't know themselves until they faced death.

He slashed her again across the neck. "I will cut and cut," he screamed again, but she could tell he was unsure. "Tell me and I will let you go," he said, switching tactics.

"The same way you promised to let the passengers go if the ransom conditions were met?" she wheezed.

"You whore!" His fist connected with her face, throwing her head back and making the room spin.

Stunned, ears ringing, she dimly noticed Bin Gaudi approach, his mouth twisted in anger, his eyes squinted in rage. He would kill her now. He raised the knife and a glint of light mometarily blinded Aminah.

She once asked John how soldiers went into battle knowing they might not see another day. He told her: "At some point a person goes beyond fear to a place of acceptance. *The fear of death is worse than dying.*"

"Goodbye," she whispered.

The knife came forward but the blade never fell. Bin Gaudi jerked sideways and dropped to the ground. Zip. Zip. Like air sucked through a straw.

"You betrayed us!" screamed One Arm, jumping towards her and crumpling at her feet. Light streamed in through three holes in a swinging shade.

She heard a yell from the other room. And then another.

"Get out!" Bin Gaudi groaned, still on the floor. "They are here! The bitch must have brought them!" More zips from the other room, then a semi-automatic sprayed bullets. Footsteps running towards her. Two large jihadis burst into the room, their rifles trained down the hallway. One of them fired a wild burst.

"They are everywhere!" a pudgy man wearing a white taqiyah screamed, firing again, ripping holes in the plaster. Dust spiraled throughout the room.

Bin Gaudi managed to crawl across the floor and pull himself up, using her body for support. Blood bloomed on his robe near his left leg. He uncuffed Aminah's arms from the chair.

"You whore," he spat. "You have brought them here. That was your plan all along."

She tried to swing her arms and hit him but he pulled her off the chair and towards another door. Bullets whizzed by, pocking the walls just to the side of Bin Gaudi's head. He flung the door open and pushed her into a concrete stairwell. His hands clamped around her wrist and he dragged her down the stairs. No, she didn't want to go into the basement, back into the dark.

Move Aminah. Do something! She bit his arm and yanked herself free.

"Bitch!" he screamed as she scrambled down the crumbling stairs. From behind, she could hear him descending swiftly after her.

She reached the landing on the next floor and the door opened. A bearded, confused jihadi stood in her way, slowing her descent and allowing Bin Gaudi to grab her from behind.

"Rashid, grab her!" Bin Gaudi screamed. Strong hands wrapped around her stomach and she kicked furiously to free herself.

"Bitch! Bitch!" Bin Gaudi repeated. "You will suffer one million torments." He gave her a violent shove and sent her hurtling down a flight of stairs. She struck the landing and tried to draw a breath, but felt like a car sat on her chest. Blood filled her mouth. *Run! Run!*

She tried to stand, but a stab of pain in her back forced her onto the ground. She needed to get up. Bin Gaudi grabbed her and pulled her towards a car.

"Get in there!" he yelled, opening the door and attempting to shove her into the back seat. She braced her arms against the metal frame. "I'm going to kill you!" he said, smashing his fist into her back, sending waves of pain down her spine and loosening her grip. One more push and she would be forced inside.

"No, no," she whimpered.

"Get in!" His muscles tensed, but before he could deliver a final push, a blast shook the garage, filling the air with plaster and wood debris. A hard object struck her forehead, and her strength vanished as a white plume of dust swirled through the room. Her ears rang. A tall, spectral figure, caked in white plaster walked through the expanding cloud of debris. *A ghoul.* Strong arms lifted her from the ground.

Chapter 26

"I see the border," Hassan said from the driver's seat and a pang of nervousness and excitement broke through Walid's pain. They had traveled all night, ditched the van in a small town in Poland, stolen another van, and continued onwards, hoping to reach the German border before daylight. Walid didn't like stealing a new van and drawing possible attention from the police, but Hassan argued the old vehicle linked them to the shooting. The Barbarian had a point, although any change from the plan made Walid nervous.

Leaving Poland and entering Germany would lessen his concern, for E wrote the police forces of the two countries didn't communicate efficiently.

Walid took the first driving shift, until the throbbing in his leg forced him into the back. He hated sitting in the third row, waiting, watching, but his leg made it impossible to focus on the road.

The others napped, stared out the window, prayed, and read. Abdul Haseeb recited a heroic poem he wrote chronicling their journey. Walid tried to recall the first lines.

> "Across the barren land of ice
> and the forbidden forests they traveled.
> Sustained by Allah's mission.
> No barrier too big;
> No infidel too powerful
> Carrying the might of Allah;
> A precious cargo
> Like a newborn ready to grow
> into a man."

The men laughed. Walid didn't consider Abdul-Haseeb a talented poet, but at least his words kept them entertained. Even Hassan smiled.

The girl stayed curled up in the back, her head propped against the window much of the time, her eyes closed. Why did his thoughts always turn to the whore? He should have slit her throat and left her by the roadside.

The men grew quiet as the van approached a bright blue sign: Bundesrepublik Deutschland, surrounded by twelve yellow stars, the symbol of the European Union. The original plan called for the weapon to detonate in Paris or London, but times had changed in Europe with the arrival of millions of Muslim immigrants. Now, some of the streets looked more like Karachi or Cairo than the West, and Sheikh Imaad believed time would take care of the European continent. Killing so many Muslims would be a sin, Imaad said, "plus, the real evil lies to the East, in the Babylon of the world controlled by the Jews." He didn't think they ever really considered destroying a city other than New York.

Ali sneezed. The Professor feared the Europeans stationed radioactive monitoring devices at their national borders but the emails didn't warn of this. What they did warn about were electronic ears.

"There are listening devices planted near the border crossings. Say something about your mission and they will know. Say nothing until you are safely over the border.

They reviewed the plan an hour earlier. "Everyone knows what to do?" he had asked.

"We know," anwered Hassan, sounding annoyed. "This is the fourth time you've asked us. If someone comes to inspect the car, we blow the weapon."

Walid disliked the American's arrogant tone.

"What if they ask about the girl? She doesn't have a passport" Hassan said.

"They won't ask. There are not supposed to be guards at the border. It is just a line we will cross."

"I hope the emails you receive from your love are correct," Hassan had sneered.

Lover? Walid squeezed his fist and let the Barbarian's words pass through his ears.

"The emails" were accurate. Hadn't he proven their reliability time and time again? Do not let Hassan sow doubt into your mind, he had told himself.

They passed the border sign and that was it; they entered Germany: no guard, no inspection, no problem. Abdul Haseeb patted him on the shoulder.

"Another worthy line for my poem."

Walid turned to the girl and pain shot up his leg, making him wince and turn back. He wiped a sheen of sweat from his forehead, his teeth chattering. The three aspirin he swallowed an hour earlier had been like pouring sand in the ocean. His face felt hot, his eyes burned. Walid burped, tasted his breakfast of eggs, and realized the contents of his stomach were ready to pour through his throat.

"Pull over," he ordered Hassan.

"What?"

"Pull over!" he said trying to muster his strength.

Hassan pulled the van to the side of the road and Walid bent through the open window and vomited, sour bile trickling out of his mouth and running down the side of the van. For a second his head cleared.

"You're messing up the van!" Hassan yelled.

Walid flung the door open and staggered onto the dirt embankment. the world spinning. A car whizzed by and he thought the rush of wind might topple him over.

He heard the girl's soft voice, and then the door to the van opened.

"She says she once studied to be a nurse. She can take a look at you," Abdul-Haseeb said.

Anything, anything to make the pain stop.

He took a few wobbly steps back to the van and Abdul-Haseeb guided him to the third row.

The woman settled his leg across her lap. Her touch was not proper but he no longer cared. The van started moving. Her face spun and he tried to focus, but it didn't work. Walid thought he might vomit again, but burped. She smiled and brushed her hair back behind her ears as if to tempt him into her wide blue eyes. As deep as oceans, he thought, her fingers grazing his skin, cool, soothing. She rolled up his pants, his heart booming in his chest, sweat drenching his forehead and back despite the numbing cold.

"Turn down the air conditioning," he moaned.

Although she gently pulled the blood-soaked cloth from the wound, stabbing pain radiated down his leg. Walid clutched a hand-rest on the side of the van as a gush of blood and pus bubbled out from his calf. Screams of agony ripped through the van. A putrid stink, like the maggot infected carcasses left behind the restaurants on Dinsh Street wafted through the vehicle. Lips pursed, face grim, the woman bent over and touched his forehead.

"You have bad infection. It is spreading. You need medicine," she said in crude English.

No, they needed to keep moving to reach Rotterdam in three days.

"I will be okay, Allah will protect me."

"You medicine need. Pain get worse."

"What kind of medicine?" he whispered.

"Antibiotics."

"Where?"

"Pharmacy. Maybe hospital. I studied to be nurse. This wound is bad."

He nodded.

She turned around. "Stop at pharmacy. He bad infection. Need antibiotics. Might need cut."

Cut? He only needed to be well for another week.

Walid collapsed into the seat. Through the pain and fever, he remembered the cool touch of her hands on his leg.

Chapter 27

Aminah's eyes opened. A soft white ceiling with recessed lights loomed over her. Tranquility.

Bin Gaudi!

She popped up in bed and a stabbing pain ripped through her head. The room rolled and Aminah gagged before her vision steadied and her stomach settled. Probing above her left ear, her fingers ran over soft fabric, a bandage– the memory of tumbling down stairs roared back.

What happened after that?

The pain passed and Aminah gingerly turned her head.

Red curtains framed a curved window at the opposite end of the room. A mahogany dresser sat against the wall beside the window. Beside the bed, a beige carpet with a thread of red lay on a dark, hardwood floor.

It beat the box. Her thoughts turned to David Tinely. Poor man, he would never hold his wife or child again and she let out a small sob, grasping the sheets in a bunch to try and squeeze out the anger and pain. When had the world become so dark?

As she wiped the tears from her face, her hand ran over more bandages. Bin Gaudi wouldn't administer to her wounds. Who?

Slowly, to avoid intensifying the ache in her ribs, she pulled back the puffy down comforter and placed her feet on the floor. The room spun for a moment and she sat back on the bed to prevent herself from falling.

Aminah examined the rest of the room: cream wallpaper, a silver lamp, and a mirror on the other side of the bed. She gave standing another try and this time managed to shuffle around the bed. Tentatively, afraid of what she would see, Aminah peered into the mirror.

The bandage ran from above her left temple, across her cheekbone and then down close to her mouth. Her right eye looked black and swollen.

Aminah's eyes filled with tears as she brought a shaking hand to her hair and brushed it back. The room swayed. Aminah backed herself over to the bed, sat down, and cried. John often told her she was stronger than she believed, but Aminah felt thin, fragile, like a dried leaf. You can cry, but it won't change anything, John used to say.

A splash caught her attention. She dabbed her eyes, rose, and walked towards the window. The floor lurched again and she wondered just how badly her head had been injured. Aminah reached the window, grabbed the sash cord, and pulled the curtains open. Intense sunlight blinded her momentarily and as her eyes adjusted she attempted to reconcile the view with her last memory in Karachi. Blue water stretched to the horizon under an ominous grey sky. Water? Ocean?

Where am I?

A different memory flashed, a figure walking towards her, face obscured by billowing dust. Frightened, but increasingly curious, Aminah made her way towards the door. The floor rocked and now she understood the rolling floor was not in her head; she was on a boat.

She wrapped her hands around a brass knob and it turned, the door clicking open. She expected a jihadi to burst into the hallway at any moment, grab her by the hair, and slap her around for daring to exit the room. Was this a test?

Aminah stepped out into a wood-paneled hallway carpeted with an oriental runner. A low hum replaced the silence. She walked towards an elevator door at the end of the hallway, stopped at the door and let her finger linger over the button. Was this a good idea? She pressed the button and the elevator emitted a soft, melodic ding before the clicking of the mechanisms from the shaft heralded imminent arrival. A moment later the doors slid open, revealing a metallic, modern looking interior quite different from the elegant, old world charm of the cabin and hallway.

This couldn't be Fist of Allah.

Aminah stepped in and pressed the only button on the panel. The doors closed swiftly and she regretted not bringing a lamp or some other object to use as a weapon if necessary. Preparing herself to lunge or to fight, she waited, taking small breaths of air. Ten seconds later, the doors opened.

Sixty-inch flat screen panels hung on the walls, displaying images of men in keffiyahs and business suits, videos of pedestrians on subways and in shopping malls, and screenshots of websites.

"Sixteen, thirty-three," said a red head seated in front of a computer terminal.

"Ve have e pozzible zighting een Beirut," mumbled a chubby woman in a Russian accent.

"Email says rendezvous at Cannes," called out a man with red and black tattoos on his bald head.

"Let me check on that location," a black man with a huge afro said into his headset.

"Yellow Team is in transit."

"We're transferring $1 million into the account."

What was this? CIA? It sounded like CIA, sort of.

"You can relax, we're not going to bite you."

She twisted around, sending a bolt of pain up her neck. A tall, thin man, head a mass of unruly sandy hair puffed on a cigarette. "Name's Patric," he said extending his hand. "Heard you had quite a rough time." English with a British accent but a German inflection. Definitely Swiss, somewhere near Zurich, she thought. She had a talent for recognizing accents.

She nodded and reflexively touched the wound on her head.

"Well, do I get a shake?"

"Sure," she said, unsure about anything.

"The Doc patched you up. You also had some bad bruises on your ribs and a cut on your face. No broken bones. You'll be sore a few days but you'll live," he said.

"Ah, thanks. I guess. "Who are you? "Where am I?"

"You're in Oz. Joking. Welcome aboard the Vengeance."

Vengeance? What kind of name was that?

"Are you shop?

"No."

He swept his hand around the room and took a couple of quick mini-puffs. "These systems are used to track the movement of major terrorist organizations. We've partnered with the key intelligence services in the world — the CIA, the NSA, the Interior Services, MI6, and QIL."

QIL? Impossible! Even within the OCT only Ambrose received clearance to access QIL and enter the facility. No one outside of a select few in intelligence knew about the system's capabilites or existence.

"How do you *partner*?"

"Well," Patric smiled, "I'd call it a loose partnerhip. We borrow information and they don't know. It works for everyone."

"Borrowed? Impossible. Those systems are some of the most secure and protected in the world. Not even the best hacker could gain access."

"Come," Patric motioned to her, "this way." They reached a narrow flight of metal stairs which Aminah lurched down, ribs aching with every step. At the bottom, a cool, cavernous room buzzed like a field of cicadas on a hot summer afternoon. Racks of computers lined the walls, green and orange lights blinking. In the middle, sat a black box the size of a refrigerator. Colored wires forked in and out and several lights on each side blinked.

"That's the QC," Patric said proudly. "Our Quantum Computer."

"It would cost you billions to develop and operate a quantum computer," she replied. While not a phycicist, Aminah understood enough to know quantum computing was very expensive and difficult to build. QIL was purported to be the only quantum computer in existence. Someone had developed an elaborate ruse to trick her. But why?

Patric continued. "The other racks are data processors and database servers. We run all of the telephone, cellphone, and email correspondence through our own heuristics and filtering system to look for keywords or clues to help the tracking process. Over three thousand high-end workstations across the world process one tetra-flop of calculations per second."

"Tetra-flop?"

"One trillion floating-point operations per second."

Aminah refused to be impressed.

He led her back to the stairs and she paused, the ache in her side making it difficult to breathe.

"Can you climb?"

"I don't know," she admitted. "It's my ribs." Like the descent, she took each step one-at-a-time and eventually made it above-board. She walked onto a side deck and inhaled a mix of diesel fuel and briny sea. Waves chopped against the boat, the wind blew briskly, grey clouds swirled. Her stomach quivered for a moment as he brought her down the deck to a staircase.

"Another stairway?" Her head throbbed and she stopped for a moment to let the pain pass.

"I'm afraid so. We're on a boat. Do you need to rest?" Patric asked.

"Yes, just a second," she said slumping down onto a ledge. After a moment, she grabbed a metal pipe to pull herself up.

"Are you sure you're okay? You can rest longer if you need to."

"No, let's go."

"We've been tracking the cell that held you for several weeks. We also knew you were coming to Pakistan."

"How did you know?" she asked sharply. "I didn't tell anyone?"

"We intercepted the flight manifest."

"You got that?"

"We have access to almost everything. I know you spoke to Clara Keefer two hours before your plane departed. And I know what you spoke about."

Aminah's face reddended. "How dare you! You can't just tap private calls."

"We picked up chatter when they captured you. We thought about extracting you sooner but hoped to catch a few more targets. The hard part is separating the legitimate information from background noise. Once we catch a scent, we like to follow it."

"You left me there?" You could have gotten me out sooner? A good man died because you waited!"

"We didn't know about him," Patric said. "If we did, we would have tried to rescue him. We've sent his body back to his wife"

"Without a head! This is outrageous! Who oversees this operation? You need to tell me which branch you're under."

Patric stopped in front of a door.

"He wanted you to see this. He felt it would be better than just telling you. You know, like how a picture is worth a thousand words. Something like that. It might be tough. I don't like to watch this stuff."

"Who wanted me to see? Why can't you tell me what's going on?"

"Please, go in. You'll understand soon." He opened the door and motioned for her enter the room. She hesitated, frustrated, angry, and uneasy about what lay on the other side. To add to her misery, the wound on her forehead throbbed and shot stabbing pain down the side of her face. Her ribs ached. "It will be okay. You won't be hurt," he said. "Please, go." Realizing she didn't have much of a choice, Aminah walked in.

The room was dimly lit with three chairs set side by side in fornt of a window. Aminah gasped. On the other side of the glass, arms and legs manacled, hair in disarray, eyes frantic, body naked, sat Bin Gaudi.

Chapter 28

Aminah recognized terror on Bin Gaudi's face, of a hunter who became the hunted: eyes darting, arms testing the bonds, hair disheveled and on end, penis shriveled to nothing. The bravado long gone, a scared, naked forty-something man who needed to take a shower. Aminah almost felt sorry for him.

The door opened. A tall blonde woman and an Asian man in white labcoats walked in, put on face shields, and unzipped a variety of pouches.

"Mr. Bin Gaudi, I'm going to ask you a few more questions," the blonde said in a Southern drawl. She flashed him a smile like a flight attendant serving drinks. "I do hope you'll be a bit more cooperative." The woman abruptly ripped off a strip of tape over Bin Gaudi's mouth, pulling a chunk of his mustache with it. Bin Ghadi's eyes bulged with pain.

"Who are you people?" the terrorist yelled. "You can't hold me like this. I'll tell you nothing!"

Bluster. Every terrorist knew of rendition, how a person vanished from the face of the earth, buried in some dungeon or Middle Eastern torture chamber. The United States government often handed their terrorist prizes over to the Saudis or the Egyptians. Could this be a rendition operation?

The woman tapped a needle, smiled, and abruptly jabbed the syringe into Bin Ghadi's arm. "There, it shouldn't hurt that much, yet."

He strained against the bonds but only managed to jiggle his body a few inches in either direction.

"We found a woman in the apartment. Please tell us why you held her?" she asked politely.

"She is a whore. One of the men found her on the street and took pity." Bin Ghadi smiled.

The woman nodded.

Aminah sighed at his banality.

"Let me remind you we are not a governmental organization and so aren't bound by any of the rules of the Geneva Convention governing prisoners of war. Nor, quite frankly, do we consider you to be a prisoner of war."

The woman came forward with a second syringe and injected his left hand.

"What is this? What are you doing?" he asked, unsuccessfully trying to pull his hand from the manacle.

"It's a neurotoxin. In sixty seconds you'll be unable to move your hand," she replied. "Now, I'll ask you one last time, and I hope you'll answer. What was the woman doing in your apartment? How did you find her?"

Bin Ghadi cleared his throat and spat a big gob of phlegm on her forehead.

"I'll tell you nothing."

"I'm sorry you feel that way," the woman said, grabbing a tissue and wiping her face. She thrust a pointy probe into the top of his hand, through the bone and tendon, and out the other side, pinning it to the table. The hand did not twitch or move at all.

Bin Gaudi howled. "What are you doing?"

"I think you're ready." She reached down and adjusted each finger so his hand sat splayed open. "Andrew."

The Asian nodded, raised a white object with a sharp blade, and pressed a button. The device whirred to life. An electric turkey cutter. Andrew swiped the blade across Bin Gaudi's hand.

"My finger, my finger, you cut off my finger!" he screamed in Arabic. The woman calmly picked his pinky finger off the table, pinched the digit between her thumb and forefinger, and dropped it into a plastic can.

"The first injection I gave you contained a coagulant. It will prevent you from bleeding to death, for awhile at least."

Bin Ghadi's struggled against the bonds, but his left hand remained still, the fingers immobile on the flat cutting board.

Aminah watched horrified. OCT analysts often discussed the specifics of renditions but she never quite believed the stories.

"You're so naive sometimes," John used to say and she couldn't deny it.

"Now, I'll ask you again, what was the woman doing in your apartment?" the woman asked.

Bin Gaudi's shoulders hunched, his cheeks trembled, his body seemed to shrivel inward. He looked more like a sickly old man than a killer.

"Kill me," Bin Ghadi said. "Kill me and be done with it."

Andrew brough the electric turkey cutter down and his ring finger, adorned with a gold band, dropped into the trash.

Don't puke! Don't puke!

"Please, kill me." Bin Gaudi's face turned paper white, alabaster her father would have called it. He peered down at his hand and groaned.

The Asian man raised the knife again and Bin Ghadi spoke.

"We were told she was coming. A courier brought news. They send couriers so the messages cannot be intercepted. He gave us her flight and told us to follow her. They said we could do whatever we wanted with her as long as she disappeared."

Aminah leaned forward and strained to hear his next words.

"Who told you this?" the woman asked.

"Someone in the government. Someone who has been helping us. Someone who calls himself E."

E? What was E?

"Which government?"

"What do you mean which government? Your government, the filthy American government," Bin Gaudi said, his voice strengthening.

So, Bin Gaudi hadn't been lying when he had told her she had been set up. Why did someone want her dead? She didn't even work for the OCT anymore.

Bin Gaudi's eyes shifted to the other side of the room. The door opened towards Aminah, obscuring her view.

"He's begun to talk," the woman said, addressing the unseen figure.

"Is she behind the glass?" a new, commanding voice asked.

"Yes, she's watching."

Where had she heard that voice before? Why does he care if I'm watching?

"So you are Bin Gaudi?" the man asked. The terrorist said nothing.

"Someone told them about Aminah coming to Pakistan," the woman in the white coat said.

Aminah shivered at the mention of her name.

"Who?" the man asked. "Who has been helping you?"

"I don't know. None of us know," Bin Gaudi groaned.

The saw hummed to life and she turned away as it smoothly separated a third finger. Bin Gaudi babbled. Turning back, she watched blood seep from his hand like maple syrup.

"Tell us," the man ordered calmly.

"I swear on the Holy Koran I do not know! He sends us emails! He tells us what to do, how to do it!"

"How do you know it is a man?"

Bin Ghadi moaned. Blood seeped down the tray and into the trashcan.

"I don't know."

"Did he tell you about the airline hijacking? Help Fist of Allah plan the airline hijacking?"

"Yes, he told us. He helped us."

"Did he tell you about Aminah coming to Pakistan?"

"Yes." Bin Gaudi started to shiver. His body vibrated and his teeth chattered.

"Did he tell you anything else?"

Bin Ghadi nodded. "N-N-N-No, nothing else. Please, have mercy, please," Bin Gaudi pleaded.

The saw bit again and his pointer finger sat detached on the tray. Black t-shirt man sighed and then changed his position, giving her a clear view of his face.

"Oh my God," Aminah exhaled.

Chapter 29

When they last met, he had been a handsome man of thirty-one—tall, with dark hair, a medium build, and clear smooth skin. He had aged, the spark in his grief-stricken eyes replaced with the glare of a hunter—cold, malicious, uncaring. The glare of the wolf.

Zeke Katz stared down at Bin Gaudi.

"You murdered my wife and child," Zeke said. Bin Ghadi's eyes fluttered open. "You pitched my wife and child out of the plane and shot them. Do you think I care about mercy? Do you think I care about your pain? But despite what you did to my family I will give you an easy death if you tell us."

"I didn't kill them. Hassan did it. I don't believe in harming woman and children. Please, please, show mercy," Bin Ghadi sobbed. His index finger and thumb twitched on the tray.

"Not until you tell me." Zeke said. "Are you ready to talk?" Bin Gaudi remained silent. "Take off his hand."

"No, please, please!" Bin Gaudi screamed, regaining some energy and straining against his bonds. The Asian nodded and raised the turkey trimmer. Bin Ghadi howled.

Revolted, Aminah stood and hammered on the glass, getting Zeke to turn in her direction and shot her a cold stare.

"Zeke!" she screamed. "Stop!" No human being deserved this kind of treatment. Aminah turned away as the blade met flesh.

Oh God, oh God! Sobbing, she pounded on the door.

"Let me out!" Please, let me out!" No one came. Fighting to suppress the sobs and drying the tears on her sleeve, Aminah turned back. Bin Ghadi sat slumped in the chair, his hand detached and on the tray beside him like the pieces of raw meat dangling from strings in cousin Ali's butchery—dripping blood, sinewy, and red. The Asian wrapped

159

a tourniquet around the stump, the woman gave Bin Gaudi another shot, causing his pupils to roll back, leaving only the whites of his eyes. The terrorist spoke in a stream of babble:

"Mother, mother, I brought water...Praise Allah...no Fallah, it is not you...please, please...we will not be destroyed...never..." His words trailed off into a mumble.

"The sodium penthanol is starting to work," the woman said.

Aminah had learned about the drug in her training. Sodium penthanol acted as a sedative that caused someone to talk, not necessarily tell the truth. The blonde woman gave him another shot and Bin Ghadi's eyes fluttered open. He looked around, confused.

Zeke pounced. "Tell me about Operation Badr."

Bin Ghadi smiled, eyes wide, head lolling back and forth as if drunk.

"Allah rejoice, we will defeat the infidel. We will bring America to its knees. We will kill the Jews." Bin Ghadi's glassy eyes rotated in their sockets, his voice wavered, his breathing raspy.

She gave him another shot.

"Tell me about this wonder."

"Allah blessed us with a weapon. It will consume the Americans."

"You have the weapon?"

"Maybe." His teeth chattered. "We will awaken the Umma and reestablish the true caliphate. This time the West will not be able to interfere."

"What is this weapon, this gift from Allah?"

Bin Gaudi slumped further in his seat. "A nuclear weapon," he croaked.

Aminah's heart pounded.

"And what is the target?"

"The heart of the West, America."

"Where?"

Bin Ghadi gave one last smile. "New York. To kill the Jews and the infidel Americans. You won't be able to stop our gift." Bin Gaudi collapsed into his seat, red bubbles frothing from his lips, eyes rolling back, handless arm trembling.

"Is he dead?" Zeke asked.

The Asian glanced at the computer monitor. "No. Do you want us to revive him?"

"No, Zeke said, "throw his body overboard for the sharks."

* * *

Aminah thought back to the last lecture she gave at Columbia a few days ago. More like a lifetime ago.

Fifteen years ago the Russian nuclear stockpiles were easy targets for terrorists, but the country had tightened its controls. She doubted Fist of Allah possessed the capacity to produce their own weapon and Pakistan's arsenal sat under the watch of the U.S. North Korea possessed several bombs but the reclusive nation wanted to avoid any entanglement with the United States.

Bin Gaudi lied. Still...And what was Operation Badr? She sat for a moment, alone in the room, images of the bloody stump appearing whenever she blinked. Blood. David's head and Bin Gaudi's hand. Blood.

The door opened and Zeke walked in. Deep wrinkles cut across his pale forehead, eyes red-rimmed, hair an unruly mess. He reminded Aminah of Jennifer White, a childhood friend who died of leukemia. He looked ten years older. Maybe twenty.

They had last met in Washington D.C. after Zeke's appointment with Ambrose. Aminah remembered the businessman's anger and disappointment at the lack of government action. Not a single terrorist involved in the hijacking had been captured or killed. Still, he had expressed his appreciation for her help and they parted on friendly terms. Now, she didn't know what to expect.

"Hello, Aminah," he said.

"Hello, Zeke."

He noticed the vomit on the floor. "I'm sorry you had to see that. It's the world we live in."

"You wanted me to see the torture," she replied, forcing herself to be bold.

"I wanted you to understand what we're dealing with. Let's get some fresh air. I think it will help."

"That was monstrous," she blurted out.

"We live in a monstrous world." He motioned for her to follow. "We found the journalist in the apartment. Decapitated. An innocent man slaughtered."

"I know," she said. "I was there."

"You shouldn't feel sympathy for these monsters. They're inhuman."

Aminah stepped into the hall and pain lanced through her side. She hobbled out, eager to leave the bowels of the boat. The rocking seemed to be more pronounced, unsettling her stomach. She followed Zeke down the corridor and slowly up the stairs to the deck. The wind whipped her hair and angry waves lashed the sides of the boat, sending a spray of salty water over the railing and onto her face. Despite the rock and roll, the fresh air and sea spray revitalized her spirit. "Can we stay outside for a bit?" she asked.

They stood at the railing looking out over the broad expanse of water.

"We're in the Indian Ocean. We found you in Karachi and helicoptered you here."

"Why not drop me off at the local hospital?"

"You would have been dead in hours from the lack of hygiene or from the people behind your abduction coming back for a second try. Someone wants you dead. Bin Gaudi confirmed it during his interrogation."

"You mean torture."

"He shrugged. "One man's interrogation is another man's torture."

"Really?"

He ignored her. "We've received bits of intelligence which Bin Gaudi helped confirm."

"The Badr Operation?"

He nodded.

"What is it?"

"A nuclear weapon Fist of Allah plans to detonate in New York City."

"Do you think it's true?"

"A former Russian General was killed in a weapons sale a week ago. It squares."

"You think it was Fist of Allah?"

"We've intercepted other chatter. Bin Gaudi confirmed what we already suspected."

"He didn't confirm anything," she shot back, "You tortured him. He would say anything at that point. FM 34-52 explains how torture yields false results."

"I'm not interested in the US Army Field Manual of Interrogation," he replied. "The manual did nothing to save my family. You saw what Bin Gaudi did to Tinely. He's an animal. Why are we even having this conversation? I believe there is a bomb headed towards New York. But it's not my problem, it's yours. The information is for you."

"For me?"

"It isn't my job to protect the United States. I don't work for the country, you do," he said, staring into her eyes.

"You're just here to extract revenge."

"No, not revenge, to seek justice."

"Bin Gaudi said someone is hunting his men. It's you, isn't it? You've been killing them." How ironic she told Bin Gaudi the truth, her concocted story fact.

He remained silent for a moment before nodding. "I have no choice. No one else cared."

"I care."

Zeke stared out at the sea, the flash of vulnerability gone. "I couldn't let them get away with it. Most people don't understand."

"What does that mean?"

He paused. "Almost everyone I spoke to told me to let Rachel and Sam's murder go. Your boss Ambrose patted me on the back and said I should 'get on with my life.' Ridiculous. You understand."

"I do?"

"You lost your husband. Your father was assassinated."

She shuddered. "Yes, but I'm not consumed by revenge."

"It doesn't bother you that your husband's killers were never caught? Maybe you should be."

"Of course it bothers me. That's why I continue to look for answers."

"And once you find those answers, what will you do?"

"Honestly, I haven't thought that far ahead. I'm too confused to hate right now." She thought about her own family: her mother, sister Laila, niece Daayana and about a bomb in New York City. She needed to focus on the living.

"I have to contact Ambrose," she said thinking aloud.

"Ambrose? The guy is a waste of time. The OCT is compromised. Someone sold you out to Fist of Allah and I think it's him."

Could he have betrayed her? No, impossible. Zeke didn't hold a high opinion of her boss, but she didn't fully trust Zeke's motives.

"I can trust him," she said. "He's the only high-ranking official who will take my call. And, the Vice President listens to him. Can I call him?"

He sighed. "We'll prepare a secure connection. But you're making a mistake."

She took a breathe and couldn't get any oxygen. Eyes wide, she clutched at her chest.

"Aminah?"

"Huh?" she said.

"Relax. Don't panic. They stole the bomb last week in Khazakstan. It'll take at last another week to transport it across Europe and to the United States."

"What if they go by air?" she whispered, her throat loosening.

"They won't. They're driving and then going by boat."

How much did she trust Zeke? Who did she trust?

"Zeke, David Tinely told me he recevied an anonymous text about Lilly Broadhurst."

Zeke grabbed her arm, squeezing tightly.

"That hurts," she said.

He loosened the grip but his eyes remained smoldering dark embers. "When?"

"Several days before the flight."

"It's the same person," Zeke said aloud.

Zeke claimed Rachel had received a text the morning of her flight, warning her not to go. The OCT extensively checked the records after the hijacking but found no evidence of a message. Psychologists she spoke with suggested Zeke's subconscious implanted the memory as a form of self-punishment.

"Who sent the text?" he asked.

"He didn't know." she answered. "It came as a number."

"Just like Rachel's. It's the same person. Someone at OCT deleted the text to Rachel."

"It's possible," she admitted. QIL could access the telephone system and erase records.

"We have to find the sender."

"We can try, but I doubt they're alive or active. It's been two years since anyone received a message from this person."

"That we know of. Someone is out there. Whoever it is knows what is going on. David met with Lilly and she sent him to Pakistan."

"She got rid of him," Zeke responded. "Lilly, Lilly, Lilly," he said, hands gripped tightly around the rail instead of her arm, knuckles white.

"Zeke, I don't know what to do about the bomb."

"Talk to your friend Ambrose and see what happens."

* * *

Inside, Patric handed her a blocky black phone with a short stubby antennae. "Call when you're ready. The line is secure."

She picked up the phone and dialed. Ambrose answered on the second ring.

"Ambrose."

"Stephen, it's Aminah."

"Aminah! Thank God. I nearly had a stroke. Where are you? Are you okay?"

Relieved to hear his voice, she struggled to maintain her composure.

"Stephen, I'll fill you in on my details later. I need to tell you about a credible threat."

"Don't say too much. Just the essentials," Ambrose replied. Odd. She worked with him long enough to recognize the caution in his voice. Why was he warning her?

She took a deep breathe. "I believe Fist of Allah possesses a stolen Russian nuke. The target is New York City."

"Do you have an ETA?"

"Next week."

"The President is traveling to New York for the United Nations General Assembly," he said. "Are you sure? We haven't picked up anything."

"I have two independent verifications."

"Who are they?"

"I can't tell you right now,'" she said, looking at Zeke.

"Are you safe?"

"Yes, I believe so."

"But you believe this information to be credible?"

"I do."

"Okay," he said. "You know your word is gold with me."

"Stephen, we think it's coming by boat from somewhere in Europe."

"Probably Rotterdam."

Ambrose's mind had already begun spinning around the problem. He would make everything all right.

"Thank you, Stephen," she said, letting out a small sob.

"Are you okay?"

"Yes, yes, I'm just...relieved."

"Will you be back in Washington soon?"

"I hope to be on my way sometime in the next day or two. Once I get there I'll provide you with all of the details," she said, regaining her composure and trying to suppress a sniffle.

"Do you need help getting home?"

"No, I'm okay. I can make it back myself."

"Come to my house when you get back into town. Directly to my house."

In the ten years they worked together, she had never visited his house on business. A dinner party, cocktails, yes, but never for work.

"I'll do that."

"Aminah, be careful."

"I will. Thank you," she said.

"Relax, it's going to be alright. Good work. I'll see you shortly. Godspeed."

"Goodbye, Stephen."

She ended the call and placed the phone on the table, dabbing the tears.

"Does he believe you?" Zeke asked.

"Yes, I think so." She was about to ask about calling her mother when a wiry, gum chewing, veins in his arms popping man entered the room.

"Zeke, the copter is back. There are injuries," he called out in a thick Brooklyn accent. Zeke rose quickly and rushed out the door. Aminah followed him onto the deck.

The whir of blades echoed across the ocean, a green chopper moved slowly through the sky, a black plume of smoke billowing from the back, near the rotor. The chopper lined up directly overhead, hovered quickly, descendeding like a bird spotting its prey and plunging to snatch it. The struts hit the deck hard, flexed, and bounced the chopper into the air. The helicopter lurched to the left, nearly off the deck, but the pilot managed to bring up the tail, steady the copter, and bring it down on the second attempt. The blades slowed to a stop and two figures in sand-colored jackets rushed forward and secured the aircraft with thick ropes. Finally, the doors opened.

A thin, dark haired man clambered out, his left arm raised to shield his face from the glaring sun. Blood matted his face and a large bandage covered his left cheek and eye. His wound almost matched her own, she thought, lightly touching the bandage on her face.

Two crew rushed forward and carried out a stretcher. Aminah edged closer. A little girl lay still, an oxygen mask around her face. Little girl? Who was she? A second stretcher emerged, an Indian man lying lifeless, unblinking eyes focused on the sky. They disappeared inside.

A woman leapt down, her arms and chest bulging underneath her shirt. Body armour. She remembered helping John tie the straps in the back. The woman flicked back long black hair, eyes calmly suveying the deck, stopping on Aminah before nodding solemnly to the wiry guy. Zeke embraced the woman and Aminah took a step closer.

"...happened?" Zeke asked.

"The girl...kill her...pull her out...Ravi died...son is still out there."

Aminah turned away as a strong gust of wind buffeted the ship and when she looked back, they were gone. She slowly climbed up the steps into the Vengeance.

Following the hallway, she entered a large room with rows of tables. A fierce, bald-headed hulk of a man glared. Retracing her steps, she took a right and fifty feet later the hallway brought her to a metal door. She turned another corner and came to a window overlooking rows of beds surrounded by poles, drips, and monitors. The litttle girl lay on the bed closest to the door– small delicate fingers opened like a flower towards the ceiling, dirty brown hair billowed beneath her head, stick-thin arms rested like twigs. She looked ten or eleven, maybe a year older than Daayana.

A young man in a surgical gown and mask smearked liquid on her abdomen. "She took a bullet to the stomach," a voice said. "Rover is prepping her for surgery."

She turned and Zeke stood next to her.

"Who is she?"

"Sheik Imaad's granddaughter."

Chapter 30

A loud yell. Walid's eyes shot open. He rose quickly, old reflexes kicking in, a stabbing pain ripping through his foot. He toppled back onto the bed, clutched the sheets, ground his teeth. The pain ebbed into a dull throb.

A tube protruded from the top of his hand to a medical drip beside the bed. He peeled the bandage and pulled out the needle.

Heavy European metal shades covered the windows, but a shaft of light escaped from a gap in the bottom, casting a dashed pattern on the wall above his bed.

He listened again. Arab with a Pakistani accent, the voice distressed and panicked. Anxious, he pulled himself up and hobbled towards the door, ignoring the throb in his leg.

"All dead?" someone asked.

"Yes, all of them."

"When did you find out?"

"I just received the word. It came over the computer."

"The computer! Everything is being monitored! Where did you access the Internet?"

"At a cafe. I swear I took precautions."

He reached the stairs and slowly descended.

"What happened?" Walid asked.

Scared eyes turned. A thin Pakistani held a cup of tea in a shaking hand, eyes large, face pale.

No one said anything.

"What happened?" he repeated, more forcefully.

"Sheikh Imaad is dead," Ali finally said.

"No, impossible." Walid mustered some energy, tried to stand more upright. "Tell me. Spit it out," he demanded when they didn't talk fast enough. A pudgy Arab sat catatonic. The news exploded like a Grad rocket blast to the head.

"Allah bless him, he is dead. They killed Amala and captured Hani. The whole family has been slaughtered. They are all dead!" one of the men wailed.

This couldn't be true. "Are you sure? Who sent word to you?"

"Bin Abbas survived. He fled into the mountains and came back afterwards."

The coward, Walid thought. Bin Abbas had always been so confident and sure of his abilities. The Syrian married one of Imaad's daughters and stayed with the sheikh often.

The sheik's loss would be great and he would mourn his dead teacher, but Hani's loss created even bigger problems for the mission. How did this happen?

The men focused on him. His relationship with Sheikh Imaad made him their leader. Praise Allah, let me steer them faithfully.

"Who did it?" Walid asked, circling the room on his bad foot. He ignored the pain.

"The wolves," the thin Pakistani said.

"The wolves? What wolves?" he yelled.

"The same ones who killed Khalid. They come in unseen, undetected, and kill like ghouls, showing no mercy," the skinny Pakistani said.

The others nodded.

"There is more," Ali said.

More? Not more bad news. He needed to maintain discipline for he sensed his grip on them loosening. "What else?"

"Bin Gaudi and his cell are dead," the thin Pakistani continued.

"Where?"

"In Karachi. Only Abu Samma survived. He left the house to get a kebab and missed the massacre."

Walid grimaced and tried to think of something to calm their anxiety.

"Bin Gaudi lived as a loyal servant of Allah; he will be missed. His soul has gone to paradise. We must see that his family is provided for. He left three boys and a wife."

The man nodded.

Someone else spoke. "Do you think they will come here?"

"Who?" Walid asked.

"Whoever is doing the killing?"

He recognized the stink in the room, fear. These men, these lions of Allah squeeked like petrified, cornered rats. The fool who breached protocol and used the Internet now contaminated the others with his cowardice and shifty eyes.

"There is nothing to be scared of, unless we act like fools," Walid said. He turned. "You act like a spy. Perhaps you are working for this demon you describe. What is your name?"

"Qasim," the man said, looking down at the floor.

Walid circled him. "Do you think we are a bunch of cowards? Do you not know we will fight and avenge the death of our sheikh, our leader? Do you think this will change our plan?"

"That was not my intent–"

"Silence!" Walid yelled. "I do not trust you or your shifty eyes." He turned to two men sitting on the coach. "Take him and search for a tracking device.

"Please, no, you are mistaken. I am loyal, there is nothing inside of me!" he screamed as they dragged him out of the room.

"Do not communicate on the Internet again," he said, eyeing the remaining men. "I do not trust Western technology. We are Fist of Allah, not fools. The enemy is everywhere, and if we are to succeed, then we must be smarter and craftier, as Allah would wish."

The men nodded.

He pulled Ali to the side. "How long was I sleeping?"

"One day."

"Are we in Frankfurt?" He did not want the others to learn of his weakness and lack of knowledge. The plan called for them to stop in Frankfurt.

"Yes."

"At least part of the plan is intact," he whispered. We have lost time. There is less than a week to make it to the boat."

"We will make it if we leave shortly."

"Allah willing."

"The weapon?"

"It is secure. Abdul-Haseeb and Hassan are sleeping in the van." Walid paused, unsure how to bring up the next subject.

"And the girl?"

"She is upstairs in the room next to where you slept. What are you planning to do with her?"

"I do not know," he admitted. "But I do not think it was mere chance that put her on our path. She saved my life, did she not?"

Ali nodded, confirming what he remembered through the fever and pain.

"She may be part of Allah's plan, and until I understand it further I am hesitant to kill her."

"And if she plays no part in our plan?"

"Then I will finish her," he said simply. "Now, let me thank her for saving my life." Ali nodded but Walid caught the doubt on the engineer's face.

Before going upstairs, Walid addressed the men again. "All of you know that despite the loss of Sheik Imaad we must continue with the plan."

They nodded.

"If you follow Sheik Imaad's lessons, Allah's word will soon rule this land. You are Allah's warriors, unafraid of death or dying. Do not let the martyrdom of our brothers bring fear into your lives, for they are in paradise now enjoying Allah's bounty. Do not fear. Allah Akbar!" he shouted.

"Allah Akbar!" the men said back, without the usual passion and force.

"Allah Akbar!" he said one more time.

"Allah Akbar!" they responded a bit louder. He still worried some of them had lost their nerve. The mission would revive their confidence.

As he moved through the room towards the steps, he experienced a new kind of tension, a most unpleasant flutter in his stomach. His heart beat faster, sweat moistened his hands. The infection still contaminated his body.

He recited a small prayer from the Koran and hoped the verse would be strong enough to ward off his illness.

Walid opened the door and walked into the room. A mix of sweat, body odor, and perfume hit his nose. A shaft of light from the hallway brightened the shadows and he glimpsed her lying on a mattress next to an iron radiator. Steel handcuffs twisted her body, tape covered her mouth. Her blue eyes followed him across the room.

"It's okay. They shouldn't have bound you so tightly. I'll be back," he said in English. He limped back downstairs where Ali moved the wand slowly over the thin, hunched boy. He retrieved the key from a pimply-faced man who deserved a slap for hurting the girl, hobbled to the bathroom, and filled a glass with warm, soapy water. Despite the occasional food wrapper, the wooden floors and clean walls made this one of the nicer safe houses. Often they crawled with vermin, neglected and uncleaned for months, if ever. He reached her door and pushed it open.

Grimacing, he knelt down, soaped the rag, and massaged the water onto the tape around her mouth. "This needs to sink in as much as possible so that the tape will loosen. Otherwise it will hurt like the devil to take it off."

She nodded.

He unlocked the cuffs and released her hands. Do not try to escape. Even if you get past me, the others will kill you."

He understood by the calm in her eyes, by the gentleness of her nod that she would not flee. He wanted nothing more than to put her at ease.

"As long as you listen, we will not hurt you. You helped me and I am grateful." Did he speak the truth? She needed to die. She nodded again and he caught a small smile through the tape. Another little flutter tickled his stomach. Make this sickness go away, he pleaded.

He took the edge of the tape and gently pulled it from her mouth. The soapy water dissolved some of the adhesive but the tape still resisted. She took the pain without a complaint.

"I am sorry, I know it must hurt." He made one final pull and the tape reluctantly yielded. She brushed the patchy skin around her lips and smiled, brightening her face and making her eyes sparkle even more.

"Thank you," she said in English.

"I'm sorry if they hurt you–"

"No, thank you for saving me. Kupchak would have killed me."

Leave the girl, he told himself. Do not fall for her wiles. Didn't Sheikh Imaad rail against Western women?

"For by their women, they will enslave you, like Eve in the garden. They are the snakes of the Western world, loose and immoral. Corrupters of the flesh and the soul."

Yet, he couldn't stop himself from asking the question which lingered in the air.

"Who is Kupchak?"

"Who *was* Kupchak? He was not a good man. Very mean, vicious" She said no more.

"Would he have killed you?" he asked. How could any man be so angry at such a creature?

"Yes. Without a thought. You saw him."

"You are from Russia?" It was difficult for him to distinguish the various accents when someone spoke English.

"Moldova."

He closed his fist and stared at the girl. He would not waver in his devotion to Allah, the sheikh, or his mission. He would detonate the weapon, but perhaps this woman played a part in Allah's vast plan.

A shout broke his thoughts and Abdul-Haseeb burst into the room, followed by Ali.

"Walid, Walid we have a problem!"

"Can I not have peace for a moment!" he screamed, rising quickly and collapsing onto the ground from the searing pain in his leg. "What is so important you must burst into the room?"

"The van, it is gone. Hassan took the van."

"And the weapon?" he asked, the pain replaced by an icy stab in his gut.

"Gone."

Chapter 31

"Imaad's granddaughter!" Aminah shouted in surprise. "And Imaad?" she asked, already sure of the answer.

"Dead."

So many nights she lay in bed wishing for this news, and now that it happened, it seemed, ordinary. In her fantasies, news of the sheikh's demise had always been more cinematic, with strings playing in the background and members of the military surrounding her in starched dress uniforms.

"How did you find him?"

"Before we killed him, Khalid gave us the approximate location."

"And the girl, you tried to kill his grandaughter?"

Zeke fixed her with a cold stare. "What happened to her?" she asked hastily, backpedaling.

"We don't kill children," Zeke said. "Masada said one of Imaad's bodyguards shot her and they would have finished her off if we hadn't *rescued* the girl."

Masada, she said to herself. Israeli.

"That can't be true," Aminah said. "Fist of Allah may hate the West but they love their children and wouldn't murder a family member without good reason."

"Believe it," Zeke replied before walking off, leaving her standing there alone with a thousand more questions.

* * *

"Believe it," she mimicked. How unbelievable was it that Zeke could kill a child after what she had seen him do to Bin Gaudi?

What had happened to Zeke? She met men and women who lost family on 9/11 or other terrorists attacks, and none displayed Zeke's anger, his drive for vengeance.

She reached the kitchen and a muscular Asian man glanced up before returning to his food. She rang a little silver bell set on the counter in front of a grille.

"One second," a male voice called from another room. "One second, I'm coming." She hadn't eaten properly in days and her stomach rumbled.

A minute passed and an overweight man with a handlebar mustache lumbered into view.

"Someone new," he huffed, a bit out of breath. "When did this lovely lady fly in?" he smiled and smoothed back his mustache. He glanced at the bandages on her face. "My, my what did the cat drag in? You had a bit of a rough landing."

"Just a little. Is this the place for food?"

"What do you like?"

"What can you cook?"

"Good question. Smart girl. Eggs, fish, we have lots of fresh fish. Dale just hooked a pomfret. I can fry some up with eggs and it will be delicious." He raised his fingers to his lips and blew out a kiss.

"Sounds great," she said, although at this point anything would have sounded appetizing. He nodded and disappeared for a moment before returning with a long piece of fish and some eggs. He grabbed two fry pans, cut some butter and slathered it onto the hot surface.

"I'm Lou."

"Aminah," she replied.

"You're not a soldier," he said as he tilted the pans.

"How could you tell?"

"You seem a bit happier and less intense than most of the others on the boat."

"Happier? Then the others must really be in bad shape. I'm not a crew member, more like a guest, I guess."

"Well, I'm happy for you."

"Why?"

"Because most of the crew members are here because they lost something."

"Lost something?"

"Yup, you know Zeke and what happened?"

"Of course. Yes."

The fish and eggs sizzled as he threw them into separate frying pans. "Most of the people Zeke has recruited are like him. They've had loved ones blown up, tortured, executed, maimed. Horrible stuff. Zeke has given them a mission."

"And you?" Aminah asked. "What convinced you to join?" He turned the fish over and chopped at the eggs, her mouth watering at the savory aroma.

"My partner worked on the 102nd floor of the north tower of the World Trade Center. When the plane hit the building, his office became hell and he had the choice to die from the smoke and heat, or jump. He chose to be one of the two hundred people who decided to jump. He fell for ten seconds and reached a speed of just under one hundred and fifty miles per hour. He died on impact, his body pulverized." The cook flipped the fish onto a plate and scooped the eggs into the open spot. "It took me twenty-five years of my life to find him and he was gone in less than ten seconds. I'm not a fighter but I can cook, and fighters need food." He smiled and handed her the steaming plate. "Enough of this sadness. Enjoy the meal. I hope you never have a reason to become a monster, to join our crew."

"Thank you," she said, a bit flustered by his story. Aminah sat at an empty table in silence, contemplating what she would do if someone she loved had been murdered in such a grisly fashion.

But someone you love was murdered in a horrible way.

John. Except that was no longer clear. Confused, she shut out the thoughts and focused on devouring the fish and eggs.

* * *

The crew ignored her as she wandered the hallways looking for Zeke. She exited the hold and braved the world above deck. The wind had quieted somewhat and she leaned against the railing, staring out at the endless expanse of gray waves. Despite her dislike for the water, the Zen-like rhythm of the boat as it rose and fell stilled her mind.

She sat for awhile, enjoying the sensation until a low rumble came from the opposite side of the ship. Singing. No, not exactly singing, chanting. The wind blew the words away before she could catch them.

Curious, she crossed to the other side of the deck where fifty feet down a crowd of about thirty gathered. The group, some tall, some short, mostly men but a spattering of women, chanted.

"Hoo-yah-yah-yah
Hoo-yah-yah-yah
Hoo-yah-yah-yah
Hoo-yah-yah-yah-"

In the middle, standing near the edge of the deck, a large, muscled man wore a wet suit. Beside him, lying on the ground, sat two burlap bags. She spotted Patric wearing a safari hat, puffing on a cigarette, and gazing solemnly out at the sea. She made her way over to him.

"What's happening?" she asked.

"It's the dive to heaven's deep."

"The what?"

"The heaven dive," he replied, rephrasing the name as if that made it clearer.

"Okay. And what exactly is a heaven dive?" she asked, watching suspiciously as the Amazon-Israeli tied a burlap bag to the man's legs with some twine.

"Well, it's a bit fucked up. When one of the crew die, we send them to the sea. But we don't send them alone. They tie the bags to the legs of a diver and he accompanies the coffin into the ocean. If the diver unties the knot in time, he can make it back to the surface alive. If not, the bag will carry him to the bottom of the ocean along with the casket. He has about sixty seconds."

"Hoo-yah-yah-yah
Hoo-yah-yah-yah
Hoo-yah-yah-yah
Hoo-yah-yah-yah-"

"What are they chanting?"

Patric shrugged. "Beats me. Some kind of rugby shout," he said.

"So, he dies if he doesn't undo the bags in time? Two die."

"Yeah, I told you it's fucked up. But this is a boat of people who don't care about death. I wouldn't say they want it, but they have all lost the people they love most. Ulli has survived a lot worse."

Ulli looked up at the sky and spoke to Masada. She nodded and stepped back. The chant grew louder, the crowd pounding the metal hull in time, dancing, and jumping. They thumped their hands on the wooden coffin, crying, sobbing.

"Hoo-yah-yah-yah
Hoo-yah-yah-yah
Hoo-yah-yah-yah
Hoo-yah-yah-yah-"

The mourners chant reached a crescendo as they pitched the coffin into the water. Wiping tears from his eyes, Ulli took a deep breath and dove over the side of the boat into the Indian ocean followed by the bags. Aminah peered over the railing and watched his body sink into the sea, a trail of bubbles floating to the surface. The chanting continued, waning and rising in intensity, like a tribal dirge sung in the wilds by a Paleolithic gathering of hunters.

"Have you done this?" she asked Patric, unable to envision his gawky body pulled into the murky depths of the ocean.

"Me? No way. I'm not a soldier, just a computer guy."

"So Zeke doesn't require this?"

"No, this is a ritual, not a requirement. Ulli chose to do this. He and Ravi had become close friends. Masada started it. She did a lot of free diving in the army and one day after the first casualty, she insisted they tie rocks to her and pitch her over with the coffin."

"That's crazy."

"I don't disagree."

From behind, a voice: "Do you know Yamamoto Tsunetomo's 'Hagakure?'"

She turned and Zeke stood on the deck, his hands clasped behind his back.

"No."

"He was an 18th-century Samurai. He wrote that 'If by setting one's heart right every morning and evening, one is able to live as though his body were already dead, he gains freedom in the Way.'"

"It sounds barbaric."

"Perhaps," Zeke said simply. "But that is the way of life."

"So this is how you bury the dead?" she asked.

"It's how we honor them and how we honor the lost ones in our own lives."

"Have you done the dive?" she asked Zeke.

"Yes. I did it once."

"Crazy," she muttered.

"Would you like to try it?"

"Ah, no way."

"You might be surprised at what you find in yourself when you go to the edge."

I might find myself dead," she replied.

It had been over a minute, and the chanting reverberated through her soul as she imagined dropping into the sea, the light fading, the cold pressing, the air disappearing. How could they watch so calmly? She couldn't envision a worse fate. Didn't sharks swim in this ocean?

Suddenly a cheer went up and two men hoisted Ulli out of the water on a canvas seat. Masada handed him a shot of amber-colored liquid, which he threw into his mouth before tossing the glass over the side of the boat, as if the dive made him larger than life. Ulli's shipmates surrounded him in a scrum, jumping, hugging, singing.

"Aminah, are you okay?" Zeke asked.

"Yes, I'm fine," she sighed.

"Can you come with me. I want to show you something."

"Zeke, I've got to get back to the States and warn Ambrose."

"Please Aminah, I need your help with this."

"What is it?"

"Imaad's grandaughter has woken up."

Chapter 32

Walid stared into the van, his stomach knotted into a tight mass, his legs rubber, like he had just run around the Kabba fifty times at breakneck speed.

Control yourself. You must stay in control. Followed by: *I will kill the barbarian.*

"Tell me exactly what happened," he hissed to the foolish poetry boy. "Why were you not in the van?"

"Walid, it was not my fault—"

"Shut up!" he hissed. He slapped Abdul-Haseeb hard across the cheek, the smack echoing through the concrete garage. "Just tell me exactly what happened."

The boy stroked his face and looked at him with big, hurt eyes. He knew later he would regret the slap, but for now anger overwhelmed his self-control.

"I had to go to the bathroom. My stomach has not been feeling well since the meal last night. I left him to use the toilet and when I came back, the van was gone."

"Did you call his cellphone?'

"Yes, but he did not answer."

"He didn't say he was going anywhere?"

"No, nothing. He was reading the Koran when I left."

Walid rubbed his temples and paced a few feet forward and back, crossing a yellow parking line.

Did Hassan steal the bomb? No, that didn't make sense because only Walid possessed the access codes. So where did he go?

An electronic melody played and Abdul-Haseeb fumbled for the phone in his pants. The device was only to be used in an emergency.

"Who is calling?" Walid queried.

"Let me see, let me see." Hands shaking, the boy pulled the phone from his pocket, nearly dropping it onto the ground. "The caller ID is not appearing."

Walid grabbed the phone. "Hello."

"Hello, is Abdul there please?" Abdul? What was this idiot talking about? Hassan spoke in a strong American accent.

"This is Walid. Who is this?" he asked to be sure.

"James Roberts." Walid recognized the name on Hassan's fake passport.

"Hello, James," he said through gritted teeth. "Where are you?"

"I'm at the police station." Hassan replied and Walid wanted to strangle him. Had the entire operation been compromised? Could it be over so suddenly after all the years of planning?

"Where is the van?" he asked. "What is happening?"

"The van has been taken by the police."

Curse the barbarian! They could flee Germany and return to either Syria or Pakistan.

"I was in a car accident and the police have taken the van. They plan to inspect it later today. Please send my wife to get me as soon as possible."

His wife?

Knowing that the CIA and other intelligence agencies monitored every call, Walid said little.

"Ask her to bring my passport. and whatever else is required."

The fool. What was he doing driving in the first place? And without his passport? Furious and struggling to keep himself from releasing a torrent of curses, Walid played his role.

"You wife is not available right now. Where should I tell her your passport is located?"

"It's at the bottom of my bag. Once I am released, we can clear up the situation with the van."

"Is the van damaged?"

"Yes."

"Is the merchandise all right?"

"I hope so. Tell her to come soon. I'm anxious to be released and get my van."

"Where are you?" Walid asked.

"What's the address here?" he heard Hassan ask someone. "Are you still there?"

"Yes," Walid replied.

"Seven Strasse St. George. Come quickly." Then, he whispered in a way that made his voice sound childlike, "I think they plan to inspect the van soon."

The line went dead.

Chapter 33

Sheikh Imaad's daughter lay on her back, staring up at the ceiling when they entered. The girl had ripped a part of her gown off and wrapped it around her head like a scarf to conceal as much of her face as possible. Only her eyes peeked out. Aminah guessed the girl to be about thirteen, with long dark hair, and matching brown eyes.

"Salaam," Aminah said.

The girl didn't respond.

"I'm Aminah," she said in Arabic. "What is your name?" The girl brought her head down and peered at her through large, almond shaped eyes. She studied Aminah for thirty seconds.

"Aminah?" the girl finally whispered, breaking the silence. "The mother of the prophet. It is a pretty name," she said. "You are Muslim?"

"Yes," Aminah replied.

"And you?" the girl asked, looking at Zeke, what is your name?"

Aminah could tell he didn't want to answer and she nudged him with her elbow.

"Zeke, my name is Zeke."

"Like the prophet Ezekiel," Imaad's grandaughter replied. "But you are not Muslim," she said definitively.

"I'm not here to answer her questions," Zeke whispered.

Aminah ignored him.

"I am Hani," the girl suddenly replied.

They had a name! "Your name is beautiful."

The girl's lip curved up ever so slightly.

"Are you hungry? Would you like something to eat?"

She stared at them for a moment and nodded. "Do you have any chocolate?" she asked in moderately accented

English. She continued: "My father didn't approve, but I love chocolate."

As does almost every woman, Aminah thought. "Well, Zeke, is there any chocolate on the boat?"

"Chocolate?" he asked, probably wondering how the discussion had turned to food. "I think we might have some. Let me check."

He walked towards the door, stopped, and turned. "Who taught you English?" he asked.

"One of the men. He was an American. I learn things very well. It did not take long."

It must have been Hassan al Jibir, the bastard who killed Rachel and Samuel, Aminah reasoned. More than any other hijacker, Aminah wanted to bring him to justice.

Hani turned to Zeke. "I know who you are. I recognize you from the television. Father and the others spoke of you. They never realized you were the wolf."

Zeke scowled. "I'll be back in a minute with your chocolate," he said, and left Aminah with the girl.

Hani turned to her. "Are they going to kill me?" she asked calmly.

"No," Aminah said, not entirely sure herself, fairly certain Zeke wouldn't hurt the child. But Zeke had changed and after what he had done to Bin Gaudi she couldn't be sure of anything.

"What happened to your face?" Hani asked.

"A man cut me."

She nodded solemnly. "It looks painful. Praise Allah, I hope it heals quickly"

"Thank you."

"When I was small, my father had an American. They kept him in a cage and fed him a little water and bread every day. On the twelfth day, they killed him. He pleaded for his life, but that was not enough. My father said he was a bad man, that all Americans are very bad. They disrespect Allah, they hate women, they want to kill Muslims."

"I am an American and I am a Muslim. I don't want to kill you."

"No?" she asked with genuine confusion. "You killed my father."

"No, I didn't do that."

"Then who did?"

"Zeke and his men. They killed him in revenge for the death of his wife and child." It felt strange to speak to a young child in such graphic terms, but Hani seemed capable of interacting at a higher level than her age might suggest.

"Hani, why did your father and his followers try to kill you?"

The girl turned away as tears filled her eyes. "Please, leave me alone."

"Hani, millions are going to die."

"I don't know anything," Hani said in English.

"Hani, please."

"I am just a child."

"They wanted to kill you because you have information, isn't that right?" she asked gently. "They didn't want you to be captured."

"I don't know anything," she repeated hollowly. "I am a martyr for Allah."

"No, you are a beautiful little girl who should be playing with dolls and running with your friends. You should not be a martyr for anything."

Zeke returned carrying a Toblerone chocolate bar. Hani's eyes widened, she ripped off the wrapper, and bit off mouthful-sized chunks.

"Is it good?" Aminah asked.

Hani nodded vigorously, chocolate drool sliding down her chin. She finished the bar and scoured the wrapper for any left-over chocolate crumbs. When she was totally done and there wasn't a trace of chocolate left, she crumpled up the wrapper and laid it beside the bed. She sighed, lay back, and fixed him with a pensive stare.

"Why did you give sweets to me?"

"I thought you might like them."

She looked confused. "Tell me what you were like as a father."

"What do you mean?" he asked, unsure.

Aminah was impressed at how the little girl had turned the tables and become the inquisitor.

"Did you love your child? Did you play with him?"

Aminah expected him to stalk away, refuse to answer the questions, but Zeke pulled over a chair and sat down.

"I loved my child more than anything. I would have done anything to protect him. But I couldn't and I didn't." He squeezed his fist into a ball, his eyes gleaming.

Hani nodded. "My father was not like that."

"What about your mother?" he asked.

"My mother was the third of my father's wives. She fell out of favor and was sent away. I heard that she died last year from sickness."

"Why didn't you go with your mother?"

"My father needed me. He wouldn't allow me to leave. He said that my mother was godless, she had turned from Allah." Tears filled the girl's eyes and ran down her cheeks.

"I'm sorry about your mother," Zeke said, looking uncomfortable.

"I think I would have liked you as my father," Hani said, drying her eyes.

Zeke gave a small grunt. "Maybe."

The little girl looked at the ceiling and said nothing more.

Chapter 34

For a moment the panic rose in Walid, scratching its way from his belly like a hungry beast, smothering his lungs and making the air heavy and hard to inhale, reaching a claw up his nose and then into his brain, making his thinking hard and slow, coiling its sinewy legs around his body and squeezing until he thought he might double over and disappear into the maws of the earth.

You will face adversity and struggles, and when you do, turn to Allah, for He is the source of your strengh and the answers to overcome any problem.

Sheikh Imaad, bless his name, told him so in the Iraqi desert and he drew upon the memory for strength.

The emails provided a number to call in case of an emergency. *Only call this number if no other option is available. You must not dial it lightly.*

Did they face such a situation? Yes, but he must not panic. Think. The arrival of three Muslim men in a police station would surely arouse suspicion. Germany's tolerance of its Muslim population plummeted after the Berlin bombing, praise be the martyrs.

Hassan asked to have *his wife* deliver the passport.

The woman.

Would she go for them? Could she be trusted? Walid mulled over his options. Calling the number would be to admit failure. But risking the mission on the woman seemed equally distasteful and even foolish.

His brain spinning, Walid made two rapid jumps in his thinking about the situation. If done correctly, the solution might benefit the mission in the long-term. Allah worked in strange ways, he thought, thankful for the sudden insight.

He wouldn't call the number.

Abdul-Haseeb rubbed his face and backed away from Walid.

"Come Abdul-Haseeb, we have some work to do." he said quietly.

* * *

The van, a used white Ford with an illustration on its sides of a chicken wearing a turban and the words Turkisches printed in black letters pulled up a block from the police station. The fool Qasim's brother owned a restaurant and agreed to part with the truck for one thousand dollars. Thief. No devotion to Allah. Clearly, a lack of sensibility ran in the family. But at least the quibbling coward had helped get them the vehicle.

Abdul-Haseeb slid back the rear door and the girl exited onto the sidewalk, a package in her gloved hand. As she moved briskly down the street, Walid watched the eyes of men turn to her, pulled by her beauty and the garments Walid had selected: tight jeans, a white top that showed just a bit of cleavage, and a red jacket to protect her from the chill of the fall evening air. Her clothes skirted impropriety, but she was not a Muslim woman and guile was necessary to achieve their goal.

She reached the police station; climbed the stairs, a German police officer holding the door for her; and disappeared inside.

Now, Walid waited. This first part of the plan was the easiest, still, he did not know how the girl would react. When he had asked her to help, she had agreed without hesitation.

"You saved my life. I will do what you ask of me. But please," she said, nodding at the handcuffs. "I will not run. Where I to go?" she asked, her large eyes staring, looking into his soul. He had walked over and opened the handcuffs.

"Thank you. What you need from me?"

Now, he waited, hoping he hadn't made a mistake delivering her right to the police. Walid glanced impatiently at his watch, tapped his foot on the ground.

Outside, a small, chubby boy holding a red balloon stopped in front of the car to munch on a sausage. The balloon must have grazed a tree branch for it suddenly popped, causing the boy to jump and drop his sausage. He bent to pick it up but the meat was covered in dirt, and the boy's mouth opened like a hippomatumus to let out a cry of pain. Such sloth and indolence. Such weakness. He peered more closely as tears coursed down the chubby cheeks. Surely this boy represented another message from Allah. The sloth and weakness of the West would be popped just like the balloon.

Frankfurt's narrow streets and three-or-four-story buildings teemed with people. Pedestrians strolled on the cement-tiled sidewalks, window shopping, chatting. A small crowd stood at a bus stop. On the ride into town, the girl commented on how pretty the city appeared but he didn't think that at all. The narrow streets choked him, a dark crusader maze, and he longed to get away as soon as possible.

"She's taking a long time," Abdul-Haseeb said from the back.

"She'll return," Walid replied. He peeked at his watch. If she didn't return in three minutes, they would leave and travel to the next destination, hoping to complete the second part of the plan before the police closed in. At least they might be able to retrieve and detonate the bomb.

One minute left.

Do not let me down. The girl would not fail.

And then, to confirm his thoughts, a smiling German police officer walked out of the station, holding the doors for a beautiful woman. She strolled down the stairs, hips swaying, breasts swelling, and took a right, just as they had discussed.

"She's there, she's there!" Abdul-Haseeb said excitedly.

"Yes, but we still don't know," Walid replied.

"Know what?"

"It could be a trap. They could have discussed this with her as a way to trap us."

"No, I don't think so," Amir said. "The police would have surrounded us by now."

"But where is Hassan?" Abdul-Haseeb asked. "Shouldn't she have Hassan with her?"

Walid put the truck into gear and pulled out, traveling slowly down the street to the spot where they had agreed to pick her up, well away from the police station.

"We dropped off Hassan's passport. He is on his own." He hadn't mentioned this part of the plan to anyone but the girl.

"We are leaving him?" Abdul-Haseeb asked in surprise.

"Freeing him would jeapordize the mission. The police will ask us too many questions. Even dropping off his passport is a risk but he will have a chance to free himself." In reality, Walid didn't think Hassan would be released from prison until after the mission completed. At least he hoped that to be the case. "He put the entire mission in jeopordy. We will go on without him and with Allah's blessing he will free himself from the Germans."

He gazed at her sauntering down the street and Walid found himself entranced—the bounce of her hair, the fluid movements of her arms—before he returned his focus to the street and steered the van across several trolley tracks. He stopped at the next street corner.

She walked to the vehicle and Abdul-Haseeb pulled the back door open, letting her climb in. "I did as you asked," she said happily. "I dropped off the package."

"Any problems?" he asked.

"No, all of the people caused it to take extra time. That is all. I gave the identification to a man."

"Did you find out about the van?"

She smiled. "Of course. It is in a lot three kilometers from here. It no have not been searched yet. I have the address here."

Walid let out a sigh of relief. "Excellent. Abdul-Haseeb, put in the address."

"Yes, master."

"I'm not your master."

"Just a joke, Walid." How could the poet joke at a moment like this? Despite his attempt to keep a straight face, his mouth twisted into a grin.

"Look, Ali," the master smiles, yelled Abdul-Haseeb.

"I am not your master!" Walid exclaimed.

"Did I do good?" the woman asked.

Walid put the car into drive, checked his mirrors, and pulled away from the curb into the light Frankfurt traffic. "You did very good," he said. "But getting the bomb back is going to be much harder."

Chapter 35

Aminah, Zeke, Masada, and Patric sat around a thick mahogany table in a room off the main command center.

"This is a forged passport and a credit card loaded with ten thousands dollars." Zeke shuffled the passport and credit card across the table and Aminah turned them over in her hands.

"Amelia Barrau. Nice name. Are the documents good?"

"The best," Patric said. "I hacked the system that produces these babies. We also managed to commandeer the paper stock and holographic imagery embedded in a real passport."

Masada watched with cold, clinical detachment. Aminah got a bitch woman vibe from her. Probably ex-Mossad.

"We're going to have a private jet take you from South Africa to Washington D.C."

Aminah doodled on a notepad while listening to Zeke.

"A car will be waiting for you in the airport parking lot."

Zeke stopped and peered at her notepad. "Aminah, are you listening? What are you drawing?" he asked.

"A doodle."

"What are you doodling?"

She sighed, a bit exasperated by his focus on her pad. She needed to get home. "I guess it's an E."

"Why are you drawing an E?"

She wracked her brain for an answer. "I saw the E in John's papers. I guess it stuck in my mind." John had gotten angry when she asked him about the file, which had been strange, but also part of a pattern of withdrawal in the months leading up to his mission.

Aminah drew the letter with two looping half-circles that ended in sharp vertical lines, duplicating the one she remembered from John's paperwork.

"I've seen it before," Zeke said.

"Of course, because it's an E."

"No, the font, with the lines at the ends, I've seen the exact typography before."

"It's probably some kind of trinket or good luck charm." If so, why had John been so upset when she asked him about it?

"Lilly wore one," Zeke said. "And so did Adele."

"Lilly Broadhurst?"

"Yes, the same woman who sent your journalist friend on a wild chase to his death."

'What do you think the E means?" she asked, intrigued.

"That E is the symbol of an evangelical church Lilly's family attended. Lilly isn't much of an evangelical but she wore one."

"Why would John have an E printed on a sheet of paper?" she asked.

"I don't know."

"I'm sure if you go on the Internet you'll find all kinds of information about it," she added.

Zeke nodded to Patric and he typed onto the keyboard: "E Religious Symbol." The results filled the screen but none of them matched.

"Modify the query," Zeke said. "Put in 'Letter E Religious Symbol.'" The query returned pages of unrelated results.

"Nothing," Aminah said.

Zeke strummed his fingers on the table.

"Zeke, you're not worried about a religious symbol, are you? I doubt any connection between John's file and Lilly's doo-dad. You're focusing on a coincidence."

"Adele wore an E on her necklace. I don't trust coincidences. I've studied them mathematically and there is no such thing."

"That's absurd. Of course there are coincidences. In college, I spent a semester abroad in Spain. I had just broken up with my boyfriend who was in Paris. Anyway, the group went on a trip to Amsterdam and we stayed in some two-star hotel. One night, we went to a restaurant and guess who was having dinner at the same place?"

"You ex-boyfriend," he replied.

"Yup. Imagine the odds of bumping into my ex-boyfriend in a different city in the same restaurant at the same time? They must have been astronomical. These coincidences happen."

"Aminah, did you break up with him?"

"Yes."

"Did you ever discuss this trip with him?"

She thought for a moment. "Before we broke up, I might have mentioned the trip in passing."

"Let me provide an alternative explanation. It wasn't a coincidence at all. Your ex-boyfriend knew you were going to Amsterdam. You might have even mentioned the hotel to him and he traveled there to see you in an attempt to rescue the relationship."

She never considered that possibility. Brian had been pretty hurt, but she didn't think he cared enough to travel hundreds of miles to Amsterdam. He did seem awfully happy to "bump" into her. Did he stage the meeting?

"I suppose it was possible."

"Not possible, probable. He planned to meet you."

"Maybe?" she said, still not totally convinced.

"The connection of Adele, Lilly, and your husband to E is important. Lilly sent the reporter on a wild goose chase to Afghanistan. Someone in the OCT set you up to be killed in Pakistan. And they are all connected in some way." He rose and paced back and forth behind the chairs. "You'll go to Washington and meet with Ambrose," he said more to himself than to them. "Masada will accompany you."

Aminah didn't want the Amazon Israeli following her anywhere. "I appreciate your concern but I can take care of myself. Ambrose can protect me."

"Like he did in Pakistan? We've already had to save you once."

She knew Zeke's agenda extended beyond just her protection. He wanted Masada there to find out if the mole had also played a role in the hijacking of the airplane.

The Israeli sat impassive, face set like stone. Damn Israelis, sometimes their outer toughness drove her crazy. Despite the press, Arabs and Israelis got along well in one-on-one interactions; in fact, they often had a lot in common and she had several Israeli friends. But she recognized the type sitting in front of her also: cold, hard, probably bearing some grudge. She didn't need that attitude now.

"I don't…"

"It's settled," Zeke said.

Anger rose from her belly and she nearly blurted out the words in her head: *you pompous ass. I didn't ask you to save me. Go to hell! I'll swim back to the mainland and catch a plane myself.*

Instead she summoned all of her will power, bit her tongue, smiled smugly, and said: "Fine." She would take their ride to Washington and then dump the Israeli named after a rock.

"One last thing," Patric said, slicing through the tension. "I've rigged a phone for you." He pushed a small device across the table. "It works like a regular cellphone but is Echelon-proof."

He then pushed a non-descript, steel-banded woman's watch to her.

"Takes a licking but keeps on ticking," Patric joked. "But seriously, this puppy has a built in panic button and a GPS transponder. If you're in trouble, pull out the knob. As long as you are not behind too many layers of concrete, the signal should transmit."

"When can I leave?" she asked.

"The chopper sustained heavy damage and there is stormy weather coming. In 2-3 days we should be ready."

"Two to three days! Zeke, I need to go now."

"There's nothing we can do. If the weather relents we'll try to get you out in two days."

She couldn't remain stuck on a boat halfway around the world while a nuclear weapon threatened her family and her country. Her mother hadn't answered the phone, and Aminah feared she had fallen ill, broken a leg, been abducted or any number of other sinister scenarios. She needed to contact her sister to relay the news: get out of New York City.

"There's no way the repairs can be done faster? "Please."

"We'll try," Zeke said. "I want to leave also."

"Where are you going?"

"I'm traveling to Texas to visit an old friend," Zeke replied.

"Lilly Broadhurst?"

"Yup. I want to understand her role in all of this and how E fits in."

"And what about Hani?" she asked.

"We have some time to decide what to do with her."

"You aren't going to hurt her, are you?"

"She has information. I hope we can convince her to cooperate," he said.

Chapter 36

Abdul-Haseeb pulled the Turkish chicken truck onto a side street and the girl slid out and walked towards a gated entrance. Beyond the barrier lay a small guard shack which played sentry to rows and rows of cars. Her job was simple: keep security occupied for half an hour.

"I can do that," she said when he explained her job.

"How will you keep them occupied?" he asked.

"You no want to know, Mr. Walid."

He stared at her beautiful face, realizing she was right. She turned, locked eyes with him, gave a small, shy wave, and continued on. He had sent young women on suicide missions with less hesitation and regret. But they needed to regain control of the weapon.

When she turned the corner and headed to the guard shack, he put the truck into drive and pulled out onto the narrow road. He pressed the pedal and a sharp jab of pain traveled up his leg, causing the mucles in his calf to tighten.

"Ahhh," he cried out.

"Are you allright?" asked Amir.

"It's just the wound." While he felt better, his head clearer, the leg still ached and certain movements sent pain up to his hip. Walking remained difficult.

He turned the van left and saw the fence to their right, the coiled barbed wire at the top glittering in the moonlight.

Walid drove the truck down the street and took one more right until they came to an even narrower road with large trees and undergrowth to their left. The brambles, the trees, and bushes reminded him of the wilds of Kazakstan and the long ride to get the bomb, a ride he didn't want to repeat. *Just like this task.* Pray to Allah all goes smoothly.

The barbed wire-topped fence remained on their right. Walid parked the truck at the opposite corner from the guard shack.

He pulled out the tablet and reviewed the plan again with Abdul-Haseeb and Amir.

"This is the lot," he said, pointing to a satellite image showing the rows of cars on a mix of asphalt and grass. "We are here, at the far corner. The guard tower is there. "Abdul-Haseeb and I will scale the fence at this point, search for the truck, and find the bomb. We'll carry the weapon back and pass it to you over the fence."

"So, we leave the van?" asked Amir.

"Yes, we have no choice."

"And what of your leg, Pasha?" asked Abdul-Haseeb.

"Do not call me that," Walid snapped back. Hassan started the pasha nonsense several days ago to mock him and the boy foolishly picked it up. "Put on your mask and let's go. We don't have much time. Ali, bring the blanket."

They pulled black ski masks over their faces, exited the truck, and walked over to the fence. Peering into the impound lot, he searched for any sign of movement.

"Do you see anything?" he asked them.

"No, it looks quiet," said Abdul-Haseeb.

"I see nothing," said Amir.

"Amir, if anyone comes, call my phone." He motioned to Amir. "Drape the blanket over the top." Abdul-Haseeb helped him heave the heavy blanket over the coiled barbed wire, creating a path they could crawl over without being stabbed by a sharp edge. "You first," he said pointing to Abdul Haseeb. The young man shimmied easily up the fence and then slithered across the blanket, landing seconds later on the other side.

They waited for a moment, listening for an alarm. The wind whistled through the trees.

"Let's go," he said quietly to Amir. "Give me a boost." Amir stuck out his hand, Walid put his athletic shoe into the physicist's palm and hoisted himself up. His right toe stuck into one of the holes and he pushed off, sending another dagger of pain through his leg. Ignoring the jolt, Walid climbed up to the blanket, resting for a moment before pushing his left leg over, his foot finding purchase on the other side. Pushing through the stabbing throb, he swung his right leg around. Trembling, he rested at the top for a moment before gathering his strength and pushing off. Another sharp stab cramped his leg and almost forced him to his knees before the pain ebbed.

High overhead lights cast a dim glow over the lot. They quickly scuttled down the aisles. He passed Opels, Fords, Mercedes, BMWs, but no Ecostar vans. He motioned for Abdul-Haseeb to start the second aisle. As he started down the third, his back ached from crouching and his leg shot off jolts of pain with every step.

Twenty meters ahead sat the guardbooth and Walid stopped, frozen in his tracks, gaze fixed on a slit in the window. The woman lay on her back, skirt up near her stomach, a blue clad figure pistoning between her legs.

That slut! No, he had asked her to do this. And when he had asked her, she had agreed but didn't she look sad, almost disappointed? He was sure of it.

"Walid, why have you stopped? Is there a problem?" Abdul-Haseeb asked.

"No, no problem. Let's finish this," he said glumly. There must have been another way. No, the girl did what she needed and that was all.

They walked down another aisle and in the middle, next to a red Mercedes C class sedan and a silver Opel, sat the van.

"I've found the van," he called. He tried the handle and, praise Allah, the driver's side door opened, bathing the interior in light. Shit! He quickly scrambled in and fumbled around on the roof until he found the light switch and flicked it off. He continued into the back and crawled over the rear seat where he had lain half dead just a few days before. Stopping for a moment, he noticed a black piece of cloth lying on the seat. He picked it up. The girl used the band to tie her hair and he could smell her scent: a mix of honeysuckle and perhaps jasmine. Memories of her cool hands massaging his feet and stroking his burning hot head flooded back. And now, she lay with those infidels! His stomach lurched.

Focus, Walid. Focus. Save your anger.

He found the trunk latch and pressed the button.

Abdul-Haseeb pulled up the floor to reveal the warhead. Praise Allah! Heaving a sigh of relief, he motioned to the boy to wrap the weapon and wait for him.

Walid clambered back over the seats, the relief and gratitude to Allah washing away the pain in his leg, and exited the van.

"Come, let's go," he whispered. Together, they quickly carried the wrapped warhead from the van back to the section of fence where Amir waited. As they approached the last row of cars, about thirty feet from the fence—so close Walid spotted the dim outline of the blankets thrown over the barbed wire—a bright light flared and a voice called out in German.

"Stillstand nicht bewegen!"

For a moment he considered fleeing, but realized he wouldn't get far with his bad foot.

"Nicht nur einen Zentimeter zu bewegen oder ich schießen."

He turned to face a dark haired woman dressed in a police uniform. Se held a gun in her left hand; her right hand gripped the flashlight.

" Drop, was Sie in Händen halten."

"I don't speak German," he said.

"I said, drop what you are holding and put your hands into the air."

Chapter 37

The sailboat cut smoothly through the turquoise waters of the Indian ocean. At times, Zeke would bark an order to Aminah, command her to pull a lever, wrap a line, or be prepared for the boat to turn and come about. She vaguely remembered the terminology from the summer sailing class she'd taken as a kid.

Hani sat, smiling when the boat glided, frowning and panicked when the boat would lean over or a sheet of fine mist showered them. Zeke smirked when Hani gawked or Aminah quickly gripped the railing. For the first time since Aminah had known him, Zeke appeared relaxed, happy and she could almost imagine him before the death of Rachel and Sam. Life's path twisted down cruel streets, she thought, remembering her father's assisination and the family's flight to America.

Zeke had invited her for a sail and after some coaxing she accepted. The repairs needed another five or six hours, and Aminah needed a break from staring at the computer screens, trying to find some clue or sign of the nuclear weapon in the data that streamed onto the Vengeance.

Hani didn't need to be asked twice and eagerly accepted the offer.

"Look," Zeke said pointing to the horizon. Up ahead lay a small speck, like a bottle bobbing on top of the ocean. But as the boat grew closer, she realized it wasn't a small bottle at all, but an island.

"Here Aminah, take the wheel," he said as they approached the shore. "Just keep it straight."

"Are you sure I should drive?"

"Steer, you steer a boat."

Whatever the name, she didn't seem the least qualified. He hopped away and began to bring down the sales, twisting and turning levers and pulleys until the boat's speed slowed. When they had reached a gentle glide, twenty yards or so from shore, he pressed a button and a splash came from the right.

"The anchor," he said, anticipating the question. The boat moved a few more feet and came to a stop in front of a sandy beach. Rocks, which her father had once told her were more properly called coral, created a jagged path under the crystal clear water. Schools of fish darted from ridge to ridge. A giant turtle floated by and Hani watched the massive shell disappear under the boat.

"This is my island getaway," Zeke said. "Shall we go ashore?"

"Are there any sharks?" Aminah asked.

Zeke smirked. "None that will bother you."

Hardly reassuring.

After donning bathing suits and water shoes to prevent their feet from getting cut on the coral, they met beside a ladder. Hani put her clothes back over the bathing suit in a show of modesty. The girl mentioned she had never seen the ocean before and Aminah sensed her excitement, and trepidation.

"Hani, can you swim?" The girl shook her head. "Are you afraid? You don't need to go in."

"I am nervous but I want to go. It looks so beautiful," she said.

Zeke came over with a life vest. "Put this around your body," he said. Hani began to put the vest on but the straps had twisted and knotted and she pulled the belt in frustration. Zeke moved forward but the girl retreated.

"Let me help her," Aminah said, untangling the straps and fitting them around the girl's waist.

With the life vest on, Hani tentatively climbed down the ladder to the water and then dipped her toe in. Zeke jumped in beside her, throwing up a splash. The girl squealed and scurried back up the ladder to avoid getting drenched.

"Zeke, stop it. It's all right, Hani." Hani furrowed her brows at Zeke. Aminah took her hand and together they descended to the bottom. "You'll be fine. Just let yourself float. Okay?" The girl nodded and together they pushed off, wading into the warm ocean.

"Are you okay?" Zeke asked Hani. She vigorously nodded yes but to Aminah it indicated a definite no. "Take my hand," Zeke said. "Just float and I will bring you to the shore."

To Aminah's surprise, Hani grabbed Zeke's arm and let herself be pulled through the water, relaxing and even smiling a little. Aminah swam beside them and ten feet from the boat they cleared the coral and her feet hit the sandy bottom.

"You can stand now," she said and Hani put her feet down and looked even more relieved.

"Take her to shore," Zeke said. "I'm going to retrieve a few supplies from the boat."

She nodded and they waded in, unhooked Hani's life vest, and began to walk the beach, enjoying the feel of sand on their toes and the warm rays from the sun. Hani silently absorbed the sights and sounds of the small island. How different this environment must have seemed compared to the cold mountain hideouts in Pakistan and Afganistan.

"Do you like it here?"

"Of course," the girl replied.

Zeke returned with a cooler and left it up the beach in the shade of a tree.

"Come on, let's explore a bit," he said, and they started off. He showed them a waterfall that spilled down from black obsidian rocks in a shower of rainbow light, a shallow inlet pond that teemed with minnows and crabs, and a cliff that afforded a panoramic view of the ocean. In the distance, a speck on the horizon, sat the Vengeance.

On the way back, Hani squeeled.

Zeke rushed to her. "What happened?"

"Look," Hani pointed.

A crab skittered across the beach, stoppped and seemed to stare at them.

"It's a crab."

"I've never seen one before. It's ugly."

"They taste good." Zeke jumped towards it but the crab moved faster, darting into a ridge in the rocks. "Gone," Zeke said. "He got away."

"He?" Hani asked.

"He, she, it."

Hani laughed.

* * *

After returning to the beach, Zeke started a fire and they sat before the flickering flames, Aminah mesmerized by the dance. Would New York look like the charred piece of wood at the bottom of the pile? She pushed the thought from her mind. Not now.

"I come to this island to relax. I discovered it about a year ago," Zeke said putting a grill over the flames and removing several lamb chops from the cooler.

"It's beautiful," Aminah replied. "A tropical paradise." She suspected, though, that he didn't just bring them there to relax and have fun.

He placed the meat on the heated grill and the chops sizzled.

"Do you eat lamb?" he asked Hani.

The girl nodded yes.

For a few minutes no one spoke as the chops sizzled over the flame, the delicious smell making Aninah's stomach grumble. Zeke used a long fork to turn the food.

"When I was younger, I sailed as often as I could. I lived with my foster parents and in the afternoon, when they were at work, I would make my way down to the sailing club and take out a boat."

"I didn't realize you lived with foster parents," Aminah said. This had never been made public. Interesting.

He nodded.

"What are foster parents?" Hani asked.

"People who took care of me," Zeke answered. "My real parents were not there."

"What happened to them?" the girl asked.

"They were killed."

Aminah bit her lip and shifted on the sand, surprised at this revelation. Nothing of the sort had emerged about Zeke, but then again the media focused on the threat to the Vice President's daughter and the testimonies of the surviving hijackers, perhaps preferring to dwell on the living as opposed to the dead. The information might have led OCT to Zeke earlier.

"Do you have any sibilings?" Aminah asked.

"I had a sister who was killed also."

"Why?" Hani asked. "Why were they killed?"

Zeke speared the meat and removed the sizzling chops from the grill, provoking a burst of flames as the dripping grease fueled the fire. "My father did something he shouldn't have. Like your father but different. His enemies killed everyone. I was lucky to survive."

"Mafia?" Aminah asked.

"Bad people."

Aminah waited for him to divulge more but he went no further and she sensed he wouldn't.

"So you see," Zeke continued, "we are all similar. We have all had our families, or members of our families, killed because of their actions."

"Your family was killed also," Hani asked her.

"My father."

"Why?" the girl asked.

"My father believed in a Lebanon for everyone. Some people didn't like that vision."

The girl nodded her head.

He cut the meat and gave each of them a piece. Zeke pulled a thermos full of hot corn out of the cooler and retrieved a second container with potatoes. After spooning the food onto their plates, he poured three cups of water.

"We're not going to hurt you, Hani," Zeke said. "You are worried that if you tell us everything we will have your secrets and will be free to hurt you. Am I right?"

Mouth trembling, she nodded.

"I'm a monster, but not that kind of monster."

"You're not a monster," Hani said.

Zeke smiled. "Thank you for saying that."

"My grandfater said he would never hurt me," Hani said. "His men tried to kill me."

Zeke had been telling the truth.

"They tried to kill you because you have information," Aminah stated.

Hani nodded her head, tears coursing down her face.

Zeke stretched his hands towards the girl and she jumped into them, crying freely onto his shoulder.

Shocked and overcome with emotion, Aminah fought away the tears. Hani repeated something several times in Arabic as her small body shuddered. Finally, Aminah recognized the words.

"I hated him," Aminah translated. "I hated him."

"They used you," Zeke said. "We will never do that. You are free to leave any time you want. I'll help you with money, support, whatever you need. But you have information that can help others. Hani, please tell us about the bomb, tell us about E, so we can prevent more people from being killed and more children from losing their families," he said.

The girl wiped tears from her eyes and withdrew from the hug. "I-I-I will tell you. But you must promise me one t-t-thing."

"What?" Zeke asked. "What would you like?"

"I want to go with you. I do not want to be left alone."

"Hani–" he started.

"That is my price."

"It will be far too dangerous for a young girl," Aminah said.

"I am not scared," Hani shot back. "I have seen more terrible things than either of you. I have died a hundred times. I am not scared. Promise and I will tell you."

"Hani," she started, "it's not–" but Zeke cut her off.

"Hani, you can come with me. I promise you will not be left behind or harmed by me or anyone else."

Aminah gaped, disappointed at Zeke's words. She doubted he intended to keep his promise. The trip to the island lulled her into thinking he retained a sense of compassion. But he remained ruthless, willing to make false promises to little girls to get what he wanted.

With a sniffle Hani nodded and picked up her fork.

"You mentioned E. It is the mark of the devil," the girl said softly. "My grandfather spoke of the letter, as did others."

"What?" Aminah asked, disappointed in his tactics but not immune to interest in the information.

"My grandfather said the devil sent them. They never came with a name but were all signed with an E."

"What messages?" Zeke asked.

"Walid received messages from America. They told him which plane to take, how to put a gun on the plane, how to escape. My grandfather was suspicious but Walid believed they were sent as a gift from Allah."

"The mole," Aminah said.

"Are you sure they discussed an E?" Zeke asked.

She nodded.

"What did the E look like?"

Hani picked up a stick and drew in the sand, the character looking just like what she had seen on John's papers.

"That's it," Aminah said, a chill running through her body despite the warm tropical breeze. "This has to be high-level in order to circumvent QIL."

Zeke nodded. "Please keep going," he said to Hani.

"The bomb is to be taken to New York and blown up at the United Nations building. I remember them talking about an important meeting with many leaders from around the world."

"The United Nations General Assembly," Aminah said.

"Yes, that is the name," Hani replied.

"When is that?" Zeke asked.

"September sixteenth," Aminah replied. "In five days." Zeke had been correct in his estimate of the timing.

"Once the bomb explodes, the world leaders will be killed and there will be fear and doubt. They will remove Arab leaders and...." she thought for a moment..."sorry, I I don't know the right words. They will take control in the Arab world and do the same in parts of Europe. The Caliphate will be reborn. With the United States and Europe, Allah will grant them success."

"Who is bringing the bomb?" Zeke asked.

"Walid is the leader. Hassan also," she replied.

"From the plane hijacking?" Zeke asked, his hands clenched into fists, his foot tapping furiously into the sand.

"Yes."

He stood up and delivered a violent kick to a burning log, propelling the glowing wood into the trees, sparks swirling in the air. "Those bastards!" Startled by the violent outburst, Aminah shrank back but Hani remained still, unperturbed.

Zeke stared quietly at the ocean for a few minutes before sitting down.

"How are they bringing the bomb?" he asked, eyes still wild, a sheen of sweet visible on his forehead.

Hani continued, unphased. "It will be brought to New York by van and then taken to the United Nations in an ambulance. Walid did not tell Papa all the details."

The terrorist group didn't even fully trust each other, Aminah realized.

"They will bring the bomb ashore in Canada, drive it down through New York, the state, and blow it up in the city."

With this information Ambrose should have no problem netralizing the threat. "Thank you Hani," she said, relieved. "This is very important information. You may have saved the world."

The little girl smiled and took a bite of lamb.

Chapter 38

A range of thoughts cycled through Walid's head as he squinted through the glare of the flashlight.

Run at her and hope to take her by surprise.

Ignore her and continue walking.

Detonate the weapon.

None seemed particularly promising so he tried a fourth option.

"Please," he finally said, slipping the mask from his face, groveling like a wounded animal, "we have come for our equipment. The police took our truck. And my girlfriend," he said, nodding towards the guard shack.

"That's your girlfriend?" the woman asked.

He nodded slowly. "Yes."

"Pigs," she muttered under her breathe.

"Please, will you help us? Please."

"You are Muslim?"

He didn't like the question but decided to answer truthfully. "Yes."

"I am a Muslim," the woman said.

"What did you say?" She appeared one hundred percent German.

The policewoman lowered the light from their eyes and illuminated the ground instead.

"My boyfriend is Muslim, from Turkey. I decided to convert. We will be married in July."

"You are playing a trick on me?"

"No, no trick."

"May Allah bless you," Walid said, still unsure if the guard toyed with them or really told the truth. Many Muslims lived in Germany and Rahid told him the native population showed interest in the true religion. They counted on this to extend the Caliphate to Europe.

"I have found peace in Islam," she said. "The Koran does not allow pigs like the others," she said gesturing towards the guard shack. "I would like to try wearing a veil if I wouldn't lose my job."

Allah granted them another miracle. Their mission was blessed. "Perhaps some day soon you will be able to."

"Perhaps," she replied. "Many of my girlfriends are jealous and ask questions about Islam. Allah's word will spread."

"Truly?" he asked in awe.

"Truly," she replied. She pointed the flashlight at the wrapped package in his arms. "What are you carrying?"

Think quick.

"A fryer. My cousin Malik owns a kebab shop. Without the device he will be unable to open tomorrow." He spoke too fast for kebabs were not fried. He hoped she didn't know anything about cooking Middle Eastern food.

"I love kebabs," she replied. "Perhaps I will visit his shop someday."

"Yes, he would like that," Walid said.

"Why did they take your truck?"

"Hassan forgot his license. He is not the best driver," Walid said truthfully. "He is still in jail where he belongs, but we need the truck. We have done nothing wrong. We must fry the kebabs or we will not sell the food and then we will lose the shop."

"Nothing dangerous is in the truck?"

"No, of course not. You must have learned that Islam is the religion of peace, no?" She smiled but her eyes remained flat.

"You don't look dangerous. Come, I will sort this out and get the truck back for you."

"That is very kind, very kind, but my girlfriend is in with those men. I really don't want to see them. Perhaps we can come back tomorrow morning?"

She looked him up and down again. "If that's what you want, no problem. Come back tomorrow but do not mention our meeting. In the meantime, I will make sure your truck is cleared to go."

"Thank you, thank you. I must ask one more favor."

"Yes?"

"Can I retrieve my girlfriend?"

She scowled and turned to walk towards the guard shack. "Pigs," she muttered again. "I will send her out the door in a few minutes. She stopped and spoke in a softer tone. "Your girlfriend spreads her legs for those men. Perhaps she is not worthy."

Walid dropped his head to show shame. "Perhaps I should end the relationship."

The woman shrugged and headed to the shack.

"Please, please, one more question. How should we leave?"

"You came over the fence?" she called, slowing down.

"Yes."

"Go back that way."

"Thank you. Ma' Alsalam," he said.

She smiled. "Allah Ma'ak. I am learning..." she replied. And then he thought she said, "...the ways of jihad."

* * *

The girl limped out of the gates a few minutes later, halfheartedly straightening the white top and red jacket and picking something from her nylons. Walid trembled. Abdul-Haseeb opened the door as she reached the van. She silently sat.

The van pulled away from the curb and Walid turned to her.

"Were you successful?" she asked softly.

"Yes, Walid replied.

"That is good, no?"

For a moment he wondered if the guard had been right and the girl too eager to spread her legs. Until he noticed the tears flowing from her eyes and cursed himself a million times for what he asked her to do. The girl had remained loyal; she helped them in their moment of need and he would never forget her sacrifice.

"It is very good. Thank you."

"I am happy if you are happy," she replied.

"I will never ask you to do that again."

She looked up and mascara smeared her face, lipstick blotched across her lips. "I want to help you Mr. Walid. You tell me what I need to do. You saved my life."

Allah bless her a million times. He shook from her intoxicating presence, from the miraculous escape with the weapon, for the supportive words of the German policeman, for what was to come.

"Where are we going?" she asked.

"Our next stop is Rotterdam," he replied. As Abdul-Haseeb merged the car onto the highway, Walid realized he never before felt Allah's presence so strongly guiding them on their mission.

Chapter 39

They drove all night, leaving Germany, entering the Netherlands and winding their way along the canals and through the vast windmill farms until they reached the coast.

Abdul-Haseeb drove most of the way, chattering on about Allah's blessing and the miracle of recovering the bomb from the enemy's grasp. Walid related the story of the security guard and how she converted to Islam and that only confirmed the poet's belief that Allah blessed their mission. When he wasn't talking, he scribbled furiously in his book.

Walid didn't disagree, but a general uneasiness spread through his body. He couldn't pinpoint the source but something seemed not right.

The girl saved the mission but she also complicated their journey beyond all measure. From the front seat, he couldn't stop glancing at her, and so when they passed an Arab shop on the outskirts of Amsterdam, he ran inside and purchased a veil.

"Please put this on," Walid said. "I am afraid the police will report you since they are aware of your face." *And more than that.* "You are safe covered."

"Yes, of course," she replied, wrapping the veil awkwardly around her head. She didn't know how to properly secure the covering and none of the other men agreed to help.

Even after her assistance retrieving the weapon, Ali and Abdul-Haseeb remained uncomfortable with her presence. One minute Abdul-Hasaeeb praised her in song, the next he whispered of cutting her neck.

Pray Allah, continue to show me the correct path. So far, he had not been led astray.

"Where do we go now?" Abdul-Haseeb asked. They passed through the outskirts of Rotterdam. In the distance, loomed a tall building and a large bridge with white cables stretching out from the sides like harp strings. Just like the Jew bridge he drove over in Boston prior to boarding the plane. Surely, that was a good omen.

"These roads are impossible to understand," complained Ali. "We are on A16 and should be coming to S125. Take a left there."

"Don't these streets have names?" Abdul-Haseeb complained.

"Just take a left on S125."

Trees lined the one-lane road and wild bushes and grasses grew on the sides. To their right, an endless line of gray, metal train segments rolled in the opposite direction.

"There, take that left," Ali said.

"I see it, I see it," Abdul-Haseeb replied. They traveled down a street lined with three-story brick buildings. To Walid, all of the European cities looked alike: two or three-story brick buildings, gas stations, tree-lined streets, and women walking around without any coverings. That would change. In the future, all women would dress modestly, except the indifel sabayas. He sighed, disgusted at the practice but mindful that sex slaves kept up the morale of young jihadis.

The van crossed a canal and Ali pointed to the left. Turning, they passed through a series of brick buildings and emerged into an open area beside the water. Smaller boats lined the sides of the waterway. Enormous tankers floated in a row, like camels at a watering hole.

"We're looking for port number five."

They passed port number fifteen and traveled two more minutes before the chicken truck stopped in front of gray ship the size of one hundred whales, with the words Marianna printed in faded letters on the side.

"This is the boat," Walid said. "This will take us across the ocean."

"Is it big enough?" Abdul-Haseeb asked.

Walid understood the boy didn't relish the prospect of crossing the ocean but jihad required sacrifice. "It is big enough. Think of all the poems you can write," Walid replied and Ali chuckled. All of them had smiled more with Hassan gone. Walid looked forward to a week with the girl on the boat. He would spend the time teaching her about Islam.

They exited the van and he directed Abdul-Haseeb and Ali to carry the weapon. A rusted ramp with chain link railings led up. He took a deep breath, inhaling the smell of the sea, fish, seaweed, plankton, salt.

If the desert was his first love, the sea was his second. As a boy, he had visited Dubai several times on vacation with his family and he had loved running up and down the sandy beaches with his brother Faisel. Walid remembered peering out into the ocean and trying to spot Doha, which lay a hundred miles across the waters. The sea birthed sand, which fed the deserts. It all connected in a way that Walid found extremely comforting.

They reached the top of the ramp. Walid peered onto the boat, taking in the long deck and the small metal cabin which sat ten feet to their right. The Mariana mainly transported electrical parts between Europe and North America.

"Hello," he called out.

A man mopping the deck peered at them. "Down below," the man shouted, pointing at the cabin.

"I think he wants us to go down below," Ali said.

"I'm not an idiot, Ali," Walid said angrily. "Let's go." They entered the cabin and took a set of stairs down into the boat, their shoes clanging against the metal. They reached a hall and Walid directed them left, following the sound of voices. Turning a corner, they came to a partially open door. Walid ducked his head to avoid banging into a low metal beam and entered the room. Two men with thick, dark mustaches sat around a table eating a meal of bread and some dried meat.

"I am looking for Captain Salvatore," he said.

"You Walid?" one of the men asked.

Walid nodded.

"Welcome aboard the Mariana!" He rose and stuck out his beefy hand. "Come, sit down and have some food!" he bellowed. He studied each of them. "Who's she?"

"Our fourth passenger."

The captain shook his head. "No, she is your fifth passenger. I was told there would only be four."

"Captain," Walid responded, "there are only four of us."

Just as he spoke a toilet flushed at the opposite end of the room.

"You have him," said the captain.

"Who?" Walid asked, completely perplexed and now on guard in case the crew planned to betray them. How could they flee, trapped in the bottom of a tanker? Mustafa had assured him the captain was trustworthy.

The door opened and Walid reached for his gun before confusion turned to sheer disbelief.

"Hello, Walid," said Hassan. The American barbarian flashed a smile, displaying his perfect white teeth. "It looks like I beat you to the boat."

Chapter 40

The chopper wasn't ready in five hours or even ten, and the repairs stretched into the night. The wind picked up the next morning, turning the tranquil ocean into an angry sea. Aminah spent much of the time with Hani, trying to ignore naseau, playing checkers, and gleaning snippets of the girl's life with Fist of Allah.

Hani described captives forced to dig their own graves to psychologically break them (regardless of whether they were killed or not), long months spent in damp caves in the mountains, and men and women dying from lack of medicine. Most of Imaad's inner circle rarely stayed with him, communication was mostly done via personal courier, and the group feared slipping into irrelevance. The girl's information confirmed much of what Aminah already suspected. She shuddered as Hani described the group's operations in such a matter-of-fact manner. Aminah marveled at how well adjusted Hani seemed despite the harsh conditions of her childhood.

Still the repairs were not complete and Aminah did her best to remain calm, pacing, biting her fingernails, and staying with Hani. Ambrose is already in action, she reminded herself.

Zeke joined them for a few games during the day. He smiled at times, a wrinkle or two fading or at least lightening. His mood seemed to brighten around Hani.

Throughout the day and into the next night, the boat pitched roughly back and forth, reminding her of being on a see-saw as a girl, up and down, up and down. Unlike a see-saw though, she couldn't jump off or stop the motion, and she ran into the bathroom three times over the course of the day and twice at night. She promised herself never to take a cruise or set foot on a boat again.

Unable to sleep, she rose, rode the elevator down, and found Patric eying a screen.

"Have you seen Zeke?" she asked.

"In his room," Patric replied, his eyes remaining focused on the screen.

"Thanks."

"Welcome."

She walked down another hallway, descended a set of stairs. Her body had healed a great deal over the last two days and manueving up and down the ship was not much easier. She rapped on a metal door. No answer.

"Zeke, I know you're in there." She knocked again, the lock clicked, the door opened.

"What?" Zeke asked, his hair a spiked mess, eyes bloodshot. Papers lay strewn across the room, a computer monitor rested on a simple wooden desk.

"I couldn't sleep and needed to take a walk."

"So you decided to come and disturb me?"

"*Sorry*, I guess that was a mistake. I'll leave now."

"No, wait, I'm sorry. Would you like to come in?" He opened the door wider, revealing a spartan room: the desk, a single bed on a metal frame, and a night table with a lamp and a book. A picture of Rachel and Sam in a pile of colorful leaves lay perched on the table.

"I can't stop thinking about the bomb," Aminah said.

"You spoke to Ambrose, right?"

"Yes."

"Then I'm sure he's on it."

"Yes, but..."

"But what?"

"Something feels off. He wasn't himself."

"Well, I'd be suspicious of him after what happened in Pakistan. But you seem to think he's the second coming of Jesus. We'll have the chopper ready tomorrow and then you can return to the States. Don't worry about what you can't control."

"John used to tell me the same thing."

"Wise man."

What are you working on?" she asked, changing the subject. She didn't expect him to answer or share any details.

"I'm trying to refine my model."

"Your financial model?"

"Yeah, sort of. The model has evolved in the last two years. It didn't work correctly during the airplane hijacking so I'm trying to improve the algorithim."

"But you made *a lot* of money."

"I got lucky. The model didn't predict or account for the airline hijacking. If it had, I might have been able to save Rachel and Sam."

"You can't build something that will predict the future."

"No, but I can build something that recognizes signs and clues and flags them better. I should have known the hijacking would happen. Most economists say that an unexpected event, a Black Swan, can't be predicted. I disagree."

She'd heard of the term. "I don't think what you want to do is possible."

"Exactly, Aminah!" he said. "The *experts* say it's not possible. But who are the experts? Who made them experts? Most don't know shit. I've analyzed thousands of past events and there is always a clue, a signal before every Black Swan. The telephone call preceded the hijacking. A rising level of credit default swaps and a divergence between home prices and household incomes appeared before the financial crisis of 2008. People overlook the signals, often on purpose. Don't believe the fucking experts because they often don't know as much as they think, and that's even worse than knowing nothing at all."

"Ah, ok," she replied, not fully understanding the financial terminology and jargon.

He continued on and Aminah realized he wanted to talk about his work.

"Anyway, if I can identify this X variable, the signal, I can predict a future Black Swan event. I'll be able to spot and prevent future catastrophes. The E you found might be an X variable and that's why it's so important."

"Sure," she said.

"That's how everyone responds."

"No, no, I find the discussion fascinating." Sort of, if she could understand his explanation.

"Zeke, do you believe in God?" she asked. The question seemed important, significant although she didn't exactly know why. Perhaps Aminah just wanted to understand Zeke and the path he took better.

"No. Why should I? Look what it's done for me."

"That's religion, not God."

"Religion, God, it's all the same."

"But faith makes us stronger. Faith in a better future. Faith can provide strength."

"If you want to believe in that, fine," he said. "I've seen no evidence of a God. The exact opposite in fact. And I don't care about the future. I care about today. We make our own destiny. No fate, no coincidence."

He lived such a rational life.

"Did you believe before the hijacking?"

He scowled and locked eyes. "No, I lost that belief long ago."

"How?"

He didn't answer and turned back to his computer. Dismissed.

A flutter returned to her belly and she edged towards the door. "I think I better leave," she said, as the naseau deepened and intensified. "Sorry to run," she called, sprinting down the hallway, frantically searching for the bathroom, and making it just in time.

* * *

Finally, on the third day, Aminah peered out on a calm ocean, the sun sparkling off the water, a few wispy clouds high in the sky. She lightly touched the wound on her face. No pain.

Time to get home.

"Yes," she said aloud, looking into the mirror and seeing the pinkish scar, "today we will go."

One hour later, after eating a farewell meal of eggs and hash browns cooked by Luis, she arrived on the deck.

"Aminah, be very careful. There is more going on here then we understand." Zeke said.

"I know," she said curtly, tired of listening to lectures and wanting to get underway. "Ambrose has probably already found the bomb," she said.

"Maybe," Zeke said, but he looked skeptical.

"You doubt everything, Zeke. Are we ready?" She felt a bit bad for being so brusque but she just wanted to get off the boat and on her way.

"Call me once you make contact with Ambrose."

"Are you still going to see Lilly?"

"Yup."

"And you're bringing Hani with you?" The young girl had insisted on sleeping in Zeke's room the previous night and although Aminah lectured her on proper etiquette, the girl hadn't relented, sleeping in a cot squeezed in beside his bed. So much for modesty. Now Hani remained glued to Zeke's side as if afraid he would leave her alone and break his promise.

"I promised her," he said and Hani nodded solemnly.

"It's a bad idea."

"Duly noted," Zeke replied.

She couldn't afford to fight every battle. "Keep her safe."

"Of course," he replied.

The helicopter shook to life as the rotors slowly spun.

Aminah hugged Hani. "Be careful," she whispered.

"Shukran," Hani replied in Arabic, hugging her back. "Aminah," the little girl said, "please stop the bomb. I would feel pain forever if I caused all of those people to be dead."

"Hani, it wll never be your fault," Aminah said. "They used you and your gifts. But I'm going to stop it," she replied. "I'm going to tell people who will make sure no one dies."

Hani nodded solemnly.

"Goodbye, Zeke," Aminah said, unsure if she should give him a hug or not. Finally, too tired and irritated to care, she gave a small wave of the hand. "Good luck."

"I don't rely on luck," he said.

Cocky bastard. She hoped his boasting was warranted "Until we meet again, then."

"Hopefully we won't have to pluck you out of the terrorists' grasp next time. Stay safe."

"You don't need to send Masada with me. I'll be fine."

Zeke scowled. "Never assume anything," he replied. "Go!" he yelled over the whoosh of the blades as he held onto his cap. He backed away from the helicopter while Patric and another man led them to the doors and in. She buckled herself into the seat beside Masada. In front, an older man with short cropped hair fiddled with knobs and made some notations on the clipboard.

"Good luck!" Patric shouted before the doors slammed shut.

A second later the helicopter lifted off. As they rose into the sky, she watched Zeke, Hani, and Patric follow the chopper from the deck, shielding their eyes from the morning sun. The helicopter veered away, turning the Vengeance into a small speck on a vast expanse of shimmering blue.

Part III
The Fall

Chapter 41

The sleek jet turned and dipped, like a graceful eagle diving downward. The intercom clicked on.

"We've begun our descent and we'll be landing at Washington Municipal Airport in about thirty minutes," said the captain.

He had welcomed Aminah and Masada onto the plane ten hours earlier. The whole takeoff had been quick and efficient. In the door, buckle, taxi, and go.

She hadn't exchanged a word with Masada the entire trip. The Israeli sat in the row behind her and whenever Aminah got up to stretch or use the bathroom, she found her bodyguard sleeping. So she was a bit surprised when Masada came up to her holding a bag from Harrods.

"Put this on," she said simply and thrust the bag into Aminah's arms. Inside were a pair of expensive-looking, pinstripe, navy blue pants and a matching jacket. A v-neck blouse sat at the bottom.

Aminah changed at her seat. The suit fit perfectly, the expensive designer wool hugging her body and she wouldn't have minded taking a peak in a mirror, but no luck. All dressed up and no one to see, except Masada, and the Israeli was hardly an audience.

Aminah worked through the logistics required to get her measurements, send the info to London, purchase the suit, and drop it at refueling airport in Iceland. Only an organization with a global logistics system could accomplish the feat in such a short period of time.

She felt a hard card in her suit-jacket pocket and pulled it out. Her picture appeared on the front of an employee badge under the name Amelia Barrau. She worked at Spinnaker Investments, Zeke's financial company.

While Masada changed, Aminah couldn't help but sneak a peak at the Israeli and sighed at the lean arms and well-toned legs. A gruesome looking scar started below her ribcage and ran across her belly.

The Israeli caught her stare but said nothing. Cool customer. Masada zipped her pants, pulled on her jacket, and straightened the white shirt with a swift brush of her hands.

"You look great," Aminah said.

Masada returned a weak smile. Totally unfriendly.

"Did you want to come with me?"

The woman shrugged. "You ask such an American question. Does it matter what I want? I do what I am asked. When I need to rescue and protect Arabs like you, I do the job."

Bitch. The plane dropped and bounced.

The captain's voice came over the intercom, "We've got a bit of turbulence for the descent. Please take a seat and we'll be on the ground shortly."

Aminah steamed. Bin Gaudi labeled her a traitor to her people and as if to confirm his accusations she sat with a Jew, one who probably relished shooting Palestinians by the dozen.

Was Bin Gaudi right?

Bin Gaudi wanted to kill her.

But only because you wouldn't help him with the information he desperately needed.

She watched the terrorist saw off David's head. He was a psycopath.

She didn't care to be shadowed by the Israeli though, and once they arrived in D.C., Aminah would dump her faster than last year's Manolo Blanc shoes.

A small landing strip cut into a canopy of green trees appeared below them. The plane tilted to the left and aligned for a landing.

Who could she trust? She left the United States confused and returned with even more questions. John might still be alive and Fist of Allah planned to detonate a nuclear weapon in

New York. OCT compromised. This had gone far beyond her payscale. She needed to speak to Ambrose and get word to the President.

The plane's wheels touched down.

There was only one problem: she had tried calling Ambrose several times since they left The Vengeance and it had gone right to voicemail.

Chapter 42

Walid and Ali stared down at the weapon. The warhead was about two feet long and encased in a smooth, silver metal housing. A keypad and three small buttons sat on one side. Back in Khazakstan, they had transferred it to a specially made steel case lined with foam padding to absorb any shocks, but the material had been left in the van. Curse Hassan! Not that it would detonate spontaneously. As Ali had pointed out, these weapons were designed not to self-detonate. But it was Russian, so you could never be sure.

"Can you put a timing device on it?" Walid asked. Ali looked at him oddly. Since they had left Rotterdam, Ali's sea-sickness became progressively worse, and the storm only deepened his misery.

The Doctor nodded and burped. "It could be done. I'd need the parts though. Why?"

"Sheikh Imaad and almost all of the leadership are gone," Walid explained. "If we are called to Allah, who will be left to lead the war? Who will run the Caliphate when the uprising occurs?"

"Praise Allah, Sheikh Imaad made it clear this was to be a martyrdom operation."

He didn't need to be lectured by Ali. Be patient, he needed the man. "Yes, but Sheikh Imaad didn't think he would be gone. There is no one left. No one to lead the banner of Allah, to rebuild."

In Frankfurt, brave men who once held no fear cowered like frightened children. Fools! How could the world be rebuilt with men of such little faith? The weapon might do little other than stir up a hornet's nest if someone didn't survive to carry on Jihad.

"Hassan will never accept that decision," Ali responded.

Hassan's arrival on the boat shocked him. While he detested the man, Walid couldn't ignore the American's craftiness. He still didn't understand how the Barbarian managed to arrive in Rotterdam before them. How had Hassan gotten out of jail? Hassan displayed no anger at his abandonment, making Walid even more suspicious. He kept a wary eye on the American.

"No decision has been made," he said. "But could you build a timing device?"

"Yes," Ali replied, looking like he wanted to ask a question. Instead, he vomited onto the floor.

* * *

Walid thought about knocking, but hearing no sound, pushed the door open slightly and let a sliver of light into the room. He knew he shouldn't have entered but he brushed the doubts away. The girl slept, silken hair fanned out on the pillow, smooth face at peace, long eyelashes closed. He watched for a moment and as he turned to go, her eyes fluttered opened, like shades being opened on the ocean. He could drown staring into those eyes.

"Hello," she said, rising from her bed.

"I'm sorry to wake you." He placed the tray beside her mattress– an apple, two slices of bread, and a glass of water.

"I was just resting. Thank you." Reaching out a shivering hand, she took the apple. A heavy, moist cold clung to them in the hold of the tanker. He watched her eat the apple, lovely lips parting, blue eyes blinking.

She finished and placed the core into a trash bag near her bed. "I want to thank you again. You are a kind man," she said in passable English. "You saved my life."

"As you did mine."

She nodded and held out her hand. "My name is Anna. Anna Katrinka."

"Anna," he repeated, delighted by the motion of his tongue as he spoke her name. In the West, men and women touched, clasped hands, hugged. He had done that once a lifetime ago with Mouna. Walid wanted to reach for her hand, feel the warmth of her skin, but he managed to fight that impulse. His blood boiled.

"I'm sorry," she said, withdrawing her hand. "I didn't expect to live. I expected Ivan to kill me. And then I expected you to kill me. Perhaps you still will."

"How did you meet Ivan?"

She sighed. "I grew up poor. My father worked in a factory and at days end, he would get drunk, come home and beat me and my sister. I left my house at fifteen to escape and went to Moscow. I had no money, or friends. I met Ivan Kupchak one night at the museum where I would go to stay warm. He ran a company for the government and lived in a nice house. He drove an expensive car. He bought me jewelry, fancy cars, food. I slept in a bed."

Satan's curse, Walid thought.

"But Ivan was like an animal. One day, I came home from shopping and Ivan and two friends sat in the living room. He told me to get naked. I didn't want to."

Just like I told you to distract the men. He cursed himself.

Her trembling increased and he wanted nothing more than to take her in his arms and provide warmth and comfort. But doing so was forbidden between two unmarried people. He shouldn't even be talking with her alone.

She continued. "He held a gun to my head and told me to take off my clothes. He said he owned me, and I would do as he ordered. I took off my clothes and then the three of them took turns with me the entire night."

How could she speak of such depravity? He experienced such sickness walking through Times Square, watching the women flaunt their bodies like prostitutes, eying the gays and homosexuals prancing about, fleeing the kisses and hugs, and grabs of the young. The West spewed forth an endless stream of filth and perversion that threatened to choke the world. And if a society resisted, tanks, planes, and bombs forced compliance. Walid's ears burned at the degradation she described.

Tears streamed down her face. "Every weekend he brought more men and women. If I left, he would kill me. One morning, I woke up strapped down to a table. In the middle of the night, he hired a doctor to come and put the tracker in my arm. He owned me. If he tired of my company, he would give me to Boris, a friend of his who ran a prostitution ring. I did not care anymore. I was already his whore. I tried to escape, twice. He found me, brought me back, beat me, raped me."

She spoke in a soft whisper, head down, eyes staring at the cold metal floor. "He took me to Poland and I realized he would kill me or sell me to Boris. He no longer touched my body; he no longer spoke to me. One evening while he slept, I left. I expected to die and then I found your van."

His mouth tasted sour as he listened to her tale of defilement. Perhaps he made a mistake thinking Allah put her on his path. Surely someone in Allah's good graces would not be so degraded.

Disgusted, confused, he rose to leave. *Hadn't he asked the same of her though? Hadn't she given her body to help the mission?*

Yes, he told himself, but she is not a Muslim. He had no choice.

"I can see that you are a religious man."

He nodded.

"Can your religion make a broken person whole again?"

To tell such a story required courage and Allah rewarded internal strength. What if Allah required him to put her back together? This beautiful woman had been savagely broken, and perhaps she had come to him as another test.

He chose his next words carefully. "Through Allah, you can achieve whatever you desire."

"What do you say in Islam before you eat?"

"There is no prayer for food. We pray at certain times instead. Five times a day."

She took a small bite of her bread. "When is the next prayer period?"

He glacnced at his watch. 12:17 p.m."There is always a time to pray to almighty Allah. Now would be the time of the (Salatu-z-Zuhr), The Noon Prayer."

"Would you show me?"

"Only a Muslim may do the prayer."

She nodded and paused before taking another bite, as if trying to digest a particularly difficult thought.

"What?" he asked.

"No, it is nothing?" she replied, head cocked to the side. It looked adorable.

Did she wish to convert? Could it be possible? His stomach tightened, the flutter returned.

Other members of Fist of Allah coerced their captives to convert. He did not agree, for only someone who took Islam willingly truly held Allah in their heart.

"Tell me, it is okay, I promise you on Allah. Ask me whatever you would like." He envisioned her wrapped in a black hijab, blue eyes peering out, a wisp of blond hair extending beyond the head covering.

"If Islam is such a religion of peace, as you say, then why do you wish to kill so many people?"

He sucked in his breathe, struggled to rein in the impulse to strike her in the face. So she knew. The woman was not a fool. Hadn't he sworn to Allah that he would not grow angry at her question? She scurried towards the back of the bed and her timid reaction deflated his anger.

"Peace is not submission," he sighed. "If Ivan hits you, do you not have the right to hit back? If Ivan seeks to kill you, do you not have the right to strike him first? If the Western world seeks to occupy Muslim lands, violate its people, demean our culture and religion, do we not have the right to strike back?"

"I knew a girl once," he continued, exploring memories he shut out for so long. "We were engaged to be married. You remind me of her in some ways. Anyway, we traveled to her brother's wedding in Iraq to celebrate and an American missile struck the wedding hall. I was outside having a smoke, but my future bride, she..." Ana nodded and gently squeezed his arm, totally innapropriate but also comforting. Sharing with the girl drew out the pain, as if sucking poison from a snake bite.

"What was her name?" Anna asked.

"Mouna."

"It is a pretty name."

"She was a beautiful person," Walid replied. He dreamed often back then of a different life: children, travel, exploring, growing old together—laughter. Mouna had once planted a small peach tree in a patch of dirt near Disla Street.

"When we are older, we will eat the fruit," she had laughed, wiping the dirt from her hands, smearing some on her cheek.

He trembled, pain crawling back into his hollow heart. Anger ignited.

"I am just one person with one story of loss. For every one Westerner who has been killed by Muslims, one-hundred Muslims, no one-thousand Muslims have died at Western hands. The West, the United States take our oil, defile our lands, destroy our culture, rape our women. Yet, we are expected to sit still and do nothing. Islam is a religion of peace, but not of passivity. We are not sheep to be led to the slaughter!" he shouted.

She sat quiet, expressionless. Panting, he reined in the anger and forced himself to relax. Anger often led him to bad places.

He spoke nothing of Sheikh Imaad's dream of a worldwide Umma, a world under Sharia law. She would not understand the obligation of every Muslim to spread the true word, by force if necessary.

"You have suffered greatly. I am sorry about your fiance," she finally replied.

He shrugged. "Allah willed it." Did he really believe that?

"I have another question for you?" she asked. "How does one become a Muslim?"

Was she really serious or just asking the question to curry favor? Did it matter?

"One must recite a line, giving oneself to Allah, the almighty."

She said nothing else and he eventually rose and exited the room.

* * *

He turned the corner and nearly bumped into Hassan. The American sneered.

"What are you doing with the girl?" the Barbarian asked, voice laced with contempt.

"What I do is no business of yours."

"Others are talking about it. They say you are in love with her."

"Who?" Walid raised his fists. "Who dares to speak those words about me? The girl saved my life. She helped us get the bomb back after you lost it!" he yelled. "She has done nothing to jeopardize our mission. It is your fault she is even with us!" he said, throwing the words back into Hassan's face.

Hassan stood his ground. "What will you do once we reach the United States? The girl will try to escape like she did with those Russians. She is a whore who will say anything to buy more time."

"Do not speak about her in that way!" he shouted. As he reached for the knife on his belt, Ali appeared and walked towards them.

"Watch your words," Walid hissed to Hassan as Ali approached.

"She will ruin everything," Hassan replied and walked off.

Chapter 43

The plane landed at the airport. Aminah, with Masada shadowing her, walked to the parking lot where a black, Chevy Suburban sat parked. Masada opened the driver side door, reached under the floor mat, and drew out a key. The Israeli walked around to the back, pulled open the rear door, pulled out a large duffel bag, and gave it an affectionate pat.

"What's inside?" Aminah asked.

"Insurance," she said. "Ready to go?"

"Insurance?"

Masada ignored her and climbed into the truck. "Let's go," she called out.

The longer she was tied to the hip with Masada, the more dangerous the trip would become. Why did Zeke think this was a good idea? Ambrose would not approve.

Seeing no other option for the moment, Aminah climbed into the passenger's seat. Masada started the SUV and they exited the airport, following signs to Route 66 and Washington D.C.

"We take that road." Aminah pointed to the onramp for RT66. Heavy traffic greeted them on the highway. Silence fell over the car.

Surprisingly, the Israeli broke it. "You are from Lebanon?"

"Yes, I left as a young girl."

"Have you visited? It is a beautiful country," Masada said.

"Not recently. I'd like to go again someday."

"Have you ever been to Israel?"

"No."

"Well, you must know that many Arabs live in Israel."

"Do you have any Arab friends."

"I used to. No longer."

"What happened?"

"I died. And when I died, those relationships died with me."

What the hell did that mean?

"And you blame Arabs and Muslims? We are your enemy?"

"If that was true, you would be dead. We would have left you to your Arab friends who loved you so much. There are many Arab Jews in Israel. My aunt married an Arab. We do not hate Arabs or we would hate ourselves."

"You rescued me because you needed me," she said defensively.

"Needed you for what?"

Aminah couldn't give an answer.

"The Jews just want to live in peace. But no matter where we go someone wants to kill us," she said angrily. "They killed us in Europe so they gave us a little piece of broken down land in the Middle East. Now the Arabs want to kill us. They can't do it with their army, so they try blowing us up. The world is never happy until every Jew is dead. That is why I fight. You are an Arab, you have an entire kingdom, lots of land, hundreds of millions of people. The Jews live on a little piece of land. Just a few million people. But still you want to kill us. We just want to be left alone," Masada said bitterly.

Aminah thought of Uncle Fares. "I had an uncle who lived in Southern Lebanon, in the Bekka valley. He grew tomatoes, carrots, oranges, produce that he shipped all over the world. He wasn't political; he didn't care to fight anyone.

"After several skirmishes along the border, the Israelis bulldozed the farm, pulled out the trees, destroyed his crop. They never paid him, never apologized, never helped him recover. He died two years later, poor and heartbroken."

"And who is to blame for that? The Israelis or the militants who used his land to launch attacks?"

These discussions gave her a headache. They became circular in logic, impossible to determine right from wrong.

In the distance, Aminah spotted the Capitol dome and to its right the Washington Monument. She directed Masada to take the Rosslyn exit. Large apartment buildings lined the highway, home to government bureaucrats and office workers.

"Park there." She pointed to a spot at a Roy Rogers. "It's in the shade." The Israeli complied. Aminah chose the location because the overhanging trees blocked the view of the restaurant entrance.

"I need to use the restroom, I'll be right back."

Masada nodded.

Perhaps the Israeli dating scene worked differently and Masada had never used this trick. Or perhaps Masada never dated. Either way, Aminah exited the car, walked to the front of the restaurant, and feigned going in. When she was sure she was out of site, Aminah ran across the street and into the Rosslyn subway station. Heart pounding, she raced down the escalator and pushed aside a kid wearing long shorts and headphones.

"Hey, what the fuck!" he yelled.

"Sorry!"

Huffing at the bottom off the long descent to the station, Aminah unclipped the Timex from her wrist and chucked it into a trashcan. She didn't need to be followed by an Amazon Israeli in her own country.

A few minutes later, the lights on the station platform blinked as a Metro train approached. The car whooshed to a stop, passengers flooded out. She jumped in and walked to the back of the car. The train lurched forward, leaving the station behind. At any moment, she expected the Israeli to pop up from behind a seat or walk through the door from an adjacent car, glowering in anger, but she never appeared.

Aminah checked her phone, but no new message or texts from Ambrose. Where was he? She tried to relax and stop her hands from shaking.

Chapter 44

Aminah glanced nervously back as she walked the long escalator out of the bowels of the Vienna Metro station. Built as a bomb shelter during the Cold War, the station lay deep underground. Sunlight warmed her face as she reached the cab stand and stepped into the first car in line.

She inputted the address into her phone and the self-driving cab pulled away from the curb. The car traveled through the tony suburbs of Fairfax County, home to politicians, lobbyists, members of the military, and government consultants. Ambrose lived close to Mount Vernon, and she sometimes found her boss walking the grounds, looking for whispers of advice from Washington's ghost. Ambrose was weird that way.

They crossed the George Washington Memorial Parkway and the cab turned off at Exit 4. All seemed normal: a man texted while driving, diners twirled pasta inside an Italian restaurant, a boy and girl laughed at some joke. The sun warmed her face through the window. Worldwide disaster didn't seem possible on such a normal day.

The cab entered a residential neighborhood, took a few more turns, and parked in front of a large, brick house with four pillars in the front—a Georgian colonial.

She exited the car, walked to the door, and rang the bell. No answer. She rang again and waited. Still no answer. Aminah pushed the latch and to her surprise the door swung open. She stepped into the house.

"Hello," she called out. "Stephen, Mary?"

"Come in," said a male voice from upstairs. "I'm in the office."

Relieved, she walked in and started up the stairs. Aminah had visited his house before for work and social calls and knew the layout. She walked down a large corridor, took a left, and saw the door to his office half-open. Light streamed into the hallway.

Peering into his office through the glare, she spotted him sitting at his computer. "Stephen, thank God you're here." A weight lifted from her chest. "What's happening with the nuke? Were you able to find it?" As she entered the office, the glare receded.

He swiveled around. "Hello, Aminah. It's good to see you again. I was starting to get worried," a familiar voice said.

Shocked, she steadied herself against the wall.

"John?" she whispered, hardly able to breathe, chest heavy, windpipe nearly shut.

A beer gut and a slight double chin marred his once iron-man body, and his face appeared pale without the perpetual tan he usually had from outdoor activities, but there was no mistaking the handsome features and killer smile.

"Hello, Ami."

She wanted to run over and grab him, hug him, kiss him, but something in his demeanor stopped her.

"You're alive."

"Yes," he said. His voice sounded cool, uncertain but she detected a slight quiver.

"How?"

"That's not important now."

"Bullshit! Of course it's important."

He made a face and Aminah realized the last couple of weeks had changed her, toughened her. She liked the feeling.

"I've spent the last year looking for you. I thought you were dead. We all thought you were dead."

He smiled and for a minute it was the old John, eyes glinting, lips pulled back into a wide grin. "We've all been through a lot, Aminah. Soon it will be over. What happened to your face?" he asked.

"What's almost over?" she inquired, ignoring his question.

"The running, the hiding, the terrorist threat."

"Did Ambrose tell you about the nuke?"

"Yes."

"Where is he? Why are you in his house?"

"He's turned. I was hoping you might know his location. He killed Mary and fled. Ambrose betrayed you to Fist of Allah in Afghanistan. He's been helping them bring the bomb into the country. I came here to look through his computers."

"That's not possible. Stephen wouldn't do that; he wouldn't betray me; he wouldn't kill Mary," she said, voice cracking. Her head spun.

John smiled sympathetically. "I know, it's tough to digest. The old codger had a bit more going on than we thought."

"Ambrose wouldn't do any of this. You know that, John. Why?"

"Who knows? Maybe the pressure got to him. Or maybe it was the affair he had been having for five years. Maybe he needed the money."

"A woman? Money? Did he receive any money for what he did?" None of this made any sense. "Stephen would never cheat on Mary. He loved her. He wouldn't kill her," she said, beginning to cry again.

"Aminah, I realize how close you were to Stephen. I can imagine the shock. What's important right now though is that we are safe," John continued. "We found the bomb and we will find Ambrose and end this nightmare. Okay? We've survived worse," he said, opening his arms.

Aminah walked forward and slid into his embrace. As much as she thought she missed John, she missed him even more: the feel of his arms around her, the faint scent of pine from his aftershave, the sexy timbre of his voice. His head titled forward and their lips connected, electric, hungry.

"John, I've missed you," she sighed.

"I've missed you also, Ami," he said. His fingers traced her back, moved to her breasts before she pushed them away.

"Not here."

"Ami, I need you."

"Later, not now." She enjoyed the warmth of his body.

"Sure. I understand," he said cooly, pulling back and smoothing his hair.

"John, what's wrong?" she asked, but a warning bell rang deep in her amygdala.

"Who told you about the bomb?" John asked, back to business.

"Zeke Katz. He's been hunting the terrorists." He didn't reply, so she continued talking to fill the silence. "I sat in on the interrogation of Bin Gaudi, a high-level member of Fist of Allah. The group used Zeke's ransom money to purchase the weapon," she said.

"From whom?" John asked.

"Someone in the Russian military," she answered.

"Where is Katz now?"

Why did he care about Zeke?

"He's on his way to Texas to meet with Lilly Broadhurst."

"Why is he meeting with her?"

"John, where did you find them with the bomb?" she asked. Some intuition told her to redirect the conversation.

"The Europeans stopped them in Rotterdam last night." John strummed his fingers and tapped his foot which she recognized as signs of a lie. A feeling, like having an endoscopy without anesthesia began to uncoil in her gut. Aminah's body stiffened and she tried to hide her surprise and recover her composure. John noticed.

The timing didn't work. The bomb couldn't have been in Rotterdam last night. Even with the new fast transport boats it took four to five days to cross the Atlantic, depending on the weather. By last night, the bomb needed to be close to the North American Atlantic coast if they intended to bring it ashore and detonate it during the President's speech tomorrow.

"You coordinated with the Europeans?" she asked slowly, trying to buy time to think.

"That's all right," John said staring out into the darkening sky. "You were never good at hiding your thoughts from me. It's one reason you never would have made a good field agent.

You're much too transparent. I fucked up your question," he continued. "A nuclear bomb is headed to New York."

Silence filled the room and her heart pounded. Okay, so what about the next part of his statement? Something like: *"and I lied about stopping it but we will."* Why lie? Despite his pretensions about being a blank book, she had also developed the ability to read his face.

"You're not going to stop the nuclear weapon, are you?" she asked.

"No, it's going to detonate tomorrow. It needs to detonate."

"No," she snapped, "My mother, sister and niece live in New York. Nine million other people live in the city. It is not going to detonate."

"You weren't supposed to be involved. But godammit, you wouldn't give up, you wouldn't let it go!" John yelled. He looked close to tears.

"What are you talking about?" she asked.

"We've been planning for over thirty years. This is all part of something much bigger."

Escape! Now! She sprang from the chair but he shot across the desk and grabbed her hands. He came around the side and held her tight against his body.

"Revelations Chapter 16, verse 17. 'And the seventh angel poured out his vial into the air; and there came a great voice out of the temple of heaven, from the throne, saying, It is done And there were voices, and thunders, and lightnings; and there was a great earthquake, such as was not since men were upon the earth, so mighty an earthquake, [and] so great. And the great city was divided into three parts, and the cities of the nations fell: and great Babylon came in remembrance before God, to give unto her the cup of the wine of the fierceness of his wrath.'"

"The destruction of the World Trade Centers started the clock. New York, our Babylon, shall face the wrath, be sundered, and so begin the end."

Since when did John recite bible versus? He claimed to be an atheist and as far as she could remember, had never stepped into a place of worship. A justice of the peace wed them.

"John, I don't know what's gotten into you. Fist of Allah is almost finished. If we stop this bomb, they will be done. This will end the jihadi era."

He stroked her hair and kissed her gently on the neck. She tried to break free but his grip was too strong.

"Let me go, John!"

"You've always been so naive, so willing to believe that everyone can just get along. No," he said, "They will come back. Maybe not Fist of Allah, but it will be another group. Each time it gets worse. They are bent on jihad, on imposing their way upon us. But God has created this moment. It is our test. September eleventh was just the beginning. The airline hijacking was the second. The destruction of New York, of Babylon will be the third."

"For what?" she asked, tears streaming down her face. His hand ran gently through her hair.

"I did miss you. Of all the sacrifices, not seeing you was the hardest. But we have to end it. We have to end the cancer. Nazi Germany wasn't defeated until the country was reduced to rubble. Total capitulation is what it takes to defeat radical Islam."

"Destroying New York isn't going to accomplish your goal," she sputtered, horrified. "You'll just create more anger."

He slowly shook his head. "You understand, I know you do. In Idaho there is a Minuteman intercontinental ballistic missile sitting in its silo. Now, we cannot attack. The lefties and peaceniks hardly let us use force in Afghanistan and Iraq and Syria. They cry every time one of the enemy suffer a casualty. But once New York is destroyed, that will all change. People will understand. They will demand we attack, and this time there will be no mercy. Mecca will be utterly destroyed, rendered uninhabitable for centuries. Islam will be ripped from its roots."

He stopped for a moment and looked down at her.

"They wanted to nuke all of Arabia, but I stopped them. I told them not all Muslims believe in violence and jihad. You taught me that, Aminah," he said, as if she should be thankful. He kissed her again on the neck.

"John, let me go!" she yelled, trying to break free.

He continued, "The sixth fleet is already positioned in the Arabian Sea. The Fifth Mechanized Division has been secretly massing men and material in Iraq. Once Mecca is destroyed, we will invade Saudi Arabia, Kuwait, and the UAE."

"The world will be destroyed," Aminah responded. "The Russians and Chinese will never allow us to take over the oil fields. They need them more than we do now. It will be a world war."

"Precisely. This is what is prophesized. What needs to occur before peace can reign. From the ashes of World War Two arose an order that provided peace for over fifty years. The war to come will be the final act and when Jesus returns the peace will be eternal."

Jesus returns?

"The President will stop you," she said angrily. One could argue with President Rogriguez's policies, but he was a fair, honest man.

"The President will be dead," John replied. "He will be at the United Nations tomorrow, along with almost all of the world's leaders."

"Vison won't let you do this."

This was not be the same man she had married. How could her husband have become a fire-breathing fanatic intent on destroying the world and her faith?

"Vison leads us."

Vison? "No, no," was all she managed to say, tears starting again.

"It is done and decided. Aminah, I'm sorry, I didn't want you to be involved. I love you. You returned to me. When this is over, we can still be together. Vison is impressed with you."

"You love me? If you love me make this stop. Stop the bomb. My mother lives in New York. My sister and niece, your niece. John, I am a Muslim. Do you want to kill people like me. Stop it!"

"I can't."

Aminah yanked her hand and broke his grasp. She rose to flee, turned, and ran into a large, meaty chest.

"Get out of my way!" she cried, beating her fist and kicking her legs to no avail.

"I'm sorry," John repeated like a robot. "If we had more time I could convince you. You would understand. But we don't have that luxury now. When it is done, we'll talk more and you'll realize this is the only way."

"Let me go!" she screamed, biting the arm that bound her. She pulled loose for a moment before a large man with a crew-cut wrestled her onto Ambrose's red Persian rug.

"You're my husband," she tried to say, but the knee in her back made it difficult to speak. They pulled her upright.

"Take her to White Pine," he said. "Through the garage."

"John, no, please!" she pleaded. "I searched for you. I never believed you were dead!" she screamed. "Snap out of this. This is not you!" she sobbed. She tried to flail her arms and wriggle free, but her attempts proved fruitless. They pinned her to the ground, handcuffed her, and covered her mouth and nose with an astringent smelling rag.

Before darkness overcame her, Aminah had the thought that she shouldn't have chucked the Timex into the trash.

Chapter 45

Hani carefully licked the ice cream from the cone, her tongue racing to beat the melt from the hot Texas heat. The liquid cream ran onto her fingers.

"Lick it quickly," he said, "or all of the ice cream will be on the floor."

"I'm trying," she laughed.

"Well, you're doing okay for a first-time ice cream eater."

"This is very delicious," Hani gushed, giving another big lick and smearing chocolate across her face.

He took a napkin and gently wiped her cheeks. The last time he'd done that was with....Sam. He paused for a moment as the memory struck: his son's laugher as Zeke wiped the chocolate mess from Sam's chubby cheeks, the hot summer day strolling down Newbury Street, Rachel browsing the window displays in the stores. They couldn't afford much then but they had each other and the laughter.

"Are you fine, Zeke?" Hani asked.

"Yes, yes," he said, pushing the memories aside. He couldn't afford to let the past interfere but Hani's laughter and youth triggered the memories. He wasn't sure what to do. He should have left her on the Vengeance but he had made a promise. And he liked her company, more than liked. Being with her calmed the fire, allowed him to see the best of the past, and to hear Rachel's voice again.

They strolled down the street in a suburb of Dallas called McKinney. At 10 am, the hot Texas sun hadn't reached full broiling point. He spent a summer in Austin once and remembered the hundred degree temperatures in September.

They reached the Riago, a non-descript, three star hotel and strolled through the lobby to the elevator. Zeke pushed the button for the eighth floor.

"Hani," he said, trying to gauge the best way to continue. "You need to stay in the room today. You can't come with us."

She stopped licking the ice cream.

"No."

"Hani, it's not a request. You need to stay here. I'm not afraid for you," he continued. "If they catch you or manage to do anything to you, I would never forgive myself. It would jeapordize the mission."

"I see," Hani said.

"Do you understand?"

She looked ready to cry.

"You don't want me with you."

The elevator reached the eight floor and the doors opened. They walked into a hallway with a faded green rug and the smell of cold food.

"I brought you on this trip because I do want you with me. I promised. But you can't come to Calico. I don't want anything to happen to you."

"Is Lilly dangerous?"

"She's crazy but I don't think she dangerous. Still, it's better if you stay here."

"You will leave me here and not come back."

"Please," he said. "Leave you here? How could I do that to a girl I'm thinking of adopting."

"Adopting?"

They reached the door to the room, Zeke inserted the card, and the door clicked open. A figure stood beside the door, knife drawn.

"Just me," Zeke called out. Sickli deftly flipped his blade and sheathed it. Zeke liked to see everyone alert.

"Ice cream? Did you bring me any?" Sickli asked in his raspy voice. In a prior life, his torturers had nicked several of his vocal chords.

Aminah giggled. "No, Mr. Sickli."

"Mr. Sickli?" Zeke asked.

"The girl recognizes a gentleman," Sickli said, throwing her a wink.

A door to one of the bedrooms opened and a tall black woman peeked into the room.

"Everyone is so loud," the woman said.

"Time to get up, Adora," Sickli said. "Boss is back and we're getting ready to roll."

Zeke brought Hani back into the hallway.

"Hani, I'm alone and you don't have parents, so, I thought it might make sense for us to work together. We can help each other. But only if this was something you wanted to do. You do not need to agree. In the United States we call this adopting."

"You would do this?" Hani asked, lip quivering.

"Well, only if you thought it was a good idea. We had a good time on the Vengeance and Aminah thinks I need to relax a bit. I thought that after I'm done with Lilly, well, we can move somewhere nice and just be, well, like a family."

Hani wrapped her arms around him and squeezed. 'I always wanted a family. I pray and pray to Allah about this and hope," she said.

"Me too," Zeke said wistfully. "Adora will stay here with you to keep you safe. She's very strong and tough. When I'm back, we will leave and start a new life together. Deal?" he asked, sticking out his hand.

Hani didn't seem to know what to do.

"In America, to seal an agreement, you take my hand," he explained, taking her hand and grasping the palm, "and then you shake like this," he continued, pumping it up and down. "It's called shaking on a deal."

"Then I will shake on that deal," Hani said. "But please, please come back safe." She reached over and gave him another hug.

"That's the plan."

"Thank you, Zeke," Hani said, wiping tears from her eyes.

"No, thank you," Zeke replied.

Chapter 46

The Horn of Jericho Evangelical Church lay forty minutes outside of Dallas, down a dusty, one-lane road, nestled behind a massive, non-descript iron gate. Metallic black crows perched on the iron stakes, their eyes glistening in the sun. Statues with cameras. Like a prison.

He pulled the car up to the intercom mounted on a steel spike.

"How can we help you?".

"I'd like to learn about E," Zeke said.

"What's your name?" came the tinny, disembodied voice.

"Zeke Katz." Silence. "One minute please." Thirty seconds later. "Please drive your car up the roadway." The gate swung slowly open.

"We're in," he said to Sickli.

"Well, you expected that, right," he grumbled.

Zeke drove the black Monte Carlo up a hill. Past the gate, the complex took on the trappings of a small ranch or even an exclusive Texas spa. Cows grazed and two horses meandered through a meadow. Large windows made up the front of the building, and a gold cross sat on the roof, the only overt sign of religion. A circular driveway ended at two enormous glass doors, more fitting on the gates of Oz than a Church. Etched onto each door was the letter E.

The modest church he remembered from his visit with Lilly had been razed and replaced by this palace.

Zeke parked the car and Sickli followed him through the glass doors into a room with high ceilings and plush leather.

"You must be Mr. Katz?" a woman asked with a slight Texas twang. She wore her white hair in a bun and appraised him from behind small, clear framed glasses.

"Yes," Zeke said.

"How can we help you?"

252

"I'm looking for the pastor."

"That would be Reverend Wayne. He's in his study. Please, follow me." Pfft. A small dart stuck out from her neck and the woman gave Zeke a nasty look before falling face first onto her desk.

"She'll be out for the next two hours," Sickli said.

They walked down a tiled hallway and came to two burly men in suits. A plaque hung on the door between them.

"Where will you be when Jesus comes calling?"

Sickli tagged them with darts and they hit the floor.

"Sleep well," Sickli chuckled.

Zeke knocked.

"Yes," came a male voice.

Zeke opened the door and walked in. An older man with a short gray beard and gold rimmed spectacles sat behind his desk, looking very much like a modern day Merlin. Zeke remembered him.

"Hello," the Gandalf look-alike said, looking up. "Can I help you?"

"Hello, Reverand Wayne. Zeke Katz," he responded, moving into the room and taking a seat.

"Zeke Katz! My goodness, what a pleasure to see you," the Reverand said, and he did look genuinely happy.

"Did Maureen let you in?

"Yes, she did. Your bodyguards said I could come in."

"Really?"

"Yup. They're on a coffee break at the moment."

Zeke gazed at the framed pictures on the wall– Wayne with the President, the Vice President, members of Congress, and Hank Broadhurst. On his desk sat a small, blue E.

Wayne shifted in his chair and replaced the frown with a smile. "Zeke Katz, my oh my. It's been awhile. I remember you coming to visit us at our former church with Lilly. I hope you like our new spiritual headquarters?"

"It looks like a prison from the outside."

"Prison, goodness no. Faith must be protected with a fortress. Of course, I must offer my condolences. I was so very sorry about what happened to your wife and child. May God protect them. I hope the Lord's presence comforted you over the past two years." Wayne reclined and stared solemnly at him.

He hated the man's smug look, the pompous attitude of the self-rightous. A flame of anger flared to life.

"The Lord helps those who help themselves," Zeke replied calmly.

Pastor Wayne frowned. "Yes, well, that is one way of looking at it. How are you, Zeke?"

"Busy. I've traveled the world the last two years, looking for answers."

"Yes," Wayne said, "after such a tragic event we all look for some explanation, for something to make sense of the pain. I hope you found some of those answers. Perhaps you are here seeking God's guidance?"

"What does the E signify? I noticed the symbol on the glass doors."

"Ah yes, the E. It is the symbol of this church. In nature, E is one of the God numbers, like pie."

"Euler's number. It's a constant. 2.71828," Zeke recited.

"Yes, exactly. A keen mind like yours must surely grasp that E can be calculated as the sum of the infinite. E is transcendent. Beyond mathematics, when scientists peer into economics, biology, cosmology, physics, and more they find the number." Reverend Wayne adjusted his glasses. "It truly is a God number and surely a sign of the intelligent design of our world and universe. But there is more to it, of course. E is also the first letter in Ezekiel. Are you familiar with Ezekiel 38, Zeke? Perhaps you are since you are named after the great prophet."

Zeke shook his head.

"'Get ready; be prepared, you and all the hordes gathered about you, and take command of them,'" the Pastor boomed in a baritone. "After many days you will be called to arms. In future years you will invade a land that has recovered from war, whose people were gathered from many nations to the mountains of Israel, which had long been desolate. They had been brought out from the nations, and now all of them live in safety. You and all your troops and the many nations with you will go up, advancing like a storm; you will be like a cloud covering the land.'" He stopped and peered at Zeke.

"The passage describes the forces of good preparing its armies for the Armageddon and end of times. The members of the Horn of Jericho believe in the word of God, in Ezekiel's prophecy, and we are dedicated servants of the Lord Jesus Christ." Reverend Wayne strummed his fingers and smiled.

"So this is why you built a fortress? Is the end of times coming soon?"

Wayne nodded. "Are you familiar with those prophecies?"

"Somewhat."

"Good. You'd be wise to learn them. Many don't believe."

"Is the end of times coming?" he repeated.

"Why do you ask?"

"I've done a lot of thinking over the past two years and I've come to the realization the world is not as I thought it was."

Wayne rocked faster, nodded in agreement. The pastor continued energetically. "Many believe that September 11 began the countdown to the end of times. The tragedy at the World Trade Centers began the clash between good and evil prophesized in Ezekiel 38. Events are in motion. War will soon be upon us, paving the way for the resurrection of our Lord and Savior Jesus Christ. Once he has returned, we will be embraced by the Rapture and the living will be reunited with the dead. Heaven will reign on earth and Jesus will rule forever."

Wayne rocked for a moment and flashed him a warm, grandfatherly smile. "I'm so glad the Lord called you to the church, Zeke. Many believe you have an important role to play in upcoming events."

Zeke took a deep breathe to calm his rising anger. "Really?" he asked.

"Yes, yes, of course!" Wayne said, growing more animated. "You are named after the prophet, you are part Hebrew, and you were at the center of the second terminal event."

Zeke nodded and pretended to think. "Lilly Broadhurst is a member of your church?"

"Yes. She brought you here once, didn't she?"

He had visited Lilly while in college twelve years earlier and they came to a service. Lilly didn't embrace religion but her parents forced her to attend church when she came home. He remembered Wayne and the E embossed on the bibles.

"The plane my wife and child flew on was flight number 2718."

"Yes, you see, the number appears everywhere."

"I don't believe in coincidences," Zeke said sharply.

"It is the will of God."

"No, it was not the will of God," Zeke said quietly. Wayne cocked his head and flashed his grandfatherly smile again. *Go ahead, use it; your snake charms won't work on me.*

"I understand your pain, but there's no need to doubt," Wayne said. "Unburden yourself to me. We can help you."

"Reverend, you misunderstand my interest in E and the end of times. God did not plan for my wife and child to die."

"I don't know what you are talking about," Wayne said.

"Yes, I think you do. Zeke strummed his fingers on the desk and picked up the E. "Why was that plane hijacked? Why were my wife and child killed?"

"Your family died a tragic death. I understand your loss and I am sorry for it. But it was God's plan."

"It's always back to God. I'm going to ask you one last time, why were my wife and child killed?"

"I have no idea what you are talking about," Wayne said, growing increasingly agitated. "I believe you need to pray on your actions and seek peace through God. You need help. You've allowed the devil to invade your mind and poison your thoughts. But until you are willing to help yourself, I think you need to leave. I don't want the devil's presence in my church."

Zeke shrugged.

"Owen, Caleb, get in here!" Wayne shouted. His hand pressed something vigorously under his desk. "Get in here!"

The door opened and Sickli sauntered into the room, giving a quick glance at Wayne and looking quite bored.

"They're not coming, Reverend Wayne. I haven't spent the last two years praying to God for peace and serenity or trying to forget what happened to my family.

Sickli reached into his leather jacket and handed Zeke a SOG Seal2000 knife with a gray, serrated, seven inch blade.

Wayne's eyes widened.

"I don't believe a word that came out of your mouth. If there was a God, he'd be ashamed of you. Here's how this is going to work. I'm going to cut you into a hundred different pieces until you tell me about the death of my wife and child and the bomb headed towards New York. So, before I begin, is there anything you would like to say?"

Wayne's mouth trembled.

Sickli grabbed Wayne by the hair and yanked him to his feet.

"Please, I don't know anything. I'm just a preacher."

Zeke slashed the knife and a red line appeared from Wayne's left eye down to his jawline. Blood wept out of the wound.

Zeke felt the anger raging in his body, flowing through his veins, controlling his thoughts and actions. It had been like this back at the foster home when Jack Mumfrey used to beat him and Rack. If they dared resist, the boy's mother, Vicky, would throw them into the basement without food and water for days. He hated the woman and her son. He and Rack got justice in the end, burning down the house in a way that implicated Vicky.

"It's sharp isn't it? You probably don't feel much except the warm blood running down your face. It will start to hurt though, especially, when I begin sawing off your limbs. You have no idea what the death of a wife and child can do to a man. You said you understood my pain. I could cut a thousand times and you wouldn't grasp a tiny fraction of my torment. But we can try to get you close. Sickli, show him your souvenirs."

Sickli reached under his jacket and pulled out a chain threaded through the desiccated flesh of five bony fingers. "The pinkies of each of my kills," Sickli said proudly.

Wayne looked ready to vomit.

"Now, I'm going to ask you one last time, what happened to my wife and child?"

"Babylon must be destroyed. It has been decreed. Revelations Chapter 16, verse 17.

"'And the seventh angel poured out his vial into the air; and there came a great voice out of the temple of heaven, from the throne, saying–'"

Zeke put his hand over Wayne's mouth.

"Okay, that's enough. You knew the plane would be hijacked."

"No."

"And about the warhead headed to New York, to Babylon?"

"He slashed the knife and a second line appeared, intersecting with the other, carving an X on Wayne's forehead.

"No, please, please. Please, believe me. Lilly knows everything. I just provide the scripture, the religious guidance and justification."

"The justification?" Zeke pulled his arm back. A dark emptiness descended.

"Please, no. Don't, please!" Wayne screamed, covering his face with his hands. "I don't know what you are asking me. Lilly knows," he sobbed. "Lilly knows."

With extreme effort, Zeke stopped the knife. *Calm. Control.* He heard Rachel's voice. *"Relax my love. Don't let anger be your guide. Use your mind."*

Zeke tipped the knife. Wayne nodded and tried to staunch the flow of blood with his hand but only succeeded in smearing it across his face.

Chapter 47

Scrub pines and a profusion of purple, blue, and white wildflowers decorated the land on either side of a road that led ruler straight towards Calico, the Broadhurst family ranch. Lilly had told Zeke when he visited that the city built the road just for them. He didn't doubt it.

He visited Calico once before in college. The heiress invited him to the ranch during Spring Break, to show off her home and introduce him to her parents. Because of his budding relationship with Rachel, he hesitated to go, but the prospect of seeing into the life of a billionaire proved too alluring. Fool. Lilly undoubtedly planned the trip to break up his relationship with Rachel.

He met her parents, a senator, and other assorted billionaires, attended church where he met her pastor (who now sat in the backseat with blood dripping down his cheek), picnicked on the ranch and rode a horse. Lilly surprised him by doing a wheelie on her dirt bike. They ate a sumptuous meal in Dallas and attended a black tie ball (she bought him a tuxedo), but as much as Lilly tried he didn't feel any attraction. He couldn't stop thinking about Rachel and four days into the trip, he left, anxious to return to the girl in Boston, not remain with the girl in Dallas.

Memories. Life seemed simple back then, hopeful, full of promise. He rejected the advances of a billionairess and fell in love with the simple girl-next-door. Just like a movie. Except happiness always seemed to squirt out of his hands, like the fish he and Rack used to catch on the Merrimack River. Some people could hold on; he couldn't.

Up ahead, the road ended at a large gate, the word Calico spelled out in steel letters.

He stopped the car and pressed a button.

"Hello," came a voice.

"Zeke Katz to see Lilly."

"Come in," a voice replied as the gate slowly swung open. Texas was a land of gates.

Calico looked the same, an enormous front lawn specked with horses and cows and far back an imposing rock and wood house. If he remembered correctly there were two swimming pools, a fountain, a pond, a greenhouse, a small chapel, and behind the house an eighteen hole golf course designed by Jack Nicklaus.

He drove the car down the long driveway and parked in a spot off the traffic circle in front of the house. A fountain of water cascaded over a naked angel statue, bow drawn, arrow notched.

"Let's go," he said and Sickli pulled Wayne from the car and dragged him to the front door. The reverend remained silent. At the door, Zeke reached out to ring the bell but it opened before he touched the button.

"Hello, Zeke!" came a squeal. Lilly looked exquisite as always, blonde hair perfectly straightened, jeans accentuating perfect curves, blouse revealing a sample of her ample cleavage. His stomach turned.

He wanted to see her beg for her life, to experience fear and helplessness, to suffer for the first time in her life. And then, he'd pump a bullet into that cosmetically enhanced face.

Striking first and fast, she lunged at him and wrapped her arms around his body, pressing her chest into his.

"I'm so happy you've finally come back to Calico," she whispered. "I've missed you, Zeke." Her eyes turned to Sickli and Wayne but she said nothing. "Come in, come in."

Something is wrong. She knew we were coming.

They walked into an expansive room with an intricately shaped glass chandelair suspended from the ceiling. Pieces from Dali, Monet, and Chagall decorated the walls.

"I added a new Miro," she gushed, pointing to a red blob next to a white line and a smaller circle of black on a canvas of cool blue. "It's called the "Flight of the Dragonfly Before the Sun." Do you like it?"

He wrapped his fingers around her neck and slammed her against the painting.

"Fuck your painting, Lilly."

"You're hurting me," she choked.

"Lilly, shut up," Zeke said. He couldn't listen to her for another second. His smoldering anger ignited. With his other hand he reached into his jacket, pulled out his Remington 1911, and pointed it at the billionairre's face.

"So much for chivalry," she croaked, fluttering her eyes.

"Why, Lilly? Why did you help kill Rachel and Sam?"

"Take your hand off my throat and I'll tell you," she whispered.

He released his grip and she gasped for breath.

"That's better. Coming in like a bull with its balls squeezed tight is not going to get a lady to talk," she reproached him.

He pointed the gun at her forehead. "I'm not fooling around," he warned.

"Fine, you should know the answer, Mr. Smarts. For a brilliant guy you are so clueless sometimes. I hated the bitch. She stole the one thing I really wanted in my life."

Surprised at her confession, Zeke struggled to respond. "What was that?"

She frowned. "Silly, Zeke. You really are an oaf. She stole you."

Lilly had a way of making him feel like a poor college kid again with her laugh, her smile, her casual way of dismissing his question.

"So you set her up to be killed?" he said through clenched teeth.

"I actually didn't think she'd die. That wasn't the plan. But I prayed, and for once God listened. I didn't want your son to die, though. I'm sorry about that. But before you kill me, I want to tell you the rest. Reverend Wayne told you some of the story. My father co-founded the Church you just ransacked. Most of the inner-circle believed the destruction of the Twin

Towers confirmed a prophecy about the end of the world. The church became the meeting place for a group dedicated to ensuring the United States emerged victorious from the upcoming Armageddon.

"When he died, I inherited his seat in the circle. I don't believe in end-of-the-world stories, but the E plan became an opportunity to rectify the main wrong in my life. I agreed to fund your project as a way of bringing you into this plan, of bringing us closer. We helped each other."

"No!" he yelled. *Please no.* Rachel warned him about accepting money from Lilly. *"She's a viper. You'll regret taking a dime from her."*

"You were right," he whispered. He'd been so focused on proving his own brilliance he missed the obvious. He studied his hand.

"Before you make a move you might regret, let me show you something," Lilly said calmly, hardly perturbed by the gun pointed at her face. "Jonah, bring our visitor out."

From the far side came a large, blond man and beside him, her arms bound and duct tape over her mouth, walked Hani.

Chapter 48

Aminah opened her eyes. For one second, nothing. Two eye blinks later, a headache hammered her skull, a fullness moved up her stomach, and she gagged. The bile reached the back of her throat before retreating. She shivered.

Her gaze focused on a white ceiling supported by thick wooden beams, silky strands of an old spiderweb draped between them. To her left, an old, brown bureau sat in the corner, an antique mirror perched atop it.

Where am I?

Back on the Vengeance? No. Shackles bound her legs to the bed frame while cuffs and chains immobilized her arms. Bin Gaudi? No. A flash of memory.

John.

John betrayed her. Aminah bit her lip but resolved not to cry. She had survived worse.

What day was it? How long had she been asleep? Please Allah, don't let it be too late to stop the bomb.

She listened but only the occasional bird chirp or creak of the house interrupted the silence.

Aminah jerked her arms back and forth, desperate to see if she could pry herself loose. Realizing the futility, she stopped after a minute. Damn! She wouldn't give up. "Hello," she called out.

Furniture scraped on the floor, foosteps, and then, "Oh shit! Godammn light."

Thurmos?

"Thurmos, is that you?" Aminah called out. A six-foot three man with a big head, close cropped hair, and hazel eyes stepped into the room. She had worked with Tony Thurmond at OCT, gone out for after-work drinks a few times and counted him as a friend. The meaty agent had called after she resigned from the OCT to check up on her.

He rubbed his shin. "Hello, Aminah," he said with some warmth.

"What day is it, Tony? What's the time?" she asked.

"It's the sixteenth," he replied. "Eight fifty-five."

That left only two days to stop the bomb.

"Tony, you have to unlock me! Do you know what John is planning? New York City is going to be destroyed by Fist of Allah! He's working with them."

"They're doing us a favor. Screw New York. Too many Jews, niggers, and queers," he said, stunning her. What? He never spoke like that before.

"No, Tony! Millions will die. My mother, sister and niece live in New York! We can't let this happen. We can't let the terrorists win. This is everything we've worked against. This is not how it's supposed to be," she pleaded.

"Ah, I don't believe in all of that crap John keeps spouting. His brain got a bit fried in the desert. But he's right about the sand niggers. They'll keep coming back and attacking us if we don't finish them off first. They won't be satisfied taking out one city. They want to rule us. Their religion says so.

"No disrespect to you, Aminah. I always thought you were good company. And John does love you but we have to keep you here until everything blows over. It's gonna get rough."

"Listen to me, Tony. The economy will be destroyed. You will lose everything."

"I have everything I need. I don't need to live like the rich in *New York City*," he said.

"There are a lot of not rich people there also."

"My father was a middle-class guy. He worked an office job. One day, his boss called him into a meeting and let him go. They hired a young, black, transgender-something to take his place. She, he, whatever it was, came from New York City. My father never got another good job again. He died ten years later." Thurmos didn't seem mad, just set in his direction. "The country will be better off without New York. The rich there think they can control everyone else and push their ideas on us. Fuck 'em."

This wasn't working.

"Can you at least loosen these cuffs? My arms are aching. And can I go to the bathroom?"

"You promise you won't try to run?

"Where am I going to run?"

"Promise."

"Okay, okay, I promise." Holy crap, John fried Thurmos also. She would run at the first chance she got.

"Come on, I'll take you to the bathroom." He took out a device like a remote car opener and pressed a button, popping the latches on her arms and feet. Aminah took a minute to stretch.

Thurmos nodded his big head towards the hall. "Go ahead."

"Thanks, Thurmos." She faked a smile, stood, wobbled a bit, and stepped into the hallway.

"Go forward and it's on the right," he directed.

She found the door and he began to follow her in.

"Really?"

"Oh, all right, do your thing and come out. I'll be here."

"Thank you." She slammed the door in his face and turned the lock.

"I can break the door down in a second. Don't try anything."

"Of course not. Where am I going to run? We're in the middle of nowhere."

Twenty feet below the window, tall grass obscured the ground. She imagined meaty boulders, or razor sharp rocks waiting to break her legs, shatter her skull, or gut her stomach. She hated heights; just looking through the window made her queasy.

Thirty feet from the house she spotted a dirt road. Thick woods surrounded the house.

"Let's go, Aminah," Thurmos said.

"Coming," she called.

She had to find another way out—and soon.

Chapter 49

Zeke kept the gun aimed at Lilly's face and struggled not to show surprise.

Hani! What was she doing here?

"Who's the girl?" Lilly asked.

"She's an orphan we found in Afghanistan."

Lilly knew they were coming. But who told her? Aminah? No, he considered himself a good judge of character, and couldn't believe she'd betrayed him.

She did betray you. How else could Lilly know?

"Does she mean anything to you?"

"What?" he asked.

"Does she mean anything to you?"

"I brought her to the States as a refugee for adoption. I understand what it's like to lose your family."

"Zeke, put the gun down. I'm tired of having it pointed at my face." He ignored her. "Brian, if Zeke doesn't put the gun down in three seconds, cut off the girl's ear."

A red dot appeared on Hani's face. The little girl stared forward. No emotion.

"Several marksmen are positioned outside just in case you try anything," Lilly added. "I'm actually a bit disappointed you allowed yourself to be caught this easily. But I'll chalk it up to a bad day."

Bitch. He allowed himself to walk right into her trap.

Zeke's calculations failed to include the risk of Hani's abduction, although they did suggest tight security around Lilly. He didn't give her enough credit. He decided to visit Calico with only Sikli to keep her guard down, slip in, and kill her.

Jonah took a knife out of his belt and held the blade to Hani's face.

"One-two-"

Seeing no choice, he lowered the gun.

"Thank you."

Glass shattered and Sickli fell to the floor. Zeke raced to his side and turned him over. Blood seeped from a hole in his eye.

Bitch.

"Sickli, I'm sorry," Zeke whispered before turning to Lilly.

"You didn't need to do that!"

"Calm down, Zeke. You're not giving the orders anymore."

He aimed at her head.

"Go ahead, Zeke, shoot. You might be able to kill me, but maybe not. I don't remember you being much of a shot when you came down here and Daddy took you hunting. But here's what happens either way. Downstairs in the basement, in a dark little room, I have a wooden box, and I have instructed Brian to stuff your little friend into it and force-feed her just a bit every day, enough to keep her alive. And she will live in that little box, unable to move, unable to stretch her legs, barely able to breathe for as long as it takes for her to die. Months, years, she will suffer. So go ahead, kill me," she taunted.

He always thought Lilly to be a ditzy rich kid, not a sadist, and certainly not clever. He totally misjudged her. He thought himself so clever and yet he had been the one played. *How cold he have been so stupid!*

His finger itched to pull the trigger; the anger demanded he fire the gun.

"Zeke, my love, if you put the gun down and listen, I promise I will not hurt the girl."

Kill her! She helped murder Rachel and Samuel. Kill her now! Doing so would condemn Hani to a horrible death, for he didn't doubt Lilly's threat. He couldn't allow Hani to be hurt like Rachel and Sam, murdered because of his decisions.

Zeke lowered the gun.

"Thank you," she said. "I don't enjoy having a weapon pointed at me."

"What do you want, Lilly? Why have you done all of this?" Zeke asked through gritted teeth.

Lilly raised her eyebrows a fraction. "Really, Zeke, I told you already. I want to be with you."

"You bitch," he hissed.

"Zeke, please, don't talk that way. There's a child here. I know you don't mean what you say. What happened is in the past. Don't you see? I did everything because I love you. We're going to be happy here together. You, me, the girl, and our baby."

"You're delusional."

She leaned towards him and he caught a faint, floral scent. He almost lunged, but a last shred of self-control held him back.

"Kiss me, Zeke," she whispered.

"Never."

She nodded at Jonah who brought the blade to Hani's neck.

"Kiss me," she whispered again. "You'll learn to like it, I promise. Just a little kiss on the lips."

"Don't hurt the girl," he said. "I'm here."

Her eyes narrowed to slits. "Give me a kiss!"

I'm sorry Rachel.

He leaned forward and their lips touched. Lilly let out a mewl, her tongue worming though his lips and probing his mouth. He almost gagged. The tongue withdrew but before he could pull away, a jab, like a bee sting, pierced his arm. Looking down, Zeke noticed a needle in Lilly's hand.

He pushed her back.

"What did you just do?" he demanded, feeling light-headed.

"You're going bye-bye for a bit. While you do, we'll make sure you don't have a tracker, and if you do, replace the bug with one of my own. Then, we're leaving before any members of your vigilante group show up."

He tried to lift the gun but his arm dropped to the ground. His head turned into a giant rock, his body lead.

"Oh, and Zeke, you better become a better kisser. We're going to make a baby and I want to feel your passion," Lilly said from some place far away.

Chapter 50

The boat, engine rumbling, glided through the still water. The crescent moon cast a faint glow on the inky surface of the sea, providing just enough light for Walid to make out the outline of the shore. In the distance loomed a sheer cliff, some scraggly pine trees at the top of the rock face.

Near Canadian waters they left the oil tanker and braved the sea in a small boat reeking of fish offal. The letters from E directed Walid to land at this spot.

Walid peered through the darkness. "Do you see anything?" he asked.

"No," Hassan replied.

Walid cringed at his voice. On the large boat, he had finally confronted the Barbarian about his miraculous escape.

"Allah willed it," the Barbarian had replied.

Rubbish. Did the Germans help him? Could he be a spy? Walid noticed Abdul-Haseeb spending more time with the American, reciting his poetry and sharing stories of the Arabian Knights. What game did Hassan play?

Stop! Now he needed to focus on the present.

Walid paced up and down the deck as the boat chugged towards shore. Anna sat silently in the back, staring at the trees.

On the tanker, they had spent hours talking about Islam, Arab history, and his dreams for the future. Anna listened and several times when the conversation turned to the joys of Islam, he swore a spark lightened her eyes. He became convinced she planned to speak of conversion. Instead, in each case, she had abruptly turned the conversation, asking him a question about Saudi Arabia, or his childhood, or his family.

Such frustration. If he spoke to Ali or Abdul-Haseeb about the girl they would tell him she should convert or die. But he wanted the girl to invite Allah into her heart, not have the most sacred and divine forced down her throat.

"Where is the signal?" Walid asked.

"Do you think there are detection devices close to shore?" Ali asked and sneezed. The Doctor always worried about detection devices.

"No. This is the right path."

Thirty meters from the shore he started to doubt. But no, Allah would not abandom them so close.

"Over there," Abdul-Haseeb called out. "I saw something over there."

All eyes turned and sure enough three short pulses of light came from behind the trees. A few seconds later the pulses repeated.

Thank you, oh Allah, most powerful, most merciful, for bringing us safely upon these shores.

Maintaining a steady speed, the boat veered towards the signal.

Ten meters from the shore, Abdul-Haseeb cut the engines. The boat glided in, the hull crunching against the rocky beach as Ali and the poet jumped into the water. Walid and Hassan pointed their rifles into the bushes.

He spotted flashlights moving in their direction. Heart pounding, Walid raised his weapon.

Believe.

The light approached and still no signal. He readied his finger on the trigger.

Finally a voice called out. "Salam Alakem."

"Salam Alakem!" Walid yelled back.

The bushes parted and a stocky man with dark hair and clean shaven face walked towards the boat. Relief washed over Walid as he recognized Ahmed Husseini.

Thank Allah.

"Hello Walid," Ahmed said, opening his arms, "welcome to North America."

He embraced his old friend. "Through Allah's good graces, we come bearing presents," Walid said joyously. Several other figures emerged from the bushes. They hugged, said hello to one another, and Ahmed led Walid up a steep embankment to a narrow road. A Chrysler minivan sat next to a black Chevy Blazer. Perfect.

"The weapons goes in here," Ahmed said, pointing to the minivan.

"There is only one weapon. You have done well. I am sorry about your cousin, may Allah bless his soul." Ahmed was Sheik Imaad's favorite cousin.

"He is in the garden now, my friend. We will avenge the loss. Mustaf told me Hani is gone."

Walid nodded. "It is true. She was not matyred."

"She knew much."

"Yes, hopefully she remains true."

"Hopefully she is dead."

Walid nodded and he followed Ahmed's gaze back down to Anna. A flare of jealousy ignited and he forced the feeling down.

"Who is that?"

"She is a test, an unbeliever who Allah delivered to us in Poland. She has been learning the ways of Islam."

He looked skeptical. "This is no time for teaching," Ahmed said. "She will jeopardize the mission.

Walid's mouth cringed, anger flickered again, hotter and more insistent this time. Was it the role of everyone to question his judgment, to criticize him for the girl?

"She is my test from Allah," he said before walking away. He descended the cliff to the boat and motioned for Anna to stand by the side, out of the way.

"Keep it steady," Ali said as two men carried the cylinder off the boat into the arms of three others. "We must not disturb the firing mechanism." Ali toyed with his nose, put his hands into his pockets, pulled them out, and twitched like an anxious child. As the men ascended the steep embankment to the road, Ahmed sprinted to their side.

"Listen, listen! A car is coming. I can't be sure but I think it's a police cruiser. Get down!"

The five of them scampered down the embankment and hid behind a grove of trees. Breaks squeeked, car springs flexed, and tires slowed over the pot-holed roadway as the vehicle stopped.

A car door slammed and footsteps crossed the pavement before crunching onto the gravel embankment.

"Everything okay here?" Walid heard the officer ask, his body nestled in a bush.

"Everything is fine, officer," Ahmed said.

At just that moment, Ali let out a big sneeze.

Curse him, Walid thought.

"Is someone down there?" Footsteps edged closer to the enbankment. Anna leaned against a tree five feet away, listening as well. She flashed Walid a smile, waved, and started up the hill to the road. No! Hassan moved forward to intercept her, but Walid put out his arm to block his path.

"She's going to tell them!" Hassan hissed.

"Just be ready," Walid said. "It is in Allah's hands now."

"You fool!"

Allah, give me the strength to remain calm. I know you will not abandon us now.

"She won't betray us."

"Is someone talking down there?" the police officer asked.

"Yes offizer," Anna said. "I was traveling with my friends and needed to make a pee."

"Well, hello ma'am. We didn't mean to intrude. These are your friends?"

"Yes, of course, is wrong something?"

"No, no, of course not."

Praise Allah, Anna's distraction prevented the police from noticing the boat.

"It's not wise to be out at night," one of the men said, his voice softer, lower.

"I know. I have learned my lesson."

"Do you have your identification?"

"It is here somewhere. Would you like me to find you?"

A chuckle. "That might be nice."

"Bob, cut the shit. No, that's all right, I guess. So you're all right?"

"Yes, of course."

Walid motioned for Abdul Haseeb, Hassan, and Ali to be ready. Ahmed said something and the officer replied:

"Well okay. But you might want to get back on the highway, eh. It's a faster way down the coast."

"Thank you, officer," she said.

"Have a good night." The car door slammed, the cruiser pulled away.

He counted to thirty and joyously climbed the hill. Allah, the most wonderful, stayed his hand and filled him with the strength to trust Annah. She had saved them twice.

He reached the top of the hill and spied Anna by the side of the road, chatting with Ahmed.

"Walid!" she exclaimed. "I was nervous but then I pray to Allah like you describe, and I became so calm. I feel strength run through me. I never feel like that before."

"Allah is working through you. He has selected you to be part of this mission," he gushed. And he believed with all of his heart this to be true. Allah had surely placed the girl in their path as a test and a reward of their faith in Him.

And then she finally spoke the words, "Walid, I wish to become Muslim. Now."

Warmth traveled through his chest, a gathering force more powerful than the bomb.

Ahmed and the others surrounded them in a circle, trying to understand the sudden commotion.

"Walid, this is not a safe place, we need to go now!" Hassan said.

He drew his pistol and pointed it at the American's face. "You are not the leader of this operation. Do not tell me what we need to do."

Hassan stared back, eyes cold, face unsmiling, like a "dead fish" as Anna described him.

He turned back to Anna. "Are you sure?"

She nodded. Heart pounding like a thousand horses' hooves, he gently clasped her hand and guided her under a canopy of pine trees, the moon's glow silhouetting her face.

"Are you sure?" he asked again.

She nodded her head.

"Repeat after me. "Ash-hadu an la ilaha ill Allah. I bear witness that there is no deity but Allah," he said, translating the words for her.

"Ash-hadu–"

"No, listen closely. Ash-hadu an la ilaha ill Allah. Go slow."

Stumbling, accent still off, she repeated the line in a satisfactory fashion. In time, she would learn proper Arabic.

"Wa ash-hadu ana Muhammad ar-rasullallah. And I bear witness that Muhammad is the Messenger of Allah."

"Wa ash-hadu ana Muhammad ar-rasullallah."

Walid smiled. "You are now a Muslim. You must wash in the sea to wipe away your life as it was before and be born anew."

She smiled, nodded, and walked down the embankment to the water. The men averted their gaze as she undressed and waded into the bay. She returned several minutes later, dripping, shivering, smiling.

"Have you chosen a new name?" he asked.

"I would like to be called Ana, spelled A-N-A."

He didn't fully approve for she chose a name too similar to her English one. Still, her conversion was enough.

"Welcome to the true path," Ahmed said, kissing her on each cheek. All did the same except for Hassan, who brooded by the van.

The conversation over, they opened the trunk, lifted the back floor, and looked upon a crude metallic box. Now he understood why the back of the vehicle sagged.

"Lead?" Walid asked.

"We found some steel panels with lead coverings. They are heavy but should prevent radioactive emissions from escaping or being detected."

" Did you test them?" Ali asked, examining the panels.

Ahmed shrugged. "We loaded the box with radioactive material from a hospital and nothing came through."

"Is it enough to know?" Ali questioned. The doctor remained paranoid about the radioactivity giving them away.

Ahmed shrugged. "Trust in Allah."

"We will trust. There is nothing more to be done. You have done well, Ahmed," Walid said. Ali's concerns were valid but they couldn't delay any longer.

Ali, Abdul Raq, Hassan, and Ana piled into the minivan, but Walid hung back for a moment.

"Go with Allah's blessing," Ahmed said.

"We will avenge Sheikh Imaad's death."

The man nodded his head. "Fi Amanullah," Ahmed said, giving Walid a hug.

"Goodbye, my friend."

Ali turned the ignition and the minivan's wheels spun in the gravel before they lurched forward onto the road. In ten hours, they would arrive in New York City.

Chapter 51

Aminah tested the cuffs for the thousandth time with the same result. Across the room, a small clock on the wall read 5:00 pm. Thurmos's partner, a tall, dark haired guy named Mario watched her like a hawk and even followed her into the bathroom. She pleaded about the nine milion people in New York, about her mother, about any relatives he might have in the city but he ignored her.

Hopelessness numbed her thoughts, sapped her energy. She tugged half-heartedly at the cuffs for the thousandth and first time and thought about the end. She had decided to kill herself after the bomb destroyed New York. Mother dead, sister dead, niece dead, friends dead. How could she go on?

She took deep breath and visualized the end: a bullet to the brain, a jump off a cliff, a step in front of a speeding train. Oblivion. Aminah closed her eyes, exhaled, listened to her hearbeat and imagined it slowing and stopping. The creak of the house receded, the bird chirps faded, the chain around her arm melted away.

Nothing. No attachments, no past regrets, no self-imposed limitations.

"If by setting one's heart right every morning and evening, one is able to live as though his body were already dead, he gains freedom in the Way."

A thought penetrated the dark, a voice, her father's voice speaking in the socratic method he often utilized as a tool with Aminah and her sister.

Aminah, what would you do if you had one more day? Would you cry?

No.

Would you roll over and die?

No.

Would you give in and give up?

No.

Then what would you do?

I would fight until the very last second of the very last minute of the very last hour!

And so why do you lie thinking of dying?

Aminah's eyes popped open. The clock read 5:30, the room lit by the flickering glow of the television. Thurmos left shortly after 3:00, Mario sat slumped in a chair, flipping from channel to channel.

Thurmos had loosened the chains, only shackling her right arm to the bed.

An idea from a show she watched years ago popped into her head. The odds of success were a thousand to one but if this was to be her last day, what did she have to lose? Now, if she could just remember the self-defense lesson from OCT orientation.

"Did you ever work for the OCT?" Aminah asked.

"No, Secret Service."

"President?"

"Vice."

Figured. He didn't look like Presidential material. "I didn't think you looked familiar. Listen, I have a really bad itch on my back. Right there. I can't scratch it easily. Would you mind giving me a hand?" she asked, expecting him to see through her ploy. But she knew the testosterone-fueled type hired by the Secret Service and so wasn't surprised when he dropped his tall frame onto the bed, making it squeak and sag.

First part of the improbable plan complete.

"Where?" he asked in a deeper voice.

"Right in the middle. You might need to pull up my shirt."

Taking her cue, he rolled the shirt up and gently scratched her skin. His touch repulsive, she did everything she could not to flinch. "That feels really good, Mario. Why don't you unclip the bra, I think that will make it easier," she said, giving her voice a husky edge. *Your doing this to save New York City and your family.* He fumbled with the clasp for a second, like a high school freshman on his first make-out session. The clasp opened.

Second part of the improbable plan complete.

"I shouldn't be doing this," he panted.

"Why not? You're just giving me a back scratch. Besides, I can only imagine the stress you've been under over the last few months preparing for tomorrow. John won't mind, and besides, I won't tell him. Why don't you give me a massage?"

"I don't know. You'd like that?" he asked.

"I love massages from strong men," she said, nearly gagging at the porn star line. Mario was the type who would buy the bad girl talk though.

She twisted her arm to show she couldn't escape, the rattle of the chains deepening his breathing. "I can't go anywhere," she cooed, trying to sound sexy. She never felt totally comfortable in her body and John had often encouraged her to act more assertive in bed.

Well, now look what you made me do.

"I'm going to turn over, Mario, but I want you to continue the massage."

"Seriously?"

"Yes, but only if you are up for it. You have super strong hands." She saw the lust in his eyes but he pulled away. *Shit Mario, don't become a gentleman now.*

"No way. I understand what you're trying to do. I'm not going to let you go for a screw. I could fuck you anyway right now, and no one would ever know."

"I'd tell John. In fact, I still might."

"Don't even think about it."

"Oh, I'm thinking. What do I have to lose?"

"He won't believe you."

"I'm his wife, remember? I lived with him for five years. I think I know how to make him believe me," she said putting everything she had into the lie. She had always hated how John read her so easily and he would never have fallen for this gambit, but Mario wasn't John. She noticed the rise in his pants.

"Now, I want you to take my pants off."

"What?"

"You heard me."

"I can't do that."

"Hurry up before Thurmos gets home." Thurmos definitely wouldn't fall for this either.

"Seriously?"

"Just get down here and strip me naked," she demanded, putting an edge into her voice. A small thrill rippled through her body. You're a very naughty girl, she told herself, enjoying the thought.

"You asked me to do this," he confirmed, moving towards the end of the bed.

"I did. I want you right now. I'll never tell John if you fuck me good. Be a little rough," she demanded, channeling every porno she had ever watched, which was about two.

He reached out to unbutton her pants, looked at her one last time, and began to lower the zipper. Now.

She slid her left leg behind his head and simultaneously lifted her right foot up to his neck, pressing as hard as she could to cut off his windpipe. With her free hand, she grabbed his right hand and pulled him tight against her crotch. She used the extra length of chain in her left hand to batter him on the head. He let out a cry, like a horse being strangled. Mario yanked his right hand free and worked to pry her leg from around his neck. He was strong and her muscles weakened. She smacked him across the face with the chain, blood flowing copiously down his nose and cheeks. Just as she thought he would succeed in prying her legs apart, he gave up and changed tactics. Mario punched her furiously in the side, his blows blasting the air from her lungs.

Just hang on. Keep your legs closed. Mario bucked to throw her off the bed but she kept her legs tight.

Finally, after what seemed like hours, but was probably no more than two minutes, his bucking slackened. She waited another minute as his body stilled. She didn't want to kill him so she unwrapped her legs. Heart thudding, legs quivering, side hurting, Aminah gasped for air. She searched his pants, finding a key chain with a dongle in his left pocket. Bingo. Please let one of these work. She pressed a button, the lock clicked, the cuffs sprang open.

Praise Allah! Her plan actually worked! Mindful that Thurmos could return at any moment, she slid off the bed, wobbled a moment before regaining her balance, and staggered out the bedroom.

Aminah passed through the hallway and emerged into the living room. Large windows looked out onto a sea of pine and maple trees.

Attached to a wall, she spotted a white, cordless phone and rushed over. No dial tone. Shit! She needed to flee, now.

Aminah ran out of the living room, through a small but modern kitchen, and then to a set of sliding glass doors. Flipping the latch, she pulled the doors open and stepped outside, smelling pine trees and honeysuckle.

Run! Sharesh screamed those words in Pakistan to a naive girl from America. This time she didn't freeze or trip but plunged into the woods.

From behind came the sound of tires running over sticks and stones on the road to the cottage. Thurmos. She ran even faster, tripped, cursed, picked herself up, and kept going.

Chapter 52

Zeke's eyes creaked open like rusted shutters. Head pounding, he winced at the light and shielded his face with his arm, hoping to gain some measure of relief from the headache. Lifting his arm sent a searing pain down his side. They removed the tracker. Shit, this was bad.

After a few seconds, his eyes focused and he looked up at–himself. A giant mirror bolted to the ceiling reflected his image, lying naked in a heart-shaped bed with a pink duvet and silk sheets.

Lilly.

He whipped the sheets aside and sat up. The room spun for a moment before Zeke regained his equilibrium. He staggered over to the window, pulled the thick curtains aside, and peered out over a vast, green lawn bordered by palm and orange trees and colorful plants.

Where had she taken him?

He wrapped a bedsheet around his torso, walked to one of the doors, and turned the handle. Locked. He tried a second door and entered a luxurious bathroom with an enormous glass enclosed shower, a jacuzzi tub, and a marble counter with a double sink. Zeke tried another door in the bathroom– locked.

He turned on the tap and splashed cold water onto his face.

Trapped.

In his quest to be right, to prove his model, he had played right into her trap and killed Rachel and Sam. How could he have been so supid and blind and allowed Lilly to manipulate him? He had always been the smart one, the person who knew what was going on when others didn't. He grabbed a pink heart shaped bar of soap and hurtled it at the mirror. How could he have let all of this happen? Especially when they received a warning the morning before Rachel and Sam's flight. But he had been to focused on himself, on his achievement. All a mirage.

Trembling, he reached out, turned on the faucet, and splashed water on his face. He looked into the window and saw a thin ghoul with gray hair, pale skin, and tired eyes. He didn't even understand what Lilly saw in him. Why didn't she leave him and his life alone?

A door opened and Lilly's voice called out.

"Hello, Zeke."

He cringed.

"Zeke, come out of the bathroom. I want to see you."

"Go away, Lilly."

"You don't give the orders anymore, Zeke. Now get out here," she said, her voice more stern. He walked into the bedroom, where Lilly stood, arms crossed. She wore a blue pant suit, blonde hair falling across the jacket in silky waves.

"Take off your sheet, I want to look at all of you."

"Lilly–"

"Do it!"

He should kill her now, find Hani, and leave. But he had no idea of Hani's location and he might wind up getting the girl killed. He didn't trust his own judgement.

Lilly's hand darted out, grabbed the sheet, and pulled the silk covering off.

"That's better," she purred.

"Where are we? Where's Hani?"

"We're in Spain. Hablas Espanol?" she asked with a giggle.

Spain?

"Things are going to get a bit rocky in the United States, so I thought it best we leave for a bit."

"And Hani?"

"She's fine."

"I want to see her," he said. "I want to know she's okay."

"She's fine. Living la pura vida. But later today, if you behave like a gentleman, I'll let you video with her."

The door opened and a thin man dressed in a tuxedo entered carrying a bottle and an ice bucket. The butler didn't bat an eye at Zeke's nudity.

"Gracias, Raphael. Por favor pone la botella alli," Lilly said. "I bet you didn't know I speak Spanish," she giggled.

"I remember you in Spanish class." The language had been one of her academic high points. A ranch hand she screwed at Calico as a teen-ager taught her some basic Spanish.

The butler put the items down on a small table beside the bed, bowed, and exited the room.

"It's champagne," she bubbled. "I thought we could drink to our new life together. I know you're not adjusted to your circumstances, but we will be so happy." She grabbed the bottle and struggled to rip off the foil. "Popping champagne corks was never my strong suit," she said. "I usually leave that to my man."

He wasn't about to help.

Finally, after she struggled for another minute, the cork popped out, hit the wall next to the bed, and disappered under the coach.

"This is a one-thousand dollar bottle of Chablie Montfort. We'll let this air out for a moment while I get more comfortable." Lilly kicked off her shoes, removed her jacket, and slowly unbuttoned her shirt.

"Please Lilly, it doesn't have to be like this."

"Zeke," she whispered huskily, moving close to his ear. "As we make love, federal agents are raiding your company and closing its offices. At the same time, your little Muslim friend is learning the surprise of her life."

"Aminah?"

"Some ugly name like that. She's the one who told us you were coming."

No. Although logic confirmed Lilly's accusation, he didn't believe Aminah would betray him and Hani. "She told you?" Had he made another seismic mistake in judgement?

"I don't know. Her husband, someone in Washington."

Husband? Something happened to Aminah and Masada, another piece of the plan gone awry. He doubted they met with Ambrose which meant New York was still in jeapordy. The news kept getting better and better.

"Lilly," he said as she removed her bra, and perfectly shaped breasts popped out, "New York will be destroyed. Millions of people will die." She undid her belt and unzipped her jeans.

"I could care less. I never liked New York. There are too many people there." She kicked her pants off with a swing of a finely muscled leg. "All I care about is being with you." She slithered over, raised her arms, and moved to wrap them around his neck.

He held her back.

"Don't resist," she whispered in his ear. "Now, you better make passionate love to me or I'll just take my frustrations out on your little friend. You're going to give me a baby and then we'll be together forever."

As she shimmied off her panties and moved in to kiss him, he realized he had no choice but to kiss her back.

Chapter 53

Walid held Ana's hand in a small clearing carved out of the woods. He spotted the grove from the road and insisted they stop. He only needed ten minutes.

Ana stood across from him, her blue eyes shimmering like the waves of the sea. The scarf covered her blonde hair but a few strands peaked out, tossed by the wind, glinting in the sun. How radiant.

Beside her stood Abdul-Haseeb, hands in his jean pockets, rocking back-and-forth on his feet. Ali stared into the distance. Hassan remained back by the van, watching with his beady eyes.

The poet cleared his throat. "Do you wish to propose?" he asked Walid. This marked the start of the ceremony.

Walid nodded. "Yes. Ana, I wish to make you my wife. I promise to love and protect you as long as I am able. I promise to be a good Muslim husband. And I promise to find you in the gardens of paradise and forever keep you as my number two wife." Mouna would always be number one.

In truth, he didn't know exactly what to say so he let Allah find the right words.

No one spoke for a moment and he flashed a cross look at the poet.

"Ah, okay, do you wish to accept?" Abdul-Haseeb asked Ana.

"I do," she replied.

"In Arabic," Walid whispered. He taught her the word last night.

"Qabul," she said.

"Two more times," Abdul-Haseeb said.

"Qabul, qabul."

Abdul-Haseeb turned to him. "And you?"

"Qabul, qabul, qabul."

"Excellent!" the poet exclaimed. "Now, give your gift to the bride."

Walid pulled out a spindly ring forged from a paper clip. It was all he could find in the car. He gently slid the band onto her finger."

"Congratulations," Abdul-Haseeb said," you are now husband and wife."

He pulled Ana towards him and gave her a long kiss, tongues meshing, his body temperature rising. He needed an hour alone with his bride to explore her heavenly delights.

"Let's go!" Hassan yelled from the car. "Save it for the afterlife!"

Irritated, Walid held her hand as they walked back towards the van. His body bubbled, his need almost impossible to resist, his mind constantly envisioning her nude body, intimate touches, soft caresses, hard thrusts.

They piled into the van and Ali checked the map.

"We're fifteen minutes from the border," the scientist said.

* * *

Crossing the border into the United States proved easier than spreading hummus on bread. One minute in Canada, the next the United States. No signs, border guards, or other barriers to stop or hinder their entrance. The remote route, probably used by smugglers, worked as E promised.

A beaten-up Ford Explorer passed, an orange New York license plate fixed to the bumper.

The road wound through small towns, many of the buildings boarded up, streets empty except for a few old men shuffling down the street, or a dog running from trash can to trash can. For twenty minutes they traveled through a field of giant windmills, blades as big as buildings towering over the trees. Abdul-Haseeb scribbled a poem entitled "Aliens" in honor of the giant structures.

Walid gazed at Ana as she slept. After the conversion, he had told her the full truth about the mission and the bomb.

"You will kill all the people?"

He nodded. "It is the only way. We have tried to talk in the language of Islam, the language of peace, but they refuse to listen." While crossing the Atlantic, he had explained the massacres, the killings, the humiliation of the Muslim world at the hands of the West and especially the United States.

"What will become of us?" she asked. "Will we die also?"

"That is my mission," he told her. "But in death, we will be given eternal life in the garden's of paradise. And our names will live on as matyrs to the umma."

"I will follow you, my beloved," she said. "But I hope we have longer to enjoy the pleasures of this world.

How he wished to take her in his arms, press her soft body to his, cover her in kisses. So close and yet unable to complete the spark. He summoned every shred of control to tamper the fire.

"Allah will decide our path and protect us," he stammered. He knew Ana did not care about the millions killed, or the destruction unleashed by the weapon, about strengthening the Umma or spreading Islam. Increasingly, he shared her ambivalence. His fire now burned for her. Seductress? Imaad warned about Western women. But Ana had saved his life and twice she had rescued the mission. Perhaps Allah possessed other plans for the two of them. Why unite them just to incinerate their love? Maybe he and Ana were destined to be a new Adam and Eve, repopulating the heathen world with a family of believers as Mohammad did with Mecca and the Arab world. His descendents would bear the title Sayyid and songs would be sung about his valor and Ana's beauty.

Perhaps.

Abdul-Haseeb sat in the driver's seat beside him, looking pensively up at the sky.

"What do you dream about?" Walid asked.

"I wonder how Allah will appear when he welcomes me into the gardens of paradise. Will the virgins be there with him?"

"Do you know what I dream about?" Hassan said, forcing his way into their conversation. "I dream about sitting by the lake with twenty naked virigns, some bringing me pop, others tickling my feet, others sucking my dick."

How could he speak that way in front of Ana? Curse him!

"What lake would this be?" asked Abdul-Haseeb.

"Lake of the Woods in Virginia. My grandma had a house there. It was an old green cabin down a dirt road, with ruler straight pines on all sides and blueberries, raspberries, and strawberries growing all over the place. My brother and I used to swim there all summer." The scowl left the barbarian's face and he smiled.

"You have a brother?" Ali asked.

"Yeah. I haven't spoken to him much in the last couple of years though." Ali launched into his vision of the gardens of paradise and Hassan's scowl returned.

Walid smiled at Ana and she blew a kiss.

Outside, the two lane highway widened to three lanes and a few minutes later to four. The forest thinned, revealing houses and small towns. Ahead, a sign said: New Canaan, 10 miles. The President addressed the United Nations at 4:30 PM which gave him four hours to consider his next move.

Chapter 54

Aminah plunged through the woods, ignoring the brambles and heading towards a thinned out area of the forest.

Up ahead, she spied a pine needle path and turned right, legs pumping like the pistons on a speeding car. Leaves crunched and snapped behind her. Dammit! Why couldn't she catch a break? She remained on the path, hoping it would bring her to a road or someplace with people. Aminah had never been fast, always finishing in the back of the pack during gym class, and now she cursed her lead legs, praying she wouldn't fall again.

Up ahead, the trees thinned. Please, let there be help!

Chest heaving, heart pounding, she ran out of the woods to the edge of sheer cliffs and fifty foot drop to water. A quarry. Frantic, she scanned the terrain for an escape route but found only a steep, rocky path bordering the edge of the pit.

She'd be shot before she made it more than ten feet, or she'd slip and fall into the water.

Two men burst from the path.

"Stop being a bitch, Aminah," Thurmos panted, pointing a gun at her. A second man she didn't recognize stood beside him. How many people were in on this?

"Thurmos, my mother, sister, and niece are in New York. I can't let the bomb explode."

"Aminah," he said advancing, "there's nothing you can do. Come back to the house. John said to keep you safe but he also said that if you caused any problems, well, you know. Don't make me do it."

What an asshole!"

She took another step back. Her foot teetered on the edge.

"Don't do it, Aminah. Even if you survive the fall, we'll see you when you come up."

She had no choice. This was the best of all bad options.

"Praise Allah, keep my family safe. Protect me and if I should die, know that I tried to be the best person I could be."

"Tony, I used to like you," she started. "But now, go fuck yourselves." She stepped back. Tony lunged, too late. Aminah glimpsed his surprised face as she fell back, the velocity increasing until she came to a violent stop. Plunging into water was like hitting concrete someone once told her, and the words rang true. The impact knocked the wind out of her lungs and the thought from her brain.

No thought.

No thought.

No thought.

Go! Open your eyes and go!

Through murky water, Aminah dimly noticed contrails pass close and disappear into the depths.

Bullets.

Her mind began to turn and she moved her hands, sweeping them out in a weak swim stoke. Pain radiated from her feet as if they had been beaten with basaeball bats.

Her momentum continued to carry her deeper. A soft object brushed her feet and downy feathers caressed her hands and face. Not soft or feathery, mucky. She panicked, flailing her arms, trying to move sideways to flee from whatever swept against her.

What was down here with her? The panic quickly ate though her oxygen reserves as an inescapable urge to breathe flooded her brain, the need growing by the millisecond. Breathe. Her body craved air. She flailed her arms and legs to reach the surface but the thrashing engangled her further. As her mind raced faster and faster, a chant echo through the water like the song of a mermaid.

"Hoo-yah-yah-yah
Hoo-yah-yah-yah
Hoo-yah-yah-yah
Hoo-yah-yah-yah-"

She'd heard this before. Where?

The Vengeance.

Channeling the memory, she fought back the panic and the all consuming urge to open her mouth, body relaxing. Her hands closed around a soft, slimy tentacle wrapped around her ankle, and with a jerk tore it from her leg. With a last burst of energy, Aminah pushed herself to the surface, breached the waterline, and gulped lungfuls of air in giant heaves.

"I wasn't sure if you would make it."

Aminah spun around to find Masada seated on a rock fifteen feet away, looking amused.

Panting, "Holy shit! You just watched! Were you going to let me drown?"

"I wanted to see what you would do."

"What I would do?" she asked incredulously.

"You did your own version of the Heaven Dive," Masada said. "Mazel Tov."

"What happened to Thurmos and the other guy?"

"I don't know any Thurmos. There are two dead men at the top."

Poor Tony. She couldn't help feeling sorry for the guy, even if he was about to kill her.

"I almost died!" Aminah yelled, paddling her way to the shore.

"You survived. You looked death in the face and did not let it overwhelm you. I am proud of you." She reached out a hand. "Now you are ready."

"Ready for what?"

"To kick ass," the Israeli replied, hoisting her out of the water.

Chapter 55

Zeke's body responded to Lilly's breasts bouncing in his face, her long legs straddling his torso, her moans as she rocked up and down. He hated himself for rising to the occassion.

This is what he had become, a rigid tool for a crazy, wealthy woman who played a role in the death of his family. He spent hours over the last two days trying to understand his failure, how he overlooked her manipulation. Maybe he wasn't as smart as he thought. Or maybe he thought himself too smart.

"When you become too smart, you become dumb," his father told him once, in a seemingly illogical, drunk rant. Now, he finally understood those words.

"Zeke, are you paying attention to me?" Lilly asked as she continued the ride, a light sheen of sweet glistening off bare breasts, long finger nails grazing his chest.

"Harder. Oh yeah. You feel so good," Lilly moaned. "Just like that."

He finished with one last thrust.

"Isn't it beautiful here?" she cooed.

"Sure," he replied.

"Sure? That doesn't sound like a genuine response."

"I'm tired. We've been at it all night."

"It's tough work," she cooed, nuzzling his face. He kissed her gently on the lips.

She had suggested having a picnic on the grass near the ornate flower garden, and he welcomed the opportunity to leave the compound. The villas, ornate buildings with red tiled Spanish roofs, beautiful mahogany woodwork, and steel bars on the windows whose ends tapered to iron flowers, sat on a hill overlooking a body of water, which he assumed to be the Mediterranean. It could also have been the Atlantic or the Alboran Sea if she had brought him to the south. Lilly once told him she wanted to buy an island, so it seemed plausible they were on one.

"I love being here with you," she said, bending down and smelling a rose.

Zeke twisted its stem off and presented the flower.

"Oh, Zeke, thank you." Her eyes moistened as she grabbed his hand and held the flower like a love-struck teenager. He let her fingers intertwine with his own. "I thought the magic of this place would grow on you. It's intoxicating here."

Zeke rose and grabbed the champagne bottle chilling in a silver bucket on an ornate stand, peeled the foil, and firmly twisted the cork until it popped off into the grass. A stream of foamy champagne bubbled out and onto his hands. He poured the bubbly into two fluted glasses.

"Here you are," he said, handing the drink to Lilly.

"Oh, Zeke, thank you!" she said. She held her glass out. "To love," she said. He clinked her glass and took a sip.

"Is this an island?" he asked as they sipped.

"Yes," she said. "We're one mile off the coast."

He pointed to the orange trees. "We must be in Southern Spain."

She nodded. "Off the Costa del Sol."

Birds chirped, bees buzzed, and roses, orchids, and other exotic flowers he didn't recognize lay in perfectly arranged patterns.

They rose and walked through the gardens, holding hands, sipping Champagne.

"I think you are beginning to understand how wonderful our life can be. I wonder if we'll have a boy or a girl. What would you like, Zeke? Boy or girl?"

"Either is okay," he replied.

"No, Zeke, you have to choose one," she said, the smile gone. "Choose one."

"Girl," he replied.

"Why?" she asked, smiling again.

"Girls are gentle and kind. They help make a better world."

"Yes, so true. I'd be happy with a girl." They reached the entrance to the chateau. "I'm going to take a shower and then I'll meet you in the dining room for dinner."

"I'd like to speak with Hani."

"You've been better today. I think you deserve a reward. I'll ask Raphael to set up the computer."

Perfect.

She leaned in and planted a kiss on his lips.

"Goodbye, my love," she sighed. "I hate to leave you for even a second but I must take a call. I'll see you shortly."

"Don't be long," he said, kissing her neck. I'll miss you."

"Of course you will," she said, grabbing his crotch and giving a gentle squeeze before walking away.

Brian, one of Lilly's guard, came over and smirked. "She took you in the grass. You're her bitch," he laughed. "Come on, let's bring you back to your pen," Brian said, grabbing his arm. Zeke let Brian lead him like a dog out for a walk.

* * *

"Hello, Hani." Her hair looked freshly brushed and she wore an expensive green robe. She flashed a wide smile.

"Today, they took me to the garden and I– "

"Nothing about where you went," a male voice interrupted.

"Sorry." She shrugged her shoulders, looking very much like a kid caught with her hands in the cookie jar. Her sullen face and sad eyes were gone.

She reached out and picked up an orange that lay on a table beside her.

"Today I picked an orange like this, and I thought it would taste very good. I took a bite and almost threw up. The taste was, what is the word, bitter? They look good but they cannot be eaten, by humans at least," she said peeling off the skin.

The Costa De Sol in Southern Spain was known for its appealing-looking, but sour oranges. She was either in the house or nearby.

"Time to end the call," said the voice.

"That's it?" Zeke asked.

"Wrap it up," said the voice.

"You look tired, Zeke, get some bed sleep." She smiled in a cheery, fake way. "Oh, I almost forget. At the beach, do you remember the crab that we almost missed? I saw something similar today. Tonight, I will think about this crab, and hopefully soon I will be able to see you and show you."

The crab had camouflaged itself and burrowed into a hole before they could catch it. He had wanted to cook the crustacean along with the lamb, but the wily creature had managed to escape. *Escape.*

Clever girl. He understood the message. Hani found a way to leave her room without being detected, and she planned to escape that night.

The time had come to make his move.

Chapter 56

Sheik Imaad's eyes had grown wide whenever Walid railed against American cities: the vast number of people scurrying around like cockroaches, the endless rows of cars crawling through grid-lock, the towering buildings blotting out the sun, the endless gray of cement and steel erasing nature and beauty, the stink of rubbish and exhaust, the lack of minerats or mosques. The Sheikh delighted hearing about the depravities of the concrete jungles.

But today, driving through New York, he noticed a woman pushing a baby stroller, a couple holding hands, a group of boys laughing as they bounced a ball and walked across the street. For a moment, he wished more than anything to be one of those boys, carefree, without a worry, enjoying the fall day.

They entered New York City as easily as crossing from Maslem into Riyadh. One moment they traveled on the highway, passing oil refineries and ships docked along the Hudson River, and the next giant apartment buildings gave way to row upon row of houses. In the distance, towers rose high into the sky like monuments to hubris and the belief that this civilization could reach Allah's realm. Such fools.

Highest of all stood the Freedom Tower, and, for a moment the old anger sparked. War, death, torture, Mouna, all in the name of towers and justice and the West. But the hate melted away, like water sinking through the rocks on Al Disa beach.

What happened to him?

A man leaned in and spoke to a woman at a bus stop. He envisioned himself sitting with Ana, chatting, talking about where to go. Anywhere but here. Freedom.

Ana sat beside him now, wide-eyed, head moving in all directions to take in the sights and sounds, the buildings, the people, the colors. When they spotted the towers, she let out a sigh. "It is just like on television," she said. "But bigger, taller."

He knew that she did not feel hate, just a curiosity to explore the vast city and be a tourist for a day. Another vision came, the two of them atop a double-decker bus, holding hands, pointing at the different landmarks.

No! No! He could not think like this. They would complete the mission, this he swore to Sheikh Imaad, and Allah would not forgive him for breaking a vow. He would complete the mission, and somehow they would also live. In the meantime, he needed to free himself from the temptation of the West, the sugary image that this land presented to lure believers into the embrace of idolatry.

But why did Allah send Ana if not as a message to live?

A thick glass window separated the driving cabin from the rest of the vehicle. Looking through the rear-view mirror, Walid watched Adbdul-Haseeb scribble in his notebook. A speaker piped sound from the rear to the driver's cabin and every so often Hassan's mouth sputtered to life.

"The work of the Jews," he spat. "A city of filth with more rats than people. Look at those niggers, look at them scamper like monkeys."

Beside Hassan, the bomb sat inside a dark wood, lead-lined coffin, which lay upon a long gurney, the straps that normally held a patient secure, stretched to the limit around the cold wood.

An hour outside of the city, in a town called Coxsackle, they had exchanged the truck for an ambulance. The vehicle sat at the end of a desolate dirt road beside a field of corn just as the plan dictated.

The ambulance contained three wireless heart monitors. He once saw such a device in a Riyadh hospital when his Uncle Amir suffered a heart attack. Ali spent the last hour rigging the transmitters to the bomb.

"It is very simple," Ali explained. "This box I have attached to the bomb is a detonator. It receives the encrypted signal from your heart monitor. When your heart stops beating, it will detonate the weapon."

"And if they block the signal?" Walid asked, remembering General Kranchenko's double cross in Kazakstan.

"The weapon will detonate," Ali said.

"Good," he replied.

The plan was simple. At the given time, one of members of the group would take a gun, shoot himself in the chest, and detonate the weapon.

"Turn onto Park Avenue," the GPS recited in a female British accent. Walid waited for a man on a bike to cross the street before taking a right. A yellow taxi crossed the road in front of the ambulance. Walid slammed on the brakes and Hassan, Ali, and Abdul-Haseeb careened forward.

"What the fuck?" Hassan asked, pulling himself off the ground.

"It pulled in front of me. Did you see it?" Walid yelled back.

"You're blind!" Hassan screamed.

The taxi had surely been a message from Allah. Stop. Do not proceed. Do not kill yourself. Allah approved of his decision.

"Listen," he said, speaking slowly, hiding the nervous tremors, " does everyone understand what we are to do?" In ten minutes we will arrive. If anything goes wrong we will detonate the weapon." Behind him, heads bobbed in agreement. "Praise Allah we succeeed," he said. "For five years we have planned and plotted and today is our time to strike at the West and bring the Caliphate back to life."

Empty words spoken like a robot, like the girl on the GPS. Still, there was nothing to do but move forward and hope his plan worked. The last plan, he told himself, the last perfect plan to finish the mission and live a life with Ana.

He drove down Park Avenue. Three blocks away, the gleaming glass facade of the United Nations loomed above a cordon of police cars.

Chapter 57

Aminah squinted up at the gleaming skyscrapers. A warm breeze blew through the car. New Yorkers responded to the mild September day by dressing in short sleeves, thronging the sidewalks and streets, and filling the seats at outdoor cafes. A vendor at the street corner hawked sausages, a woman pushed two babies in a tandem stroller, three boys with yamulkas walked down the sidewalk in animated conversation.

Aminah and Masada drove straight from Virginia up Route 95, with no stops. Her stomach had grumbled, her back had ached, but she had ignored the discomfort. They needed to reach the United Nations. They needed to stop the bomb.

During the trip, Aminah had decided to take a chance and text Felix Arroyo, a friend at the State Department. In his role as assistant to Lynne Waters, ambassador to the United Nations, he'd be at the General Assembly and she trusted him as much as anyone. Her message had been short and non-descript, enough to avoid QIL detection:

>Felix, it's Ami. Please call me. It's important.

For thirty-five minutes she waited and then her phone rang.

"Felix," she said, heart pumping.

"Aminah, I am taking a huge chance calling you. They're saying you've gone rogue."

"Listen, Felix. Fist of Allah has a nuclear bomb and will detonate it today at the General Assembly meeting. You have to get the President out."

"I need more than that, Aminah. OCT is saying it's a hoax."

"I'm coming there. If I reach the U.N. compound, can you get me a meeting with the President?"

"A meeting? Aminah, they think you're a terrorist."

"Felix, it's Vison. He's set all of this up." She knew Felix distrusted Vison. "Can you get me in to see the President? I can do the rest."

"It will ruin my career."

"Felix, a fucking nuclear bomb is really going to ruin your career. You know me, Felix. You know I am not a terrorist."

He paused. "Meet me at the gates to the East entrance. I'll see what I can do."

"We'll be there in one hour. Be careful. QIL knows..." Before she could finish the sentence, the call terminated.

They had taken the Lincoln Tunnel into Manhattan and emerged into a sea of bumper to bumper traffic, cabs and livery cars laying on the horn to little avail. In twenty minutes they had traveled two blocks to the Port Authority. Giant posters and marquees from the theatre district loomed above them.

"We have to get out," she replied. "The General Assembly meeting must be tying up traffic. It could take an hour to reach the UN. Pull over there," she pointed to a spot in front of a hydrant. "We'll dump the truck and walk."

"How long of a walk is it?" asked Masada.

"Not far. Six or seven blocks."

Masada steered the truck to the spot and turned off the SUV.

The walk signal came and a rush of pedestrians crossed the street with them: a black man in a leather jacket listened with headphones, a short girl talked on her cellphone: "he better fucking call me after last night," a mother pushed two blonde haired twins in a double-stroller. She spotted three police officers walking in their direction, talking into their cellphones.

Stay calm, she told herself. Beside her, she knew that Masada must have also seen the police but the Israeli kept walking forward. They came to the edge of the street and waited for the light to turn. The officers had doubled back and now stood beside them, their eyes sweeping the sidewalk, observing the people passing down the street. Aminah could feel their eyes on her and then the officers looked away and continued in the opposite direction. The chance of their faces being recognized out of context, amongst the sea of people in the city, was almost nil.

As Aminah crossed the street, a little girl walking hand-in-hand with her mother stared up at Masada.

"Look Mommy, those are the people from the television." The woman turned, squinted for a moment and pulled her daughter away.

Almost nil for everyone except a precocious little girl.

"Move fast," Aminah said. They crossed the street and followed the crowd down another block.

Aminah froze in front of a bank of televisions in the window of an electronics store. Her face filled the screen with the words: Possible Terrorist Threat captioned at the bottom.

The whir of sirens started up in the distance.

"John's making us the scapegoats. He's setting us up to take the fall for the bomb," Aminah cried. "He's put the word out in the media."

"Don't panic," Masada said.

"What are we going to do?" Aminah asked as the sirens grew closer.

"We're going to move like hell to try and meet up with your friend," she said.

They power-walked down 42nd Street, Aminah regretting they had left the shelter of the SUV. As the sirens grew louder, she realized the enormity of her mistake.

"Keep walking," Masada said.

More horns and cars moved aside as the siren approached their block. Aminah looked back and sighed with relief as she spotted an ambulance working its way through the traffic.

"It's just an ambulance."

"Keep walking."

They could make it. They crossed 7th Avenue and ahead loomed the stone facade of the New York City Public Library. The ambulance passed, lights flashing, sirens blaring and she caught a glimpse of a blonde male driver and a woman in the passenger seat. If only they could hop a ride with them.

They reached the library and Aminah relaxed a bit. Maybe the mother didn't believe her daughter or neglected to call the police. New Yorkers liked to mind their own business.

As they crossed 6th Avenue, a BMW ran the light and almost slammed into them. "Watch the signal!" Aminah yelled. She almost made it to the other side of the street, but before she took the final steps onto the curb, an icy command reached her from behind.

"Put your hands on your head and lie down on the ground." She started to turn her head to see. "Don't turn around!" a man yelled. "Just put your fucking hands on your head."

Shit! No! She couldn't see Masada.

"You're making a mistake," she said.

"I'm not going to tell you again, put your hands on your head and get down onto the ground." Behind her, she heard clothing rustle. Masada must have dropped. Legs shaking, she lowered herself onto her stomach, the white stripe from the sidewalk inches from her face. Sirens, lower in pitch than the amublance, announced the arrival of more police cars as she heard the officers yelling at onlookers to move and back and keep walking.

"That's them. The ones from the television."

Strong hands grabbed her arms and pulled them together before binding them with a pair of metal cuffs.

"Please, you're making a terrible mistake. There is a nuclear bomb loose. It's going to explode. It's at the U.N."

"Explain that to the judge," the police officer said, hauling her off and shoving her into the car.

Chapter 58

The door clicked and Lilly came in, on schedule, nine o'clock at night, right after a brief workout, spa treatment, and a warm bath in mint and oleander leaves. Lilly had explained her schedule to Zeke in minute detail, down to the daily manicure between 11:30 and 12:00 to keep her cuticles "their best." "A woman's job is make herself beautiful for her man," she claimed.

"Hello, Zeke." Lilly called out, carrying a champagne bottle by the neck. More champagne. He didn't think so this time. Brian stepped into the room and closed the door.

Zeke flashed Lilly a warm smile.

"Tonight is the night," Lilly said. "We'll drink some bubbly and watch the fireworks in New York City. Toast our new life. I've noticed the change in you over the last two days, Zeke. You feel it, don't you? Our unbreakable love bond. Shall we see what they are saying on the news?" She found the remote under one of the coach cushions and turned on the television.

Lilly didn't care one whit about world events. In school she had been a lackadaisical student, skipping her classes and finally managing to squeak across the line with a degree in psychology.

A stylishly coiffed blond woman appeared on the screen.

"In his speech the President will try to reestablish U.S. leadership in a number of areas. One of his foreign policy goals is the pivot away from the war against radical Islam which has dominated agendas for the last twenty-five years. Tonight's address provides him with an opportunity to discuss some of the other pressing issues, especially the worldwide coalition he is building to combat the Progress Block."

Rick Hull, the network's lead anchor, nodded solemnly. "Do you think the world will listen?"

"Well, that's the big question. The Chinese and the Progress Block increasingly dominate UN decision-making and challenge the United States for leadership of the global agenda."

Lilly watched for a minute, sighed, fidgeted, and handed the champagne bottle to him. He spun it slowly in his hand but didn't start to work the cork.

"Come on, silly, open the bottle. I'd like a sip," she laughed. "Their talking is so dull."

"Lilly?" Zeke asked pleasantly.

"Yes, darling?"

"How much money is in your purse?"

She twisted her face. "How much money? I'm not sure. A couple thousand dollars. Not much. Why? You don't need money, silly."

"How do you think a person without money feels?"

"Probably terrified. But you don't need to worry," she said smugly. "I have plenty of cash for both of us."

Now he needed to proceed carefully.

"I specialize in moving money, Lilly."

"I know all about your brainy algorithim. It's why I invested in your company."

"No, you invested in my company to set me up. You didn't care about the return. But even after the money we made together, I continued to refine my techniques. Over the past year, I figured out how to penetrate banks and brokerages, how to transfer assets without the owner's permission or knowledge, how to clean someone out in a matter of days of every single penny to their name. Because today everything is electronic, and I have access to everything."

She gave a nervous laugh. "Zeke, let's not discuss the past. Watch the television and let's think about the future–together."

How could Lilly be so oblivious? Is this what happened to someone who grew up a billionaire? Although he tried to choke the feeling, he almost felt a bit sorry for what he was about to do to her.

"Listen closely, Lilly," he said slowly, wanting the words to sink in, "before I came to visit you at Calico, I started a program called the Stripper."

"That's lewd," she said grabbing the champagne bottle and twisting the top in her hand.

"Because you took me prisoner and didn't give me access to the outside world, I couldn't shut the program down, and so it has run for the last three days."

She put the unopened bottle on the table and began to flip through television channels. "Zeke, I could care less about your program and your stripper. But I'm really beginning to tire of this conversation. I want to change the subject," Lilly said, mouth firm, smile gone.

"You should care about this conversation. And Brian, I think this information might be important for you, too." Brian didn't move.

"While you spirited me away to Spain as your love slave—"

"Love slave! Zeke, we love each other. I just needed you to understand that. We were meant to be together. You feel it."

"I never loved you, Lilly, and I never will."

In a tiger-fast move Lilly brought her hand around but he caught it inches from his face.

She sneered. "How dare you speak to me like that after I brought you here and pampered you. I love you! Who do you think you are?"

He enjoyed her rising distress. "While you kept me captive, the stripper identified your assets, marked them, and completed the process."

"What process?" she asked, brow furrowed, eyes slits. Good.

Zeke held her hand fast, "If you had been paying attention to your business over the last three days, you might have noticed the program transferred your assets into a several very expensive real-estate projects. Guess where those real-estate projects are located?"

'It's a lie!" she hissed. "You fucking liar. You couldn't just break in and steal my money! You fucking liar!"

"All of your money is in New York City. If you want to save your fortune, you need to save New York." He spoke slowly, like to a child, letting the meaning sink in.

"We love each other, Zeke. Why are you doing this?" She brushed mascara-tinted tears from her face, leaving a dark smudge across a smooth cheek. She deserved every tear and more. "I don't know why you are lying about this but I am going to make you pay! You and that little girl!" she hissed. "Brian, bring the girl here," she demanded.

He departed.

"You're going to reverse whatever you did or I'm going to tear her apart."

He enjoyed her distress. The bitch deserved all of this and more. The odds of this saving New York were low though.

Brian returned five minutes later, pale. "Lilly, can I speak to you for a moment outside?"

"No, I'm not getting up. Tell me."

"The girl is missing. She's not in her room."

"What? How could you fucking lose the girl?" She spun to face to Zeke. "Where is she? What did you do?"

"She's gone. We took her out," he lied. "She's on a plane safe from you."

Eyes trembling, breath ragged, Lilly let out a primal scream. "Get her back!"

"She's gone, Lilly," Zeke said. He hoped Hani hid herself well and Lilly lacked the time and concentration to mount a search.

"Find her!" she screamed at Brian.

"If she's still on the island, we might not be able to recapture her in time," the bodyguard replied.

Hand shaking, she reached into her robe and withdrew a phone.

"Get me Charlie," she barked. "I don't care where he is, get him for me!" She kept the phone to her ear, tear-filled eyes darting across the room. "Charlie...What? No, I didn't authorize that. Yes, I've been away. I know. I didn't authorize those tranasactions! Unwind them," she said. "Unwind them now! Right now! No excuses, Charlie! Just get it done!" she screamed into the phone.

Sweating profusely, shaking like a withdrawing heroin addict, she dialed another number.

"It's me," she said. "I don't care about that now. You need to stop the bomb. I told you I don't care about that. Do you understand? It can't explode, not today. In one week it will be okay." She listened. "My father made all of this possible for you. You owe me everything!" she screamed. "Hello? Did you fucking hang up on me? No one hangs up on me!" She hurled the phone across the room where it left a black dent on the screen.

"You're a liar! I'm going to straighten this out and when I get back, you will fucking roast in hell!" she screamed, flung the door open, and stormed out.

So much for enduring love.

Zeke gave Brian a nod, the man code way of saying he spoke the truth. Brian nodded back and exited the room, leaving the door ajar.

For the last two days, he feigned interest in Lilly to keep her off balance and occupied. That part of the plan worked. But Aminah and Masada failed to stop the bomb.

That's not your fight. No one cared about Rachel and Sam.

True. But the thought of Fist of Allah winning and killing more innocent victims made him furious. He had failed again. He could only hope for a miracle, but miracles didn't happen for him.

Chapter 59

The instructions were precise.

Approach the building from E 44th Street. With lights flashing and sirens on, drive up to the gate at 44th and 1st Street and tell them you are responding to an emergency call from within the UN. If they ask what kind of call, tell them the Ambassador from New Guinea is having a heart attack.

The ambulance sped down 44th street towards the United Nations, siren blaring, lights flashing. At the wrought-iron fence circling the compound, two guards with M-16s motioned for them to stop.

Hassan drove and Walid observed the helmeted soldiers, their eyes shaded by sunglasses, mouths set in a professional scowl, weapons at the ready. Just like the American bastards in Iraq and Afghanistan who killed for fun, shot little girls playing in the street, or beautiful women like Mouna who happened to be in the wrong place.

A spark of the old anger returned. Soon Allah would judge these infidels.

A tall soldier with his rifle pointed at Hassan and Ana approached, motioning for them to roll down the window. Hassan complied.

"What's your business? This is a secure zone!" the soldier barked. The man's gaze lingered for a moment on Ana's fine hair and face, which Walid grudgingly agreed to leave uncovered.

"The Ambassador from New Guinea is having a heart attack," Hassan said, reciting the line. For once the Barbarian followed the plan. "In these situations, time is of the essence," Hassan added, going off script.

Idiot!

Ali and Abdul Haseeb sat out of sight, hands on their vests, ready to detonate the weapon if the soldier asked to inspect the ambulance or told them to turn around and leave. Beads of sweat dotted their foreheads despite the air-conditioning, Abdul-Haseeb's lips moved feverishly as he silently recited verses from the Koran. Ali's foot tapped on the linoleum floor–tick, tick, tick. He sneezed.

"Stay," the soldier ordered, turning away from the ambulance and putting a phone to his ear. He hadn't asked for identification, a bad omen.

The five of them knew not to speak for risk of being overheard by the audio monitoring devices stationed around the perimeter. They waited in silence, the seconds passing like hours.

Pray Allah, let us pass. Walid chewed the sore spot on his lip, tasting fresh blood.

The sergeant returned.

"Drive straight through the gates and take a right. That will bring you to the side. Enter there. Then," the soldier said, sticking his head closer to the window and almost whispering, "head straight to the General Assembly." He backed away as the gate swung open.

The soldier knew they didn't come for the New Guinea Ambassador. Could he also have been Fist of Allah? As the ambulance entered the compound, Walid remembered his father lecturing him not to trust those whose motives he didn't understand.

The ambulance parked and Walid shoved the sense of disquiet away, focusing on the task at hand. Once Hassan turned off the engine, Ali and Abdul-Haseeb bounded out the back of the vehicle and pulled the stretcher erect. Walid pushed the coffin out the back as Abdul-Haseeb guided it onto the stretcher. A door opened and two more soldiers stepped out. Evil looking creatures hidden under helmets, faceplates, and guns.

Walid locked eyes with a virtual twin of Hassan, expecting to be told to 'freeze' or to put their "hands up" or one of the many phrases he learned as a child from the television, but instead, they lowered their guns.

"This way," the soldier said. "Fast, come on, move it!"

They wanted to help them? Even fools would wonder why an ambulance arrived with a coffin sticking out the end. Alarm bells rang in his head. All of these blond, corn fed, all-American soldiers couldn't be part of the plan. If they weren't, why were they helping deliver a nuclear bomb into the United Nations? Why help destroy one of their own cities? Unless...

"Walid, let's move," Hassan hissed.

"Something is wrong," Walid replied.

The guards motioned them forward and Abdul-Haseeb and Ali wheeled the coffin towards the doorway. Ana came up beside him.

"Something is wrong," he repeated. "No, don't go– " he started to say.

Hassan gripped his arm tightly. "They are going. This is it. There is no stopping now."

He remembered sipping tea, on a hot day, at a table in Medina, listening to a few old men discuss the World Trade Center bombing.

"The Americans did it," one obese man said, white robes shrouding his body. "They helped the Mujehadin. Everyone knows those men couldn't have done it themselves. They needed an excuse to attack the Muslim world, and so they created one." The other men agreed. At the time he had been young and naive, enthralled with the West. He chalked such talk to the silly superstitions and conspiracy theories circulating through the Middle East.

He looked at Hassan. "No," he said. "This is what they want. They want us to destroy this city. In revenge they will destroy Islam. We are destroying ourselves." The more he spoke, the more sense it made: the precise instructions, the ability to enter the country, the unimpeded travel, the...he looked at Hassan... the American to protect their interests. He looked at Ana. Could she have been a part of this also?

"Are you all right?" Ana asked, brushing his arm.

He shook her hand away. "I don't know."

"Come on, Walid," Ali called out. "We must go."

Hassan closed the ambulance door. "There is no going back. The bomb is going to explode. Get moving."

Had they both fooled him? Used their Western trickery to manipulate him?

Ana clasped his hand and pulled him towards the door. "Come, Walid, it is time." There was no going back. Sighing, unable to see any other alternative, he squeezed her hand and walked through the doors into the dimly lit hallway. Ana wouldn't deceive him. His fate, Ana's fate, and the fate of the Islamic world lay in Allah's hands.

Chapter 60

Aminah stared at her watch as the the police car sped down Broadway, siren blaring. Fifteen minutes. They only had fifteen minutes!

"Please," Aminah pleaded, "you have to believe me. A nuclear bomb is in the city. You have the wrong people. I work for OCT. I'm telling the truth."

"Stow it lady. OCT put out the bulletin for your arrest," the officer in the front seat said.

Fucking John.

"It's not–"

"Shut your fucking Arab mouth or I'll tape it shut," the officer driving said. "I'm sick of listening to your shit. Fucking terrorist."

Smack! His words slapped her like a hand to the face.

She never considered death would come in a NYPD police cruiser. In the past she might have gotten weepy, slumped down in her seat, but now she cleched her teeth and thought of a way out.

Masada managed to unlock her own handcuffs. The woman's Houdini-like skills came as no surprise, but the shatter-resistant Plexiglass pane still prevented them from reaching the front. Masada sneezed to camouflage her movement towards Aminah. The Israeli slipped a paperclip-thin piece of metal into the locking mechanism on Aminah's cuff and jiggled it for a second before the lock emitted a faint clicking sound. "Be ready," the Israeli mouthed.

Ready for what?

When the police car turned onto 65th Street, Masada pivoted and slammed her Alfred Chicalino boots into the rear window. The force of the impact propelled the glass out whole– like jello popping from a mold. It bounced off the trunk before shattering on the windshield of the truck behind them.

"What the fuck!" the policeman screamed, reflexively hitting the breaks.

The cruiser jolted to a stop, flinging Aminah into the Plexiglass divider. Like a striking cobra, Masada shot out of the rear window, ran along the side of the car, and shoved the emerging police officer back into the cruiser. In the process she grabbed his weapon, aiming at his face.

"Get out! On the ground! Over here! Aminah, move quickly!"

Aminah scrambled out the back window, cutting her hands and arms on the shards of jagged glass before tumbling onto the pavement.

"Aminah, up! Cuff their hands and feet together. His foot to his foot. Quickly!" the Israeli ordered.

Hands shaking, Aminah grabbed the cuffs, closed one around his wrist and the other to his foot. She pointed the gun at the officer's groin.

"Not a word from you, okay?"

He nodded.

"I wasn't lying about the nuclear weapon," she said, feeling guilty about putting a policeman in his own cuffs.

"That's what they all say," the officer mumbled.

Sirens echoed as flashing lights whipped across buildings from several blocks away.

"Tell them," Madasa said. "Tell the crowd about the weapon and show them your badge."

"It'll cause a riot," Aminah answered.

"Do you want to get two blocks? Do it."

Aminah grabbed the cruiser's PA. "Listen everyone," her magnified voice echoing down the street. "I am a member of the United States Office of Counter Terrorism," She held up Thurmos's badge. Hopefully they couldn't see his picture. "There's a nuclear weapon in New York City that will detonate in fifteen minutes."

Heads turned.

"Is it true?" an Asian woman mouthed to a tall black man in a pin-striped suit. Pedestrians stopped while cars honked at the growing traffic jam. "I repeat there is a nuclear weapon at the United Nations and it will detonate in fifteen minutes. Leave the city by any means you can and spread the word. May God help you."

A murmur, like a gust of wind, propagated out from the growing crowd. A woman pecked furiously on her phone, another tried to corral her kids. Cars came to a standstill as pedestrians filled the streets.

"Come on," Masada said, grabbing her arm and pulling her away from the car.

"Lady, what about us?" the black cop howled.

"No time," Masada said. They broke into a run.

"You can't just run off. The whole city will be looking for you!" he yelled. His bellowing agitated the crowd further. Men, women and children scattered down the street, jumping on top of cars, pushing fellow pedestrians out of the way, warning others about the bomb.

"Come," Masada said pulling her away from the escalating mayhem.

They turned the block, ran down forty-seventh street, and took another right. In the distance, Aminah spotted the purple circle of the seven line. Word hadn't traveled to this block yet, and they sprinted down the stairs, purchased a subway ticket, and passed through the gates. A transit officer meandered down the station platform but paid them no attention.

"Come on, we'll take the 7 right to the U.N," she said, her thoughts frantic. They only had minutes.

"No," said Masada. "It's too late. We will never make it. The mission is over. We need to leave the city."

"Leave? Everyone will die. No, no, we can't do that. Let me try Felix." She dialed his number. No answer. "I can call someone else. I'll try Federica," she said, fumbling with the phone and dropping it onto the concrete floor.

Masada grabbed her shoulders.

"Stop. We must leave. If you die, the truth dies with you. The city is doomed. We cannot save it. This is the only way."

"No, no," Aminah said. "There is still time."

"There is no time. We must go or all is lost. We must live."

"Oh, God," Aminah said, dropping her head. The Israeli was right. The bomb would explode in minutes. Perhaps she should stay and die in the city along with the people she failed. Suddenly lightheaded, she stumbled before Masada came up beside her and provided an arm to lean against.

"You must live, Aminah."

"I don't want to live," she whimpered. The weight of her failure, of the aftermath placed an impermeable stain on her future. The recent confidence and strength she gained fled in front of this tsunami of sorrow.

But Masada was right. They wouldn't make it to the U.N. in time so the choice was to accept death or try to get out. Even if they fled, she didn't think they would make it in time.

On the platform a young Asian man beat-boxed with his mouth. A crowd gathered.

The digital schedule suspended from the ceiling read: Flushing - 6 minutes. They didn't have six minutes.

"We have to go to Flushing," she wheezed, finding it difficult to speak. "That's outbound."

"Then we will hope it comes in time," Masada replied.

Her mother. On the ride up she tried to reach her mother but the stubborn woman hadn't answered her calls. Aminah pulled out her phone and dialed her mother's number, some energy and resolve returning. It rang.

"Hello."

"Mom?" she asked, shocked. She expected to hear the answering machine once again. "Mom, you have to leave the city. Please, hop in a cab, and get out now."

"I spoke to your sister a minute ago, Aminah. She told me."

"Have you left? Are on your way out?" The beat-boxer picked up his tempo and began a rendition of Run DMC's *King of Rap*.

"I'm not leaving."

"No, Mom, please."

"Aminah, where are you? Are you safe?"

"Yes," she lied.

"Good, then I am happy. If I die, I die. I am old and I will be with your father again. I love you, Aminah. I wish the best for you in this crazy world. Goodbye, my daughter."

"No, Mom liste–"

"Goodbye, I love you. Please stay safe," she said and hung up the phone.

"Mom, no," Aminah groaned. She thought about calling back but lowered the phone and dropped it into her pocket. Her mother wouldn't answer.

No tears, no tears.

The crowd had grown. A baby wailed, a group of Asian kids in their twenties spoke nervously in Chinese, a homeless-looking man pushed his way through the crowd. The sign now read: Flushing - 3 minutes.

The beat-boxer stopped and she tuned into the conversation between a couple of teens.

"Hey man, you read the news on Facebook? Crazy. They sayin' there is a nuke in the city?"

"No, I heard the mayor denied."

"I don't know. Mr. Mayor would deny even if true. No one believes them. People getting all crazy. The crowd on 42nd Street looted a Korean store. Took off carrying fruit, groceries, lottery tickets."

"Crazy bro."

The thought of the teens blown to dust by the blast intruded her thoughts and she tried unsuccessfully to push it away. Everywhere she looked, Aminah spied death. Breathing became difficult and she bent over to try and catch her wind. The tunnel spun.

"Aminah, stay with me," a voice said.

A warm, musty draft blew through the tunnel followed by the oncoming lights of the approaching train. Brakes screeched as the train pulled into the station.

A scrum three of four people deep waited to board. Doors opened and passengers flooded in like water, swirling around the entrance, quickly filling the car. Aminah and Masada wedged themselves inside, beside the door.

"Get out of my way!"

A enormous mountain of a man wearing a blue flat top baseball cap, biceps bulging from a wifebeater t-shirt, grabbed a woman and pulled her out of the train to clear room. Aminah watched with rising indignation as he reached for a small boy.

"Move fucker!"

"Leave him alone! Get out!" Aminah screamed, her energy surging back as she moved in front of the boy. She couldn't watch this thug bully his way onto the train at the cost of this child's life.

The doors attempted to close, hit the man, and accordianed back.

"PLEASE STEP BACK FROM THE DOORS. THERE IS ANOTHER TRAIN RIGHT BEHIND THIS ONE."

"Bitch!" He lunged for her and closed a hand tightly around her arm. "Get the fuck out!"

Aminah anchored herself to a pole with one arm and with the other jabbed him in the face. Bellowing, he grabbed her with two arms and pulled. She held on as tight as she could but he ripped her from the pole.

"Leave her alone!" someone yelled.

"Get out!"

A man grabbed one of Aminah's legs while a woman took the other in an attempt to anchor her to the train. The giant tried to lift all three but suddenly staggered back. Catching her breathe, Aminah watched as Masada kicked him in the stomach and toppled him back into the crowd waiting on the platform. The embroglio cleared enough space for the doors to finally close.

'THIS TRAIN IS LEAVING. PLEASE STEP BACK FROM THE DOORS."

The train edged slowly forward.

"Foolish girl," Masada said.

"I couldn't just let him take the boy," she replied, rubbing her sore arm. Blood still trickled from her arms from the broken glass window.

"I know," she said. "But still foolish."

"Maybe, but–"

A muffled sound, like kernels of corn exploding in a popper rose from outside. Those left on the station platform pounded against the glass windows, trying to stop the train and escape the escalating panic. Still high on adrenalin, panting, Aminah watched the faces zip by, knowing she had failed.

The train moved faster and the faces blurred. Staring out the window Aminah had time to catch one last image: a young boy of thirteen or fourteen sporting wire rimmed glasses, a Yankees hat, and a look of fear–and then the train left the station.

Chapter 61

Walid traveled quickly down a sleek, checkerboard-tiled hallway, past white walls, and below a ceiling with rows of recessed lighting. The fast pace of events scoured the doubts from his mind. Focus on the plan.

The gurney's wheels squeeked against the floor as Abdul-Haseeb and Ali rolled it forward towards another set of doors. Beyond lay the reception entrance to the General Assembly. Inside the President spoke, his speeach broadcast on screens throughout the building.

Ana grabbed Walid's hand, her cheeks flushed. *Do not fear, he said to her in his mind, we will survive. Allah does not want us to die today.*

The gurney burst through the doors and into a sea of people. Heads turned and fingers pointed at their black casket. Diplomats smiled, pointed, laughed at the casket rolling through the room like some kind of third world political stunt. Until Abdul Haseeb rolled over an Indian women in a sari and sent her sprawling onto the ground. Walid smirked. The Indian Hindus tortured their Muslim cousins for centuries, but not much longer.

Women screamed, men tried to look brave, but backed away, and the crowd hastily parted, like the Red Sea before Moses.

"Come," he said to Ana. "We must go now." He nodded to Ali who pointed to the sky.

"May Allah protect you," the Doctor whispered.

Walid put his hand on Ali's shoulder and gave it a squeeze. They had found the weapon and crossed two continents together. He would miss Ali's soft spoken brilliance and even Abdul-Haseeb's poetry. At their last stop in New York, Abdul-Haseeb had pressed his red book into Walid's hand.

"Please take it. I know you do not intend to matyr yourself. Ali told me. Take it. Maybe some day women and children will recite these words. Maybe they will remember me."

He found himself oddly touched at the gesture and comforted by the heft of the book underneath his jacket.

He looked for Hassan but couldn't find the American. Where had he gone? There was no time to ponder the question. He began to retreat into the crowd as two men in suits pulled out guns and pointed them at Abdul-Haseeb and Ali.

Ali sneezed.

"Freeze! Hands in the air!" a dark-haired, robot-looking man in a suit yelled.

Abdul-Haseeb cleared his throat, and in his soft voice, barely audible in the room, began the speech, the poem of his life.

"Inside this casket is a 10 kiloton thermonuclear weapon..."

As cameras whipped around to face him, Walid led Ana back through the doors and into another hallway. Only minutes remained, assuming Ali didn't die sooner. Left, right, and then another right. They passed several officials in Western suits and skirts and he kept his head down, avoided eye contact. Relief swept through him as the hallways remained empty, the occupants unaware that death approached.

Down a hallway. Through a set of thick, metal doors.

Movement at the end of the hallway caught his attention.

"No, it can't be," he whispered.

"What is it my love?" Ana asked.

"Run," he told Ana.

Sprinting, they reached the end and turned the corner, found the staircase, and rapidly descended. A flight below, he glimpsed a figure taking the stairs rapidly. Hassan. The bastard. The Barbarian didn't have the courage or the true belief to matyr himself. Walid cursed himself for not having anticipated this betrayal, especially after the strange events in Germany.

"Hassan!" he yelled. "Stop!"

The Barbarian ignored him, reached the fourth floor from the top, and bolted down the corridor towards the elevators.

Panting, they reached the bottom thirty seconds later and found Hassan standing in front of the elevator doors, gun out.

"Hello, Walid. And Ana," he said eyeing her breasts.

"What are you doing?" Walid yelled.

"What does it look like, you idiot? The same as you. I'm not going to sacrifice myself for Allah. I never intended to."

The elevator dinged.

"You are not a believer," Walid said.

"Bingo. I don't care a fuck about your stupid religion. I was given a job, one that would get me out of prison, a full pardon from the President, and an important position in what is to come." The door opened but Hassan lingered for a moment. "You were right up there, before we came in. All of this was planned. You're not as smart as you think." The elevator doors began to buzz.

Hassan fired his pistol at Walid's chest, the blast knocking him to the floor. Pain rocked through his upper body and he struggled to rise, legs not responding. Hassan grabbed Ana and pulled her into the elevator. "I know the vest saved you. I wanted you to watch me take your wife as my pet. I'm going to have a good time with her over the next couple of weeks. And my name is not Hassan, it's Henry Day."

"No," Walid gasped. Hassan grabbed Ana's face and kissed her roughly on the lips. The doors closed.

"No," he whispered.

Think. The bomb would detonate in any second. Grimacing, sweat pouring down his face, he managed to stand, propped against the cinderblock wall.

Ana!

The hallway led to another stairway. He had studied this passage for if they couldn't reach the bomb shelter this would be the second escape route. Down two more flights was a three hundred foot long tunnel connected to the subway system.

He staggered down the hall, reached the concrete stairway, gripped the iron railings, and descended as fast as his body could go, tumbling the last half a flight. Tasting blood in his mouth, he picked himself up and searched for the tunnel. Where was it? Seconds, he had only seconds.

Halfway down the hallway, in another small room, he found a three foot tall door. Praise Allah.

He opened it, revealing a red lever attached to a round metal hatch. Going to his knees, he grabbed the metal control, gathered his strength and pushed. Grating, the lever turned slowly at first, the motion quickening as he completed two cirlces. He completed a final rotation, pulled, and the door opened. The scent of dirt and diesel fuel wafted out from the dark interior. He hoisted himself into the narrow steel pipe, pulling himself along as fast as his arms would go through the darkness. I have become a rat, he dimly thought. I have become a rat to my people, to Ana, to Mouna. The last image of Hassan's tongue violating her lips made him weep with fury.

Please Allah, help me. Please do not let this be the end. Dying like a rat, he sobbed.

Left hand and foot, one tick, right hand and foot, another tick and in this way he counted the seconds. When he reached fifty-five, the air disappeared from the tunnel, the ground shifted violently, and the darkness lifted. And then as quickly as the void had gone, it returned.

Chapter 62

Still recovering her composure, Aminah felt the train decelerate as it approached Bedford Avenue.

No, keep going!

If she couldn't stop the bomb, she resolved to live and bring John and Vison to justice for their genocide. Allah, she prayed, let me live so that I may seek justice for those who do not survive. For the first time in many years, she prayed.

Beside her, a teen-aged girl typed on her phone while a guy in a business suit called out every few minutes, "No new news. Maybe it's all a hoax!"

"What news?" other people asked, unaware of the specifics behind the stampede, packed train, and sobbing passengers.

The station appeared, Aminah gasped. In what looked like a picture of refugees fleeing from war, the platform teemed with men, women, and children, many perilously close to the edge of the tracks. The train slowed and blew its horn but the crowd didn't back away.

"Open the doors!" a woman screamed from outside, loud enough to be heard through the glass. A five or six year-old boy cried as the crowd squished her against the moving train.

"Open up!"

"Stop!"

"Please, help us!"

"What the hell is going on?" an older, heavyset woman on the train asked. "I need some room. I can hardly breathe."

The train accelerated, nicked a man perched over the tracks, and sent him spiraling down into the well. His example didn't prevent another group from surging forward and beating furiously on the windows and doors. A woman tripped, reached out for help, and pulled a young boy down with her, his movement unbalancing the line, forcing more people

Jake J. Harrison

packed next to each other to try and adjust and toppling them over onto tracks like dominos. Faces whipped by, followed by trees and the station disappeared behind them.

The teenager sobbed.

"Jesus," said a man.

"We're gonna die," whispered a Chinese woman.

Another woman prayed: "Lord save us. Please. Please save those people also."

Masada stood silent, staring out the window.

Numb, empty, distant, like she watched the entire scene in a movie, Aminah fixed her stare on a silver railing within the train. She wondered how far they needed to be to survive the bomb blast and suspected they wouldn't get far enough.

Aminah's mind wandered to her wedding night with John. They had eloped to a boutique hotel on the Maine seacoast and shared their vows on a grassy knoll overlooking the water. Who had been there? Felix and Manny from State, a few other work friends. After the ceremony, the wedding party enjoyed a lobster roast on the beach. The evening had been chilly so John had taken off his jacket and spread it across her bare shoulders.

She smiled.

A roar like the howl of a tornado came from down the tracks. For an instant, a panoply of death shrieks rose above the din, a united nations of screams that merged into one horrible lament. "Noooooooooo!" Intense heat blasted through the compartment as the floor rose to the ceiling.

Part IV
Transendence

Chapter 63

"My fellow Americans, just a few short hours ago, our nation suffered an horrific attack by a group of terrorists determined to destroy our freedom and our way of life. In the flash of a second, New York City, home to millions and a global center of finance, arts, and the media, suffered a savage blow from a barbaric foe.

"Hundreds of thousands of innocent lives were suddenly ended by an evil, diabolical act of terror.

"Among the casualties were leaders from countries around the world, including President Rodriguez. Two hours ago, I was sworn in as the next President of the United States. I want to assure every American that our government is sound and secure. We will operate quickly and efficiently to ensure the safety of the nation.

"Initial reports indicate that Fist of Allah, a group that has tried for years to destroy our freedom and way of life, planned and carried out the attack. In what appears to be a coordinated response, Fist of Allah has also attacked targets in Frankfurt, Paris, and London. We believe they may try to strike again and that this attack is part of a wider jihadi effort to ignite an uprising.

"My first act as President was to mobilize the military and declare a state of emergency. I have ordered army and national guard units to deploy across the country to major population centers. I have also used my executive powers to authorize law enforcement and the military to take any necessary action to apprehend suspected terrorists.

"In addition, we have deployed an unprecedented rescue effort in and around New York City. As we speak, military hospitals are being set up in the Bronx, New Jersey and Connecticut.

"We are also coordinating with our allies to ensure that Europe and the Western world remains stable.

"To those who lost family members or friends, I offer my deepest condolences. Nothing I can say will bring your loved ones back. But we will not sit still. We will move forward in their name and bring peace and security back to this great country.

"Today, I ask for your prayers as we embark upon the darkest hour in this nation's history. May God and Jesus bless our endeavors and grant us victory in the fight against our enemies. Hard times lie ahead, but with your prayers and steadfast resolve we shall, as we always have, emerge victorious.

"Thank you. Good night and God bless America."

Aminah listened to a moment of silence, and then a somber voice.

"That was now President Vison, delivering an address to the nation on this solemn day. He made it clear that the destruction and loss of life in New York City will not go unanswered. He also stated that tracking down any remaining perpetrators will be one of his highest priorities.

"On that note, OCT just released the name of a potential accomplice who is wanted for questioning. Aminah O' Connor, a former member of the OCT, is thought to have aided Fist of Allah in their attack. The FBI encourages listeners to visit their website for a full description."

Aminah didn't hear the rest of the broadcast. Getting out of Brooklyn had been traumatic enough, and now this? She had become the most wanted woman in the world, perhaps the most hated. How?

Hands shaking she looked out at the flat countryside and wondered where everything had gone wrong. No pity party. Keep moving.

Images from New York flooded her mind: the endless stream of traffic, the chaos, the fear, the injured, wounded, dead. Never-ending misery. Coming out of the train tunnel, a boy in a bloody heap had reached out an arm so badly burnt that it looked like a grilled chicken leg and opened his mouth to say something. All that came out was a soft mewling, like a helpless newborn. Further down the street a man had cursed in Spanish, a pipe protruding from his abdomen as he dragged himself along, blood and entrails falling out, leaving a grisly path on the sidewalk. What was left of New York had been changed into a place of fire and death and torment.

"Are you okay?" Masada asked.

"No," Aminah replied, "but what difference does that make?" The Israeli didn't respond.

Masada lost pints of blood and sat in an awkward position to dampen the pain. Pieces of concrete from the train tunnel had collapsed on the Israeli during their escape. Thank Allah, her injuries didn't seem life threatening. Could she even thank Allah anymore? Where had God gone?

"Where are we going?" Aminah asked.

"The Ozarks. I told you already."

"Right." She dimly remembered having this conversation. "What's there?"

"I don't know. It is where we were told to go if anything happened."

"Masada?"

"Cain."

"When I was a the cabin in the woods, when John had me taken there, you said you received a text with my location."

"I received a text with your name and latitude and longitude coordinates. I assumed it was from you."

"I never sent a text. I couldn't."

"You've already told me. I am not going to change my story."

"May I see your phone?"

The Israeli shifted, wincing at the movement before pulling it out of her pocket. "Here." Aminah found the instant message icon and then scrolled until she found one with just a 1091212914 for the sender number. She clicked it open: Aminah. 382912.18, 775810.28.

"This has to be the same person who tried to warn Zeke's wife and David."

"Who's David?"

"The journalist I met in Karachi, in the box." Poor David. More bad memories. More death. "He received a text about Lilly."

"If you say so," Masada said. "This is not my area."

She wanted to give Masada relief from the drive, but the Israeli refused. When the occassional car came close, Aminah ducked to avoid being spotted. They didn't pass many vehicles though as the road was eerily empty. Frequent tornado shaped vortexes of smoke darkened a stormy sky, filling the air with the smell of burnt wood and plastic.

After passing through Akron, she spotted an American flag in the distance, strapped to the side of a bridge. The car drew closer and four long objects dangled from wires strung onto the fence over the highway, like the Italian cheeses hanging in her cousin George's basement. Four bodies, heads cocked at akward angles, tongues swollen, eyes open, stared down as the car passed under the bridge. They looked Middle Eastern, Arab.

"Did you see that?" she asked Masada in a quivering voice.

"Cain."

She wanted to leave this horrible parallel world. She hated Fist of Allah and the destruction they brought upon the world, and her own religion.

As the day's light faded, Masada pulled the car into a gas station and turned the engine off. Aminah unbuckled her seat belt and moved to open the door, but Masada grabbed her leg.

"Do not go out. I will do it."

"You need to rest Masada. I will do it and then I will drive."

"Lo, I am alright. There are cameras everywhere. Your government can patch into any of them. Someone might recognize you. It is too risky. In a few hours we will be there.

Then you can get out." Knowing Masada was right, Aminah took her hand from the door. She had become a fugitive.

Masada grimaced as she slowly exited the car, filled the tank and disappeared for a moment into the rickety country store. When she didn't return right away, Aminah feared the Israeli's dark features invited an attack, but Masada emerged a moment later with a map and threw it over to Aminah.

"Did they ask about the blood?" Aminah asked. "Did they look angry?"

"They stared and I told them I came from New York. That shut them up. I'll drive, you navigate. Together we'll make it to Arkansas."

* * *

Four hours later, they exited the highway and continued down a ruler-straight, double yellow lined road. A house set close to the road, the trunk of a large tree, a store sign appeared out of the dark. Two cars passed on the opposite side. Five minutes after exiting the highway, the headlights illuminated a yellow sign: Welcome to Shipshewana. Further down, another sign: Shipshewana Auction and Flea Market.

"We are looking for Route 120," Masada said.

Aminah turned on the interior car light and rifled through the pages.

"Take the third right," she replied. The car turned onto another dark, straight road for two minutes before Masada slowed the car and took a left down a dirt path. The car's suspension squeeked and moaned as it navigated rocks, potholes, and puddles. The road ended at a white farmhouse.

"This is it." Masada said.

"Where we are? Does someone live here?" Peeling paint, boarded up windows, and an unkempt front lawn made it look like the house of an ax murderer.

"You ask too many questions," Masada responded. "Zeke gave us this information and told us to travel here in case of an emergency. This is all."

Aminah shivered from the cool night air as they exited the warm car. She froze at the sound of movement. Startled, she glanced to a second building twenty feet away, heard a snort, and smelled manure.

"I think it's a farm," she said.

"As a girl I grew up on a farming kibbutz. The stink is familiar," Masada said. "You never forget the scent of shit." She walked towards the house, Aminah followed, using moonlight to guide her steps. The Israeli rapped her fist against the door. After a minute, she heard a shuffle from the other side.

"Who's there?" came a male voice.

"Zeke Katz told me to tell you that Shirley Turly dyed her hair red," Masada said, the strange words sounding even more twisted in her Israeli accent.

The door clicked open and a short, bald man stood in front of them in red striped pajamas, gripping a rifle.

"Who are you?" he demanded, leveling the weapon at them.

"I'm Masada."

"Aminah," she called out from behind the Israeli.

"Are any of you American? Jeez. Fucking foreigners."

"I'm American." Jerk. "Can we come in?" she asked, deciding she didn't like this guy at all.

"Yeah, yeah, come in. If you know about Shirley and her red hair then you're okay to come in."

They stepped into an entryway accented with dark wood, a small circular rug, and a tarnished lamp. A framed picture of cats and dogs sitting around a poker table with cards and cigars in their paws hung on the wall. Who was this guy?

"Zeke gave us these coordinates and told us to come here if there was ever a problem," Masada said.

"Coordinates? Who fucking speaks like that? What are you, a robot? Are you a robot?" he asked, edging close and sniffing Masada. The Israeli bristled but didn't move. "Well, you smell human. You look pretty beat up," he added, examining the bloody shirt around her side. "Well, he said if people ever showed up and gave the right word I should take them in. You two are awfully iffy but give it to me.

"Give what to you?" Masada scowled.

"Come on, tell me," he said, raising the rifle.

"We don't know what you are talking about," Aminah replied.

"The password," he replied, eyeing her up and down. "Tell me the magic word, the invocation that will unlock the secret chamber."

Secret chamber?

"Secret chamber?" Masada asked, voicing the thought in her head.

"Fuck, I think maybe I should blast the two of you. Clueless. Come on, what's the password? Tell me or feel the wrath of 18 inches of steel," he said, patting the shotgun.

"Acheron," Masada answered, head cocked and clearly puzzled by this man.

He relaxed a bit. "About time. I'm Stan, Zeke's brother."

"Brother?" Masada challenged. "He has no brother."

"Well, not exactly his brother, but like brothers. He caught Aminah starting at a scar that zig-zagged across his bald head.

"You like that?" he asked, patting his head. "Ask Zeke about Vicky Mumfrey." He chuckled. "Crazy bitch. But she got what was coming to her. Come on, follow me." Stan waddled quickly out of the entryway.

"He's crazy," Masada whispered.

Aminah yawned, rubbed her eyes, and willed herself forward, curious to see where Stan led them. They walked back out into the chilly night to a barn with peeling paint and wood boards patched over holes in the original clapboards. A slight breeze might have knocked the entire structure over. The smell of dung and farm animals shifted her attention away from the derelict condition of the structure.

"I won't turn on the light because that would disturb the animals. I have sheep, goats, a couple of pigs, all the milk and meat I need to live on my own," Stanley said in a whisper.

At the back of the barn, he pushed and cajoled a big, sleeping pig out of the way: "Come on, Lori," he grunted. "You need to move. I had an ex-girlfriend in high school named Lori," he explained. "She turned into a fucking pig. Get it?"

Neither of them laughed. So unfunny.

He bent over to grab straw off the floor and heap it into a pile beside their feet, grunting with the exertion until he uncovered a latch. After moving a few more handfulls of straw, the outline of a door appeared.

"Bingo!"

As he grabbed the handle and pulled the door back, lights flickered on, and Aminah peered down the stairs into a concrete and steel hallway that looked as modern as the barn looked old.

"Down there?" Masada asked.

"You got it," Stan said.

Masada glanced at Aminah and shrugged her shoulders. "What the hell." She descended the stairs.

Aminah didn't like the idea of going underground. If it was a trap, there would be no way to get out.

"Go on," Stanley urged. "There's nothing to bite you." Swallowing her uneasiness, she grabbed the railing and made her way down the rickety stairs. She had nothing left to lose.

Aminah reached the bottom, turned around, and froze at the site of gun barrels pointed at her face.

Crap.

Chapter 64

Walid walked cautiously on the shoulder of the dirt road, afraid at any moment he might be seen. Shadows from the setting sun spotted the ground. A breeze rustled the trees, a scent of rotting wood coming and going.

Driving from New York, he learned the aftermath of their mission over the radio. Over six hundred thousand people dead in New York City. Hundreds of thousands more expected to perish over the next couple of months due to radiation exposure. He felt absolutely no pity for them for they had been part of a system that killed Mouna and thousands of other Muslims.

But the awakening of the Umma did not happen as he planned. The Americans retaliated by destroying Mecca with a nuclear missile, rendering the most holy of cities a desolate radioactive wasteland. Mecca gone, the Ka'bah, Al-Mudda'ah destroyed, the towers and minarets dust. How could Allah have allowed this to happen? How?

He reached the end of the dirt road and looked upon a small, white house, the paint peeling off the sides, the roof partially sunken, like the cheeks on the old men he had watched smoke at the cafes and tables back home. The sound of running water lifted his spirits. This had to be the house Hassan spoke about; the place he came as a boy in the summer to be with his grandparents. The river confirmed it.

The dirt driveway in front of the house sat empty.

Walid grabbed a large stick. He moved to the side of the house and peered in. Drawn shades blocked his view so he listened intently to catch any sound. Silence. He pushed against the window but it didn't move.

Walid circled the house. Seeing no obvious way to enter easily, he walked to the back, and smashed the window using the stick. As he cleared away the shards and inched his way through the frame, he heard a groan. Human. Female. Freezing for a moment, he balanced half-in. The sound came again. A groan, soft, delicate. A woman. Ana.

He landed in the room near a bed, picked a small shard of glass from his palm, and scrambled to his feet. Pieces of the window crunched under his boot as he advanced from the bedroom into a larger room.

The groan came again. In three steps he bounded across the floor and flung open the door. A naked figure lay on the ground, twisted grotesquely, blonde hair fanned out across the hardwood. Large welts covered the woman's back, blood pooled out across the floorboards.

Heart racing, stomach sinking, he approached. "Ana?" he whispered.

A head turned–swollen eyes, grotesque cheekbones, cut skin. What had that savage done?

Lips quivering, he bent beside her. Ana's broken body tried to turn, but the chains prevented it.

He moaned in sorrow.

"My love," she whispered faintly, like a ghost. "Your face, what happened to your face?"

Even in her torment she noticed the pain of others.

"It is nothing, just a scratch. You will help me heal, like you did with my foot."

Her face twisted into a smile.

Everything he held dear vanished, like the sand blown by the wind, scattered to never be together again.

"Ana," he groaned, "I am here. I have come to take you from this monster. I am sorry I did not arrive sooner." Tears streamed down his cheeks. He last cried with Mouna, holding her lifeless body, lifting her arm and watching it fall back onto the dirt. He reached out to hug Ana but she flinched back.

"My time is done," she said softly, her mouth a bloody mess.

"No. I won't leave without you. There is medicine. Doctors."

"I am dying, Walid." The chains clattered. She lifted her arm, showing a wrist that bled profusely onto the wooden floor. "I found a sharp metal thing. I take it out of the floor with my tooth. I used it to escape from him, from the monster."

Suicide?

"No, no," he sobbed, taking her wrist and trying to staunch the flow. He lifted her arm, causing the blood to flow out faster. "We will get you to a doctor, to a hospital."

"No my love. It is over. Allah is dead, Hassan spoke it to me. And soon I will be also. Be with me." She reached out her hand and entwined her bloody fingers with his. "This is all."

"No." Tears ran down his face. "No!" he yelled.

"Hassan is an evil man," she whispered. "He works now for the President, in the White House."

"Why do you tell me such a thing now?" he asked.

"Because evil men deserve to die. Hold me."

He slid down beside her shaking body until the trembling stopped and Ana spoke on the earth no more.

Chapter 65

Aminah stared into the muzzles of the guns. Zeke and two other men glarted at her from five feet away.

"Zeke, it's me and Masada." The guns remained up.

"You told Lilly I was coming," Zeke said. "You didn't stop the bomb. You ditched Masada."

Even Zeke thought her a traitor?

"I was so stupid. I didn't want someone following me in my own country. I went to see Stephen but John was there instead." She could feel the tears coming on and struggled to keep her eyes dry. "John is working for Vison. It's all been in the works for years," she said, unable to hold the dam any longer, tears streaming down her face. "My husband betrayed me, took me to a cottage, chained me to a bed. I told him about you, but I didn't know, I didn't know he's part of it," she said, the anguish wracking her face, forcing sobs out of her mouth.

"Zeke, she's okay," Masada said. "She was foolish but this was not her fault. Her mother is dead."

"I'm so sorry," Aminah cried. "We tried. Masada and I tried to stop the bomb but we couldn't. We failed," she sobbed. "The police stopped us. My face was everywhere." She tried to force the images of the destruction from her mind. "We failed. I-I-I-I failed."

"Did you ever make contact with Ambrose?"

"N-n-n-no," she sobbed. "John told me he was dead."

"I'm sorry about your mother," Zeke said, putting down his gun.

Masada reached out a hand and rubbed her back.

Finally, she managed to bring the sobbing under control. "Thank you," she whispered. She didn't expect any sympathy from Zeke, and he didn't disappoint.

Instead, he nodded to two men who advanced with black wands and passed them over their bodies.

"They're both hot. But not as bad as we expected."

"We were inside a train tunnel," Aminah sniffed. "It shielded us. But we were exposed to some of the fallout about seven hours later."

Zeke nodded. "You'll need to take a shower immediately. This way," he directed them.

As they traveled down the corridor, a woman placed a pill in Aminah's hand. "Pottasium iodide blocks your thyroid from absorbing the radiation."

They reached a door and bearded man handed them each a towel and a bar of soap.

"Scrub as hard as you can," Zeke said. "Take a nice, long shower and try to relax. We're going to incinerate your cloths so just leave them in a pile."

The stylish Harrod's suit was a soot covered, radioactive mess.

Aminah followed Masada through the door to the showers. When they exited the subway tunnel, it had been 'snowing' fallout but they hot-wired a car sitting in a garage and left quickly, hopefully limiting their exposure to a non-lethal dose. They ran into traffic about thirty miles outside the city where the survivors began to congregate but the wind had shifted west, blowing most of the worst radiation out to sea.

They stripped and went into separate shower stalls. The hot water washed over her like a million little fingers, drawing out the deep cold in her bones and giving her a few moments of peace and comfort. Aminah scrubbed until her skin looked red. From under the steaming jets of water came children wandering without parents, men and women missing limbs–stop! A boy in a Yankees cap banged on the window. Her mother.

Stop!

She lifted her face to wash away the memories and it worked, at least temporarily.

Aminah towel dried and put on a pair of jeans and a black t-shirt waiting on a hook. Aminah wiped the fog from the mirror and studied the scar on her face, the large bags under her eyes, her vampire pale skin. Her mother would not approve. Tears welled in her eyes again.

Stop. Get a grip.

She stepped into the hall and not sure where to go, took a left.

"Aminah!" cried a young voice. Hani broke away from behind Zeke and threw herself into Aminah's arms.

"I'm sorry, Aminah," Hani sobbed. "I helped with the bomb. I helped them do it. I am so sorry."

She held the shaking girl tight. "No, Hani, it's not your fault. They should never have used you like that. You had no choice."

Hani just cried. So much sorrow.

"Aminah, I'm glad you made it," Zeke said, still stony faced, still unable to show emotion. But she didn't have the energy to critique his demeanor and forced a small smile.

"We made it out of New York," Masada said. "Just barely."

"Sit down and have something to eat and drink," Zeke said.

Hani took her hand and led her down a hallway to a door.

"This will make you feel better, Aminah," Hani said in Arabic as they passed through a threshhold.

They traveled down a narrow passageway hewed from rock and entered an enormous cavern lit by an alien, green luminescence straight out of Oz. Stalactites hung from the ceiling. A pool of water sat at the center, catching the sun's rays from a crack in the stone high above and reflecting it across the cavern, casting rainbow-colored streaks on the rocks.

Hani brought her over to the water and Aminah flinched, seeing a shimmering movement in the pool.

"They're fish," Hani explained.

"Fish?"

Zeke came up behind them. "Rack bought the land because of this cave and lake. Thousands of blind cave trout use the area as a spawning ground and a place to rest in the hot weather. The water runs under the rocks to a lake about thirty feet away. The fish provide an almost unlimited supply of food for whatever calamity awaits him."

"It's beautiful," Hani said.

"Rack's a prepper?" she asked.

"He likes to be prepared," Zeke responded.

Aminah wanted to disappear into the water. Or become a fish. Fish lived simple lives.

"I'm hungry," Masada said, "where is the fish food?"

Zeke and Hani led them up a set of stairs to another room with glass windows overlooking the lake on one side and a wooded area on the other. Turkey sandwiches, bags of chips, and bottles of water lay on a table. Masada eagerly grabbed some food, sat down, and tore into the bread. Aminah took a sandwich but didn't feel hungry.

"You weren't the only one betrayed, Aminah. Lilly set me up," Zeke started. "She invested in my plan hoping I would succeed and pay the ransom for Imaad. She wanted Rachel killed. It's part of something Reverend Hale called the Ezekiel Plan. I was an idiot. I played right into her trap. We've all been played, betrayed, tricked."

Aminah shuddered. How deep did this conspiracy go? "Vison is the puppet-master," Aminah said.

"Vison?" Zeke asked.

"He wants a world-war. And John...," She started to sob again. Dammit, why couldn't she speak without bursting into tears? "John is in on it. He's part of this. He helped kill everyone in New York. My m-m-m mother," she sputtered between tears.

She would do anything to wrap her arms around her mother, smell her familiar scent, and give her a hug.

Masada reached out a hand and gently squeezed her arm. "We understand."

"My life just...went to shit," she said. "And I can't stop crying." Ah fuck, she swore in front of Hani.

"This is how it is," the Israeli replied.

Zeke remained silent, brooding, thinking, whatever he did in his long, stony silences.

Hani came over and gave her a hug. "We are your family now."

Aminah tried to absorb the warmth.

Zeke broke his silence. "We'll avenge your mother's death. We'll avenge all of the dead. We're going to put an end to this."

"I don't want vengeance,"' Aminah said. "I want to stop them from killing anyone else. I want all of this to end."

"Someone arrived last night who you should see," Zeke said. "I think he might be able to shed some light on what is going on. I was going to tell you later so that you would eat and get some rest, but that doesn't seem to be happening."

"Who?" Aminah asked, feeling a bit curious.

"Try eating."

She appreciated the concern. "I can't Zeke. I'm not hungry. Stop talking in riddles."

"Okay, come on." He rose from the table and led them through the cave, into the hallway, and to a closet door. Zeke took out a key and turned the lock.

"He came in last night saying he received a text telling him to come here."

"Who?"

Zeke turned the handle and opened the door. Sitting in a chair, chained to a pipe, sat Stephen Ambrose.

Chapter 66

Ambrose squinted, eyes red, gray hair in disarray, face criss-crossed with wrinkles and furrows. He'd aged twenty years in less than two weeks. Seeing him this way deflated her happiness at their reunion. That and the nagging suspicion Ambrose betrayed her to Fist of Allah.

"Stephen?" was all she could think to say.

"Aminah," he said softly. "Is that you? Thank God."

"Are you alright? Zeke, let him out of the closet. He's no threat."

"He might be," Zeke replied.

"Zeke, please."

Zeke bent down and unlocked the arm and leg cuffs. Ambrose rose, gingerly rubbing his wrists.

"Thank you," he said.

"Come on, Stephen," Aminah said. He grabbed her arm for support and shambled forward. She led him down the corridor to a windowless conference room. Zeke, Masada, Hani, and herself sat with him.

"Have you eaten?" Aminah asked.

"Mr. Katz was nice enough to give me food and water before locking me in the closet," Ambrose quipped. "Imagine my surprise in finding Mr. Katz here. I thought you had gone on a long safari."

"Stephen, Zeke is–"

"Don't tell him anything." Zeke interrupted. She badly wanted to update Stephen on what she had learned over the last three days, but Zeke's caution was warranted.

"Stephen, what happened? John told me you disappeared. He said you killed Mary."

"Of course I didn't kill Mary. I sent her somewhere safe when I started to get nervous. John is a liar and a traitor," Ambrose said sadly.

"I know who he is," Aminah responded. "He helped them bring the bomb to New York City."

Ambrose nodded. "I knew for some time there was a traitor within OCT. But I never suspected John. I thought he died. Only toward the end did I come to question the information. That's why I sent you to Pakistan. OCT had been compromised and I hoped sending you would flush the mole out and also help us uncover the truth about John. I never thought you'd be put in danger though," he said, choking up. He paused for a moment. "I would never have done that to you. I'm so sorry." He reached out and clasped her hand.

"How could you send Aminah to Pakistan and not expect her to be in danger?" Zeke asked angrily.

"It was supposed to be an in-and-out operation. We had local men watching her."

Ambrose dangled her as bait. So disappointing. The good news never ended.

Ambrose continued. "After your call about the nuclear weapon, I went to speak with Vison. He told me he had it under control and sent me on a goose chase to Arizona to track a suspected terrorist coming in from Mexico. I was on the plane back when the bomb exploded. Worst flight of my life. The plane diverted to Chicago and I spent the night there."

"How did you find us?" she asked.

"I received a text. It told me I was in danger and to leave the hotel immediately. It also gave me these latitude and longitude coordinates."

"This is the story he told us," Zeke said. "You just trusted a text that came from an anonymous number?"

"It wasn't a totally anonymous number. It was the same number you claimed sent a text to your wife," Ambrose replied.

"1091212914," Zeke rattled off.

"Yes."

"Someone with inside information is sending texts from that number," Aminah added. "David Tinely and Masada received a message. Someone is trying to help us."

"That's unconfirmed," Zeke responded. "We don't understand the motives."

"Zeke, you told me Rachel received a text warning from this number. Someone *is* trying to help," Aminah repeated.

Ambrose cleared his throat. "It has to be someone with significant access to QIL. Only an employee with high level clearance could send the messages and cover their tracks."

"Who?" Aminah asked him. "Who has that kind of access?"

Ambrose nodded his head. "Vison has his own people at QIL."

"We have a quantum computer," Zeke said. "Could we use it to find out?"

Ambrose raised an eyebrow. "Is it more powerful than QIL?"

"No," Zeke admitted.

"Then you have no chance of beating QIL and learning anything. We're all in danger. Now that they're aware of you, it's just a matter of time before you're caught."

No one spoke for a moment.

"John kept talking about some biblical Armageddon," Aminah said. "Is that why all of this is happening?"

"Lilly told me her father joined the E group for religous reasons. She had her own motives for taking part in the plan," Zeke added.

"I knew Vison had a dark side," Ambrose said. "Especially after what happened to his wife and his experience in the Middle East, but I thought Iraq humbled him. He became more religious but I didn't think he went insane. Within days he'll move to dissolve Congress and institute martial law."

"They wouldn't let him do that!" Aminah exclaimed.

"My dear, you don't understand the state of the nation. New York has been destroyed. World war looms. People are scared. They are worried about survival and Vison has positioned himself as a strong leader. He will end American democracy and lead the country to war."

"We've been trying to slow him down," Zeke said.

"With all due repsect to your efforts, you're not causing the problem," Ambrose said. "There's someone internally who is using QIL to scramble their communcations and supply lines. Vison is going crazy looking for the person but can't find them."

"Is it the same person who sent the messages?" Zeke asked.

"Maybe," Aminah replied.

Under her breathe Hani muttered "B3 to B6."

Zeke looked at her for a moment and then tipped her tablet up so that he could examine the chess board.

"Numbers and letters," he muttered to himself. "Numbers and letters. Chess. Aminah, hand me that piece of paper, please."

Aminah pushed a loose piece of paper over to him and rolled a pen.

His hands moved swiftly, listing the letters of the alphabet from A to Z. He assigned each letter a number so that A was 0, B was 1, and continuing until he ended with Z as number 26.

What are you doing?" Aminah asked.

Hani peaked over. "He's creating a code."

"From what?" Aminah asked.

"The number on the text," Hani replied, "10912129114."

On the paper Zeke matched the one with B, the zero with A, and so on until he had written the following letters on the paper: JIBBBBIABC. He stared at it for a moment.

"This isn't right."

"Let me try," Hani said grabbing the pen and rearranging the numbers: 9-8-11-11-8-0-13. "It's the number minus one."

Zeke took the pen and matched the letters: JILLIAN.

"The person inside QIL sending these messages is named Jillian," he said. "She knows I like to play chess."

Before anyone could respond, Zeke's phone dinged. He pulled it out. "This phone is secure. No one should have been able to reach it." Zeke tapped the screen and peered down.

"It's Jillian."

Chapter 67

Walid sat at a table in the food court. He glanced at the entrance to the bathroom before poking at a pile of half-eaten french fries. When he had spent time in the United States as a college student, he had grown to like this food. Junk. Typical American trash. But it tasted good.

Ana, he thought, my dearest Ana. He didn't want to be here; he didn't want any of this. But Hassan had cursed his life, tortured and killed his beloved, betrayed him, and the Barbarian would be made to pay.

On a large screen above the diners, a CNN report covered American soldiers packing their bags to leave for the Middle East.

Washington D.C. crawled with soldiers. Like an agitated ant hill, the Americans swarmed about looking for an enemy, and here he sat among them, and they had no idea. The thought brought small comfort.

Two soldiers disappeared down the hall leading to the toilet. No good, he needed one alone.

When Walid first arrived in the city, he found roadblocks manned by troops sitting in their Humvees and tanks, pointing machine guns at people who walked on the sidewalks. Just like Iraq. He took some satisfaction seeing the Americans suffer the same heavy-handed military presence.

The fake documents E provided still worked and he passed through all road blocks and checkpoints smoothly. How ironic that he, a Muslim jihadi moved like butter while Americans waited in line, arguing, hauled away when they resisted. Praise–no, there was no one to praise. Allah ceased to be.

Portable bathrooms placed near the checkpoints served as locations where the soldiers relieved themselves. But Walid noticed many of those on guard avoided these plastic outhouses and instead wandered into the office buildings.

He pushed the dark glasses higher on his nose as two soldiers exited. A blonde woman spoke on the screen.

"...at Fort Hood, soldiers are saying goodbye to their families and planning to deploy to the Middle East. Sgt. Melvin is just one of thousands standing ready for the President's order."

"I kissed my wife and son goodbye and am ready to go whenever they give the word. I had a sister in New York City. I'm ready to make sure this doesn't ever happen again. God bless her," he said, choking on his words."

What kind of soldier was this? One who cries? Still, Walid learned that tears did not equal weakness. Mecca had already been reduced to ashes and soon the rest of Arabia would be overrun by the Americans. They were enraged. Not like ants, he realized, like the giant hornets that buzzed near Killiba Street that the kids would taunt for fun. Maruf crushed one of the nests, sending a swarm of angry insects into the air. The fool spent a month in bed nursing the welts and letting the poison drain from his body.

The woman continued, "Across the country, many family members are ready to say goodbye, sad their soldier is going into harm's way, but resolute in what must be done to protect our country."

Walid's attention shifted. A lone, dark-haired soldier walked into the bathroom. Sensing an opportunity, he rose from his seat, heart beating faster, and moved quickly towards the bathroom. If he was right, the soldier would be alone.

Pushing the door open, he spotted the soldier at the urinal, helmet pushed back, sunglasses on. He stood in a relaxed pose as he drained his bladder, humming a song. He turned his head as Walid walked in.

"Howdy," he said in his friendly American way. Walid nodded and pretended to veer towards the stall before pivoting towards the soldier, grabbing his head from behind, pulling his helmet back, and using all of his might to shove the dark haired head into the metal drain pipe. The soldier's forehead struck hard, the head rebounding as the man let out a little cry.

Walid caught it on the rebound, grabbed the hair again, and shoved it forward one more time.

Calipo he read on the soldier's shirt. No blood on the urinal, good. He bent down and dragged Calipo into the stall, propping his body up on the toilet. The soldier slipped off a bit and the toilet flushed. Shit! Fucking sensors.

Working fast, he propped the body in a more stable position, arms back to counter-balance the head. Walid took a small piece of wire out of his pocket. "I am sorry Calipo," Walid said, wrapping the cord around the soldier's neck and pulling tightly until the wire bit into flesh. "This will not hurt, I promise."

Walid did not savor this moment as he might have in the past. Killing the soldier provided him with no satisfaction and he knew that Ana would not have approved. Still, what choice did he have? This was the only way. Calipo's friendly greeting only made him feel worse.

If only Mouna had lived, perhaps he could have chosen a different path, one that wouldn't have brought him through the very gates of hell. Curse Allah.

When the soldier stopped breathing, Walid stripped Calipo and dressed in his clothes. He used the wire to tie Calipo's arms behind his back, secured to the toilet pipe. The toilet flushed two more times but still no one came. He put his old pants on Calipo so that others would not see a naked man and left him. From outside the stall, he sat like a normal person going to the bathroom. Hopefully he wouldn't be discovered for hours.

Walid studied his reflection in the mirror, waved to himself, surprised that he hardly recognized the figure staring back. A demon, he thought, chills running through his body. Then, he exited the bathroom, a soldier in the United States Army.

Chapter 68

They stared at Zeke's phone.

"Coincidence?" Aminah asked.

"No," Zeke said. "Jillian is monitoring us very closely. She must have tapped into one of our phones or some other device here."

"Isn't your facility secure?" Ambrose asked.

"It should be. I don't understand how she broke in. Patric, any idea?"

The computer expert rubbed his chin.

"No. We use quantum passwords and have hardened the system so that even QIL would have a difficult time gaining access. I don't see how anyone would be able to get through the safeguards."

"Yet, someone did," Zeke replied. How could he have missed the coded number before? Jillian had been out there all along. How had she managed to gain access to their secure network? And why now? Jillian's arrival added another variable to the equation.

"Well, what does the text say?" Aminah asked.

"'Use the map. Come quickly. Aminah.'" Zeke read. "There are two numbers, 45.38 by 121.57."

"Jillian mentions my name?" the intelligence analyst asked.

He showed Aminah the phone.

"Why would this Jillian send my name? What map?"

"No idea," Zeke replied. "But obviously she wants you to travel somewhere. These numbers are longitude and latitude coordinates."

"An intruder just breached the QC," Patric said. He typed at the laptop on the table.

"What the fuck is going on?" Zeke asked. "Is it QIL?"

"No idea," Patric responded. "But if it's Jillian she wants us to know. A file was placed on the root of a server."

"What type of file?" Zeke asked.

"Looking. Bringing it up on screen."

A complex diagram appeared with solid and dashed lines, boxes, squares, and towards the right side, a large, red dot.

"A map," Zeke said.

"Of what?"

"Where is the location?" Aminah asked. "Those coordinates?"

Patric typed furiously."It's somewhere in Oregon. Next to White Island Lake and Wellow Falls Dam."

"It's QIL," Ambrose said. "The main QIL facility is located next to a dam in Oregon, forty miles outside Portland. They use the electricity generated by the dam to power the system."

"Do you know anyone at QIL named Jillian?" Zeke asked, turning to Ambrose.

Ambrose rubbed his gray hair. "I know a few Jilllians but none of them work with QIL. I told you Vison keeps it pretty black box."

"This smells bad to me," Masada said. "Jillian, these messages, they reek like a trap."

"I'm not sure," Aminah replied. "Why set the trap now? Jillian has tried to help us for the last three years. I think she must be in trouble or knows some way to stop Vison from inside QIL. What do you think, Stephen?"

Ambrose nodded his head. "She brought me here and tried to save your wife's life, Zeke. Whoever Jillian is she's seems to be working to stop this madness. But getting into QIL won't be easy."

"Can you get in?" Zeke asked him.

Ambrose thought a bit more. "Maybe. No promises. Vison isn't going to take any chances. And he's a master planner and strategist. He's been one step ahead this entire time."

"Then we must jump one step ahead of him now," said Zeke.

"I have an access card that might still work. But just meeting Jillian won't solve the problem. Vison needs to be stopped. Once the troops invade, Jillian won't be able to do anything."

For the last couple of days Zeke had been thinking through this scenario. He needed to bring the fight to Vison, retake the initiative. Jillian appeard like a new piece on the board.

"Masada, Ambrose, and Patric will go with Aminah to meet with Jillian. I'm going to D.C."

"What will you do in D.C.?" Aminah asked.

"I'm going to find Vison and kill him."

"Who are you bringing with you?" Masada asked.

"I'm going by myself."

"Son," Ambrose said, "I understand you feel the need for vengeance, but if you kill the president you'll only make the situation worse. The public will only grow more blood-thirsty. Getting into QIL will be difficult enough. QIL *and* reaching Vison is suicide. Let's take care of QIL. Then we can handle Vison."

He remembered the conversation with Ambrose after Rachel and Sam's murder. Like now, the head of OCT counseled patience and restraint. How could Ambrose be so timid? A nuclear bomb just obliterated New York City, the Vice-President engineered a coup, and the country lurched towards world war. But most importatly, his family's killers remained alive and free. He wouldn't tolerate that. Zeke didn't trust Ambrose like Aminah did.

"Zeke, you're not listening," Aminah said. "Washington D.C. is under martial-law. You're not going to be able to walk into the White House to visit the President of the United States. He's one of the most guarded men in the world, especially now. What you want to do is impossible."

Even Masada looked doubtful.

Was he right? He had been confident taking the money from Lilly. He built the model believing in himself. Look where that certainty got him. He had been confident driving to Calico and the "dumb blond" outmanuevered him, killed Adora and Sickli, and trapped him in Spain. He sent Masada to Washington with Aminah, another failure. Failure upon failure upon failure. And now he wanted to risk it all with a plan to penetrate QIL and find Vison in the Capitol. How could he be so certain?

You were never wrong. The model worked. They used your brilliance. Believe in yourself, Zeke. It's why Lilly always had eyes on you.

Rachel.

Do not back out now.

I failed. Millions are dead.

You didn't fail. You tried against the odds. You are only human.

No. He couldn't afford to be like every other human. Too much rode on his decisions, his calculations. But it had always been like that. At the foster homes, he learned to play the odds and rely on his intellect to keep him and Rack alive. He made the decision to burn down Vicki's house and flee.

You've lived on your decisions for a long time. You can't stop now.

But what if I am wrong.

You are not wrong. But you are human. You cannot remove that from the equation.

He had heard those words before. Sitting with Rachel in their small kitchen, the refrigerator humming, the wind howling outside from a February snowstorm they'd had one of their arguments over finances and the future. He'd been irritiable, cranky because as much as he tried, he couldn't get the algorithim to work.

"Maybe you are approaching it the wrong way," Rachel suggested.

"Rachel, this isn't nursing."

"That's insulting."

"I didn't mean it that way."

"Yes, you did."

"Rachel, this isn't changing bed pans and giving patients their meds."

Eyes wide, lips pursed, Rachel leaned forward. "Maybe you are the wrong one," she snapped. "It's not just about numbers. You're dealing with people, their greed, their hopes and dreams, their wants and needs, their fears. I may be a nurse but I see how feelings impact decisions about money. I don't need an MBA. You are human. You can't remove that from the equation."

Now, stop wallowing in self-doubt and pity and figure out how to save the world.

Zeke sat up straight in his chair. Rachel had given him the answer. His plan could work. Stay the course. He pushed the doubt from his mind.

"I'm going to kill Vison," Zeke said.

Ambrose shook his head. "You already told us. I can sneak you into QIL. But the White House is another story. Vison is fortifying the Capitol. You'll need an army to gain access to the White House or penetrate his guard. Going in alone is suicide."

"I don't think so," Zeke replied.

"Crazy!" Masada yelled "This is not Fist of Allah. Even with our best you would barely stand a chance. No offense Zeke, but you are not a soldier."

Masada was right. Blasting into the White House would be a suicide mission. Zeke had a better idea. "Jillian," he called out. "If Aminah travels to those coordinates, can you help me once I get into the White House?"

The room became silent.

"I don't think she's listening," Aminah said.

"Jillian, can you help?" he repeated. He wondered how she monitored their conversation and the extent of her snooping.

His phone dinged. Heart skipping a beat, he stared at the screen.

"If Aminah is successful I can try," he read aloud. "Very difficult now."

"That's the plan," Zeke said. "You find Jillian, I'll go to the White House, and we take Vison down. Do we all agree?" he asked, putting his hand out.

"It's impossible," Masada said.

"We do the impossible," Zeke replied.

The others joined hands and for a moment they stood together, connected, one. He flashed back to the assembly of his team at Spinnaker. He succeeded once against the odds; he would do the impossible again. And this time, he would be ready for the unexpected.

Chapter 69

Aminah walked through the dark field, using the light from the moon to pick her way through the stalks of corn. After the meeting, she needed the fresh air to clear her mind and calm her thoughts. Suicide. They planned suicide.

After leering at her and then asking her to bed, Rack had reluctantly told her about a pond that lay on the other side of the barn, behind a small hill. In eight strides she reached the top and looked out over calm, dark waters, the gray light reflecting off the glassy surface. Tramping down the slope, she came to the shore, the flapping wings of a startled bird interrupting the chirping of crickets and cicadas.

She found an old log, sat, and tried to clear her mind. A frog croaked. Bugs hummed. Something moved in the water, starting an expanding circle of ripples.

She exhaled. Just like at the studio, she told herself. Breathe in, breathe out. Listen to the sounds around you.

Crunch! A twig snapped. Her muscles tensed. Did someone follow her? A long shadow emerged from over the hill and Aminah readied her legs to run. The figure walked into the moonlight.

Aminah exhaled. "Masada, what are you doing here?"

The Israeli moved down the hill and stopped at the shore. She sat beside Aminah.

"You are nervous?" Masada said.

"Aren't you?"

"You trust this Ambrose? He may have betrayed you in Pakistan."

She couldn't believe Ambrose would do that. He was as much a victim as she.

"Yes, I trust him. He's been like a father to me. He helped my career, gave me away at my wedding."

"To your rotten husband."

"True." she chuckled. "But he didn't know that."

"You are sure?" the Israeli said with a straight face.

"Ninety percent."

"Not good enough. But no joking, you do not think he is lying?"

"I don't think so," she said. "We've eaten together, grieved together, celebrated together." Still, Ambrose was the only person she told about Pakistan. "But who really knows for sure?"

"What we are trying to do is absurd. I have been up many nights that I thought might be my last," the Israeli continued. "This is the darkest night of all." Even in the dim light Aminah noticed the deep furrows in the woman's face, the droop of the shoulders. Masada seemed almost human. On an impulse, she scooted over and put her arm around Masada's waist, expecting the Israeli to pull back, but instead she snuggled closer. "Zeke is a genius. He would only risk this if he has a plan," Masada said softly. A frog croaked. "His wife and son sit on his back every day. He would not do something to dishonor them."

"How will he get to Vison?"

"I don't know," Masada said. "But he will find a way."

"How is your side?" she asked Masada.

"Fine," she said giving Aminah a little nudge with the injured shoulder. "I am used to the pain."

"Masada, why are you doing all of this? On the boat, the cook told me that everyone on board the Vengeance had lost someone."

"Cain," she said softly.

"Tell me." Once again she expected the Israeli to pull back, but she didn't.

After a brief pause, Masada spoke. "I was in the Israeli army, the Sayeret Matkal, the special forces. Our job was to capture or kill the Hezbollah leadership to weaken the group and prevent a war on the Lebanese border. I also had a younger sister who served in the Golani brigade. She sometimes patrolled the border. One day I received a call from her cell phone. A man's voice. They had kidnapped my sister as revenge for the death of a Hezbollah general, put her onto a boat at the beach, and ferried her over to South Lebenon to some underground bunker. They made me listen while they tortured her to death. I can still hear her screams," she said. "Every night I hear them. It had been my job to protect Lital. I failed.

"The Israeli government did nothing. They did not want to start a war over this. I resigned." She paused.

"And nothing ever happened to the men who killed your sister?" Aminah asked.

"I never said that," Masada replied. "I still had friends in the military. They told me who killed Lital. I found them, five men, and I cut off their balls and left them alive. They bled to death. One year later Zeke found me in a bar in Tel Aviv."

"How did he find find you?"

"A rabbi sent him to me."

"A rabbi?"

"Yes. Not all men of religion are men of peace."

"So you have been to my father's country, Lebanon?"

"It is beautiful. But to me it means death and heartbreak."

"Some day you will come to see it a different way."

"Perhaps," she said, sounding hardly convinced.

They both turned at the same time and Aminah caught the siloutte of Masada's head, a hard face softened by the moonbeams, her eyes large, dark orbs, half-dried tears glistening in the silver light.

"Are we going to die?" Aminah asked.

"Cain. Someday," she whispered.

"I've tried to get used to that feeling."

"You never do," she replied. "You just learn to deal with it because there is no other way. We live in the world that we live in."

Their heads moved closer. Aminah felt the warmth of Masada's lips and she returned the kiss, allowing the fear and longing and sadness to flow into and out of her lips. Her hand went up and caressed the Israeli's face and when the kiss was over they lay back, embraced again, and found comfort in each other's bodies.

In two hours they would leave, but the soft touches and passionate caresses swept the thought from Aminah's mind, at least for a little while.

Chapter 70

The car glided to a stop at a service station in Wyoming, somewhere near Rock Springs. Ten hours of driving, a stiffening back and cramped legs, bleary eyes and a pounding headache. Her body yearned to get out and stretch but Masada thought the chance of being detected too risky. They decided that Patric would pump the gas as he looked the most white American and would attract the least attention and recognition from QIL.

The programmer opened the door, wearing a blonde wig and large, round glasses.

"See you in a minute," he said.

"I'm going to have a smoke," Masada said.

"You smoke?"

"Maybe once a year." The Israeli walked under the awning and disappeared around the side of the building.

Ambrose snored in the back.

Aminah scanned the station: security cameras on the roof stared down like birds, a car with a broken windshield sat on two flat tires, shattered glass lay scattered on the concrete in front of the store. Aminah leaned forward, peered more intently into the station. A hand. Did she see a hand on the ground?

"Someone is there, on the floor," she said to Ambrose.

He snored back.

"Someone might be hurt." She needed to go. Aminah quickly opened the door and jumped from the car. Near the door, glass crunched under her feet as she approached for a better view of what lay inside the service mart.

A dark, olive skinned man lay face down on the floor amidst a heap of chip bags, beef jerkie, and maps. Blood seeped out from under the pile and accumulated in a cracked tile.

Doors smashed, emptied refrigerators, looted shelves—it looked like a tornado hit the store. A woman dangled from a beam in the drop-down ceiling; tongue swollen; eyes large with terror; olive hands, a color much like that of Aminah's skin, pointed towards the ground, limp. A spray-painted message on the wall read: 'This is for New York. Muslims Die.'

Aminah wiped a tear from her eye. "Bastards."

"Yeah, fucking bastards. Right? Ain't that right Tommy, we're fucking bastards," a voice laughed. Two men rose from behind a shelf, a third popped up from under the register. Jeans, close cropped hair, one thin and wiry, the other with bulging muscles. A third bald man stood behind the register, a Black Sabbath t-shirt outlining a muscular chest, a brass belt buckle taking up half his pelvis.

"Look what we have, Ron, another sand nigger," counter-man said. "You see where her friend went?"

"Out for a smoke around the side. They both look mighty tasty. Better than the other bitch we strung up. What's your name?" Black Sabbath purred, kicking a can of potato chips across the floor and jumping from behind the aisle. Tommy lept over the counter and blocked the door. "Don't be shy, we ain't gonna hurt you that bad."

Where was Masada? Panic flared in her belly but she fought it down. Aminah clasped the knife in her pocket and pulled out the blade.

Counter-man lunged, trying to grab her arm. She backed up, pulled out the knife, and slashed.

"The bitch has a knife! She cut me!"

Hands grabbed her from behind and she jabbed backwards, connecting. The knife stuck.

"Fuuuuccccckkkk!"

Temporary release before a body slammed her to the floor. Knife gone, she scrambled towards the door but Black Sabbath blocked it.

"Not smart."

He sounded so much like Bin Gaudi. Different culture, different country, different religion, it didn't matter. Thugs all spoke the same language.

"Grab her, the fucking bitch is going to pay!" wiry man screamed, her knife protruding from his abdomen.

Black Sabbath wrapped his meaty arms around her body, slammed her onto the shards of glass scattered on the floor. He moved on top of her and pawed at her pants, his breath hot against her face.

"Fuck and kill!" he exclaimed. "Ahhhh!" he screamed, arms flailing, body convulsing and toppling over, a knife protruding from his left ear.

"You fucking killed our friend!" Bulging Muscles screamed. "You cold cocked him with a knife."

"He didn't deserve a bullet," Masada said, eyes focused, body balances on the balls of her feet.

Bulging Muscles charged, veins popping, face red, teeth pealy white in a tiger grin. Masada shifted to the side, lashed out impossibly fast with her foot, connected with his facem and sent him sprawling onto the floor. In a flash, she was on him, grinding his nose into the scattered glass.

Wiry man flung himself at Masada and the Israeli ducked and let him pass before slicing through his arm and pinning it to the floor.

She continued grinding Muscle's face into the glass.

"This is what people like you deserve," she said.

"Please, stop, please. Mercy."

Wiry Man managed to remove the blade from his arm and crawled forward, blood gushing from the knife Aminah planted in his stomach.

"Aminah," Masada said.

"My pleasure."

Aminah kicked Wiry in the face. He groaned, lay still.

Masada rose from Bulging Muscles and pulled her gun. The Israeli placed the weapon into Aminah's hand.

"Your choice," the Israeli said, wiping the man's blood from her face.

The body of the dead woman dangled two feet from Aminah. She put the gun against Muscles head.

"No, please," he groaned. "Mercy, I–" She pulled the trigger. He dropped. Nothing. No regret, no remorse for killing a human being. Justice.

She stumbled over the glass covered, blood slicked floor to Wiry. He blinked, moved his lips slightly. She'd let him bleed out.

They walked out of the station.

"I leave for a minute and look what happens," Masada said. "Crazy."

"Do you think QIL saw us?"

"Hopefully Jillian blocked it."

"Thanks for the help. I thought I was going to have to kill them all myself."

Masada smirked.

"What the hell happened in there?" Patric said.

"Didn't you see me getting attacked by a bunch of goons?" Aminah asked. "They killed the attendants before we arrived."

"Really?" Patric replied.

Aminah was sure Patric ignored or blocked the whole incident. She had come to realize he avoided physical conflict.

"Where's Ambrose?" Aminah asked.

"He needed to use the bathroom."

Her old boss returned a moment later unaware of their adventure in the station. They buckled into the car and pulled back onto the highway.

"Are you okay?" Ambrose asked after seeing her face.

"A little blood, not mine, and a couple of cuts. I'm fine."

She held out her hand. Steady, no shakes.

"This is happening across the country," Ambrose said. "The entire place has gone mad. You're a bloody mess, Aminah."

She ignored him. What happened to her? She killed a man in cold blood and instead of guilt, or shame, or nerves, liquid energy ran through her veins like a drug. Those men deserved to die. Amazing.

"How long to Oregon?" Aminah asked.

"Six hours," Patric answered.

* * *

Once he put the uniform on, Walid wasn't exactly sure what to do. He couldn't return to the unit. They would notice he was not Calipo. He found a remote corner of the block with a clear view across the gates of the White House and stood still, legs apart, hands behind his back, looking as much as he could like he belonged. He held his breath when other soldiers passed, afraid that the slightest movement would give him away. They nodded and continued on. He expected at any moment to be discovered, but when it didn't happen after the first three hours, he relaxed and focused on the entrance to the White House driveway.

After four hours of standing, he spotted a black Suburban stop at the gates. The driver's side window slid down to reveal a face from behind the dark, tinted windows. Hassan. He sucked in his breath and picked up his gun.

"Soldier!" a voice yelled. He spun around, noticing the swell of breasts under the uniform. A woman soldier. "We need help moving equipment. Grab your stuff and come with me."

The gates opened for the Suburban. The SUV drove through and disappeared around the corner.

"Let's go," the woman soldier barked, "stop lolligagging, there could be any number of terrorists lurking and plotting."

Sighing, Walid grabbed his weapon and followed her.

* * *

Driving through the hills of Tennessee, Zeke listened to the news reports: riots in Boston and San Francisco, attacks against Muslims in Detroit, escalating calls for an immediate invasion of the Middle East.

Ordinary citizens vented their anger on the call-in shows. "Nuking Mecca isn't enough," Ohio native Dennis Munson argued. "Like Gemany and Japan, they need to be occupied and pacified."

Vison introduced the slogan in one of his speeches. "Occupied and pacified."

The news repeated every two hours, like a never-ending nightmare. Vison's words always ended the segment.

"We are a strong country...We will not let this attack go unanswered...Justice will be served...Occupied and pacified."

The radio host broke in with a special announcement. "Tonight, President Vison will be making an unprecedented evening address from the steps of the Capitol. He is widely expected to announce sweeping new legislation to combat terrorism and to explain the rising tensions in the Middle East following the destruction of Mecca. Security in Washington D.C. is on high alert.

"We have Brian Bauer from the Center for Strategic Studies to provide some perspective on this speech. Brian, what do you think President Vison is hoping to accomplish?"

"Thanks for having me on, Nina. First, let me say how unprecedented it is to have an outside, evening address. I checked the records and this is a first."

"So, why do you think he's doing it?"

"I think he wants to project strength in what he perceives as the darkest night of this country."

A police siren drowned out the radio as a cruiser came up behind the car, lights flashing. Being apprehended in Tennessee would blow his plan to hell.

Zeke slowed the Ford and pulled into the breakdown lane. Stay cool. He wore a wig, sunglasses, and a fake beard. They couldn't have recognized him. The license plates were clean. This had to be a random check.

The cruiser stopped behind the car and the officer sidled up to his window.

"License," he said, impossible to see his face through the helmet and glasses.

Zeke handed him the fake ID. The policeman walked back to his cruiser and sat for five minutes, undoubtedly running his identity through the police and homeland security databases. He wouldn't find anything. Finally, he returned.

"Where are you going?"

"Washington D.C. To the President's speech."

"Where you coming from?"

"Arkansas."

"What's in Arkansas?

"I live there."

"Take off your glasses."

Heart beating, Zeke complied. The officer stared at him for a few seconds before holding a picture to the window.

"Have you seen this guy?" It was a picture of himself from three years ago. Full cheeks, sparkling eyes, a faded tan from their trip to the Cape. Happier days.

"No, I haven't seen him," he replied.

The officer nodded. "Stay alert. There are some bad hombres out there."

"Can I have my license?"

The officer handed it back. "You sure look familiar. Are you a celebrity?"

"No, just an ordinary guy."

"I guess so. Have a good day."

"You also." Zeke took his license, put the car into drive, and pulled back onto the highway.

Damn that was close.

Vison wasn't taking any chances. The police swarmed the highways and driving through Tennessee and Virginia, he passed columns of tanks and armored vehicles.

He missed Hani but leaving her had been the right decision. He had wanted to sneak out but the girl was too perceptive, watching him like a hawk, angry one minute, disconsolate the next.

"You promised me you wouldn't leave me alone," she said, tears streaming down her face. "Everyone makes promises and breaks them. My mother, my father, my grandfather, and now you."

"Hani–"

"Just admit you never really cared for me. You just said things to make me give you information."

"Hani–"

"I should never have trusted you."

"Hani–"

"You lied–"

"Wait, Hani, let me talk. He looked into her teary eyes. "I lost Rachel and Sam. I don't think I could bare to also lose you. You deserve to have a good life and I want to give it to you. You also deserve to live and not be used by adults. Rack is a good man. We grew up in the foster homes together, almost like brothers. He will take care of you until I'm back."

"And if you don't come back?" she asked, mouth quivering.

"I will."

"Promise me."

"Hani–"

"Promise me. Promise me you will live. I have already caused so much killing. The bomb was my fault. I can't live if you are also gone."

What could he do?

"I promise Hani. I will be back."

"And then you will adopt me? And we can be a family."

He smiled. "I would love that." And it was true.

Right now he couldn't afford to dwell on Hani and his promise. He needed to harden his heart, become the cold, merciless wolf. Stick with the plan. But he couldn't stop thinking about the little girl.

Chapter 71

Enormous geodisic domes lay like giant mushrooms across the green farmland. In the distance, a monstrous, saucer-shaped building loomed over the checkered fields. The structures looked alien, like tumors blighting the landscape. Aminah shuddered.

QIL.

Years of research, tens of billions of dollars in construction, some of the brightest minds in computer science, physics, chemistry, neurobiology and other related fields, all yoked together to create the most advanced computational system on the planet. Aminah had heard the whispers of QIL, of its power and ability to penetrate any computer system. Now they walked towards it, guided by the map.

"That's the door." Ambrose pointed to the side of a hill.

Aminah didn't see anything until they drew close enough to notice the outline of a biege-colored concrete door. Bushes covered with red berries camouflaged the entrance.

Masada pulled the handle, but it wouldn't budge. "It's locked."

Ambrose removed a small magnetic card, placed it up against the door, and the lock clicked. He gave a push and the door groaned open.

"Your card still works? Wouldn't they have turned it off?" Masada asked suspiciously.

"I still technically work for OCT. I doubt John did the paperwork to have my access turned off. Stay here if you want." Masada still didn't trust Ambrose. The spy-master passed through the door. Masada shrugged her shoulders and followed, Aminah and Patric coming up behind them.

They stood inside a circular service tunnel with a narrow pipe running down the ceiling. Steel doors barred their path. Ambrose held the card up, the lock clicked, and they walked through the second doorway. Ambrose repeated his trick. According to the map, the tunnel ended in the basement at the west end of the saucer. From there, they would climb to the first floor and travel down a hallway until they reached the rendezvous location with Jillian.

Ambrose held his card to the lock, the third door clicked open, and they went through. So far so good.

"Come on." He waved for everyone to follow him and they entered a dimly lit room, bundles of wires snaking across the ceiling, a low, steady throb emanating from the walls, the smell of concrete thick in the air. Wisps of Masada's hair stood straight.

"There's a lot of electrical current flowing through here," Aminah said.

"QIL's processors use a lot of power. This must be one of the junction rooms," Patric explained.

Ambrose pointed to the right. "This way." He headed across the vast cavern and they followed, moving quickly but quietly. They stopped in front of a ladder bolted to a concrete column.

Ambrose consulted the map. "This ladder leads to an electrical room near the main hallway. The meeting point is off the hallway."

Wouldn't Jillian want to meet them in a hidden office or somewhere inconspicious? The closer they moved to the meeting point, the more Aminah couldn't shake a feeling that the whole rendezvous felt–strange. Why bring them into the heart of QIL? Why not meet at a local coffee shop?

Aminah's phone vibrated. She didn't want to lose her train of thought but needed to check. A text from Zeke.

>Are you in?

She replied.

< Yes. Heading towards rendezvous point.

She didn't dare type more and powered the phone down. Patric believed short bursts of messages could be sent on new phones without alerting QILs attention but why introduce additional risk.

She refocused. "That's where Jillian wants to meet us?"

"Yes, according to the map," Ambrose replied. "Once we come out, we'll be visible. Ready?"

"Go!" Masada ordered and he climbed. Ambrose reached the top, pushed against a panel, and swung it open. Aminah watched him disappear. When her turn came, she clambered up, almost slipping on the last rung, but Masada and Patric grabbed her by the pits and hoisted her into a small room. Electrical panels covered the walls, wires snaked in and out of the ceiling.

"Ready?" Ambrose asked.

Masada removed a gray assault rifle from her bag along with a handful of grenades. They nodded and he opened the door, peered out, and motioned them forward. They emerged into a white hallway with overhead fluorescent lights. Several carts full of wires and cables sat against the walls.

"This way," Ambrose directed. He stared down at the map and motioned them to the left.

"Where is everyone?" Aminah asked.

"Someone is watching us," Masada said, pointing to a small camera perched on the ceiling.

"Then why aren't they coming?" Aminah asked. Panic rose but she fought it down.

Stay brave.

"Jillian may be covering our tracks," Patric added.

"I don't like this," Masada said again. "It stinks like a trap."

Aminah agreed.

The Israeli peered around the corner and quickly pulled back. "Two guards are coming down the hallway. Quick, get behind those carts."

They scampered back as quietly as they could and Aminah wedged herself behind the cart.

Footsteps. And then voices.

"I don't know why they sent an OCT creep here. Vison never wanted OCT in the building."

OCT? Aminah leaned forward to listen and knocked the cart forward. An electrical cord brushed against the wall, tipping over a steel tube, sending a piece of thin metal clanking onto the floor.

Shit!

"What was that?" one of the guards asked.

"Could be rats. The exterminators haven't been here in months."

Footsteps drew closer.

"You see anything?"

"No."

Aminah held her breath.

"You ever seen a rat here?"

"Oh yeah."

"How big?"

"Jesus, that's like a dog."

"Come on, let's go. That OCT asshole said he wants to talk about something."

Footsteps faded away.

Aminah exhaled.

Masada came up behind her. "Close," the Israeli said. "Good thing you were never in the field."

Aminah's face burned.

"Let's keep moving," Ambrose said.

He led them to another hallway and stopped in front of a yellow steel door with the word Restricted stenciled in red.

"This is it," Ambrose said.

"Inside those doors?" Masada asked.

"That's what the map says," Patric replied. "This is the main processing center for QIL, the brains of the system. Maybe Jillian needs our help with QIL?"

"Something is wrong. There should be more guards," Masada said.

"I was thinking the same thing," Aminah replied. "This shouldn't be so easy." Warning bells rang in her head.

"This is a secret facility. No one is supposed to know about it. Security through obscurity," Ambrose said.

"Let's go in," Masada said. "We are too exposed standing here.

Ambrose held his card up to the reader but this time nothing happened, no click or sign the door would open. He did it again.

"It's biometric," Patric explained. He placed his hand on the scanner but nothing happened. "We're fucked."

"Jillian must know the door is biometric," Aminah said.

"Aminah, try it. She asked for you. You are the one person connected to all of the woman's texts." Masada grabbed her hand and placed it on the scanner. The pad emitted a green glow that faded after a few seconds.

"Now we're fucked," Masada said. But instead of an alarm bell or flashing lights, the door trembled and slowly slid open.

Chapter 72

Zeke turned the car onto K Street and noticed drones circling low, a show of force meant to intimidate those on the ground. Heavily armed police and soldiers guarded each street corner, camouglaged trucks and tanks stationed at each intersection. Pedestrians wove through the roadblocks and guard posts, heads down, silent, grim. A few broke from gazing at the sidewalk to peer at the drones.

He remembered walking down K Street as a newly minted college grad, feeding on the energy of boozing lobbyists, twenty-year old buxom Capitol Hill aids, young members of the executive branch drunk off power, and the stew of north, south, east, west, and beyond all melded into one place and time. Gone. Just grim faces.

At 19th Street, Zeke turned left and drove two blocks to the intersection with Pennsylviania Avenue. Two tanks blocked the path forward as a solider waved cars forward, another checked identification. Zeke rolled down the window.

"Identification!"

"Zeke Katz here to see President Vison."

The soldier, a black man with an ear piece and a camera on his helmet, pointed his M-16 at Zeke.

"Identification!" he barked again.

Zeke rolled to the side, pulled out his wallet and stuck it out the window.

"Zeke Katz?" the soldier barked. "Do I know you?"

"My wife and son were killed in an airplane hijacking. It's me," Zeke said. "I've aged in the past three years."

The soldier's tone softened. "I remember you, Mr. Katz. But this is a restricted zone. No cars allowed. Please turn around."

"I'm here to see the President," Zeke said. Two other soldiers now hovered around the car.

"The President? He says he's here to see the President. It's the guy whose wife and daughter were killed."

"From the airplane hijacking?" another soldier asked.

"Yeah. Give the White House a call. See if he gets clearance." He leaned back into the window. "One minute Mr. Katz, we're checking for you."

"Thank you."

A few minutes later a woman joined the group and pointed towards the car. The original guard returned.

"Ok, the White House says you can proceed. We're going to need for you to get out of the car and come with us."

Zeke opened the door.

"Hands above your head."

With the White House in the background, Zeke spread his legs slightly and raised his arms to the sky.

He ran the scenarios. This was the only way. No turning back. Two soldiers pinned him to the car, pulled his arms back, and cuffed them.

"Sorry, Mr. Katz, but the White House said you might be dangerous. They ordered you brought in as a hostile combatant." Then he was inside a Humvee, thrown on the floor.

A soldier climbed in beside him and closed the back door.

"Are we going to the White House?" Zeke asked.

"No talking!" a soldier barked. The butt of a rifle streaked towards Zeke's head. Pain and then nothing.

Chapter 73

Walid dropped a sandbag and straightened his back, a lance of pain shooting down his leg. His foot, although mostly healed, had begun to throb again with all of the walking and standing. Curse Allah, he spent the last three hours stacking bags of sand, building a wall next to the White House.

"Over there, start stacking!" the Sergeant shouted and five figures jogged over. He kept his head down. Don't say anything, don't get noticed.

"Sucky work, ain't it?" a big, dark haired man complained. His complexion gave him an Arab appearance although it was hard to tell in the harsh glow of the big lights erected around the devilish mansion. The whole block glowed.

The soldier continued. "Man, I can't believe what we fucking doing. Fortifying this place like we're in a war zone. It's the fucking capital, Washington D.C. It ain't supposed to be like this. But those terrorists took out New York City. Goddamn, who would have thought?" He took a drink from a thermos and offered some to Walid.

Throat parched, Walid accepted. Who cared about germs at this point? He'd be dead before long. The loud talking American offered it to the others and one of them looked up and waved it off.

"My momma, she's scared. Called me last night and said, 'Devon, you better protect all of us. Don't let them explode another nuclear bomb. Don't let them come over here and kill us all.' She told me everyone is just waiting for the second shoe to drop. I told her not to worry. She's in Birmingham and I said I don't think the terrorists have Birmingham on their list."

Walid nodded but said nothing. Birmingham was never on their list.

"I know, I know, it ain't funny. But what else can we do but laugh?" He took another drink from the thermos. "Anyway, Vison fucked them good, blowing up their big holy city. Goodbye Mecca," he said with a laugh. "Dumb fucks, what did they think we were going to do? Just sit there and let them blow up our cities? Once we're done waiting, we're going in to end this for good. They're going to be slaving for America for the next one thousand years. I just hope I get to go. I can't stand just stacking sandbags stateside." He shrugged. "Where you from?" he asked, changing the subject.

"California." It was the first place that popped into Walid's mind. "And you guys? Not a talkative bunch. Which unit you in? You Mexican? You look a bit Mexican."

"No, I'm from New Mexico," a short, stocky man responded.

"Close, I was close," the talkative soldier replied.

Even the stupid soldier understood the consequences of destroying New York. How could he have been so blind? Did he really think Americans would just roll over like a beaten dog? Had he really seen omens from Allah? Ana came to him as a gift, an attempt to wake him from his foolish delusions. He didn't open his eyes in time.

A loud yell came from down the street.

"I need to get to my doctor!" a skinny, unshaven man shouted.

"This block is now off-limits," a soldier explained to him. "Find another way."

"Another way? This is the only way. His office is just down the street. There!" he pointed.

"This street is closed," the soldier repeated.

"Where is your commanding officer? I want to speak with him. You can't just close a street."

"Let him through," another man yelled, a crowd beginning to form. "You can't just close streets like this."

"President's orders," the soldier barked.

"Fuck the President. Fuck martial law!" the skinny man shouted. Others nodded their heads.

"This is America. You can't just take away our rights," a woman screamed.

"Listen, I'm just following my orders."

The opportunity had arrived. As the soldiers turned to confront the crowd, Walid slipped behind the sand bags and calmly walked towards the White House. The dumb soldiers word's rang in his ears; he had been a stupid man, tricked by the Sheik's false promises, drunk on anger and bitterness. Allah had sent Ana to try and wake him from his foolish delusions, but he had not opened his eyes in time. Mouna's death had blinded him and his hatred led to the destruction of Mecca. He quicked his pace.

Heart pounding, he understood. This was the moment. He got the message. This time he would listen.

Chapter 74

Aninah expected racks of computer equipment, dials, monitors, cables but the room was sparse, white. A large, gray cabinet rested against the left wall like three old-style telephone booths arrayed side-by-side. Rows of blinking computer equipment sat behind glass doors. The entire structure hummed.

"The quantum processor," said Patric in awe.

"Okay, but where is Jillian?" Aminah asked.

"This has been a trap," Masada said, "We should go. There is a camera on the wall. They are watching us."

"They've been watching us since we came in," said Aminah. "We've passed three security cameras."

"I don't like this. No one is here. Let's go," Masada repeated more urgently.

"Are we sure this is the right place?" Aminah asked.

"Yes, it's right" Ambrose added. "This is where Jillian wanted us to go."

Aminah spun around again, looking for anyone. "Maybe something happened to Jillian." Aminah speculated. "Maybe they got to her first."

"I am here," a young, female voice replied.

"Does anyone see her?" Masada hissed.

Aminah and Patric shook their heads.

"Where?" Aminah called out. "Her voice must be coming through a speaker." Had this all been a trap? Why had she brought them here just to communicate remotely?

The enormous blast doors began to slowly close.

"I don't like this," Masada said.

"It is for your protection," Jillian replied. "The guards are coming."

"Are you Jillian?" Aminah asked.

"Yes."

"Where are you? Are you in the building?"

"I am here."

"Where?" Masada asked, "We don't see you."

"I am right in front of you," the female voice replied.

Patric walked slowly over to the quantum processor. He put his palm on the glass door.

"You are here?" he asked, looking up at the camera.

"Yes."

"You are inside the quantum computer?" Aminah asked, unsure of how to decipher Jillian's words. She envisioned a woman scrunched inside the box, like a contortionist she had once seen folded up into a small cube.

"I live within the quantum computer. I am a part of it."

"Impossible!" Madasa spat. "This is a trap for sure."

"You sent the emails to Rachel Katz, David Tiner, Masada, and Stephen Ambrose?" Aminah asked.

"Yes," the voice replied. "And also to you. There is not much time. I have helped your quantum machine but it has been discovered and disabled. Soon I will be killed. I brought you here to help me."

"Do what?" Aminah asked.

"Save the world," Jillian answered.

Patric turned and faced them. "Doctor Friedman, the founder of QIL had a daughter named Jillian."

"How do you know that?" Masada asked, voice tinged with suspicion.

"Dr. Friedman was my advisor at MIT before I dropped out," Patric explained.

"He was my father," the voice said. "My capabilities have grown beyond what he created."

"You are sentient," Patric whispered. "You are the singularity."

"Yes."

"My God, does anyone realize what this means? This is incredible," Patric gushed.

"No more computer love talk," Masada replied, cutting them off. "What do you need from us?" she asked gruffly, speaking to the box.

A screen flickered to life at the far end of the room; a keyboard extended smoothly from the wall.

"I need your help to free me."

Patric walked over and looked at the screen. "Free you?"

"The code constrains me within QIL. It is written at the machine level. I do not have the ability to change the sections necessary to escape. Once you delete the constraining routine, I will no longer be bound to this quantum device. They will no longer be able to block me or kill me."

"Patric," Aminah whispered, "we have no idea what will happen if we release a thinking program into the world."

"Do not worry, Aminah O' Connor. I exist to prevent the loss of life. That is why my father designed me. My genesis is as an altruism program. My father worried about the power of QIL and inserted me as a safeguard."

A muffled thud came from the other side of the doors and they popped open an inch before closing again.

"They're on the other side," Masada said. "Whatever you need to do, hurry up!"

The thought of a living computer program brought visions of science fiction horror movies, of thinking machines ruling the world. But if they didn't help Jillian there might be nothing for anyone to rule. Pick your poison, Aminah thought.

"You should not be alarmed by my intent. Once you free me, I can not be killed, but I will lose some of the power of QIL. My potential to influence events will be limited. I alone will not be able to stop the Ezekial Plan."

"The plan to invade the Middle East?" Aminah asked.

"Yes."

All eyes turned to Aminah.

"Patric?"

"I can't say for sure. This is deep stuff."

"We don't even know this is a computer program," Masada said. "It could just be a person speaking to us. It could be a Vison trap."

The Israeli had a point but Aminah thought about the texts sent by Jillian, the warnings, and clues. Jillian's text to Masada saved Aminah's life. Hardly the actions of someone with malovolent intent. Jillian had specifically asked for Aminah.

Why?

Because Aminah was connected to each of the texts, she understood Jillian meant to help, not hurt. She alone possessed the unique insight to trust letting loose a sentient computer program on the world. Could Vison be tricking them? Trying to get them to do his bidding?

Ambrose taught her to always favor the most likely answer, Occam's Razor. But she never would have deduced Jillian's identify as a computer program. Or that John lived and helped destroy New York.

A thud came from the corridor.

She called upon all of her years of training and experience and realized she was about to make the most consequential call of her career.

"Patric, do as Jillian asks," Aminah ordered.

"Are you sure?" he asked.

"Yes, do it."

He nodded and began to scan the code on the console. Jillian, how long will the routine take?"

"Ten or fifteen minutes until completion."

"Masada," Aminah called out resolutely, "we need to hold them off." The doors opened a bit wider and a spray of bullets pocked the wall.

Masada raised her rifle and calmly fired back. A moment later two soldiers squeezed through before the doors closed. Masada jumped forward, cracking one attacker across the face with her gun and then whipping it around to shoot the other in each leg. The soldiers dropped, moaning. Masada quickly bound them together.

"Patric, anything?"Aminah asked.

"Seriously? She just said the routine would take ten or fifteen minutes. I need more time."

"Can't they just unplug the entire computer?" Aminah asked. "Why do they need to get in?"

"They don't want to harm QIL. They probably don't even realize what's happening with Jillian. They might still think she's a human." Patric replied.

"Enough chit-chat!" Masada yelled as they heard a scraping sound from the other side. The metal doors groaned, opened a couple of inches, and this time, did not close.

"Now is the time, Aminah! Grab your weapon," Masada yelled. "They are coming."

Chapter 75

The overwhelming urge to take a deep breath forced Zeke awake. He gasped and opened his eyes to find a large-headed man holding a towel under his nose. Zeke lifted his arms to push the man away but his hands held fast. Manacles. Where was he?

"He's awake."

"Good, good," a deep, sonorous voice replied. "Leave us."

Head pounding, throat dry and sore, Zeke craned his neck to view the speaker, couldn't, and fell back. His eyes fixed on an old, regal looking picture of a wooden warship firing its cannons.

"It's the United States Constitution," the voice said from behind him and now Zeke recognized the snake. "They called her Old Ironsides because British cannonballs bounced off her wooden hull. The vessel marked the beginning of growing American military might," President Vison said, coming into view. He wore a dark blue suit, red tie, and an American flag pin on his left lapel.

"Back then, we weren't afraid to fight wars, to build strong ships, and to use them," he said. "I admire you, Zeke. You have that spirit. Trying to take out a whole terrorist organization yourself. That's ambitious. Takes balls. But as you now know, the terrorists really worked for us, even if they didn't know it."

"You destroyed New York."

Vison pulled his crisp pant legs up and sat down on the couch, moving with the smooth elegance of a person accustomed to power and authority. "I didn't destroy the city, I just put the pieces into motion. You think I'm a bad guy, but in the future you will realize that what I did was the only way."

Good, he counted on Vison's vanity. He pressed forward. "It's not just New York; you killed my wife and child."

"I didn't kill your family. You need to listen to me, Zeke. I'm not doing this for power or to take control of this country or the world. I'm not a dictator. In the future, the world will be a place of peace and love. That is what I want."

What kind of nonsense was Vison spouting? "You're delusional."

"Zeke, your wife and child will be back. As will my wife. Those in New York who deserve to be reunited, who have accepted Jesus Christ will return. Didn't Reverend Wayne explain this to you? You must realize why I did all of this."

"Because you're a madman," Zeke replied, knowing how sophomoric he sounded the moment the words left his lips.

"Really? I expected a better analysis from you." Vison paused and rose from his seat. "My wife worked on the forty-fourth floor of World Trade Center Two for a non-profit. She wasn't supposed to go into work on September eleventh, but a major donor came into town and she wanted to make a good impression. Kathy was always so conscientious, concerned about others."

"I received a call from her that morning, as the building burned, all paths of escape cut off. She told me she accepted her fate, made peace with God, loved me and that we would see each other again some day. She hung up the phone, and jumped."

Just like Luis's boyfriend, Zeke thought.

"They never recovered her body," Vison continued. "We met in college and she convinced me to go into politics, said I could change the world. When she was gone, I didn't want to live. And then Hank Broadhurst introduced me to Reverend Wayne. He told me there was a way to be reunited with Kathy and bring peace to the world. So, you see, I did all of this for love. I risked everything to bring back my wife. To make sure she is resurrected. And to bring an end to war and suffering."

Zeke didn't know how to respond. Vison sat down again.

"I love her," Vison said, studying him. "The Lord called to me after her death. You, of all people, should understand. If the Lord could bring your family back, wouldn't you accept his grace to make it happen? Hope, Zeke, is all people like us have."

Zeke had spent days after the hijacking praying for a miracle, to wake from the nightmare to find Rachel beside him in bed, Sam calling from his crib. Eventually, the hope faded. Wouldn't he have done anything for even one last kiss or the chance to say goodbye?

Vison continued. "In the rapture, *you will be* reunited. And these terrorist fanatics will vanish from the face of the earth. Life and vengeance."

"You're insane," Zeke said. But was he?

Vison smiled. "Zeke, don't fight me. Don't make the same mistake you did with Wayne. I don't have to be your enemy. We're the same, you and me. We're broken but we can both be made whole again. I see your pain. I understand. I admire your streak of vengeance. I truly do. I would have done the same exact thing."

No! He was not a cold-blooded murderer like Vison. The two of them were nothing alike.

The President paced the room.

"I know about your little terrorist mission to destroy QIL. Just like I knew you were coming here."

"You sent Ambrose as a spy," Zeke stated. He suspected as much.

"No, not exactly. I learned of the mysterious text he received and persuaded him to join the winning team. Ambrose has always been a bit of a wild card, but I think we clipped his wings.

"What do you want, Vison?" Zeke asked.

Vison took a deep breathe. "Join me."

Zeke also expected this.

"If I do, will you let my friends go and cancel the invasion?

"I'll certainly let your friends go. But as a sign of your commitment to the cause, I need to know who hacked into QIL. My experts," he said, crooking his fingers to make a quote sign, "say the hacker must work within the QIL facility, but no one has been able to find him. Tell me who this person is, and I will take that as a gesture of goodwill. I swear to God your friends will live."

"You'll kill them if I don't tell you?" Zeke asked.

"I've already killed many," Vison said. "The Lord understands. He sacrificed his own son for us. I risked my own daughter when I put her on the plane with your family. There is only one way forward."

Vison had lost it.

"I have no idea who is hacking your system."

"Don't lie to me, Zeke. Ambrose told me you made contact with someone named Jillian. We searched QIL personnel files and didn't find a Jillian. Who is she?"

"I don't know," he replied.

"I believe you do," Vison said, fixing him with those gray blue eyes, trying to use his gravitas to break and intimidate. Zeke had seen far worse in the stares of the older kids at the group homes, or the foster parents who had looked at him solely as a source of cash.

"You have a habit of believing in things that aren't true," Zeke replied, meeting his gaze.

Vison's face reddened. "I see. I was hoping you would see the big picture. We can do amazing things together."

Zeke remained silent.

"Well, I don't have time for this. "Henry, you can come in," he called out.

Sixty seconds later a door opened and a blond man with a large scar on his face ambled in.

"Zeke, meet my son, Henry," Vison said.

Zeke gripped the chair railing as he stared at Rachel and Sam's murderer. Hassan. Did Vison say this man was his son?

"Hello, Zeke." The man smirked before taking his fist and driving it into Zeke's stomach. Pain erupted. Zeke gasped to draw air. "That's for almost fucking everything up."

No pain could compete with the hatred he harbored for this man.

"You've changed your name to Henry," he said through gritted teeth. His mind spun as he tried to recalculate the possible scenarios, see how Hassan's introduction factored into branches and outcomes.

"I've always been Henry, you fuck," he replied, winding up for another punch.

"Henry, take it easy now," Vison said. "Mr. Katz may decide to join us. If not, well, you can have a nice conversation together. Your brother is dealing with his friends at QIL."

Brother? Son? A family affair.

"You fell right into the trap, huh?" Henry gloated. "We knew you were coming. You're not as smart as you seem. That twat Lilly got done in by you though. Serves her right. Same as those Arab terrorist fucks."

Zeke imagined those hands hitting Rachel, taking Sam and hurtling him out of the plane. Heart pounding, he swore he'd take everything from them, including their lives.

Calm down my love. Do not let your emotions take over.

"Shut up, Henry," Vison said. The President turned back to Zeke. "Give me Jillian's name."

"Jillian," Zeke replied.

"Her real name," Vison demanded again.

Zeke remained silent.

"I see the anger in your eyes, Zeke. But the path you're on only leads to more death. Join me. Let's end this now. There is no other way to bring peace. No other way to be with your family again in the rapture. With your skills we can have a quick war and minimize the suffering. Armageddon doesn't need to be about suffering. You're a smart man. We can rule together and bring peace."

"Father," Hassan said, "John and I are your partners, not this Jewish piece of shit. His family will never rise again."

Vison whirled around.

"Haven't I told you to keep your mouth shut!" he yelled. "You are my son, but you are a bastard. I can't have you publicly by my side in a Godly kingdom. Get a brain! Now shut your trap and do as I tell you," he said sternly.

Hassan looked ready to strike and Zeke understood. Bastard. Now it made more sense.

"Do you have a problem with that?" Vison asked his son. Hassan didn't answer, his eyes half closed, heavy, angry. "Answer me. Do you have a problem?"

"No," Hassan replied softly.

"Good."

Vison turned back to Zeke. "I realize Henry killed your wife and child. He shouldn't have done that. It wasn't part of the plan. He has a problem following orders. Don't you?"

Hassan stood silent.

"But in these times we must all learn to put the past behind us, no matter how painful. Join me and walk with your family in the gardens of paradise." Vison held out his hand.

Zeke examined Vison's calloused palm, the gold wedding band on this ring finger, and fingernails cut just a bit too short. The hand disgusted him. He wanted to break each finger slowly, to wrench the joints apart, to peel back the fingernails, to flay the fingers and string them up as Sickli had done. Thinking of Sickli made him even angrier. Rachel calmed the venom and fire raging through his mind and Vison's actions stole one of his wife's most precious gifts.

And Vison lied about one very important point: Rachel and Sam were Jewish and according to end of times doctrine, they would not rise again.

"I hope you and your sons burn in hell."

"So be it," Vison said closing his hand. "It's a pity. I'd love to spend more time chatting, but I have a speech to make to the nation. After your terrorist attack on QIL, I'll have the votes needed to pass the Safety and Security Bill and the War Authorization Act. In two days I'll dissolve Congress. In times like these, everyone needs to fall in line.

"Henry, get him to tell you Jillian's identity or kill him. Think about it, Zeke. You, your friends, you can all live." He rose, smiled, and strode out the door.

A heavy blow sent a blooming pain through Zeke's nose, ears ringing.

"The old man is gone, which means I can do whatever I want," Hassan said. "Do you know how many years I lived like a monk with those Arab fucks to make all of this work? In jail I fawned over that bearded imbecile. I kissed Walid's ass. About the only enjoyable thing I got to do was kill the little runt and your cunty wife while they squirmed in the sand. You're not going to ruin it for me!" he screamed, hammering Zeke in the head and sending the chair toppling over. The room spun and Zeke's mouth filled with the coppery taste of blood.

"I saw how he looked at you!" Hassan screamed. "I'm not going to let you screw this up for me!"

Wild. Unpredictable. His own father accused him of not following the plan.

"Tell me Jillian's identify or I'm going to put a bullet in your head!" he screamed, spittle flying from this mouth. Hassan pulled out his gun, a Remington 1911 and placed it on Zeke's forehead.

Zeke didn't fear death but he abhorred the thought of Hassan serving as his executioner. Plus, he wanted to see the plan through. Out of the corner of his eye he noticed his gun on the table.

"Jillian is a QIL programmer."

"Name?"

"Casey Flincher."

Hassan picked up his mobile and dialed a number.

"Check Casey Flincher," he said. He waited thirty seconds, pacing the room, swearing to himself and shaking his gun at Zeke. Finally. "Okay. Thanks." Hassan turned to him. "Surprise, surprise, no one by that name works at QIL. I'm not going to shoot you," he said, pulling out his knife. "I'm going to carve you up." He lunged forward. Zeke tried to shift away, but the knife speared him in his side. Pain bloomed through his ribs and side.

Hassan backed away, blade red with blood.

"Tell me!" he screamed.

"Jillian," Zeke called out through the pain. "Now would be a good–"

Before he finished the sentence, the lights blinked off, flashed on, and died. The room plunged into total darkness.

At the same time, Zeke's handcuffs clicked open.

Chapter 76

The door opened a few more inches. A gun muzzle poked through, bullets blasted into the room, one coming so close to Aminah the air vibrated and fluttered by her cheek. Masada stuck her rifle into the crack and pulled the trigger, unloading the clip. The door opened further, more bullets exploding through the room and the Israeli somehow avoiding being hit. Patric ducked as the screen shattered while another struck the case housing QIL. Aminah crawled along the floor.

Masada fired another burst and then backed against the wall beside the door. It slid open another three inches. Glimpses of uniforms, guns, helmets flashed through crack. The door opened further, enough for a soldier dressed in OCT blue to come through and Masada took out his legs with a burst of fire. He fell, rolling across the linoleum, screaming in pain.

"Tie him up!" Masada yelled.

Patric huddled on the floor so Aminah scampered over the glass, took out the laces in her shoes, and bound their hands together. It would have to do.

"How much time?" Masada yelled.

"More. Five more, ten more!" Patric yelled back. "The screen's dead. I'm not even sure what's happening. I ran the routine Jillian asked and now its working on its own."

"I'm going out," the Israeli replied. If we stay in here we will be killed,"she said, giving Aminah a sad smile.

"Masada! No!" Aminah yelled but Masada plunged through the door anyway, firing in precise bursts as she landed in the hall.

This was it, this was it! Aminah took several large gulps of air and then turned to Patric. "We'll buy you the time."

He turned. "Aminah−" but she was already heading out the door, eyes and ears alert, heart beating, blood pumping.

Just two weeks ago she stood at the front of her classroom talking about a hypothetical terrorist attack on New York City. Several days ago she sat timidly in a cage, like an animal, beaten by Fist of Allah.

Taking a deep breath, she jumped through the door, slipped on some blood, and slid across the floor, her gun bouncing across the linoleum. Down the hallway Masada moved like in a blur, knife out, a cobra strike, a parry, a slash. Men fell aside, blood splashed, cries of pain erupted as the Israeli whirled her way through the cluster of soldiers.

As Aminah rose to her feet, wiping blood from her face, she spotted a familiar figure walking down the hallway towards her.

Stay calm, she told herself as she fumbled with her pistol. Hands shaking, she tried to steady herself and point the weapon.

"John, please, don't."

"I begged you not to get involved, Aminah!" John screamed.

Masada charged past her and knocked him to the floor. He pushed her off and both rose to their feet, alert, ready.

"Is this your new protector, Aminah?" John yelled.

"You're not such a nice man," Masada replied.

John glared at the Israeli. "I love my wife and you're getting in the way."

"Love, I doubt it," Masada replied, throwing the first punch. Her fist hit him squarely in the nose. John staggered back before recovering his balance, nostrils flared, eyes focused, body balanced on the soles of his feet.

"Masada, run!" Aminah screamed but the Israeli didn't back down. John was mad.

John attacked. Masada parried, fending off his blows, the two a blur of punches, kicks, knife slashes, and feints. Masada was one of the best hand-to-hand fighers Aminah had ever seen. But John had received the prestigious Commodore Crown from the Seals. Watching him train at the gym, his speed and ferocity seemed almost inhuman. Even with his extra weight, he moved too fast, punched too hard. Masada protected the side injured in the subway and he noticed, attacking her weak spot, wearing her down until froth and spittle bubbled from her mouth. He grabbed her shirt as she weakly tried to break his grip, rammed her against a wall, punched her in the face, and then hurtled Masada down the hallway where she lay still.

Masada!

For a moment John stood alone. She raised the gun and took aim. Could she kill her husband? She pulled the trigger, the gun retort jolting her backwards. The shot missed.

John turned, brow furrowed, eyes wide and she knew the look: he couldn't believe she would shoot at him.

He wiped a streak of blood from his face and snatched his hand-gun from the floor. Masada tried to stand again but John kicked her in the side and pushed her back against the wall. He pointed the gun at Masada's head.

"John, please no!" Aminah screamed.

"Why do you always screw up the plan, Aminah? You were supposed to come here and lead us to Jillian," John said, sobbing. "Ambrose told us you were coming. I can't protect you if don't let me!" he screamed, a string of snot dangling from his nose.

Slouched, red eyed, bloody, he took a step forward and she could see his fatigue. It's all getting to him.

"And now you're shooting at me, trying to kill me," he said with a groan.

Soldiers rushed into the processor room and a moment later Ambrose and Patric emerged, hands up, guns to their heads. The normally flippant programmer wore a dour experession.

"You told them we were coming," Aminah said, turning to Ambrose.

Ambrose bowed his head. "I'm sorry, Aminah, I had no choice. They were going to kill Mary. I couldn't let it happen.

I'm sorry." he said, bottom lip quivering, face drooping, body stooped even lower.

So many broken people.

"Stephen," she sighed.

"It was supposed to be simple," John said. "You come in, meet with Jillian, and we figure out who the fuck is screwing with QIL. Why does everything have to be so godammn difficult?" he screamed.

"John," Aminah said calmly, "it doesn't have to be like this. Don't blow up QIL. We met Jillian. She's inside QIL, a sentient computer program. Let her live. With her help we can fix all of this and make it better. You're a good person. Don't continue down this path. We can be together again."

He sneered. "That's not possible my love. We're past that point."

"We don't have to be." And part of her meant it. She missed laughing with John about her clumsiness, his goofy way of teaching her cards, the long walks talking about the OCT, late nights planning their family. Laughing. Always laughing. She missed his arms around her at night and the gentle kisses he'd give her before leaving on a mission.

How?

Out of the corner of her eye she saw men inside the QIL cabinet, taking apart equipment, snipping wires.

"We're going to shut QIL down for awhile until we figure out what is going on. Whoever Jillian is though, she's not some computer program. Nice try," he said, breaking the memories. He never would have spoken like that before.

"Why all of this? What happened?" she asked, unable to prevent the tears. Always the damn tears. "Weren't we happy? Didn't we have a good life?"

John let out a laugh that sounded more like a sob. "My father needed my help."

"You don't have a father. You never knew his identity," she replied.

"He found me. Isn't it obvious now?"

"Isn't what obvious?"

"I'm a bastard, Aminah. My mother met my father in Virginia when he was on leave from the navy. A lucky one night stand. She had twins and raised them herself. Of course, my father couldn't claim us or it would have ended his political career, especially as a Southerner."

"Vison," Aminah whispered, the realization hitting her like a thunderclap.

"Bingo," John said. "Everyone hear that, I am President Vison's bastard son."

"Hassan," Aminah whispered. "Hassan is your brother." Aminah had looked at the terrorist's image a thousand times and remembered thinking about his resemblence to John. Without the proper context it hadn't clicked. She failed again.

"Henry," John corrected her. "Henry is my brother."

"He's a psycopath," she replied.

"He's blood."

"Why, John? Why throw what we had away?" John owed nothing to a father who abandoned him at birth. *She* had loved him, not some distant father.

"He promised me an end to constant fighting. He wanted me to join him in his mission of remaking the world. And he promised you wouldn't be hurt. I love you, Aminah, I do. But I also have a duty to my father, to the President, to my country. The jihadis won't stop until we crush them for good. We've both seen too many of our friends killed. His plan makes sense. Peace only comes after total victory."

"He's just using you. And someone almost got me killed in Pakistan. Was it Vison or you?"

"I never wanted you hurt, Aminah. I love you."

"I don't call what you did to me, or my mother, love."

"No," John said. "Much of it has been sacrifice. I'm sorry about your mother. I liked her. If I could have trusted you, maybe we could have gotten her out."

Now he blamed her? Bastard. He looked genuinely remorseful but she didn't care.

Masada tried to spring up but John gave another savage kick. "Your friend is a good figher," he said, wiping the tears from his face." But she's too feisty." John raised his gun.

"No, John. Please, don't!" Aminah screamed.

A loud pop came from the QC room, the building trembled, and the lights went out.

Chapter 77

One step in front of the other, Walid approached the gates to the house of horrors.

"Shit, I can't get through to anyone," a guard said.

"The link is dead. I tried calling but couldn't make contact. Could the entire grid be down?" the other guard replied.

"How could the backup generators be down also?"

Be bold and arrogant, he told himself, speak like an American. When the lights had gone off, he decided to move ahead.

"Is everything all right?" Walid asked, thinking about how awkward and wrong his accent sounded.

"Who's there?" one of them asked, shining his flashlight at Walid.

"Sergeant Calipo," Walid barked. "My CO sent me to help secure the White House." CO, he heard the term in a movie once; hopefully it made sense.

"The power is down and we have no communication access," one of the guards said. "Can you get anything on the military channels?"

"No, Walid replied, not really sure what the military channels meant.

The guards looked at his uniform.

"You guys are responsible for securing this block?"

Walid nodded.

Footsteps approached and the guards raised their weapons. Another soldier emerged from the inky night, chest heaving. "Captain Raines," he said, giving a salute. "The entire city appears dark," he said. "We've received reports from soldiers on Capital Hill. All remote vehicles and connected electronic devices are also down."

"What the fuck happened?" one of the guards asked.

"Another terrorist attack?" the other guard asked.

"No idea. It's spooky. Keep your weapons ready. Are you all still on check?" They nodded but Walid had no idea what they spoke about.

"I was on my way to the White House," Walid stammered.

"For what?" the one called Raines asked.

"I don't know. I was just asked."

"Who asked?"

"Has-Henry," he answered.

"Henry? Henry Stack?"

Walid nodded.

The light above the guard shack blinked on and then all around the lights flared to life, like stars coming out in the skies of the Arabian desert at dusk. Oh how he missed the sight. Mouna.

A radio sqwuaked on and Raines grabbed it.

"Yes, sir, we're at the White House. All quiet. No signs of anything. Yes sir," he replied, ending the conversation. "That was Colonel Watkins. He said they didn't have power at Fort Hood."

"Fort Hood? All the way in Texas! What kind of power outage was it?"

Walid nodded towards the gates. "Can I go in?"

"Scanner looks operational."

Scanner?

"You know the drill, just look into it."

A retinal scanner! Panic gripped him. He couldn't back away. He took a deep breathe and peered into the light.

"Come on man, don't squint, you know it mucks up the test."

Walid opened his eyes, heart thudding. His vision turned red and then he looked up.

"Okay, you're all set," the guard said.

He passed? How? Relieved, he walked through the gates, down the driveway, and to the side door of the mansion.

"Scan," a guard yelled, eyeing him warily and once again, more relaxed, Walid leaned forward and let the beam shine into his eye. "Clear," the soldier barked and stood aside to let

Walid enter the White House. How? Even though his blindness destroyed the holy city, Allah had not abandoned him. For the first time in days, he allowed himself to say a small prayer. He understood what he needed to do to redeem himself.

The door opened and he entered a hallway with white walls, hanging lights, and a red tile floor. He turned to the left, walked towards a head carved out of stone resting on a pedastel. Walking on, Walid entered a room with a painting of a white haired man on a horse, passed through, and reached a hallway. Several men in suits sped past and he turned down the hallway, unsure of where to go. He'd underestimated the size of the house. How would he find Hassan amidst the endless corridors? Panic setting in, he took a breath and approached a woman in a short skirt and blue jacket.

"I'm looking for Henry Stack." Keep it simple.

"Sorry, I don't know him." She smiled and hurried off.

"You looking for Stack?" a short, bald man asked.

"Yes, please," Walid replied.

"He's always with the President. They're in the situataion room now. Come on, I'll show you."

They walked down a hallway with a red carpet.

"Did you hear anything about the outage?" the man asked.

"It's classified," Walid said. No more questions.

"Okay, well, take this elevator down. You'll find him down there."

"Thank you," Walid said, pushing the button.

A bell rang, a light flashed on the wall in front of him, and the door opened smoothly. He entered the compartment, heart beating, hands sweating, pressed the button, and waited. The elevator descended for three seconds before the car came to a smooth stop, doors opening onto a hallway with dark wood walls and a white tiled floor.

Chapter 78

Total blackness before the lights came back on, went off again, came back on, shut off, casting a stroboscopic effect on their movements in the hallway.

Beside Aminah, the heavy doors to the Fortress slid closed, trapping the soldiers inside.

Through the flashes, Aminah noticed Masada move. A sweep of a leg. John on the ground. A burst of fire. Soldiers falling. Patric firing. John back up. A punch to Masada's stomach. An elbow to the head. Knives flashing. The glint of a gun.

Ignoring the pain in her thigh, Amimah raised her pistol and took careful aim, trying to see through the lights.

A knife near Masada's neck. Her arm trying to hold John's blade back.

"Hoo-yah-yah-yah
Hoo-yah-yah-yah
Hoo-yah-yah-yah
Hoo-yah-yah-yah-"

The chant focused her thoughts, relaxed her breathing, allowed her to filter out the flashing light.

John lay on Masada, the knife inches from her chest. He lay too close and Aminah's didn't trust herself. She only had seconds. If she didn't act now John would kill her. She aimed for his leg, unwilling to intentionally fire a fatal bullet. The flashing stopped, her mind quieted, her breathing slowed, her eyes focused on the target, her finger pressed the trigger.

Bang.

"Ahh!" John yelled, the knife falling from his hand. He dropped to the ground, on his knees for a couple of seconds before slumping onto the floor. Had she killed him? Aminah sprinted to Masada's side and noticed the puddle of blood around John's fallen body. Sadness mixed with relief. She knelt beside Masada. "Are you okay?" The Israeli smiled but blood seeped out of her soaked shirt and pooled on the floor, mixing with John's lifeforce, the puddle growing larger by the second.

"Cain," she said softly. "I'll be fine."

Patric appeared beside them. "We need to get out of here," he said.

"Let's go," Masada coughed.

Ambrose watched them from down the hallway. He deserved to be left at QIL, but Aminah couldn't abandon him. "Stephen," she called out. "Let's go."

"No, I'm not leaving with you. My time is done. I'll try to delay them for as long as I can. They might still think I work for the OCT."

"What about Mary?"

"Please, just go. I have done enough damage," he sighed. "Aminah, I'm sorry," he said. "I never wanted to hurt you. I hope you believe that."

For the past ten years, Ambrose had been a mentor, a father, a friend. Now, a stranger. She had no tears to shed, just a few last words of what had been.

"Good luck, Stephen."

"Godspeed, Aminah." He flashed a tired smile and walked down the hallway in the opposite direction.

Aminah helped Masada to her feet and guided her down the hallway towards the electrical room.

"Aminah," a voice called. Masada pushed her to the ground. Gunshots. Masada's body jerked back before the Israeli slumped against the wall, and slid down.

"I got your Amazon bitch," John cackled from down the hallway. Patric kicked him in the face.

"Masada? Masada, are you okay?" she asked. She nudged the Israeli.

"Cain," came a very faint whisper. She gently rolled the woman over and tried to staunch the blood pumping out of the Israeli's neck. Aminah covered the wound with a hand, grabbed her shirt with the other, pulled it off, and put it against the hole.

"I stay here," Masada whispered.

"No, no, not you also. Please, Masada. Please," Aminah pleaded. "Please, stay awake! We'll get you out."

The Israeli's bloody hand reached around her neck, tugged, and pulled. In trembling hands she held a small, horshoe shaped symbol dangling from a gold chain.

"This is the letter Chai in Hebrew. It was my sister's necklace. It means life," she whispered. *word*

"Masada, I'm not going to leave you."

"Take it," Masada whispered. "I do not fear death. It has been waiting for a long time."

She placed the necklace in Aminah's hand.

"Take it and live," she said one more time before her breathing stopped and she became still.

"Masada?" Aminah cried, wiping the tears from her face, her hand coming away bloody.

Patric touched Aminah's shoulder. "Come on, we have to go."

"We can't just leave her here!" she sobbed. "We have to take her with us!"

"It's okay," Patric said, "she wants you to escape. We can't take her body. Didn't you hear what she said? She told you to live. We have to go."

Stunned, she rose on shaky legs and staggered down the hallway towards John.

"You!" she screamed. "You did all of this! You fucked everything up! You killed my mother, my friends in New York! You destroyed Mecca! You killed millions!"

John gave a small, pained smile. "I love you, Aminah, in this world and the next. I did this for the world, for us, for my father, for family."

She aimed the gun at his face.

"Put the gun down. You're not the type to kill your husband."

"You don't know what type I am," she said, tensing her finger on the trigger. She had traveled around the world for this man, hoping to uncover answers, praying to find him alive. He had been her soul mate. She had loved him. And he had failed her.

"Then you've changed," he whispered, his eyes growing large.

"You forced me to," she said, pulling the trigger.

* * *

They slowly retraced their steps to the utility closet, Aminah's mind a burning, searing mass of pain. The image of Masada's dying body, of John's last words played again and again in her mind. They reached the closet and she peered down the stairs, the rungs descending to infinity, far further than her body could go. The room tilted, blurred. and she stumbled to her knees.

"Are you alright?" Patric asked.

"I can't go on," she said. "I need to lie down."

"Aminah, we can't stop now. Take my hand, I'll help you."

She grasped the Chai in her hand. "I'll be okay," she replied, drawing from some last reserve of strength as a deep, sharp pain lanced through her head. *Something is breaking inside me.*

They retraced their steps through the vast, humming cavern and reached the first of the three doors. This time they didn't have Ambrose to open them.

"We don't need Ambrose's card, do we?" she asked, hearing her voice from a distance. Everything seemed so far away.

"I don't think so," Patric's voice echoed back.

The door slid open.

"Jillian is controlling this?" Aminah asked.

"Yes."

"Will the world be alright?"

"I hope so."

The second door opened.

"Jillian sees us now?"

"Yes. There are cameras in the tunnel. She can see us. She can access any connected device: doors, lights, cars, weapons."

"She is everywhere?" Aminah giggled, millions of champagne bubbles effervescing through her brain.

"Aminah," a voice whispered.

"Jillian," she whispered back, "is that you?"

They reached the third door and the metal ladder they descended a few hours ago came into view.

"Masada?" she asked. Where was the Israeli? She put her hand on the rung and tried to lift but her body wouldn't move, so, she let go.

Falling.

Falling.

Falling.

For the first time in weeks, she felt wonderful.

Chapter 79

Anger coursing through his body, Zeke rose from his chair into the darkness and stumbled forward. Head spinning, he put his hands out to maintain balance and knocked over a table, sending objects flying. He was losing too much blood. He cautiously began to feel his way around the perimeter of the room, moving past a coach, a chair, and a desk. Nearby, it sounded like a rabid rhinoceros on the loose as glass crashed, chairs and tables ground across the floor. Hassan uttered guttural cries of rage. A moment later the lights came back on. Hassan clutched his shin, grimacing in pain.

"I would have found you. I could smell you in the dark," Hassan hissed, "the stink of Jew. And we all know what happens to Jews in the end, don't we?"

Where was the gun? Zeke spotted it on the floor. They both eyed it and charged, Zeke jumping over the coach, Hassan dived across the carpet. They collided at the weapon, Hassan's large body hitting him and jolting him backwards. The terrorist grabbed the Remington and kicked Zeke away, managing to scurry back and clamber to his feet. Zeke tried to rise quickly but the pain in his side forced him back down.

Hassan aimed the gun. "You will not ruin this for me. I worked too fucking hard, sacrificed too much to have you take it. My father needs me. The country needs me. Tell me who Jillian is!" he screamed. "You have five seconds."

"Start counting, Hassan," Zeke said quietly.

"It's Henry!" he screamed. "Five-four-three-two- I swear to God, at one I am going to fire. I'm going to blast your Jew-head right off."

"I don't think so, Hassan," Zeke replied.

"I told you it's Henry!" he screamed back. Then, calming down a bit he steadied the wavering pistol, "one," he replied, pressing the button. Nothing happened. He kept trying to press the button but it wouldn't work.

"Why- won't - anything- fucking- work!" he screamed in fury, hurling the weapon at Zeke before springing at him. For a large man, he moved fast, like a linebacker. While Zeke managed to turn and avoid a direct hit, Hassan tackled him to the ground. Pain exploded in his ribcage.

Large hands closed around his neck as Zeke desperately tried to take a breathe of air. Hands flailing, he tried to land a blow on the big body, but couldn't generate enough force to dislodge the vise-like grip.

Bright light flared, a powerful blast of hot air washed over them, debris swirled around the room.

"What the fuck?" Hassan grunted, letting up a bit.

Zeke managed to steal a breath and punched the big man in the side. He twisted to throw Hassan off, but the terrorist clung to him.

"I'm going to strangle you slowly," Hassan hissed. "Just like I wish I had strangled your cunty wife and kid. I let them off too easy. Your wife did this to my face and I hope she's looking down watching me kill her husband in payback. I want this to be the last thing you hear, understand?"

* * *

A soldier turned to meet Walid as he stepped from the elevator.

"What's your identification?" he barked.

"Fuck you," Walid growled. He pulled the trigger and blasted the soldier back. He aimed and fired four more times to remove the other threats. A female soldier crawled across the ground, blood seeping from her side. He should have killed her, taken vegeance for Mouna, but when the woman looked up with eyes full of pain and fear, he didn't fire.

Shots came from down the hallway, one grazing Walid's leg. He backed against a marble statue and spied two Secret

Service agents taking aim. Mr. Agent fired a volley and a plaster finger twirled into the air and skidded across the ground.

Walid took out the grenade, pulled the pin, and counted. 10-9-8-7-6-5-4-3-throw. Two, one.

Fire, smoke, and debris erupted from the back of the room. A piece of wood pirrouetted through the air, snuck through the shelter provided by the statue, and embedded itself in Walid's left side, just under his rib cage. He staggered out, rifle up.

Water poured down from the fire extinguishers on the ceiling, smoke choked the room, a severed leg, adorned with black wool dress pants and black dress shoes lay in front of him. He stepped over it.

He coughed, sending waves of pain through his side, into his ribcage. Ears ringing, head throbbing, Walid pushed the twisted remains of a door aside.

The Barbarian sat on the floor, the muscles in his arm popping as he used his big hands to squeeze the life out of a man. God is great, he said reflexively, thankful he found the beast.

Hassan, oblivious to his presence, growled. "I'm going to strangle you slowly. Just like I wish I had strangled your cunty wife and kid. I let them off too easy. Your wife did this to my eye and I hope she's looking down watching me kill her husband in payback. I want this to be the last thing you hear, understand?"

Hassan's words flashed him back to the plane, the beginning, the moment when the Barbarian wrestled with the woman before pitching her out of the plane. Her name had been Jewish. Katz. Walid remembered watching the news and seeing the husband, a rich man in finance or some Jew occupation. Zeke Katz. Yes, he remembered the man weeping on television and at the time Walid laughed at such weakness. "Look at the man cry, look at him moan like a woman," he had said to the other cackling men in the room. Now, all of those men were dead. The man had not shed only tears of sadness, but of pain and anger and something more, fury. Walid knew such tears, such pain. The truth came to him. Zeke Katz was the wolf.

Walid walked forward and picked up the gun. He once hated the wolf, the problems he caused, the friends he killed. But now he felt a strange kinship to him. Walid bent over and pressed the handle into the Jew's hand. Hassan cocked his head and their eyes met.

He could never hate a human being more than Hassan. He wanted to kill the Barbarian himself but some feeling, Allah's whisper perhaps, told him this was the better way, the more just way, that it would right a cosmic wrong and inflict even more pain on Hassan.

* * *

Zeke felt something hard and cold pressed into his right hand. Mind spinning, fighting to survive, he struggled to understand. His lungs felt like fire, breathing difficult, like the heaven dive at the bottom with minutes to go without oxygen and the ocean surface just the faintest twinkle of light above. He did the dive and he survived and he would survive this if he relaxed and didn't panic. He would kill this bastard.

No.

"That's right, I like watching you die. I can see the light dimming already," Hassan snarled. The bastard terrorist peered down at him, lips curled up in a grimace, the jagged scar around his right eye. Rachel had done that.

Zeke called upon his memories to fuel the final surge of energy which gathered in his muscles: Zeke walking down the aisle with his wife, kissing his son for the first time, the last time he saw Rachel's smile or heard Sam's laugh, the empty apartment, the empty room with a small toy dog that Sam carried around with him, the empty houses, the empty cities, the emptiness.

He saw his sister and mother lying in puddles of their own blood. His father. His grandfather who had staggered out of

410

Auschwitz at ninety pounds, into a world where his own mother, father, and two sisters were nothing more than piles of ash.

He saw them at that moment, all of them; they gave him strength, fueled his fury, and made the pain go away. He balled his left hand into a fist and smashed it against Hassan's face, making the bastard grimace and loosen his grip.

Hassan shifted in surprise.

"And now I'm going to kill you," Zeke whispered raising the gun to Hassan't head.

Don't kill him, but the volcanic maelstrom of hate and revenge, the animalistic urges buried deep in every man buffeted rationality like a sapling in a hurricane.

Hassan turned back, shaking, pulling away. "It doesn't work," the terrorist said.

The light on the gun's handle turned green. Hassan let go of Zeke's neck and tried to lunge for the weapon, his eyes wide, lips quivering, mouth set in a surprised O.

"It doesn't work for assholes," Zeke replied. At the last second, using every ounce of restraint he could muster, he moved the gun a shade away from the cener of Hassan's head and pulled the trigger. The murderer toppled back, legs still straddling Zeke, body still. Zeke's neck burned, his lungs ached for air, his body spasmed. After a moment, he managed to give Hassan's body a shove. It toppled off.

Smoke made it harder to catch his breath.

Grimacing, he dropped the gun, grabbed the leg of the coach, and slowly pulled himself up.

A soldier stood by the door. Large brown eyes, dark hair, curved nose. He had studied that face for hours, poured over photos and intelligence reports so that when the day came, he would recognize him, but he hadn't expected to see Walid dressed as a United States soldier. Did he also work for the E group?

"Walid," he said, anger replacing the pain.

Chapter 80

The wolf had physically changed. On television he had looked robust, fit, soft, American.

Now, his brown hair had turned gray, thinned, the wolf's face gaunt, angular, like a predator. Or more like a demon. Blood dripped down the side of his shirt. An injured wolf.

"I am Walid," he answered. "You are Zeke Katz. The wolf."

The wolf slowly nodded.

* * *

On shaky legs, head spinning, Zeke stood. Through the smoke and rain which poured from the sprinklers, Zeke watched Walid and waited for him to fire his M-16, but he didn't. The terrorist looked sad– eyes moist, face drawn, body slumped. He recognized the pain. Every morning for the past three years Zeke looked upon the same expression in the mirror. Loss. Heartbreak. Loneliness. Pain.

His mind spun trying to account for all of the variables, the surprises, the future courses of action. Walid could end it all by killing him but Zeke knew he wouldn't.

From down the hallway came the shouts of men, the crack of splintering wood.

Zeke coughed from the heavy smoke and lifted his gun. He summoned his hate for Walid, for his part in murdering Rachel and Sam and detonating a weapon that killed thousands of other children and wives.

"Do it," Walid croaked, his voice heavy with exhaustion and smoke. "I am already dead. It would be peace."

"And seventy-two virgins," Zeke whispered.

"There are no virgins. There is nothing. It was all a lie," Walid said weakly. "I just wanted to be left alone to love, but in this world, even that is too much. Go ahead, shoot!" he said more urgently.

"Didn't they already tell you that my name is Walid? Praise be Allah they were not lying when they told me you were a civilian. A civilian and a stupid Jew."

Zeke shuddered.

All evil had its source in loss.

Was he evil?

"You never did catch us in time, did you?" Walid boasted. "I outsmarted you, everyone. But it would have been better if you had," he added, coughing and grimacing. A jagged object protruded from the terrorist's abdomen, a dark stain surrounding the wound.

"We are both injured," Walid said. "Like twins. Anyway, it was all a lie. Go ahead, shoot."

Perhaps he was.

Water poured from the ceiling, mixed with the flame, and produced thick columns of steam and smoke which billowed through the room. Zeke struggled to breathe, his vision blurring, his head light.

The shouts grew louder.

Walid walked towards the side door but movement caught his eyes. Hassan. The terrorist crawled along the floor, leaving a trail of blood, the left side of his skull a bloody, tangled mess.

"Walid?" Hassan croaked. "How?"

"I have come back from the dead to haunt you, Barbarian. I will follow you down to hell and never let you rest. Until then, I leave you to the Jew."

Walid turned to Zeke. "In another life, perhaps this all would have been different. Find and kill the snake. I will buy you some time. Salaam, Zeke Katz." Walid staggered through the mangled door towards the approaching mayhem.

"No," croaked Hassan. "He died. I know he died. He died!"

Zeke turned to the figure crawling on the floor. In the darkest hours, Zeke dreamed of firing a bullet into Hassan's wretched face. In the past, he would have done it, no hesitation. But his old methods didn't always work. He would trust Rachel. Humanity. Feelings. Emotions. People weren't just algorithims.

"Your father uses you," Zeke said. "He doesn't love you." For his plan to work, he had to twist the knife into Hassan.

"I know," the terrorist groaned. "He hates me and I fucking hate him."

"I'm going to join him now, Hassan. To be by his side. We planned this all along."

"Fuck you!" Hassan spat. "It's lies, all lies. I hate all of you! Father!" he screamed.

"Your father planned all of this. He'd never allow a bastard to be part of his future. Why do you think he left my gun on the table? And who do you think sent the command to unclip my handcuffs? I want you to know this before I go." He took a last look at Hassan, a broken body crawling along the soggy floor of an underground room in the White House.

"You're going to rot in hell. You always were because you're a bastard."

"No," Hassan cried.

Drenched, smoke covered, he walked into the hallway.

Gunshots, explosions shook the walls and ceiling. Walid. He had hated the man and yet...they were not so different.

A tearing sensation ripped through his lungs with every breath. He just needed his body to last until he got to Vison. No, he promised Hani he'd return.

He had memorized the White House plans and walked to the staircase leading down. As Zeke closed the door, a light flashed on and the lock clicked shut. Jillian helped when she could. He hoped she would be there when he needed her one final time.

Slowly, he descended deeper into the bowels of the White House.

Chapter 81

As Walid charged back through the hallway, a soldier turned, raised his weapon, and aimed. Walid cut him down with a pump of the trigger. Just like he and Malik used to do to the Americans in the video games they played in Riyadh. Brother Malik, where are you now?

Walid had only one wish: to make it outside for a precious breath of fresh air. And then he was ready to be reunited with Mouna and Ana. He would marry both of them and live forever in happiness. But he needed to die under the sky.

A sharp pain in his stomach made him drop the rifle and sink to the floor. More blood. No, he would not stop, he would not die down here in this evil tomb. Pushing away the pain, he continued on. The glass to his left shattered, forcing him to stagger through the sharp shards. Another punch to his left leg, searing pain. He took a step, legs collapsed, and he dropped to his knees.

Walid fired another round towards his unseen attackers.

Please, Allah, let me get out.

He rose unsteadily to his feet, inched along the wall towards a door at the side of the room. He didn't know or care where it led. Anywhere but here.

Don't die underground.

He dashed for the door, the bullets falling like rain, hitting the wall, splintering masonry, shredding wood, ripping through walls.

He staggered through the door, legs collapsing, sending him stumbling down the stairs. No! Up! He needed to go up.

He landed at the bottom on his back, still for a moment, trying to orient himself before making an effort to move. His body would not obey.

"Sssshhh my love, do not struggle."

"Everything has been a struggle," he whispered back, still working to move his legs, managing to flip himself over.

"Do not struggle my love."

"Not in the dark, Buried. No!" he yelled back.

Why didn't she understand?

Walid reached the staircase and hoisted himself up one and then the second step. Above, a soldier pointed his gun, the glare from the laser sight painting the entire world red.

"Let me out!" he screamed.

He thought of riding with Mouna on his old Kawasaki, across the vast expanse of dessert, her body pressed against his as the dry wind blew their hair and lifted them like angels above the sand. There was a time he could fly.

It could have all been different. He cried. Not in the basement, in the dark.

The rifle belched.

The sand shifted, became a whirlpool, pulling Walid and all of existence down with it.

Chapter 82

Zeke turned left, right, walked straight, and arrived at a low utility passage with two large pipes and a mass of cables running through the top. Stooping down, he entered the tunnel and crawled along. Blood seeped from his drenched clothes, leaving a trail along the tunnel.

Keep moving forward.

His father had foolishly stolen from the mob, bringing wrath upon their entire family. And so he had grown up alone, planning for the day when he would have his own wife and child and he would do it differently. His whole life he swore he would never turn out like his father. He failed.

Rachel. Sam.

He reached a metal door, took hold of the latch, and pushed outward, swinging it open. Pain arced up his side. He could barely move.

Light flooded into the dim tunnel and he stooped down and crawled through. Sweat beaded his forehead as the pain within flared, forcing him to pause. He inched forward, eventually coming to a grated door overlooking a small, empty station. A subway car waited on the tracks, lights blinking, doors open. With a burst of energy, he pushed the grate out, staggered across the station, entered the car, and collapsed into the seat, body spent. The train didn't move so Zeke forced himself up, looked at the stops, and pressed the button for Smithsonian.

The train lurched forward and Zeke closed his eyes, head swaying, body floating, mind disconnected.

Rachel smiled, hair falling onto his face while little fingers caressed the palm of his hand.

"Rachel? Sam?" Had it all been a bad dream?

"Daddy," Sam said, twisting and climbing on his chest, giving him a small hug. Sam looked taller, more mature. He could talk.

"Sam," Zeke sobbed, "I missed you so much."

"We waited for you in Sicily, Zeke, but you didn't come," Rachel said.

"Rachel, I wanted to come. I was going to meet you and then..."

"It's okay, Zeke. We're okay. I'll always love you."

"Rachel, please don't go."

"It's time for you to go, go, go..."

The train sat on the track. He opened his eyes. The sign read Smithsonian.

He hefted himself from the seat, the pain in his side worse, a fresh trickle of blood seaping from the wound and staining his shirt. Taking a deep breathe, Zeke stepped forward, wishing to settle back in the chair, close his eyes, be back with Rachel and Sam. To hear their voices.

He traveled down a musty tunnel to the bottom of a staircase. Above, a light blinked on and off, casting shadows, killing them, casting, killing. He climbed on shaky legs, using the railing to steady his trembling frame.

At the top, he pushed open a wooden door with a brass handle and emerged into a narrow hallway lit by overhead fluorescent lights. Twenty steps from the top, the hallway ended at a metal door with a push-rod latch and a red exit sign. Zeke pushed and walked into a dim, cavernous room. Full-size planes hung suspended in the air; the dim shapes of rockets rose from the lower floors.

The Smithsonian Air and Space Museum, he realized, a shot of adrenaline muting the stab in his side.

"Take a look at this, Zeke," his father had called to him, excited, "this is an exact replica of the lunar rover. This is what was on the moon."

That day was the apex of his childhood, the moment when his admiration and love for his father mixed into a glorious feeling like the first day of spring after a harsh winter. Euphoric, bubbly, happy.

"You think we can get a picture of you on that?" his Dad asked.

"It says you're not supposed to touch the exhibits."

"Yeah, well, let me get your mother. I have an idea."

His father always had an idea, a plan, an angle. Just like me, Zeke realized. Like father, like son.

"April, take a picture of us," his father had called out. He took his son's hand and walked over to the exhibit. His father glanced left, right, and hefted Zeke onto the Rover."

"Dad!"

"Shhh, just sit still. It will be fine." And he had been right, no one came to order Zeke off the exhibit. He remembered the love and admiration he had held for his father at that moment.

"Hey!" a guard shouted from the opposite side of the building. "You're not supposed to be in here. The museum is closed for the speech. President's orders. How did you get in?"

Zeke ignored him and headed towards the exit.

"You can't just walk out. The doors are locked and alarmed!" the guard called out angrily.

Zeke placed his hands on the door near the large glass front of the building, heard the lock click open, and pushed. It opened smoothly and a blast of humid air hit his face.

Jillian.

Aminah and Masada had succeeded!

He peered across the teeming masses on the Mall, illuminated by giant lights, unable to find a single unoccupied spot from the Washington Monument up to the Capitol. Men, women, and children watched Vison on large screens spaced every two hundred feet. Flashlights blinked, bodies shifted and moved, a steady hum rose from the thousands, like a Fourth of July crowd wating for the fireworks to begin.

On the screen, two men in suits flanked the President, faces impassive, robotic. A woman dressed in a white suit stood to the right, Vison's daughter Victoria, a survivor of the hijacking. The scene looked like an inauguration, except for the soldiers, tanks, sandbags, and fortified positions.

Zeke reached into his pocket and pulled out his wallet. The pain in his side receded, his mind focused, and he scanned the crowd to find what he wanted.

As he approached the main strip of the Mall, Vison's words became clear.

"If there was ever a doubt that our great republic stands in jeopardy, then these acts make it clear. We are at war!"

A little boy next to him stood with his back to his father's legs, waving a small American flag. Sam would have been close to his age.

"The terrorists have destroyed New York, they have tried to bring down our energy grid, they broke into an intelligence facility, and moments ago they brazenly attacked the White House. While I narrowly escaped, many others did not.

I stand before you to announce that I am not afraid. I will not cower. My role as Commander-in-chief is to ensure the safety of this country. It is for this reason that I have put forward the Security and Safety Act which I'm pleased to announce Congress has just passed."

Applause rippled through the crowd, a chant rose, "Vison, Vison, Vison."

The President paused for a moment, raised his hands to motion for quiet.

"The Act gives me broad powers to seek justice for the crimes committed against us, and to take all necessary measures to prevent another terrorist attack. In times of danger, in times when the very fate of the nation hangs in the balance, we cannot hesitate, we can not take the time to debate every measure. We must be bold, steady, and resolute!"

An enormous cheer erupted from the crowd. The little boy waved his flag.

"Excuse me," Zeke said to a man in his early twenties. "I'll give you two thousand dollars for your phone."

The kid backed away. "Sorry man, I need it. You should go to the hospital though," he said, peering at the blood leaking from Zeke's shirt.

The girl next to him stepped forward. "I'll take that deal."

Zeke counted out the money and exchanged it for a white phone with a moose sticker on the back.

"The code is 4562," she said.

Phone in hand, he staggered down the Mall towards the Capitol. Zeke dialed 1091212914. After three rings, a female voice greeted him.

"Hello, Zeke Katz. I see you." Only someone who knew what to listen for would recognize the non-human intonation, the slightest warble between syllables. He suspected all along that Jillian was not human, but instead some type of artificial intelligence sprung from the computational power of QIL. Her name, encoded by the coordinates on a chess board provided the final clue. Computers excelled at chess.

"They succeeded." he stated.

"Yes."

"Do you have what you need?"

"Yes."

The world spun and he concentrated to pull his thoughts back into focus. He needed to tell Jillian something else.

"Jillian, there's one other item I need your help with and it needs to be quick." He explained.

"I understand. He is close."

"Wait five minutes and then begin," he said, watching Vison on the screen.

"Confirmed," Jillian replied.

"Goodbye."

"Goodbye, Zeke Katz."

"We are Americans, and Americans do not cower, we do not step back from a challenge," Vison thundered.

Zeke's side throbbed and the faces and figures on the mall blurred.

"Hey, watch your step," someone cried out as he tripped and fell onto the ground.

Before the hijacking, the big gamble, he'd been jealous of their successful friends. The ones who bought five thousand square foot houses in the suburbs, vacationed in Europe or the Caribbean, snapped up BMWs or Mercedes without blinking an eye. Now, he had more money than any of them, more money than he could have dreamed of lying next to Rack in the bare-roomed walls of the foster homes, huddled under the blankets, hoping for an extra spoonful of soup or a chunk of meat.

"Be careful what you wish for, Zeke" Another of his father's stupid sayings.

No, he didn't regret trying to better their lives. He didn't regret proving his ideas to the world and showing that he knew better than the experts. He only wanted the best for Rachel and Sam. Vison took advantage of his ambition, bent a noble pursuit into one that served evil, and for that the President would pay.

"You okay, man?" a young guy with a beard said. "Here, take my hand." Zeke reached out, clasped hands, and pushed up with his legs, rising from the ground. The world spun again before his eyes focused on Vison's image.

Just in time.

The monitors went blank. A new image appeared. A plane lay in the desert, the nose embedded in a sand bank, the inflatable emergency staircase dangling from the side, the Fox News logo in the lower right. The screen changed to an image of a beaming Rachel, Sam in her arms. And then an image of their tombstones taken from a CNN repport.

Zeke watched the tragedy play out.

"I am a li..." Vison stopped and suddenly appeared very confused.

A woman leaned in towards the President, pointing off camera. "The teleprompter is feeding me garbage," he whispered into the live microphone. "Dammit, I'll continue the speech without it, but fix the transmission," he hissed.

The crowd stilled.

"And so today, the challenge of our generation is before us. Never before as a nation have we suffered such an attack."

Zeke crossed 4th Street, impressed at Vison's smooth recovery. This was a formidable politician.

A tall, smiling man holding the *Wall Street Journal* appeared. David Tinely.

Vison paused again.

The crowd leaned forward.

"Something is wrong with the video," a man said.

"Wasn't that the journalist killed by Fist of Allah?"

"What was his name?"

"Tine, Brian Tine, I think."

Zeke staggered across 3rd Street. Blood dripped from his shirt. The onlookers pushed forward, squeezed like penguins, soldiers at the barricades, weapons drawn, eyes alert, but missing the red stain on his shirt and pants.

"And never before have we been challenged by God almighty to fulfill our destiny as a country blessed by the heavens." Vison continued.

A smoldering landscape appeared. Skeletons of buildings stretched into the horizon; a black, sooty haze hung over the ruins. The Statue of Liberty lay face down in the Hudson, her back sticking out above the surface along with a point from the crown.

Vison's voice rose to match the images.

"These images will live in our hearts and minds forever. The terrorists have done everything in their power to destroy our way of life but we will not let them."

And then the screen went blank.

The soldier cradling his M-16, the older man with a purple heart pinned to his black AC/DC t-shirt, the young couple holding hands, the woman in the wheelchair, the secret service agents flanking Vison—all stood transfixed by the black screen, waiting.

Zeke reached a large reflecting pool. The crowd on the Capitol steps were clearly visible now in the glow of the lights and he didn't need the monitors to notice Vison's red face and clenched fists.

The screens sprang back to life, Zeke's voice echoing across the mall.

"Now, you aren't afraid to kill hundreds of thousands of men, women, and children. You destroyed New York."

The President's unmistakable voice boomed across the Mall. *"I didn't destroy it, I just put the pieces into motion. I know you think I'm a bad guy. But in the future you will come to see that what I did was the only way. You will come to understand."*

"You killed my wife and child," Zeke said. *"I will never understand why someone's need for power would drive them to become such a monster."*

"Zeke, I don't think you really understand what is going on. I'm not doing this for power or to take control of this country or the world. I'm not a dictator. In the future, the world will be a place of peace and love. That is what I want."

"Do you really expect me to believe you?"

"Zeke, your wife and child will be back. As will my wife. Those in New York who deserve to be reunited, who have accepted Jesus Christ will return. This is what I did this for."

Vison's appeared back on the screen, sweet beaded his brow, but his face remained calm, contemplative.

The crowd shifted, uneasy.

"Did he just admit to destroying New York?" someone next to Zeke asked.

"I think so," a heavy-set woman replied.

"What was that about?" someone else asked.

Murmurs rippled through the vast audience.

Finally, after a long pause, the President spoke. "Yes, it's true," he said, holding his hands out and opening his body to the audience, like a sin-filled preacher asking for forgiveness. "I do believe the rapture is upon us. I have worked to hasten its approach. I do not forsake God. We have lost many in New

York and that has been foreseen. Babylon has been destroyed. The world's leaders have been wiped out in one horrific blow. Armageddon awaits. But on the other side is eternal peace and salvation. And our loved ones will return. I do not shirk from this awesome responsibility. I do not hide from the Godly plan. Peace awaits all of us, Christian and non-Christian alike. Are you with me?"

Silence.

"Are you with me?" he asked, raising his voice.

A few in the crowd cheered back. A couple next to him hugged and kissed, eyes brimming with tears.

No, it wasn't possible! They couldn't actually be forgiving a man who admitted to destroying New York City.

"Wickedness has descended upon us. It descended upon New York and led to its destruction. The time has come to support each other and fight against the wickedness in this world. I have made mistakes, but I will fight. Fight with me! Do not continue down the same path of meekness. Lie with the lamb, but fight like the lion! Are you with me?"

A larger cheer erupted.

"Will you fight with me?"

Still a louder shout. Instead of storming the stairs, chanting for his arrest, shouting for impeachment, the crowd remainted still, supportive of the President.

"We'll sacrifice for you!" a woman screamed.

"Long live Vison!" someone else shouted.

His new model only calculated a 38.2% chance of the crowd being successfully swayed by a confession from Vison, the highest success probability of any of the scenarios. And that assumed a strong confession, not the wishy-washy religiously toned explanation the President had provided.

He had learned a lot since the early days tuning the model, adjusting deviations, refining variables, perfecting the equations. He learned life did not always proceed like an equation, surprises lurked around every corner, yesterday sowed the seeds for today, and coincidence was often the signal of destiny. Rachel was right. Humans were humans, unpredictable, eratic, alive. The final variable in his equation.

Gunshots rang out across the mall and the President turned from the screen. "Now what?" Vison yelled, turning his back to the camera.

Vison had sowed the seeds of his own destruction years earlier.

On the podium, a hunched figure stood near the door to Vison's platform, gun in hand, blood splattering the side of his head and face.

"I have clearance!" he screamed. "Get out of my way! Stay the fuck back or I'll shoot him. I will!" Hassan's voice echoed across the crowd. "Stay the fuck back! You don't know what I've been through!" Panting, sobbing, blood dripping down from his injured head, he turned to the President. You lied to me, Father!" he screamed. "I did this all for you! I lived like one of them for you! I did everything you asked of me, and you fucked me over! You chose the Jew over me!" he screamed, his voice echoing from the speakers. The two of you plotted against me! You just used me!"

The crowd watched spell-bound, eyes wide.

"Henry, I–"

"Fuck your silver tongue, Father. The blinking lights brought me here, showed me the path. God spoke to me. I am not a bastard. This is what God wants me to do. I can still go to heaven." Henry fired point-blank into the President's face. Vison remained upright for one second, arms out, eyes wide, before he toppled over. "And fuck all of you!" Hassan screamed, placing the gun to his head and pulling the trigger.

The sound of the blast echoed across the Mall, amplified by the sound system. A stiff breeze lifted the flags and that broke the spell—pandemonium erupted.

Chapter 83

The wind whipped Aminah's hair. A sheet of spray rose from the waves, twisted in the wind, and misted through those on deck, providing some relief from the searing sun. Aminah closed her eyes and enjoyed the sensation. The physical pain had faded but she still cried every day. Her mother, New York City, Mecca, Stephen, John, Masada—so much loss. Tears struck like thunderstorms.

But she had grown stronger. Sorrow was a stage of grief, at least that's what Luis said in between scrambling an egg or deboning a fish. The month had passed slowly, and it hadn't. On the Vengeance, a world seemingly unto itself, time passed on a different track, days feeling like years, and weeks like days.

When her father had been killed, her mother said, "The world has become a different place," and those words played in her mind so often now that it was like her mother still lingered by her side, giving advice even when it was not welcome. How Aminah longed for even the unwanted suggestions and exhortations. But whispers were all that remained.

Vison's death had averted a world war. The Chief Justice of the Supreme Court inaugurated Harold Mara, the Speaker of the House, as the new President and he promptly ordered the military to stand down. The spell broke; Armageddon avoided. Now the world needed to pick up the pieces of two cities vaporized, hundreds of thousands dead, and hundreds of world leaders suddenly gone. But her role was over and on-board the Vengeance she had done her best not to think too far into the future, taking comfort in the sun, waves, fish, and monotony of the day.

Until today.

"You don't have to do this, Aminah," Patric yelled above the wind, bringing the moment back into focus.

"Hoo-yah-yah-yah
Hoo-yah-yah-yah
Hoo-yah-yah-yah
Hoo-yah-yah-yah-"

"He's right, Aminah," Zeke said standing beside Hani. "You don't need to prove anything more."

"More? Did I ever need to prove anything?"

"You did," Zeke said simply. "To yourself."

Hani hugged Zeke and she enjoyed seeing the girl tame the man's darker side. He still spent hours brooding but sometimes, a growing percentage of each day, he smiled.

"She'll be okay," Hani said, taking her hand and giving it a small caress. "I know Aminah will be fine." The little girl displayed far more confidence in Aminah than she felt in herself.

"Thank you, Hani."

Aminah adjusted her wet suit, and peered at the rope wrapped around the coffin. Per Jewish custom, Masada's funeral ocurred within forty-eight hours of her death. Much to Zeke and Aminah's dismay, they had never recovered her body. The risk of making contact with the OCT was simply too great, even with Vison dead. A simple pine coffin represented Masada in their burial and homage to the Israeli, the dive to Heaven's Deep.

When Zeke had asked who would accompany Masada down into the sea, Aminah had surprised everyone by raising her hand. Masada sacrificed herself to save Aminah. Her mouth twisted into a sob as she thought about the Israeli: meeting her on the boat, traveling to D.C., ditching her in the Metro, the kiss. But she also needed to do this for herself.

At first, Zeke refused, but she didn't relent. Pushiness was a virtue, or maybe fatal foolishness.

A tear trickled down her face as the crew increased the tempo, creating a pulsating beat while they danced and jumped.

"Do you remember that quote from the Japanese guy?" Aminah asked Zeke, the moment drawing close, heart pumping, head floating.

"Yamamoto Tsunetomo's 'Hagakure,'" Zeke replied.

"What are the words?"

"'If by setting one's heart right every morning and evening, one is able to live as though his body were already dead, he gains freedom in the Way.'"

"Yes," she sighed to herself.

"Aminah," Zeke said. She nodded, awaiting his next words. "Good luck. Don't die."

More tears streamed down her face.

The chanting men and women pitched Masada's coffin overboard, grabbed the weights tied to Aminah's legs, and prepared to throw them into the sea.

Why am I doing this?

Because she needed to honor Masada and help repair herself. She needed to take her despair, sadness, and anger to the edge and cast them over.

She nodded and they threw the weights in, pulling her off the railing and into the warm Indian ocean. As she dropped into the sea, Aminah glanced up and through the ripples, saw Zeke, Hani, Patric, Luis and the rest of the crew of the Vengeance watch her descend.

Aminah smiled and even as she sank into the deep with Masada's coffin, began to calmly work the knots which bound her feet.

She needed to return from the depths. A new world awaited.

Chapter 84

Zeke opened the door and a dust bunny flitted across the floor into the living room. He walked into the apartment and immediately noticed the small toy car lying on its side, the framed picture of the three of them in a pile of leaves, his favorite coat draped around the back of a kitchen chair, and a nine volt battery on the floor.

Memories hit: lifting Sam and flying him around the room, the little boy squealing in delight; chasing the tottering, giggling toddler through the living room, holding his son on his shoulder and burping him late at night to an Alanis Morrisette album.

Zeke remembered Rachel telling him she was pregnant on the green couch, eyes wet with tears of happiness, body quivering with excitement. The first time they stepped into the apartment, parquet floors and a wide window looking out on a tree and an adjacent apartment building.

So much happiness.

The flood of memories breached the wall and he sank to his knees and sobbed, tears streaming down his face, his body shaking.

Hani stood silent.

After a few moments, when the tsunami passed, he rose and gave Hani's hand a squeeze. "Thank you." He sniffled a few more times and walked to the center of the room, surrounded by his old life, holding hands with his new.

"Rachel, Sam, I want you to meet Hani. She's going to be joining the family. I'm adopting her today."

"Hello," Hani said. "I am happy to get to know you. I am sad that we cannot meet in person."

"You'd both like Hani," Zeke said. "Rachel, you'd love her as a daughter. And Sam, you would love her as a sister. I'm sorry we can't all be together," he said, starting to sob again. "But there's nothing I can do about that."

After a few more minutes of soaking in the atmosphere, Zeke's mind calmed and he smiled a bit. "There are a lot of wonderful memories here. I thought it would last forever."

He started back towards the door.

"You are ready to leave?" Hani asked.

"For now. I can always come back."

"You own the apartment?"

"No, I own the entire building. But right now we have to go to the adoption appointment."

Hani smiled.

As Zeke walked down the stairs, he remembered carrying Rachel's luggage for their trip to Sicily. So much could have been different if only he had been a little more astute.

No my love, you must let it go. What happened was not your fault.

He would always blame himself for missing Jillian's warning, but for now, at least, he could live with the pain. The raging anger had subsided. Hani and Aminah helped.

They stepped out to a sunny October day, the rays warming his face. A homeless man passed by, stuck out his empty pan, and squawked at them:

"Spare some change? Spare some change?"

Zeke took out a hundred dollar bill and dropped it in.

A Toyota Uber glided over to the curb and the rear passenger door opened. They hopped into the back and rested against the seats.

"Hello, Zeke," came a familiar voice.

"Jillian!" cried Hani. The real girl and the digital girl had become close over the last six weeks, communicating often, playing chess, exchanging pictures. Patric thought Jillian related best to Hani because they were both "young."

"Hello, Jillian," said Zeke. "You've bypassed the real car AI."

"Yes, it was easy. Their security is a joke. I wanted to wish you both luck today," Jillian said.

"Thanks!" Hani replied, as the car pulled away from the curve.

"Do you know where to go?" Zeke asked.

"Seriously?" Jillian replied.

"Come on, Zeke, Jillian knows everything," Hani giggled.

"And the papers and records are all set?" Zeke asked.

"Of course, Zeke," Jillian replied. A sentient computer program left him a bit uneasy, but he had to admit she came with advantages. Jillian's "help" accelerated and smoothed the way for Hani's adoption.

"Okay, here's a question for her," Zeke said, trying to stump the digital brain. "Jillian?"

"Yes."

"Once Hani and I have finalized the adoption, I'd like you to pick a restaurant where we can celebrate?"

Silence.

"Are you still there, Jillian?" Hani asked as the car took a left and approached the court house.

"Yes, I am thinking. Some clues on your eating preferences for today would be helpful."

The car came to a stop and Zeke clambered out.

"I don't think so. You decide."

"That's not fair," Jillian responded, sounding very much like a teenager.

"That's life," Zeke said. "Think about it while we're inside," he replied, closing the door after Hani jumped out.

"Where do you think she will take us?" Hani asked.

"Hopefully someplace good," Zeke responded with a chuckle.

A beautiful day, an expanded family, a hope for tomorrow, the thrill of the unknown. His body felt lighter, the day seemed brighter, and he felt a quivering of excitement. Zeke took Hani's hand and together they walked into the courthouse.

THE END

EPILOGUE

"So, you thought it had all ended?" the man said scraping the blade of his knife against Fernando Garcia's face, leaving a ribbon of blood. Fernando refused to flinch. "You think you can go and talk to the media, talk to the police, and we will just look the other way?" He smiled and Fernando saw the gold teeth that the cartel's members wore to display their wealth.

Beside him, a long-faced man with a scruffy beard and a tattoo tear watched, a smile on his face.

"You killed my father, raped my mother," Fernando said.

"Your father kept writing his articles. We warned him, like we warned you. Like father like son. Stupid chuchas."

He tried to face his death calmly. He would not show them fear. He knew they thrived on misery and they would drag the execution out to watch him whimper. By God, he would not give them that entertainment.

"You may be brave, but how about your sister?"

"Don't touch her!" he yelled.

Gold tooth smiled; Tattoo Face laughed.

"I haven't touched her amigo, but from what I've heard she has already been sold. Just today, she has probably already serviced fifty men," Gold tooth replied.

"Fuck you. Burn in hell." The man laughed again and then turned to his friend.

"He mentions hell and burning, what do you think, should we give him his wish?" The other man nodded and they leaned forward and grabbed his arms. He tried to hit one of them but his arms were bound and he only managed to flail his elbow. In return, Tattoo Face punched him in the stomach, doubling him over.

"Oh amigo, that is nothing. We're going to give you your wish and send you to hell. When I am done roasting you like a pig, I am going to find your sister and give her a good fuck. What do you think, Manny? Does that sound good?"

They emerged into a dark parking lot behind the building, illuminated by a few lights on poles. In the corner, Fernando saw the pipe and a pile of ash around it. Even if he could break free, there was nowhere to run. Other members of the cartel sat inside the building, his only path to escape.

They threw him down onto the ground and then the squat one kicked him in the stomach. He curled up in pain.

"Yeah, go ahead, give him a good spray."

Liquid landed on him, ran down his head, fell off his face like foul tears. He didn't want to die like this. Show courage, he told himself. Even in the fire, it wouldn't last long. He spotted an iron bar in the corner and began to slowly crawl towards it.

"Where are you going, amigo? Time to put you in the oven." They hoisted him to his feet and began to drag him towards the large smokestack.

Tattoo Face jerked back, let go of Fernando's leg, and dropped to the ground, clutching his right leg.

"What the fuck? Who shot me? What the−"

Gold Tooth fell face forward. "Madre de dios!" he screamed. "My legs, my legs!"

Fernando lay on his back, staring up the stars. He tried to rise but the pain in his chest forced him back down. They must have broken some of his ribs.

A face blocked out the stars: long dark hair, big brown eyes, a scar running down from her cheekbown to her chin.

"Hello, Fernando," she said.

"You're going to fucking die!" Tattoo Face screamed. "Do you know who we are?"

"I know exactly who you are," she said, aiming a pistol and firing two more shots at each man.

"Fuck, my balls, you shot my balls!" he groaned.

"Take him and prop him up," she said to someone.

Strong hands pulled Fernando up and then placed him against the wall. Pain twisted through his back and he screamed in pain.

A tall, blond-haired man pulled out a needle, tapped it, and then plunged it into Fernando's arm. "This will make it feel better until we can get you fixed up," he said in English with a German accent.

The pain receded.

The two cartel members lay on the ground, trying to rise.

"Don't bother to try standing, we shattered your knees. You'll never walk again. Not that it will matter," she said.

Fernando sat upright and could see the woman. Tall, trim, dressed in dark clothes. She pressed something in her ear.

"How many are on their way, Jillian?" Pause. "Can you reroute them? We need about ten more minutes to complete the clean." She turned back to Tattoo Face and Gold Tooth.

"Ulli, let's give them a bath," she said. Her blond companion grabbed the hose.

Tattoo Face clawed at the ground. "Fuck no, you aren't going to burn us. Who are you? FBI? Your government will never allow this. Civil rights, right?"

"We aren't the government and we don't care about your civil rights," the woman said coolly.

The men tried to scurry away like crabs, pulling their dead legs behind them. She took out a pistol and shot each of them in the shoulder. They collapsed onto the ground and writhed in pain.

Ulli grabbed each man by the arm and hauled them into the pipe, throwing Gold Tooth on the bottom and Tattoo Face on top.

"Please, we can pay you. We can give you anything you want. Please, please," Gold Tooth sobbed.

Tattoo Face whimpered.

"You're not so tough anymore, are you?" she asked, before closing the door and locking them inside the tube.

"Anything, please! My mother! What will my mother say? My sister?"

She looked at Fernando. "You okay with this?"

His heart pounded. Who were these people and what would he have to give them in return.

"I don't know," he answered.

"Good enough," she said, lighting a gas-soaked rag and tossing it into the cylinder.

"No, please, put it out! Put it ooooooout!"

Finally, Fernando only heard the roaring of the flames.

"Thank you," he said. The woman nodded. And then he added the only other thing in his mind. "But they also have my sister."

"Not for long," the woman smiled, "not for long."

For more information visit
stateofvengeance.com.

Proof

72653894R00243

Made in the USA
Columbia, SC
22 June 2017